Poppadom Preach

ALMAS KHAN

**SIMON &
SCHUSTER**

London · New York · Sydney · Toronto

A CBS COMPANY

First published in Great Britain by Simon & Schuster UK Ltd, 2011
A CBS Company

1 3 5 7 9 10 8 6 4 2

Simon & Schuster UK Ltd
1st Floor
222 Gray's Inn Road
London WC1X 8HB

www.simonandschuster.co.uk

Simon & Schuster Australia
Sydney

A CIP catalogue record for this book is available
from the British Library.

ISBN: 978-1-84983-211-3

Typeset by Hewer Text UK Ltd, Edinburgh
Printed and Bound in Great Britain by CPI Cox & Wyman

To Ismael, Danny and Eric, for being the sunshine and laughter of my life.

Prologue

Princess Dilly of Sharnia had it all. Her beauty was legendary throughout the kingdom. Her eyes were the colour of sparkling emeralds, her mouth as soft as a rosebud, and her long hair fell about her shoulders in a thick silky pool of gold.

Hers was a pampered life, her every need met by willing handmaidens. For nineteen years she'd avoided contact with people whom she considered to be beneath her – the 'common folk', as she called them – staying away from the noise and smell and the hustle and bustle they created as they went about their pitiful lives.

Given a choice, she would have preferred to be back at the royal palace now, plotting ways to rid herself of the evil Queen Gongal while King Shah was away in far-off lands.

But the King's word was law, and that's why she was standing in a queue at the Bradford Interchange at two in the morning, waiting to board a National Express coach bound for Manchester Airport. Sighing inwardly, she paused for a moment at the bottom of the stairs. What was that she could smell? A nasty warm concoction of unwashed bodies and diesel fumes. Her stomach heaved and she suddenly felt nauseous. She was dimly aware of her three maids pushing impatiently past her as they clambered aboard the coach.

Surely, the Princess thought, it would have been so much more civilized to make the journey by glass carriage, pulled by her four white Lipizzaner stallions.

Why had the evil King insisted on her travelling in such a demeaning manner? In fact, why did she have to go at all? It wasn't even her wedding. How preposterous that she, heiress to the Kingdom of Sharnia, was being forced to attend the wedding of a simple maidservant. It was unheard of . . .

She was jolted from her reverie by a sharp shove from behind.

'Dammit, Dilly, get a bloody move on – you're holding everyone up.'

The warm wispy clouds of dreaminess vanished in an instant.

'Sorry, Daddy,' I mumbled. 'I was miles away.'

'Just get on the coach,' he barked.

As I reluctantly took my seat beside my sisters at the back of the coach, I stared out from behind my veil at the holiday-hungry passengers already tucking into sandwiches and bottles of pop. A small child ran up and down the gangway, shooting a plastic cap gun. A young couple were studying a map and giggling excitedly. The blonde woman in the seat in front of me looked up from her Thomas Cook brochure, turned to glare at me, and sniffed indignantly.

'What's your problem?' I asked angrily.

'You lot,' she replied tartly as she went back to reading her brochure.

My sisters were sitting together in a huddle of gloomy silence. Meanwhile, my father had his nose buried in a cricket almanac. It was a tatty dog-eared volume that he'd already read several times. I don't think he was even reading it; it was just an excuse for him to ignore his daughters. I wondered if he knew how much we all hated him. I guessed that even if he did he wouldn't have lost much sleep over it; he was that sort of man.

He would have been more concerned had he known about the plan that was beginning to form in my head, a plan that would allow me to finally escape from him and my mother.

All my life I'd been a prisoner, but, unlike Cinderella, I'd given up waiting to be rescued by a dashing young prince and had decided to figure it out for myself. I knew my struggle for freedom would be long and hard-fought, for my shackles had been forged by the evil witch Rasheeda, many years before I was even born . . .

Chapter 1

1967 was a fruitful year. Twix and Smash were born, Elvis married Priscilla, and, on 21 March, as Engelbert Humperdinck sang, 'Please release me, let me go ...' my mother pushed me out into the world. There were already two boys in the family – my brother Monkey and my cousin Doc – but Mammy wanted another, and I don't think she ever really got over the disappointment of having a girl.

A year later, she was disappointed again when she gave birth to my little sister, Egg. In 1970, she was doubly disappointed by the arrival of twin girls (Daisy and Poppy), and that's when Mammy decided to give up on childbirth altogether.

From as far back as I can remember, all the Shah kids could speak two languages – English and Punjabi. You'd think that would be enough. But when I was eight my mother decided she wanted to teach me Urdu as well. She said Punjabi was such a guttural, vulgar language, whereas Urdu was cultured and refined, and maybe learning it would soften my rough edges. So, one sunny afternoon during the summer holidays, she sat me down at the huge oak table in the kitchen, handed me a text-book, and told me to do the first lesson while she got the dinner ready.

I took one look at the book and knew it wasn't going to be a good day. The lesson went:

1) Translate the following words into English: **din, rah, jab, kar, kam**.
2) Practise the pronunciation of each word.

'When you've done that, Dilly, take a look at the next page and answer those questions as well,' Mammy said as she peeled an onion the size of a melon.

I turned the page and looked at the next lesson. She had to be joking.

1) Write ten sentences using **yakayak**.
2) Write ten sentences using **baad**.

I laughed out loud. 'Mammy, they've spelt this one wrong. Isn't that meant to be "bad"?'

'No, you idiot; it means "after".'

'Oh, I see,' I said, feeling foolish. 'So what's a *yakayak*?'

'For God's sake, just get on with it.'

'And this word here, Mammy, what's *dar*?'

'Be afraid,' she replied.

'Why?'

'No, that's what *dar* means,' she said impatiently. 'If you read the bloody thing with a Yorkshire accent, you'll never get it right.'

I didn't like the way she kept waving the knife in the air, so I slouched down at the dining table, positioned *Exercises in Urdu* in front of me, and quietly practised singing Bay City Rollers songs to myself.

*　　*　　*

Half an hour later, my mother looked over my shoulder and saw I was still on the first question.

'Oh my God,' she groaned. 'Why are you such hard work?'

''Cos this is boring. Can't we go shopping?' I asked hopefully.

'Why would I want to go shopping with you?' she replied impatiently. 'I asked you to do one simple thing, and you can't even be bothered to do that. You're so lazy and ugly, I don't know how I'm ever going to find you a husband from Pakistan, but at least if you make the effort to learn Urdu you might be in with a chance.'

'That's *baad*,' I said, feeling proud that I'd used one of my new words in a sentence.

'No,' she replied as she lit the cooker with a long strip of cut-up cereal carton. 'What's bad is your attitude. You can't just think about yourself all the time. When you're married, your husband becomes your boss, and you have to do whatever makes the boss happy.'

'Bollocks to that.'

My mother gave me a stinging slap across the face. 'Get out of my kitchen, you little bitch!' she shrieked.

And that was it. I'd got what I wanted: I was free to play.

Leaving her to her cooking, I grabbed Hamble, my favourite doll, and headed out into the back garden. It was a beautiful sunny afternoon. A gentle breeze was rustling through the leaves of the giant oak trees on the other side of the back alley.

From somewhere came the distant hum of a lawnmower, and the tinkling of Harami's ice cream van. Next door, Batool's washing was dancing on the line, and the familiar scents of Daz and Lenor came floating over the wall to embrace the aroma of frying onions that was escaping from the open kitchen windows.

I gave Hamble a bath in the water coming from the drainpipe. She was my pride and joy. I'd bought her at a school jumble sale, and she was special because she was darker than me. I didn't know anyone who had a doll like Hamble. The minute I saw her little black foot poking out of a box of toys, I knew I had to have her.

A dripping wet Hamble and I had just started to hunt for caterpillars in the vegetable patch when the back gate opened and suddenly my father was standing there, glaring at me with a manic look in his green eyes.

And that's when I learned that sugar can fly. A two-pound bag, cruising at an altitude of four feet, narrowly missed my head. Like a fat white pigeon, it flew across the garden and landed with a soft thud on the doorstep.

The bag ruptured, and I watched in fascination as the sugar trickled out to form a little white mountain. Another bag followed, and it dawned on me that my father was armed, dangerous, and busy reloading. It was time to run for cover. As Hamble and I cowered in a corner of the garden, Daddy reached down into the two huge hessian shopping bags on the ground next to him. With me out of sight, he decided to turn his attention to the house.

It was a tin of tomatoes that broke the first window. My father looked like he was playing cricket as he bowled a big red apple straight through the jagged glass. Good shot, I thought. One by one, every item – potatoes, eggs, cartons of milk, bags of flour, tins of soup, bunches of grapes – was thrown across the garden and into the kitchen through the broken windows. Finally, out of ammunition, he went charging into the house, spreading chaos in his wake.

'You useless cow!' he shouted at my mother. 'I've lugged that shopping all the way from Rawson's Market and you couldn't even be bothered to open the front door!'

'Did you ring the bell?' she asked in a deadpan voice.

'No, I didn't ring the bloody bell.'

I sneaked up to the kitchen doorway so I could get a better view. Daddy was raging, surrounded by broken glass and scattered groceries.

'So how was I supposed to know you were there?' Mammy asked.

'You knew I'd gone shopping. You should have known I'd be back.'

'Don't be stupid. I've got better things to do than sit and look out of the window all day. Maybe next time you'll remember to take your key.'

It was a bad choice of words. Daddy picked up a tin of spaghetti and hurled it through the last unbroken window. Then he grabbed more of the weekly shop and sent it flying again – only this time it was all going out of the kitchen and into the garden.

When, at last, everything was in the back garden, I crunched my way through the glass, picked up some tins, went into the house and put them on the dining table in front of him. It wasn't often I was handed an opportunity to humiliate both my parents at the same time.

'Here you are, Daddy, I brought these back so you can chuck them out again.'

He stared at me in disbelief.

'What the hell are you doing?' my mother shrieked.

'Keeping your boss happy,' I replied. 'Go on, Daddy, chuck them out and I'll fetch them back for you.'

He was too embarrassed to speak. As his rage subsided and his shoulders sagged, we all stood and surveyed the mess.

'You're going to have to mend those windows,' Mammy snapped as she stepped gingerly across the kitchen floor.

'Yes, Gongal, I'm well aware of that,' he said through clenched teeth.

'I'll help you, Daddy,' I offered eagerly.

'Get lost,' he hissed. 'Go on, get out of here.'

Disappointed that the show was over so quickly, I shoved my hands deep into my tartan flares and skulked back into the garden. A moment later, my mother followed, grabbed the yard brush and started to sweep the path furiously.

'The neighbours are going to love this,' she muttered to herself. 'The man's crazy. One minute he's fine, and the next he's acting like a rabid dog. It's as though someone's done voodoo on him.'

Daddy strolled casually out of the kitchen. 'Gongal, I need you to help me fix the windows.'

'Go to hell. You broke them, you fix them.'

'Aw, come on, love,' he wheedled. 'I can't measure the glass on my own.'

'Why don't you get your daughter to help? She's obviously on your side.'

'Oh shut up, woman, and get inside. You're going to help, whether you like it or not.'

She glared at him, then carried on sweeping. The bangles on her wrists jingled, and, with each movement, tiny sparks of red and orange light glinted off the gold and darted round the garden.

But it wasn't long before my mother gave in, as she usually did, and my father got his own way, as he usually did. Together, the two of them cleared up the mess, with constant interruptions from people wanting to know what had happened. My parents didn't say anything, but I think the neighbours knew anyway. The whole street would have heard Daddy, and I'm willing to bet they'd all stepped outside to listen.

Chapter 2

My father was a very religious man. He prayed five times a day, and every evening he'd line all the kids up in the back room and make us read verses from the Koran. Recitals would go on for hours and, by the time I got to bed, Arabic words would be spinning round in my head like clothes in a tumble dryer. And when I went to sleep I'd dream that the alphabet was chasing me down the street.

But one day, by chance, I discovered that if I read my verses for my mother, before my father got home from work, I wouldn't have to read again in the evening. Mammy was always too busy to pay much attention to how much time I'd spent, and my cunning little plan worked well for a while – until the day I made the mistake of lying down on my stomach in the back room to read the Koran. Mammy came in unexpectedly, took one look at what I was doing and blew her top.

'What the hell?' she shouted. 'How dare you be so disrespectful?'

'I was just trying to get comfortable,' I said, sitting up quickly.

'I've never seen anything so disgusting in all my life,' she exaggerated. She slapped my face and frog-marched me to the cellar, shoved me inside and bolted the door.

I hated that place. It was where all the demons conjured up by a young and vivid imagination would hunt. It was cold, the air was always damp and heavy, and in winter the walls would run wet with condensation. It was my idea of hell; there were black rats skulking around down there, and huge spiders like the Martians from *The War of the Worlds*. But worse still was the vapour monster that Monkey had told me lived in the hole in the stairs. As a little girl I spent a lot of time in that dungeon beneath the house, being punished for whatever it was I was supposed to have done wrong, and worrying about the monster that was creeping slowly up the stairs on all fours to come and devour me.

My mother would leave me in the cellar for hours. Occasionally someone would rattle the handle and I would hear her telling them to come away. After each trip to the cellar I would tell myself there was no way I was going back in there again, and then I'd do something wrong and find myself sitting in the dark, begging to be let out.

However, on this particular occasion I did something I'd never been able to do before. I reached up on tiptoe and discovered that, at last, I was just tall enough to reach the light-switch. For the first time in my life, it wasn't such a scary place after all.

There was no sign of the monster, so I made my way downstairs. There were piles of junk everywhere: old newspapers that would be used as firelighters, broken furniture and old mattresses being kept for bonfire night, and empty paint tins that Monkey and his friends used as targets when they were practising with their BB guns in the back garden. There was a huge chest freezer, boxes of tools and tins of food that were kept for emergencies, and lanterns for whenever the miners were on strike or Daddy forgot to pay the bills.

I hurried over to the sash window, clambered up on to the sill and undid the locks. The window groaned as I pulled it up, then a soft breeze came into the room. I climbed out quickly, closed the window to cover my tracks, and headed out into the street.

Gomshall Road was full of rows of large terraced houses, all locked together like huge chunks of Lego. Many of them had been converted into bedsits, which were inhabited by a variety of tenants: students from the university, immigrants from Pakistan, OAPs, single mothers with small children, and people stopping off en route to somewhere else. Behind the houses on our side of the street was a cobbled back alley, and beyond that a high brick wall separating the alley from the railway tracks. On the opposite side of the street there was a gap in the terrace with a path that led down to Titus Park, which was sometimes used as a gypsy camp. At the far end of the park were the haunted woods that no child had the courage to explore.

I loved my street. It was full of noise and colour, the sort of place where everybody knew each other. There were always lots of people to watch: the boys would be playing cricket and football, while the girls jumped rope or played Jacks. You could usually find the older children, including Monkey and his best friends Scully and Mark, sitting on a wall, flicking back their ridiculously long, poker-straight hair, trying to out-Ozzy Osbourne each other, while eating sweets and drinking Irn-Bru they'd stolen from Toadie's, the shop by the entrance to the park.

There was always at least one small child looking after a baby in a huge Silver Cross pram because their mam was knackered and she'd told them to 'piss off out and take the baby with you'.

There wasn't much to thank my parents for, but I was grateful they'd chosen to settle at 38 Gomshall Road. I couldn't imagine living in any other street. Everything about it was etched in my mind: the familiar faces, the back alleys crawling with children until late in the evening, the sun shining at a certain angle on the windows across the street; in summer dandelion seeds dancing in the breeze, and in winter the air thick with the metallic smell of frost and the snow falling in plump grey flakes from an even greyer sky. Gomshall Road was my favourite place in the world.

Today Scully's sister, Sue, was skipping outside her house across the road. I went over for a chat.

'What are you up to?' she asked.

'Not much,' I replied.

'I'm waiting for Sharon. Did you know she's got her first bra? It cost ninety-nine and a half pence.'

'What's the big deal?' I asked, thinking I'd much rather spend the money on a catapult.

'I can't wait till I get one,' Sue said. 'I'm gonna go to John Street Market with my mam, and we'll choose one together.'

Not to be outdone, I replied: 'Yeah, well, me and my mam are gonna get mine from Busby's. She said I can have a pink one.' I knew hell would freeze over before Mammy ever took me to Busbys'.

Sue climbed up on to her garden wall. 'I didn't know your mam could go out. I thought Pakis didn't let their women go shopping.'

'Yeah, but we're British.'

'Only when it suits you.' She giggled. 'Hey, your dad's home – shouldn't you be going in for your tea?'

'Shit! I'm supposed to be locked in the cellar. My mam'll be coming to let me out.'

I waited until my father had gone into the house, then raced across the road. But, to my horror, when I tried to open the cellar window it was stuck tight and I couldn't get it to budge.

Cursing loudly I tried again, but it was no use. There was only one thing to do, so I did it. I rang the bell.

The front door opened, and my mother stared at me as though she was seeing a ghost.

'What the . . . ?'

'Hi,' I said as I brushed past her, following the smell of frying parathas into the kitchen.

'Huh?' she questioned, unable to articulate.

My father was already feasting on saag aloo; there were long slivers of green chillies and a puddle of butter floating on the surface of the bowl in front of him.

'Hello, love. Where've you been?' he asked good-humouredly.

Shaking her head in disbelief, my mother said, 'I locked you in the cellar – how did you get out?'

'I got fed up of waiting for you, so I let myself out.'

'Dear God!' she said in disbelief. 'What sort of demon is this?'

Instead of showing concern about the fact that my mother's main method of punishment was now useless, Daddy just laughed. Mammy, angry that she'd been outdone by an eight year old, stormed over to the stove, picked up a paratha and slammed it down on my father's plate, sending buttery fragments flying in all directions.

'That girl's got no respect. You should've seen the way she was reading the Koran; you'd have killed her. She was lying on her stomach.'

My father's attention was no longer on his meal. 'Dilly? Is that true?'

'Yes, Daddy, it is,' I replied sheepishly.

'Go upstairs and wash. Then come back down and get your Koran. You're going to sit and read it, and give it the respect it deserves.'

'But I've already done that, Daddy.'

'Well, now you can do it again. And this time you'll sit up properly, and you'll continue to read until I tell you to stop.'

It was five hours before my father was satisfied I'd learned my lesson. He taught me well; I never made that mistake again.

Chapter 3

Two monsters inhabited the Kingdom of Sharnia. The vapour monster lurked in the cellar, while upstairs in the attic lived my father's older sister, the she-monster known as 'Auntie Climax'.

Climax had lived in Sharnia since before I was born. She and her son, Doc, came to England soon after her husband had caught her in bed with another man. Her mother, Rasheeda, horrified by the scandal, packed her daughter off to live with my father in Bradford, far enough away that any future indiscretions wouldn't be trumpeted all round Jallu, their village in Pakistan.

Every night, I would hear her clumping around overhead as I tried to sleep. Sometimes the smell of a Woodbine would float down the stairs, accompanied by the wails of Asha Bhosle and Lata Mangeshkar.

Climax wasn't a good-looking woman. Five feet nine tall, with size-eight feet, she could have been the bastard offspring of Desperate Dan and Dick Emery in drag.

She had the biggest breasts I'd ever seen, and wasn't ashamed to flaunt them for all to admire. She knew it wound my mother up, so she would deliberately dress in clothes that did little to hide her voluptuousness; her kurta tops all looked like they'd been welded to her skin, and she used old nappy pins to hold together the zips whose teeth had twisted out of shape and could no longer be done up.

Whenever my mother told Climax to cover up, because parading around the house in revealing clothes was shameful, Climax would say, 'Don't look if it bothers you so much. I can't help being gorgeous, can I?'

It wasn't uncommon to see one of Climax's enormous bras dancing wildly on the washing line, each cup big enough to accommodate a Galia melon. She'd use the clothes stick to hoist the line up in the air so that every passer-by in the back alley could get an eyeful, then she'd have a good laugh as Mammy hurried outside to peg a towel over the top of the bra.

If she was feeling particularly playful, she would wash two weeks' underwear in one go, and Mammy wouldn't have enough towels to cover everything up.

I admired the way she refused to be bullied by my mother. Of course, her boldness and self-confidence were bolstered by the knowledge that, as Daddy's older sister, she was virtually untouchable. Unlike every other female in Sharnia, Climax could do more or less what she wanted, knowing that my father would turn a blind eye. Her reputation was already in tatters, so there was simply nothing left to preserve.

She couldn't even be bothered to look after her own son – most of his pitiful upbringing was done by my parents. Doc shared a bedroom with Monkey; Climax would drop in now and again, like a visitor, to see how he was, but I never saw her being affectionate towards him (or anyone else, for that matter).

Climax baffled me. How could a woman who was such a negligent mother be such an excellent cook? I loved to watch her when she was preparing a meal; she reminded me of a mad scientist as she danced around the kitchen, opening cupboards, pulling out bottles of spices, mixing and measuring, wiggling her hips and humming away to the tune in her head.

My mother was a hopeless cook – her food tasted watery and weak, as though she'd deliberately rinsed out all the flavour. When Mammy cooked, it was in black and white; but when Climax cooked, it was like she was working with a rainbow.

If Climax could have been persuaded to spend more time in the kitchen, how different mealtimes would have been. But sadly she could only be coaxed in front of the stove on special occasions. It was Mammy's slops that we had to endure on a daily basis.

Climax wasn't an easy woman to get close to. One day I found her in the back room, reading *TV Times*. I clambered onto her lap, put my arms round her neck, pulled her face close to mine and said, 'Why can't you cook for us all the time?'

She snorted, pushed me off her lap and turned her attention back to the magazine. As I tried to climb back up, she put a manly hand on my forehead to keep me at arm's length.

'If you loved me, you'd give me a cuddle and you'd cook for me every day,' I insisted.

'Look, Dilly,' she sighed, 'let's get something straight right now. I don't love you. Come to think of it, I don't even like you. But then again, I don't really like anyone in this house. Now piss off, I'm trying to read.'

Maybe my words hadn't come out quite right, but I'd done my best to compliment her and all she'd done was throw my affection back in my face. Feeling confused and downhearted, I took Climax's advice and headed off into the street.

Monkey, Doc and a group of their friends were playing football in the middle of the road. I raced over to join them, but Doc shoved me roughly out of the way and said, 'Piss off, Dilly, no girls allowed.'

'Hey, Monkey!' I shouted. 'Please can I play?'

'You've been told, now piss off,' came the reply.

There was no point picking a fight with him; he was six years older than me and didn't have a problem using his fists. Compared to the rest of his gang, Monkey was a beast of a boy – tall and muscular, with demon-green eyes and long brown hair usually tied back in a ponytail. He spent most of his schooldays truanting, and whenever there was a fight in the street he was always in the thick of it. He'd already had his nose broken twice.

Dejected, I sat on the kerb and watched the game jealously. Scully was on the ball. He skipped past his marker and smacked a shot straight at Doc, who was goalkeeping between two parked cars. The ball bounced off Doc's leg, hit a blue Ford Anglia, and flew into the front garden of Number 43.

A collective groan went up.

'Not again!' Monkey shouted at Doc. 'You retard!'

Doc hurried over to where I was sitting. Although he was only two years younger than Monkey, and almost as tall, he was weedy and spotty, and his watery green eyes and pale skin made him look as though he was permanently suffering from some sort of vitamin deficiency. Doc idolized Monkey, and did what he could to emulate his hero, but he lacked his cousin's charisma.

'Dilly,' he said in a low voice, 'go get the ball, or I'll kick the shit out of you.'

Feeling my hackles rise, I scrambled to my feet and faced him. Doc had clearly learned a lesson from living with my parents: whatever the problem, threatening violence was usually the solution. But, as Monkey ambled over, Doc's tone suddenly changed.

'Look, Dilly,' he wheedled, 'if you get the ball, we'll let you play.'

Refusing now wasn't an option; I couldn't afford to be branded a coward. I was desperate to be taken seriously by Monkey's gang, and this was a chance to prove myself. But everyone knew that Estie, the Jamaican lady who lived at Number 43, was as big as a mountain because she ate children in between meals. I'd lost count of the number of times that Monkey had told me he'd seen a child's bones poking out of Estie's rubbish bin.

Full of false bravado, and with the eyes of a dozen older boys upon me, I walked slowly up to the wooden gate and hesitated, my heart beating furiously and my legs shaking. Standing on tiptoe, I tried to peer into the garden, but the thick privet hedge was too high for me to see over.

Doc ran up behind me, opened the gate, shoved me inside and pulled it shut.

A moment of panic gripped me when I realized I wasn't alone in the garden; Estie was sitting on the bench under the front window, wolfing down a bag of chips.

'Please, lady,' I mumbled, 'can I have the ball back?'

'Lady?' She chuckled. 'I haven't been called that for a while. If you like, you can call me Estie, 'cos I'm the bestie. Want a chip?' She held out the bag. 'They're nice and hot – I just got them from the fish-and-chip van.'

'I dunno,' I said. 'You might eat me.'

Estie threw back her head and roared with laughter. 'Now where did you get that notion from?' she said as tears rolled down her cheeks. 'I think someone's been pulling your leg.'

Throwing caution to the wind, I sat down next to her on the bench and dipped my hand into the chips. They were delicious.

'You can have some Lucozade, if you don't mind sharing my glass,' Estie offered. I was just about to take it from her when a nervous voice came from the other side of the hedge.

'Dilly! Are you okay?'

'Go away. I'm busy,' I called back.

'Now then,' Estie said warmly, 'I expect those boys will be wanting their ball back. But I say let them wait. Why don't you just sit here a while and tell me about yourself.'

The next hour was sheer bliss. That day I'd been told to piss off three times by members of my own family, but here was a complete stranger who was happy to spend time with me.

Later that evening, Estie came over to our house with a bagful of Woolworths' pic 'n' mix and a huge bowl of homemade vanilla custard. I was overjoyed to see her again, but it was my parents and Climax she chatted happily with for hours. And, when she finally left, it was Mammy who ate all the custard.

Chapter 4

With Daddy at work in the library all day, and Climax showing little interest in housework or her son, the job of raising six children fell to my mother. She found it difficult to cope.

Monkey and Doc were too boisterous to be stuck indoors for long, so Mammy would kick them out into the street and then spend hours tense with worry over what they were getting up to. Of course, she couldn't go out to check on them, because she wasn't allowed out of the front of the house without my father – and the boys, aware of this, were too smart to play round the back.

My three sisters added to my mother's stress, in different ways.

Egg was a frail, stick-thin fussy eater, who avoided mealtimes as much as possible. Poppy was clingy and demanding; when she wasn't asleep, she was usually throwing a tantrum.

But worst of all was Poppy's identical twin, Daisy, who wasn't even living with us. Daisy suffered from pustular psoriasis, and when she was a baby her scratching and crying used to keep my parents up all night. During the day, Mammy was supposed to treat Daisy's skin frequently with emollients, but she never had the time to do it thoroughly and the neglect made things worse.

So much so that, by the time Daisy was two years old, Daddy had had enough. He decided it must be the damp Bradford air that was aggravating the problem, and made up his mind to send Daisy to Pakistan to live with his mother, Rasheeda, in Jallu.

Mammy hated Rasheeda, and she was horrified when she heard of Daddy's plan.

'You can't do it,' she cried hysterically. 'I'm not going to let you give my baby to that witch.'

'You can't stop me,' my father shouted. 'That child's driven me up the bloody wall. I can't take it any more.'

A week later, father and daughter were on their way to Jallu, while Mammy sank into a deep depression, and took to her bed.

It was a joyful time for me, because Daddy wasn't around and Climax did all the cooking.

Three years later, memories of Daisy had become blurred in my mind. It would have been easy to forget about her altogether, but for the fact that my mother would often burst into tears and plead with my father to bring her home. His response was always the same: 'Stop nagging, Gongal. She's in good hands. There's no one I'd rather have raising her than my mother. She'll be fine.'

Sometimes, when Daddy wasn't around, Mammy would say, 'I don't trust that Jallu crowd. I know what they're like. When I lived with Rasheeda she treated me like shit. Why would it be any different for Daisy?'

I'd heard so many conflicting stories about Rasheeda's cruelty (according to my mother) and saintliness (according to my father), I didn't know who to believe.

It was impossible for my mother to speak to Daisy, because neither family had a phone, so Mammy had to rely on occasional letters from Rasheeda to find out how her own child was. The letters all followed the same theme: gushing with enthusiasm about how well Daisy was doing on the farm, her skin almost healed by the country air and sunshine. She even had her own pet goat that Rasheeda's husband, Pappajee, had bought for her. At the end of every letter, Rasheeda claimed that Daisy didn't want to come back to England, but did miss her sisters and maybe my father should consider the importance of Daisy's feelings, and send over one or two of the girls to keep her company.

Instead of reassuring my mother, each letter would send her into a frenzy. 'That lying old bag's full of shit! How can Daisy miss her sisters? She doesn't even know them. As if one isn't enough, now she wants all my daughters. I just knew this was a bad idea.'

Then, in July 1975, Asif, one of my father's friends from Jallu, who now lived in Keighley, called round for a cup of tea and a chat. He said his father was ill, so he was going back home to visit his family soon. My mother waited until my father had gone to the toilet, then she pleaded with Asif to check up on Daisy, as she was out of her mind with worry.

A fortnight later, Asif returned with bad news: all was not as Rasheeda had led us to believe. Daisy, who had been in Jallu for three years, and was now five years old, was so neglected she was more animal than human. Asif had seen her, half-naked, squatting in the road and shitting like a dog. When he'd tried to speak to her, Daisy had shouted obscenities and thrown stones at him.

My father decided it was time for Daisy to come home, but he couldn't take the time off work to go and get her. So he sent a telegram to Rasheeda, saying: 'SEND DAISY BACK'.

It was the dead of night when the sound of the doorbell woke everyone up, and the whole family gathered in the passage to see what was going on. My father opened the door to be met by a weary-looking man.

'Mr Shah?' he asked timidly.

'Yes,' my father replied, making no attempt to conceal his irritation. 'What do you want?'

'Sorry to disturb you at this hour. I've just got back from Jallu and I'm on my way home to Leeds. I promised your mother I'd do her a favour. She asked me to drop this little one off.'

As he stepped to one side, a skinny, long-haired doe-eyed girl emerged from behind him; she bore a striking resemblance to Poppy. I felt my mouth drop open in surprise.

'Daisy?' my father said shakily. 'Is that you?'

'Oh my God!' my mother cried, clasping her hands together in delight. 'It is! It's Daisy!'

'Come in, love,' my father gushed, throwing the door wide open. 'It's so good to see you.'

'You motherfucker, you sisterfucker, I wanna fuck your granny's cunt. Come here and suck my dick,' Daisy replied.

There was a sharp intake of breath.

It appeared that Asif hadn't been exaggerating.

Chapter 5

The next morning, Mammy spent hours furiously shampooing Daisy's hair with nit lotion. Then she combed out all the dead lice (of which there were hundreds), filled a matchbox with them, and posted it to Rasheeda.

Now that Daisy was back, my mother tried to salve her guilty conscience by spoiling her rotten. Daisy was aggressive, greedy, foul-mouthed, cunning and selfish. She was terrified of falling into the toilet, so whenever she could get away with it she'd shit in the back garden. She was a savage.

I hated her for coming back and monopolizing my mother's affection. When I asked Mammy why she didn't make Daisy sleep in the shed with the rabbits, I was told not to be so silly, and to play nicely with my little sister.

I didn't expect anything different from my mother, but I was appalled when Egg, who was supposed to be my best friend, decided to take our new sister under her wing, and the two of them would play happily together, unaware of my growing resentment. Egg even gave Daisy the one-legged teddy bear that I'd given her as a birthday present.

Frustrated at being edged out by the newcomer, I began to channel a lot of my negative energy into making Poppy's life miserable. She was easy to scare, would cry a lot, and was too young to defend herself. She was perfect bully fodder.

My mother kept a huge milky-pink conch in a cupboard in the back room. We weren't allowed to play with it as it was fragile, but sometimes Daddy would let me hold it, and I would put it to my ear and listen to the rolling waves.

It was scary to think that the sea still haunted the insides of a shell it had surrendered many years ago.

'How does it do that?' I would ask.

'It's magic, Dilly,' Daddy would say.

But then I discovered that the shell had other amazing powers. Poppy was terrified of it – I could get her to do almost anything I wanted, just by threatening her with it.

One evening, I was chasing her with the shell when I dropped it and snapped off one of the spikes.

'How many times have I told you not to play with that?' my mother yelled.

'I was only showing Poppy.'

She snatched it from my hands, and then slapped my backside.

'Daddy said it's magic,' I sobbed.

'And he's right, you little bastard. Watch it disappear. You'll never see it again.'

She gave Poppy a cuddle and sent me up to bed.

When Estie found out about Daisy, she invited herself round. I was delighted to see her, and even more thrilled at the sight of the huge tray of cupcakes she'd brought with her. But then she said the cakes were for 'the little one from Pakistan'. Daisy stuffed as many in her mouth as she could, and I wanted to cry at the injustice. It seemed as though everyone was oblivious to my torment, treating the new arrival like royalty, while I was being overlooked. Estie was meant to be my friend, yet she hardly noticed me as she set her massive bottom down at the table, took a bottle of Lucozade from her handbag and asked my mother how she was.

The two of them chatted happily while Mammy made chapatis, then Estie asked if she could have one. Instead of eating it, she placed it on her knee and said, 'Ah, Gongal, that feels so good. Make me one for the other leg.' And the two of them howled with laughter at the sight of Estie sitting there, warming her knees with freshly cooked chapatis.

The amusement ended abruptly when Daisy shouted, 'Black cow!' at Estie, and threw a cupcake at her.

Estie rolled her eyes in horror. 'Gongal,' she demanded, 'are you going to let her get away with that?'

Mammy sighed dejectedly, and said, 'I'm so sorry, Estie, but Rome wasn't built in a day. It's going to take a long time to teach her manners; she's been living with savages for years.'

'Really?' Estie's eyes lit up at the whiff of gossip. 'Tell me more,' she implored. 'I'm not in a hurry to get home. Nathaniel won't be back for ages – he's gone to a church dance.'

My mother rinsed her hands under the tap. 'Well, in that case,' she said, 'why don't we go in the other room?'

Mammy piled the chapatis and remaining cupcakes on to a plate and led Estie into the back room, where they made themselves comfortable. I groaned inwardly at the prospect of another of my mother's stories about the evil relatives in Jallu, but I still followed them, because I wanted to be with Estie. As soon as she'd sat down, I climbed on to her lap. She felt warm and cuddly, and smelt of coconut oil. She tweaked my pigtail affectionately.

My mother scowled. 'What do I have to do to get a bit of peace and quiet around here? Dilly, get lost.'

'Oh leave her, Gongal,' Estie said. 'She's no bother. Now come on, girl, pass the chapatis and tell me everything.'

'Well,' my mother began, beaming with joyful anticipation. It was rare indeed for her to have the floor to herself; most of her friends just treated gossip as a way of trying to outdo each other. But then most of her friends came from Pakistan, and none of them liked their husband's families. 'Where shall I begin?'

'Start at the very beginning,' Estie sang. 'It's a very good place to start.'

I shuddered, and put my hand to my forehead. I knew this could take hours.

And so it was that Estie heard my mother's life story. About how her own mother had died, leaving her father, a dirt-poor farm labourer, to bring up three children in poverty, all of them living in a shack they shared with their chickens and goats.

'Life was hard, Estie,' she sighed. 'I spent most of the day working in the fields alongside my father. I never even got a chance to go to school.'

Estie tutted sympathetically, and shook her head. 'But you're all right now.'

'Am I? All I did when I got married was trade one set of problems for another. Sometimes I wish I'd never met Shah.'

'Why did you marry him, then?' Estie asked in surprise.

'I didn't have a choice. I lived in Chowki and Shah used to ride his bike over to see me on his way home from college. He's a cousin of mine, so no one thought much of it. But you know how one thing leads to another, and before I knew it I was pregnant with Monkey.'

Estie guffawed. 'Men, eh?'

My mother nodded. 'You're telling me. Shah knew Rasheeda would never approve of him marrying a pauper, so we sneaked off to the mosque and got wed in secret. Then he took me back to his house in Jallu, and all hell broke loose.'

Estie clapped her hands loudly. 'Girl, this is good! Tell me about the hell.'

'It was the first time I'd met Rasheeda, and we hated each other on sight. I think she was jealous of me. You should have seen me back then, love.' Mammy sighed nostalgically. 'I was gorgeous. I had skin the colour of honey, hair down to my waist, and I was as slender as a reed. Mind you, I was only thirteen at the time. But what really put her back up was that I'd ruined all her plans. Shah was doing a Business Studies degree, and once he graduated Rasheeda wanted to pack him off to England to get a job so he could send money back to her. She had big plans for that money. Every day I'd hear the same speech, over and over, until my ears bled: half the families in Jallu had sons in England who were sending money back home to their mothers. All the neighbours were racing their shiny new tractors around Jallu, and Rasheeda's pathetic husband was still using a stick to poke a cow across a field. So the last thing she wanted was for me to be on the scene, ready to reap the benefits once Shah started earning.'

'Silly cow, what did she expect?' Estie asked. 'A good-looking fella like Shah, he's not going to stay single all his life, is he? Blimey, I wouldn't mind copping a feel of that arse.'

The two women roared with laughter. Estie's lap bounced up and down alarmingly, and I struggled to hold on. When the rumbling finally subsided, I settled back down as Mammy said: 'It was sheer hell in that house. Everyone bossed me about. I was nothing more than a housemaid. Worse than that, Rasheeda brainwashed Shah into believing that he was some kind of king, and that his wife and any daughters we might have were worthless, and were there just to serve him. "Rule them with a rod of iron, or they'll all become whores," she used to say. That witch poisoned my own husband's mind against me. He'd punch me in the face just to make her happy, even when I was eight months pregnant. By the time he left for England, I was glad to see the back of him. As soon as he'd gone, Rasheeda put me to work in the fields. The day after Monkey was born, I was fetching water from the river for the livestock.'

Estie reached forward to grab a cupcake, and I tumbled on to the floor. I tried to climb back up, but Estie held me off.

'Gongal, I take my hat off to you. If my mother-in-law had tried that with me, I'd have knocked her block off.' She glanced at her watch. 'I'm going to have to make a move. Nathaniel will be back by now, and he'll be wanting his tea.'

'But you can't go,' my mother said. 'I haven't told you about Daisy yet.'

'Just five more minutes, then, and I can blame you if Nat's cross.' Estie slumped back into her chair and took a big bite out of her cake.

'Where was I?' my mother asked.

'Daddy's left for England,' I said. 'The next bit's about the money.'

Mammy shot me a dark look, then said: 'You know what, Estie? The whole time Shah was in England, he was sending money back for me, and that bitch Rasheeda was stealing it. I never saw a penny. When I finally got my visa and came to Bradford, she was furious because the money dried up and she still didn't have enough for a new tractor. But then Shah sent Daisy to live over there, and of course Rasheeda wanted lots of money to care for her. So for three years she's been getting money again and doing God knows what with it, while my child has been left to run wild like a savage. It's going to take me ages to undo the damage.'

Estie shook her head slowly. 'Dear Lord, preserve us. What's the world coming to when you can't trust your own blood? But don't you worry, Gongal, the Lord Jesus sees everything, and that woman's got it coming, for sure.'

I cast a sneaky glance at my mother, to see how she'd react to the idea of Jesus helping her out. I was mildly surprised to see that she was nodding her head in approval.

Chapter 6

In the world outside our house, everyone loved my father. He was six feet three inches tall, with green eyes and freckles. He'd been shaving his head ever since he'd seen the first episode of *Kojak*. He was educated, amiable, hard-working and always willing to lend a hand. The Pakistanis in Gomshall Road thought he was fantastic, not just because he was captain of the local cricket team (the York Shah Terriers), but also because he could read and write English, and helped them to fill out forms.

Throughout my childhood, we had a steady trickle of illiterate visitors, and it was always the same story: a smiling man would call round on the pretext of saying hello, and would then pull out some official document. With a perplexed look, he'd hand it to Daddy, who would waste no time in filling in the paperwork, while his guest drank tea and sang his praises.

If I'd ever summoned up the courage to tell any of these visitors that my father was a bully and a tyrant, they'd never have believed me. For them, Mr Shah was beyond criticism.

Whenever Daddy left the house he would be immaculately turned out, and would think nothing of weeding the front garden in a new suit and tie – which made him very popular with all the ladies on our street, except for my mother. Gabby, the alcoholic tart from Number 37, would hang out of her bedsit window and holler, 'Shah, that's a fine arse you've got there – can I have a squeeze?' And Daddy would pretend he hadn't heard, so she'd come bounding up our path, her floppy boobs swinging under her grubby white T-shirt, and say, 'Lend us a fiver, love.'

While he was protesting that he didn't have any money, she'd be stroking his head and saying, 'Bald men are such a turn-on.'

He'd smile and reply, 'Well, your hairy armpits aren't,' and chuckle to himself as he went back to his gardening.

I loved it when he was being given all this attention; it made him easy to be around. My mother, confined to the house and unable to do anything to stop the flirting, would sit in the window, bobbing her head up and down angrily like a budgie trying to frighten its reflection.

It wasn't just among the women on our street that my father created a lot of interest. He was the only male employee at the library, and there was never any shortage of female colleagues wanting to come over for dinner – which, of course, Mammy and Climax would have to prepare.

A week before the end of the summer holidays in 1975, Daddy threw a dinner party to celebrate his recent promotion to Head Librarian. This wasn't the first time he'd given a party, but on this occasion he went to extraordinary lengths to ensure that everything went without a hitch. He told his children and Doc he expected nothing but the best behaviour; he insisted on making the yogurt chutney and the shami kebabs himself, because he 'wanted the salt just right'; he even went out and bought a pineapple-shaped ice-bucket to chill the bottles of Coke and lemonade that he'd bought from the drinks delivery van. In a house full of psychedelic wallpaper, shag-pile rugs and mismatched furniture that he'd picked up from various house-clearance sales, a cheap plastic ice-bucket was the cherry on the cake. Most surprisingly of all, he persuaded Climax to spend all day in the kitchen.

By evening, the whole house smelt fantastic. Climax had roasted Juicy Anne, the big fat hen that Daddy had slaughtered especially in the back garden that morning, and there was a huge vat of mutton and potatoes bubbling away on the back burner. The dining table was groaning under the weight of stacks of poppadoms, buttery parathas, pans of pilau rice, kebabs, homemade cheese, sauces, and semolina pudding.

While Mammy was preparing the salad, Daddy was preparing himself. When he finally emerged from the bathroom, he was wearing his new white cable-knit tanktop over a starched white shirt, tweed trousers, and his head was glistening like a new cricket ball under a slick of olive oil.

My mother was baffled. She said he hadn't even made this much effort when they got married.

All became clear when the new assistant librarian walked through the door. She was tall, slender, had beautiful wavy red hair, and was wearing a tiny baby-doll dress that showed off her long white legs. My mother hated her on sight.

As soon as she got the chance, Mammy dragged Daddy into the kitchen and hissed, 'Who's that woman, and why's she here?'

'Jolene's new, so I invited her. It would have been rude not to.'

'I don't think there's enough food to go around. Climax has cooked for fifteen, and there's sixteen here now.'

'Don't worry, I've worked it all out mathematically; it'll be fine. Fifteen plus one equals sixteen, minus you makes fifteen. What's the problem?' he asked.

Mammy was still scratching her head when he continued, 'To be quite honest, Gongal, you could do with losing some weight.'

I headed into the back room to check out the gaggle of chattering women. Everyone was so glamorous in their summery frocks and flowing kaftans, I immediately felt uncomfortable in my blue polyester flares, green nylon blouse and sensible red Clarks shoes.

Daddy's boss, Mrs Fortune, was rummaging around in the ice-bucket and asking, 'Did anyone bring any wine?'

Jolene smiled at me, and I smiled back; she took a sip of her Coke and then dabbed her lips with one of the cloth napkins that only appeared when we had visitors.

During dinner, a lot of eye tennis went on between Daddy and Jolene. Once the last guest had gone, Mammy, who'd been silently fuming all evening, finally blew her top.

'Do you think I'm blind?' she shrieked at my father. 'I saw the way you kept brushing up against her. You made a complete ass of yourself.'

'Don't talk rubbish,' he replied. But I noticed the red flush that stole across his face.

'Who the hell does she think she is? She's lucky I didn't smash her glasses through the back of her head. Skinny white whore, coming into my house, eating my food and trying to steal my husband!'

I didn't know why anyone would want to steal my father, but with any luck she wouldn't bring him back.

The next day, there was a knock at the front door. Mammy peered through the nets to see who it was.

'I don't believe it – it's that ginger slut again! Dilly, go and see what she wants, but *do not* let her in.' The 'do' and 'not' were said slowly and emphatically, just in case I missed their importance, then she scuttled into the back room and hid.

I opened the door and Jolene smiled sweetly. 'Hi, Dilly, is your dad in?'

'He's out playing cricket,' I said, inhaling her perfume, which hung in the air like a dirty secret.

'And your mam? Is she home?'

'Yes, but she's too busy to talk to you.'

'Well, do you mind if I come in and wait for your dad?' she said as she breezed past me into the passage.

'But I don't know how long he'll be,' I replied lamely, conscious of the fact that I'd just let the red-headed tart into the house even though I'd been ordered not to. I left Jolene standing in the passage, and ran to get my mother.

As soon as I entered the back room, she caught hold of my arm. 'You were supposed to send her away,' she whispered, cuffing my head with the back of her hand, her green eyes flashing angrily. 'Get rid of her now!'

I sailed back into the passage, not really knowing what to say. I couldn't believe it: Jolene was sitting in the front room, as though she owned the place.

'My mam says you've gotta go. Daddy won't be back for ages.'

'It's okay, I'll wait for him.'

I didn't want to go back to break the news to my mother. In fact, I didn't know what to do, so I sat down on the sofa opposite Jolene, and counted the ornaments on the mantelpiece.

Jolene crossed her long legs and, as her dress rode up, I caught a glimpse of stocking-top. Her black shoes had incredibly high pointed heels. I was desperate to try them on, but I didn't have the nerve to ask her. She was oozing sexuality; no wonder my frumpy housebound mother didn't like her. Daddy had a gazelle for a girlfriend, and a warthog for a wife.

Jolene sat and smiled. I sat and smiled back. Mammy continued to hide. Finally, Jolene glanced at her watch, sighed dramatically and got to her feet.

'I've got to go. Will you be a good girl and tell your dad I called?'

There was no doubt in my mind that Daddy would know soon enough that Jolene had called, but it wouldn't be me telling him.

My mother settled down to wait for her prey. As soon as he came through the front door, she pounced.

'What the hell's going on?' she demanded.

'I don't know,' he replied, shrugging his shoulders.

'Why was that bitch here?'

He looked puzzled. 'I don't know what you're talking about.'

'Red hair, glasses, slut. Does that ring any bells?'

'Calm down, dammit, there's no need to shout,' my father told her.

'I'll shout if I want to. So you're just going to keep me to do all the work, and then you've got her to have fun with, is that it?'

'I can't help it if she finds me attractive.'

'Attractive, my arse! You want to have an affair? Do it somewhere else. Pack your things and get out.'

Daddy suddenly turned on me: 'You!' he said. 'Get me a towel and a bag.'

I ran to oblige.

'What do you want those for?' Mammy asked. I could tell she hadn't finished shouting, and now she was frustrated as well as furious.

'I'm off swimming,' came the reply.

My mother opened and shut her mouth silently like a goldfish. Eventually, she forced a word out. 'What?'

'Swimming,' he replied. 'Where are my underpants?'

'You can't go swimming in your underpants – this isn't Pakistan!' she yelled. 'And since when did you go swimming?'

'Since now,' he replied, as he brushed past her. 'You and Climax put too much ghee in the food. I need to get fit.'

He stormed off down the path, carrying his plastic bag awkwardly so it bounced off his leg as he walked.

While Daddy was out, Mammy stuffed some of his clothes into a battered brown suitcase which, according to the faded nametag, belonged to a Mr Jones (another good find from a jumble sale). As soon as she was out of the way, I dragged the case upstairs to the bedroom I shared with my sisters.

I told the twins to get lost because I wanted to play with Egg, who was busy making Plasticine models. But they refused to leave until I'd bribed them with orange-flavoured aspirins from the bottle that my mother kept by the fireplace.

'Come on, Egg, let's play,' I said, sucking on an aspirin. I handed two to her.

'What's in the case?'

'Daddy's stuff. Mammy's chucking him out.'

'Okay, so why have we got it?'

''Cos you're gonna be Daddy and I'll be Jolene. We're gonna run off together.'

She put on my father's suit and said she felt a bit weird, so I gave her another aspirin.

Chapter 7

I was woken in the middle of the night by a loud wail. Switching on the bedside light, I was surprised to see Egg lying on top of the bed we shared. She whined that she felt ill, and then she threw up all over the duvet.

Daddy hurried to the phone box on the corner to call Dr Johnson, who arrived a couple of hours later and said he couldn't find anything wrong with Egg, but suspected she'd picked up a bug of some sort. He said she needed plenty to drink, and suggested Lucozade. Suddenly I wished I was sick as well, because my friendship with Estie had given me a taste for Lucozade: the smell, the bright orange colour, the cellophane wrapping (which could later be used to make X-ray specs), the glugging as it left the bottle like a fizzy golden waterfall, the tiny bubbles jumping out of the glass and popping in the air. The only way I was going to get any of that Lucozade was if I played nursemaid to Egg. So I nursed her as well as I could, and took sneaky swigs from the bottle when no one was looking.

Egg was in bed for a week, during which my mother's mantra was, 'I can't understand it. Why does her vomit smell of oranges?'

As soon as Egg was up and about, we went to play in the back garden. We decided to grind some spices for our dolls, the way Mammy ground them for her curries. So I dug up pieces of stone, and Egg mashed them to a fine powder with the hammer I'd borrowed from my father's toolbox. As I squatted to join her, I farted as loudly as I could. Laughing as she bashed the hammer down, she missed the stone, and crushed her finger instead. The skin bubbled, ruptured, and then blood started to ooze out.

Mammy bandaged the wound with cotton wool and gauze, but the blood began to seep through almost immediately.

'Why's she bleeding so much?' Daddy asked, picking Egg up. 'I don't understand. It's only a little cut. I'd better take her to the hospital.'

Egg's fat plait of silky brown hair bobbed up and down like a tail as Daddy hurried down the path to the car.

With a heavy heart, I sat on the front step and waited for Egg to come back. I hoped she wouldn't die; she was my best friend. She was the shy little butterfly with all the pretty colours and vulnerable good looks, while I was the loud-mouthed brat whom everyone mocked. Considering how much time we spent together, it was surprising that none of my brashness had rubbed off on her. Her emerald-green eyes, freckled face and olive complexion won her a lot of attention; at school she was constantly mollycoddled by Mrs Thomas, the headmistress, who'd pick her up and say she was so light she could be a fairy on top of a Christmas tree. Every time I asked her to pick me up she'd say she couldn't, because I was too fat and if I didn't enjoy my food so much then maybe I'd be as slim as Egg. But there was no way I was going to curb my passion for two scoops of mashed potato, boiled carrots and watery cabbage followed by chocolate pudding and a ladle of custard, just to get lifted into the air.

A few hours later, Daddy returned with Egg. She had a thick bandage over her hand, and was sporting a sticker that read: 'I was very good at the hospital today.'

That evening, she just lay in bed, clutching Turd (her scruffy rabbit, who'd come from the same jumble sale as Hamble), and smiling serenely now the drama was over. I hovered nearby, wanting to look after her, and not really knowing how to, but hoping there'd be some Lucozade to aid her recovery.

I was busy tucking her in and rearranging her pillows when my mother came into the bedroom carrying a jug of water and her latest knitting project, a brown tank-top.

Egg whined that her finger was still hurting, so I went to the fireplace and grabbed the aspirins.

'Dilly, what are you doing with those? Put them back.'

'I'm gonna give Egg a vitamin treat, Mammy.'

'Yeah, they taste all orangey,' Egg added.

My mother looked horrified. 'Oh my God!' she shouted, as she slapped me across the face. 'I'm sick of you, you're nothing but trouble.'

I felt my heart sink with despair as she called out: 'Shah! Come upstairs now!'

But when my father arrived he surprised us all by taking my side, accusing my mother of being unfit to raise children, and saying, 'It's your fault, Gongal, you shouldn't be keeping medicine in the kids' room.'

'She hands out tablets like she's a doctor, and you're blaming me? I'll kill her!'

As she lunged at me, I ran and hid behind my father, using his legs as a shield to protect myself from her grasping claws.

'If you lay a finger on her, you'll be sorry. Just leave it,' Daddy said firmly.

I had temporary immunity, and she knew it. There was no way she could touch me without disobeying a direct order; if she tried to hit me now, she'd be in big trouble.

'Stay away from me, Dilly,' my mother said, as she snatched up her knitting and left the room.

'You'd better keep out of her way, the woman's mad,' my father said to me, and followed her out.

From downstairs, the familiar sound of angry voices rose and fell in waves, one minute muffled and indignant, the next thunderous and furious. I knew the aspirins weren't the real reason why Mammy was so upset; it was the prospect of losing Daddy to a white woman that was really preying on her mind.

Things finally reached crisis point a few days later. I was playing in the bedroom with Doc's Tonka car collection, when my mother came in. I could tell she'd been crying.

'Your father wants us to go to Pakistan,' she said.

My heart soared. We'd never been anywhere as a family. Daddy had often promised to take us out for the day, but he'd always changed his mind at the last minute. And now we were off to Pakistan. I rushed over to hug her.

'When are we going?' I asked excitedly.

She held me back and said, 'Why are you so happy, you stupid girl? Your mother's about to be booted out of her own home, and you're rejoicing? He's infatuated with that cow, and now he wants to marry her. If he thinks it's so easy to get rid of me, he'd better think again.'

All hope of a family holiday was dashed.

She held her hands out. The knuckles were swollen and bruised.

'What happened, Mammy?'

'He hit me.'

'Why?'

'Never mind, I'll get him back,' she said coldly.

Thanks to my parents, I'd experienced elation, disappointment, horror, confusion and apprehension, all in the space of sixty seconds. It was just business as usual in Sharnia.

A week later, my mother was crowing. 'It serves him right: my prayers have been answered.' She was talking to herself, but I stopped playing and listened to her monologue. 'The red-headed harlot's turned him down,' she tittered. 'He asked her to marry him, and she told him she's already engaged to someone else.'

I decided to look up 'harlot'; it sounded brilliant. I was going to use it on Hamble as soon as I found out what it meant. Mammy was still gloating as I hunted for the dictionary.

'Bloody fool, he got the right-sized slap for his ugly face. He wanted a white woman on his arm so he could show off. He thinks he's so smart, but he's a moron. That'll teach him to think with his dick.'

For the next few weeks, my mother seized every opportunity to poke fun at my father's failed affair. She taunted him mercilessly, and would sing, 'I'm not in love, so don't forget it . . .' every time he came in from work.

She even found a photo of Jolene hidden away in his briefcase, and used a black biro to give the harlot a big handlebar moustache. He was fuming when he saw what she'd done, but all he said was, 'Bitch!' as he stormed out of the house with her laughter ringing in his ears.

Chapter 8

In October 1975, our cat, Trumpet, had four kittens. Suzy, a girl in my class at Fox Hill Primary, said she'd be my friend if I gave her one of them. Mammy told me to wait until the kittens were old enough to be separated from their mother. So, when they were five weeks old, I put a tiny blue-eyed kitten in my coat pocket, and took it up the hill to school.

Suzy decided she didn't want it after all. I was so angry that I tried to flush her coat down the toilet, but it got stuck and the toilet overflowed and flooded the cloakrooms. The kitten was adopted by the caretaker, while I was smacked by Mrs Thomas, told I was stupid, and made to stand at the front of the classroom wearing a dunce's hat.

Later that day, I was sent to the book corner, to give me time to consider the consequences of my actions. It was there that I discovered *A Book of Princes and Princesses* by Ruth Manning-Sanders. My love affair with fairytales had just begun. Up until that moment, I'd always considered reading a chore, not a joy.

Within a week, I'd devoured *A Book of Dwarfs* and *A Book of Ogres and Trolls*. In the evenings, while I was busy reading, Egg would be copying the pictures and cooing at the princesses in all their beautiful clothes.

At night I would lie in bed and imagine what it would be like to be a princess. I wanted to wear a dress like Snow White's, and I wanted my hair to look like Rapunzel's.

Sometimes Egg and I would take the net down from our bedroom window and drape it over our heads and pretend we were princesses who were about to get married.

In December, I asked my mother if she could make me a ball-gown; her eyes lit up as she said, 'Ah, Dilly, I've got something even better than that.'

My heart danced a little jig as I imagined a buttercup-yellow dress and matching silk slippers; but no, it was just a crappy purple salvaar kameez.

The next morning, she told me to wear it to school. I kicked up a huge fuss.

'I can't go in this,' I cried. 'We've got rehearsals for the Nativity, and I wanna be Mary.'

She shuddered. 'You want to be Mary?'

'Yes, and if you make me wear this stupid thing then I might as well not bother, 'cos there's no way Mary wore anything so dumb. If I wear this I'm gonna end up being a shepherd – or worse, one of the animals.'

'Oh my God, what am I going to do with you?' She caught hold of me, and through clenched teeth she said, 'You listen to me, Dilly Shah: you're going to wear these clothes today if you know what's good for you.'

When I got to school, Egg skipped off in her English clothes, abandoning me to the taunts of my classmates, who spent most of the day singing, 'If you're baggy and you know it, clap your hands . . .'

My teacher, Miss Henderson, told me I looked really nice, but I didn't believe her. 'That colour is beautiful,' she said, stroking my hair. 'You look so sweet.'

'I don't wanna be sweet. I can't run in these stupid baggy things, and the other kids have been calling me Dilly Bongo.'

Even she couldn't fight back a smile. She put her arms around me and held me tight. 'Sweetheart, your clothes are lovely. You look so exotic.'

I had no idea what 'exotic' meant, so I made a mental note to look it up in the dictionary.

Jane Baxter was cast as Mary. I hated her, with her perfect round freckled face; the way her hair fell soft, brown and long down to her waist. I was cast as a shepherd and ended up wearing a costume that was way too big, and a checked tea towel on my head, but it didn't make me feel as ridiculous as I'd felt when I arrived at school that morning.

After the Nativity, it was time to prepare for the Christmas party. Miss Henderson told the class she wanted everyone to dress up as a character from a fairytale. I knew straight away who I wanted to be – Rapunzel! Egg told me that her class was going to dress up too, and she wanted to go as Snow White.

That afternoon, when we got in from school, we made a beeline for Mammy and asked her to make the costumes. She said she'd see what she could do. I was so excited at the prospect of dressing up as a princess, it felt as though I'd swallowed the sunshine. I was afraid to speak in case all the sunbeams trapped inside my body escaped.

Come party day, Egg and I awoke to find that we were going as ourselves. As we walked up the hill that morning, it seemed that every fairytale princess known to man had escaped from the pages of the Ruth Manning-Sanders books, and was heading to Fox Hill Primary. Some of the princesses were carrying trays of iced cupcakes or bowls of Angel Delight; others were holding on to their conical hats and giggling as they skipped happily along with their mothers. I was holding Egg's hand and a plastic bag of sweaty samosas.

Chapter 9

Mammy was in the kitchen, feeling unwell and looking for sympathy. She put on her most pathetic face, as she watched Daddy gathering together his cricket gear. 'I'll be in the park if anyone needs me,' he said.

'But I need you,' she wailed. 'I can't get rid of this damn backache. How am I supposed to look after the kids when I'm in this state?'

'If it's that bad, go to bed. Dilly can sort the kids out,' he said distractedly, heading for the door.

My mother turned to me, and said, 'You heard your father. I'm off to bed, so you're going to have to see to things. And please, for God's sake, make sure those kids keep the noise down.' She grimaced with pain as she got up and made her way towards the back room.

I looked out of the window. It was a beautiful sunny day, and Egg, Daisy and Poppy were busy playing hopscotch in the garden. Egg's slippers made a lovely slapping sound on the path as she threw a twelve and hopped crazily up and down.

My mother reappeared. 'My ankles are hurting – give me a massage,' she said.

We went into the back room, and she climbed into bed. As I rubbed her feet, I could hear three happy voices coming from the garden, and I thought about how much

I resented my mother. I especially resented her when she was pretending to be sick, which was becoming more of a regular occurrence.

'That's enough. Leave me alone. I need to sleep,' she said abruptly.

'Okay,' I replied, only too happy to escape.

As soon as I stepped into the garden, the balmy spring sunshine warmed my face. It felt wonderful. Egg was lying on her back on top of the garden wall, looking up at the sky. There was no sign of the twins.

'Hey, Dilly,' she said. 'Come and check out the clouds – you can see some really cool shapes. That one there looks like a dolphin.'

I lay down on the wall a few feet away from her, and stared up at the wispy cotton wool clouds.

'It makes me feel dizzy,' I said, as I squinted at the sun.

'What was that?' Egg asked. She sat up suddenly, looking alarmed.

'What?'

'That noise,' she replied.

I strained my ears, but all I could hear were the usual sounds of spring – nothing that might be classed as strange by Gomshall Road standards.

'I can't hear anything,' I mumbled.

'Shhh! Listen, I heard something.'

'What did it sound like?' I asked.

'It was weird.'

'Yeah,' I said, climbing down from the wall. 'That's what you get when you lie around all day looking up at the sky. Come on, let's get sommat to eat.'

'There! Did you hear that?' she whispered, looking excited. 'It was a goat.'

'Yeah, right, course it was,' I said.

'I'm telling you, it was a goat.'

'Look around you, Egg. This is Bradford, you know, not Jallu.'

'Must've been a Yorkshire goat, then,' she said, getting off the wall and putting on her slippers.

'That's daft,' I said. 'Maybe it was Mammy.'

'You retard,' she mocked. 'Why would she be bleating?'

'Dunno, but I'm gonna go and check on her.'

I was halfway down the path when I heard a 'maaaaa, maaaaa'. I paused and stared at Egg.

'I told you, didn't I?' she beamed. 'It's a goat.'

'Come on,' I said. 'It must be in the back alley.'

But when we opened the gate and poked our heads out, there was no sign of a goat; just Daisy and Poppy coming down the alley, carrying Lolly Gobble Choc Bombs.

When they came into the garden, Egg wasted no time in telling them what we'd heard. Daisy finished her lolly, then climbed on to the wall that separated our garden from Number 40's. The house had been empty for ages, and the garden was overgrown with a sea of weeds as high as a man, punctuated by wild rose bushes that spread out vicious thorny branches, waiting to scratch the skin of the unwary explorer.

'Oh wow!' Daisy exclaimed, as she stood on the wall. 'You lot, come here quick.'

We all climbed on to the wall. I couldn't believe my eyes – wandering through the thick vegetation was the cutest little billy goat I'd ever seen. 'Aw, it's so sweet,' Poppy said, as she hugged herself. We all cooed in agreement.

'Where d'you think it came from?' Egg asked.

'Dunno,' I replied. 'Come on, I've got a plan. We're gonna climb over the wall and bring Little Boy round here.'

Egg looked alarmed. 'What if we get caught?'

'So? It's not as if we're breaking any laws. I bet you any money the gypsies stole it off the moors and dumped it here.'

'Oh, that's all right then,' she said brightly. 'It's about time someone stole sommat off them.'

Catching Little Boy wasn't easy – he was very agile for such a tiny scrap of a thing, and he kept darting into bushes to avoid capture – but eventually he gave up, and Daisy managed to grab hold of him.

Dragging Little Boy by his collar, we herded him into our garden. He bleated loudly while four pairs of hands all tried to stroke him at once. I was desperate to cuddle the little thing; I hoped he would be ours forever.

'Oi, Daisy, go back next door and get lots of grass,' I ordered.

As Daisy climbed on to the wall, she spat on me, then jumped down before I had a chance to hit her.

'I hate her,' I said. 'Wouldn't it be brilliant if there was a lion hiding in there, and it gobbled her up?'

Egg let out a deep booming laugh, and Little Boy jumped with fright. As Poppy patted the goat's head, I announced, 'This is our secret pet; Mammy and Daddy mustn't know about him. We're gonna hide him in the shed.'

'We can't keep him in there,' Egg said.

'Why not?' I asked.

''Cos Daddy'll find him the next time he goes in there.'

My mind was racing. What would my parents say when they found the goat? Would my father let Little Boy live in the shed? What would happen if the gypsies came back for him? If this all went horribly wrong, would I be able to blame somebody else?

'You lot stay here with the goat; I'm gonna see if Mammy's up yet. If we keep her sweet, maybe she'll let him stay.'

When I went into the back room, my mother was beginning to stir.

'What have you been up to?' she asked.

'Nothing much.'

'I'm feeling a bit better. Make me some tea, Dilly,' she said.

'Mammy, have you ever thought about getting another pet?' I asked.

'No, why?'

'No reason. Would you like something about the size of a dog?'

'What are you on about? You know I hate dogs – those things are disgusting. The angels won't come in the house if there's a dog.'

'Will they come in if there's a goat?' I asked.

'What?'

'A goat. How do angels feel about goats? Do they like them?'

'Dilly, what on earth is wrong with you?'

'Nothing, Mammy. I was just thinking out loud.'

'If you ask me, goats aren't much better than dogs.' She scrutinized my face. 'You're up to something, aren't you?'

'It's okay, don't worry, Mammy. I have to go.'

I ran out to check on my new pet. The poor thing

looked miserable – not surprising, really, as he had three Shah kids fawning all over him.

'You lot,' I said, 'we can't tell Mammy and Daddy about the goat.'

'Why?' Daisy asked. 'It's not a big deal.'

'Yes, it is. Mammy doesn't like goats; if she finds out, she'll get rid of him.'

Little Boy chose that moment to wriggle free from his captors, and sprinted for the kitchen door with all of us chasing after him as fast as we could. He raced through the kitchen and into the passage. His little hooves made the most wonderful clippety-cloppety sound as he dashed across the tiled floor into the back room, where my mother was lying on her back with her eyes shut, dozing gently.

Little Boy bleated loudly as he zigzagged across the back room, narrowly avoiding my lunges.

'What the . . . ?' my mother shrieked, almost falling off the bed in surprise.

'It's okay, Mammy,' I said as I finally caught hold of the goat's collar. 'He's ours.'

Egg, Daisy and Poppy all piled into the back room and skidded to a halt.

'Ours?' my mother squawked, as she tried to collect her thoughts. 'Since when?'

Nobody spoke.

Suddenly, a look of rage flashed across my mother's face. 'I knew it,' she hissed. 'That bloody man. He's been hiding it in the shed, hasn't he?'

Four pairs of eyebrows reached for the ceiling. But this unexpected development looked promising, and no one saw the need to correct my mother's misunderstanding.

'I can't turn my back for one minute without him doing something stupid,' she wailed.

I patted Little Boy's head, and watched in fascination as black marbles dropped from his bottom onto the carpet.

'Get that thing out of here. I don't bloody believe this; just wait till he gets home – I'm going to kill him.'

When my father came home, my mother was sitting up in bed waiting for him.

'Have you started making dinner yet?' he asked, as he poked his head around the back room door.

'How the hell did you think you were going to get away with it?' she snapped. 'It's not staying. I want it gone.'

'What do you mean, you want it gone? Want what gone?'

'Don't take the piss,' she spat. 'If you want to be a farmer, go and be one somewhere else.'

'I've got to go, or I'll be late for mosque.'

'What do you mean? You've only just come in. I haven't finished with you yet,' my mother said, but he'd already gone.

Relieved, I rushed out into the garden, where Little Boy was grazing enthusiastically on my father's coriander. We all played with him for a while, then the front doorbell rang. It was my father again.

'There's a thief about,' he said, as he strolled in.

'Really?' I replied, and followed him into the back room.

My mother sat up. 'Right,' she said. 'Now we can finish our conversation.'

'Never mind that – I've got something to tell you.

When I went to mosque, some of the men were talking about Anwar. He bought a goat, and someone stole it. Anwar's fuming.'

'Take a look out of the window,' my mother said.

'What?'

'Your daughter reckons she found it,' my mother sighed, folding her arms in a gesture that said, 'I told you so'.

'Dilly, please tell me you didn't take it,' my father said, shaking his head. 'Those people are going to say I stole it.'

'No they're not, Daddy. I found it.'

'What do you mean, you found it? It wasn't lost.'

'You have to take it back,' my mother said, clearly relieved that this was now my father's problem, leaving her free to snipe from the sidelines.

'Sometimes I really hate my children,' my father snarled, stomping into the garden with me close behind.

'It's very small,' he said, as soon as he saw Little Boy. 'I can't believe they're making so much fuss; there's hardly any meat on it.'

'Can we keep him, Daddy?' I asked. 'Please, Daddy, I'll look after him.'

'No way!' my mother shouted from the kitchen doorway. 'Never! No way! It's not staying!'

'I'm never going to live this down,' my father said to me. 'You have to take it back.'

'I didn't steal him. What sort of moron leaves a goat in someone else's back garden?' I asked.

'What sort of moron takes a goat from someone else's back garden?' he replied, then, pushing me aside, he plucked up Little Boy in his arms and plopped him over the wall into the garden of Number 40.

'I'm not going to have people calling me a thief,' he said. 'I'm going to tell them that you bastards were just playing with it, and as soon as I found out, I made you put it back.'

'They won't believe you,' my mother said.

'For once, Gongal, you might have a point.' He looked at the miserable faces staring up at him, and said brightly, 'Cheer up. I'm going to get my own goat. And it's going to be a lot bigger and fatter than that scrawny little thing. That'll show them I wouldn't need to steal Anwar's.'

My father smiled at my mother as he strode purposefully past her, pausing only to grab his keys before he was gone once again.

'Mammy, has Daddy gone to buy a goat?' Poppy asked hopefully.

'Not in my lifetime,' she replied.

'But Mammy,' Egg said, 'you know what he's like. It might not be today, but one day he'll come home with a goat, and there'll be nothing you can do about it.'

Chapter 10

My parents were happy for us to talk to any of the neighbours – except for the gypsies, who came every year. Whenever they were camping in Titus Park, my father warned us to stay away; he said they were dangerous. Once, desperate to see what bad things they got up to, I sneaked out of the house and hid in the long grass next to the camp, so I could watch them. It was all very uninteresting – the adults were doing household chores, while the children played around the brightly painted caravans. My father caught me, smacked me hard, and dragged me home.

According to Daddy, the trains were even more dangerous than the gypsies. He said he would thrash the life out of anybody who so much as tried to scale the wall to get on to the tracks. What he didn't know was that Monkey and Doc often climbed over and put pennies on the rails to see how flat the trains would make them. One day, I decided to do the same. I was as disobedient as the boys, but not as devious. They always posted a lookout, whereas I just took my chance – and got caught by my father, who smacked me hard, and dragged me home again.

Mammy was fuming. 'You so much as look in the direction of the trains and I'll poke your eyes out.' She slapped my face and threw my flattened penny at me. 'Get upstairs and wash your ugly face.'

As I rushed past her, my father said, 'Gongal, she's a menace. Keep an eye on her.'

The smacks and the warnings were soon forgotten, and three days later I was on the tracks again, flattening more pennies. This time, Daddy gave me such a beating that his fists left bruises all over my back. The next day at school there was a medical; when I refused to take my frock off, the nurse took me to one side and forced me to remove it. When she asked me what had happened to my back, I was faced with a dilemma: I could tell the truth, and suffer the consequences, or tell a lie, and it would all be forgotten about. My mother had warned me often enough what would happen if I ever told anyone about the beatings at home: 'Social Services will take you away, put you in a care home with rats and spiders, and they'll make you eat pork every day. Is that what you want?'

But I was even more afraid of what would happen if I told the truth and Social Services *didn't* put me into care and I was left at home to face the wrath of my parents. So I took the easy option, and told the nurse that Doc had beaten me up.

That evening, I was just about to sneak off to the park with Monkey's binoculars, to see if the gypsies were doing anything bad yet, when my father appeared out of nowhere and demanded to know where I was going.

'Birdwatching in the street,' I answered, as casually as I could.

'I wasn't born yesterday, Dilly,' he snarled, as he seized

me by the arm and dragged me into the kitchen, where Mammy and Climax were sitting at the table eating custard creams.

'Gongal,' he roared at my mother, 'you're supposed to be watching this little bastard, not stuffing your face. I just caught her again.'

My mother jumped to her feet and shook me, making the binoculars bounce up and down against my chest. 'What were you up to?' she demanded angrily.

'I was just going to look for birds,' I sobbed.

I thought my father was going to fly into a rage, but he just shrugged his shoulders and said in a very flat but determined voice: 'Dilly, you've blown it this time. You're banned. No more going out to play round the front. From now on, you stay in the house, the back garden and the alley. You can only go in the front garden if I'm there. If I see you anywhere else, I'll break your legs.'

I suddenly felt cold with horror, as the significance of what he'd just said sank in.

'Don't say you weren't warned,' he added, then strolled out of the kitchen without another word.

'Serves you right,' my mother said coldly, then turned her attention back to the biscuits. 'Look at her, Climax. Who does she think she is, Johnny Morris?'

Climax chuckled.

I tried to speak, but the lump in my throat was so big that it refused to go up or down, and no words would come out.

That night, as I lay in bed, I prayed that my father had just been in a bad mood, and would change his mind in the morning. But the next day, he stuck to his guns, and told me I couldn't go further than the back alley unless I was on my way to school or mosque, or running an errand for my mother. He also went to great lengths to point out that the Ban would be in force until I was married; after that, it would be up to my husband to decide where I could and couldn't go.

With bitter irony, I realized that the next time I could play in the street would be when I was too old to enjoy it.

I spent most of the day sitting in the window, watching my sisters playing in the front garden and wishing I was dead.

Chapter 11

Sunday, 20 June 1976 was the date of the annual Titus Park flower competition – a single day in the calendar, but, as far as Daddy was concerned, the culmination of three months' intense preparation. After many failures, he was determined that this year, finally, he would walk out of the park with a winner's rosette, and it would be his pansies that would be the talk of the neighbourhood.

For weeks he'd lovingly tended to them. Every evening after dinner he would be out there, working his magic: dousing them with bone meal fertilizer, arranging little blue force-fields of slug pellets around the pots, and covering the flowers with plastic bags at night to protect them in case there was a frost.

The pansies were enormous. Planted in dozens of terracotta pots, they were various shades of purple, ranging from light to almost black. Some petals had a frill of cream, and the eye in the centre of each flower was a deep sunshine yellow. They reminded me of the velvet fabric swatches in my mother's sewing box.

Whenever Daddy went out to water them, I would watch in fascination as the beads of water rolled off the petals, like a string of pearls that had just snapped.

* * *

It was late one afternoon when Egg and I offered to help shell the peas that my mother had picked from the back garden. The dining table was a sea of green. Mammy and Climax were already busy squeezing pods, playing 'one for the pot and two for me' – and who could blame them? The peas from the back garden were always deliciously sweet and tender.

We sat ourselves down at the table, reached for a pile of pods, and sang: 'As sweet as the moment when the pod went . . .' and then we both put our index fingers inside our cheeks and made the popping sound from the advert.

'For the love of God,' my mother snapped. 'Will you two stop that noise? It's getting on my nerves.'

Climax threw a pea at Egg; it hit her on the cheek.

'Try again,' Egg said, and opened her mouth wide, like a seal trying to catch a fish.

As Climax took aim, my mother scowled at her and said, 'Why don't you act your age, you old bag?'

To which Climax replied, 'What's your problem – wrong time of the month, love?'

'No, wrong time of the day. Shah's going to be home any minute, and dinner's nowhere near ready. There'll be hell to pay, and all you lot can do is muck about.'

'Like I give a toss,' Climax said dismissively, as she threw a pea at my mother. 'Do you want a gobstopper? The sugar might do you some good.'

'Don't you think you're a bit old for kiddies' sweets?'

'Can I have one?' I asked hopefully.

Climax reached inside her bra and pulled out a paper bag, which she tossed onto the table. 'Help yourself.'

I was just about to thank her when Daddy came flying into the kitchen with a look of terror in his eyes.

'Who did it?' he bellowed.

Mammy looked alarmed. 'Who did what?'

'Some bastard's chopped the heads off the pansies.'

'Oh, is that all?' she sighed, and popped a pea into her mouth.

'What do you mean, "Is that all"? Those were my prize pansies!'

'Oh, okay,' Mammy said. 'Never mind; I'm sure they'll grow back.'

'Why don't you call the police?' Climax asked. 'Maybe they can dust for fingerprints.'

Egg and I watched in silence as Climax and my mother fell into fits of laughter.

'Is that it, then?' Daddy thundered, almost blue with apoplexy.

'Well, surely there can't be more?' my mother said.

'You're at home all day, and you couldn't even keep an eye on the garden,' he barked at her.

She swallowed her laughter, and said, 'Honestly, do you think I've got nothing better to do than sit in the window all day? If they were that special, you should have kept them round the back. You were just trying to show them off to the neighbours, weren't you? Well, that'll teach you: God doesn't like braggers.'

'Take it easy, Shah, you look like you're going to have a heart attack,' Climax said. 'If it's any consolation, these peas you grew are bloody brilliant. Do you want me to fry some up for you?'

My thoughts instantly flew back to the last time I'd had peas à la Climax; straight from the garden, sizzling in a pool of Kerrygold with garlic granules, black pepper, grated rock salt and chopped mint, cooked until they turned into a dark chewy purée, then spread on slices of home-baked white bread, with a topping of Heinz salad cream. One look at Egg confirmed that she was taking the same trip down Memory Lane.

I was jolted from my reverie by Daddy pulling me out of the chair.

'Was it you?' he shouted angrily.

'No, Daddy, it wasn't.'

'Hah, that makes a change,' Climax said sarcastically. 'I bet you any money she knows something.'

'Honestly, it wasn't me,' I said. 'But I did see Doc hanging around out there earlier.'

Daddy didn't wait to hear any more; he was already on his way to find his nephew.

Climax shot me a withering glance. 'What the hell did you do that for?'

'Why not?' I asked. 'If you can blame me, then I can blame Doc. He always looks guilty, anyway.'

'You little cow,' Climax snapped.

'Oh, shut up,' I said.

My mother reached over and slapped my face so hard that the gobstopper tucked away in my cheek flew across the kitchen, bounced several times on the floor, and rolled under the cooker.

Climax smiled smugly as she picked up the bowl of peas and plonked it in the sink. 'That'll teach you to talk back,' she said.

Later that evening, a mean silence descended over the dining table. Doc sat next to his mother, eyes red from crying. Daddy sat regally at the head of the table, satisfied that justice had been done.

Meanwhile, the stolen flowers were wrapped up in Izal toilet paper, fast asleep inside the pages of the old *Oxford English Dictionary* on the bookshelf in the front room.

As soon as they were dry, I was going to make a Father's Day card and decorate the border with the pansies. This year, Daddy wouldn't be able to say that all his kids were useless, and that not one of them had even bothered to give him a card. I even harboured a faint hope that he would be so moved by my thoughtfulness that he would lift the Ban.

As Father's Day wasn't until 20 June, which was still almost two weeks away, I felt safe in the knowledge that, by then, he would surely have forgotten all about the flower competition. I couldn't wait to see the look on his face.

My smugness disappeared that night, when I overheard Doc telling Monkey what he'd do if he ever found out who'd stolen the flowers. His voice was dribbling with venom. In a panic, I crumpled up the pansies and flushed them down the toilet.

Chapter 12

During the blistering summer of 1976, the tar in the back alley melted. It looked like liquorice as it bubbled up between the cobbles; Egg and I gouged it out with broken twigs, rolled it into little balls, and told Poppy it was aniseed Bazooka Joe gum, and that she really should try it because it was delicious. She got her own back by filling our bed with hundreds of ladybirds that she'd collected from the pear tree in the back garden.

Daisy spent most of the summer in the back alley, riding her bike up and down, pretending to be Evel Knievel. Somehow, she'd acquired a Raleigh Chopper. No one could work out where it had come from, but she let us all have goes on it, so we didn't ask too many questions.

On the rare occasions that Monkey and Doc showed their faces, they'd convince us the best place to stay cool was under a tree, and then shake the branches so we'd be showered with greenflies.

Climax spent the summer in the back garden, sunbathing on a mattress she and Doc had rescued from the railway embankment. She was totally unconcerned by the attention she attracted from the neighbourhood children who would come by to take a look at this whale of a woman, baking in the sun. She'd lie there for hours on end, with her kameez tucked under her bra and the legs of her salvaar rolled up above her knees. She was an impressive sight, with her flabby stomach spreading out like a spongy mountain range; it was a sickly yellow colour, illuminated by shiny stretch-marks that looked like lightning strikes.

My mother had just been diagnosed with high blood pressure, and ordered to lose some of the weight she'd been piling on for the last few years. The hospital had told her that, at five feet five inches and now weighing fifteen stones, she was obese, and had given her a diet and exercise plan, which she'd thrown in the bin the minute she'd got home. She spent the summer indoors, popping pills, watching TV and feeling sorry for herself.

Every day, my father would come home from the library, sweating in his work clothes, and hook the hosepipe up to the kitchen tap, then spend the evening trying to save his precious plants, while keeping a lookout for snoops from the Water Board. But it was a waste of time; by the end of the summer, everything in the garden had turned to dust.

The weather was still beautiful when I started at Holly Field Middle School in September. On my first day, I met a girl called Angie. We were both late, and, as we ran across the playground, I realized we were heading in the same direction.

'Are you in Mr Smith's class?' she asked.

'Yeah,' I said, panting. 'Are you?'

'Yeah. Hi, my name's Angela; all my friends call me Angie.'

'Hi, I'm Dilly. If I had any friends they'd call me Dilly.'

We found our class, and when we got inside everyone stopped what they were doing to watch us. I squirmed with embarrassment, mumbled an apology to the teacher, and sat down.

Mr Smith, who had shoulder-length blond hair, said, 'See me before you go for your lunch, please, girls.'

At lunchtime we waited for him to speak to us.

'I've never had anyone late on their first day,' he said, smiling at us.

'I'm sorry, Sir, I missed the bus,' I told him.

'I slept in, Sir,' Angie said.

'Just don't make a habit of it,' he said, as he glanced at his watch. 'Right, off you go.'

I heaved a sigh of relief and went in search of the canteen. Holly Field felt like a maze to me – it seemed to go on forever. The boys wore black pumps inside the building, and the girls wore Scholl slippers; I was the only girl in the whole school who didn't have any. It was so embarrassing to have to wear plimsolls because Scholls were too expensive.

Wandering down endless corridors, we finally found the canteen. As Angie and I stood in the queue with our trays, she talked non-stop; it was nice not to have to say too much, as I was still finding my feet. Middle school wasn't what I'd expected; in fact it was a huge shock to my system. I was no longer one of the older children; I was now one of the youngest, and it was quite terrifying to see the size of some of them, especially the boys. Everyone came across as much more grown-up than at primary school.

Moving quickly down the line, I handed my plate to the dinner lady and she tipped some boiled potatoes and carrots onto it. I was about to pick up a knife and fork when I felt a sharp push from behind. I turned and found myself facing a huge boy.

'Oi, watch it,' I said.

'No, you watch it.' He jabbed me in the arm. 'Out of the way, Paki.'

'What did you call me?' I asked furiously.

'Paki,' he said, as he put his face up close to mine. His breath smelt stale, like he hadn't bothered to clean his teeth.

'Don't call me that.'

Laughing loudly, he caught hold of my plait and pulled it sharply. 'Shut your face. You Pakis should go back to your own country.'

'Leave her alone, Webster,' a voice said.

I looked around to see who was brave enough to challenge him; it was a freckle-faced girl with a shocking mass of light-brown curly hair.

'Why don't you pick on someone your own size?' she demanded, coming to stand next to me. Without waiting for an answer, she propelled me and Angie towards a dining table.

'You all right?'

'Yeah,' I replied shakily as I sat down. 'Thanks for that, but there was no need, I can stick up for myself.'

'I'm sure you can, but Webster's a shit.'

'He called me a Paki,' I fumed.

'Keep out of his way,' she said. 'My name's Gail. What's yours?'

'Dilly,' I said glumly. My eyes filled with tears as I realized that the safety of primary school was a thing of the past; I was way out of my depth at Holly Field.

'Aw, don't cry,' she said, patting my hand.

I felt a sudden panic when Webster came and took a seat opposite me. 'So, Gail, is this your new scabby pet? What's that shit on her face?' he scoffed.

'Go away, Webster,' said Gail. 'Why are you picking on her?'

''Cos she's a Paki and she's covered in boils.'

'Yeah, and you're a sack of white shit,' I spat. 'And they're not boils – it's eczema, you ignorant git.'

He sniffed the air theatrically and said, 'Man, it stinks of Pakis round here.'

'You'd know what they smell like, Webster, 'cos there's usually one bouncing your mam, isn't there?' Gail said bitchily.

'What are you defending a wog for?'

Without thinking, I picked up my tray and brought it crashing down on the top of his head. It made a lovely whumping sound. A huge roar of laughter went up from the children who were listening and pretending not to. All of them were white.

'Watch your mouth, you prat,' I said, my face hot with rage. I got to my feet to walk away, but he jumped up, grabbed my arm and pulled it behind my back. 'I'm gonna get you after school, and then you're dead.'

At the end of the day, he was waiting for me outside the school gates, where a group of children had gathered to see Webster vs the Paki, round two. Desperate to give him the slip, I scurried out of the playground as fast as I could. He followed me.

'Where ya going, Paki?' he asked spitefully.

I was too afraid to speak, so I hurried into the bus shelter, hoping in vain that there would be an adult there to protect me.

'I asked you a question,' Webster sneered. He snatched my satchel out of my hand.

'Give it back,' I sobbed, as I watched him empty it onto the ground.

'Make me,' he laughed, kicking my new books all over the pavement.

I looked around for someone to help me. There must have been at least ten children, all older than me, just standing there waiting to see what would happen. When I crouched down to retrieve my books, someone said, 'Go on, mate, hit her.'

Webster kicked me in the back as his friends laughed and cheered.

Yelping with pain, I tried to get to my feet. He grabbed me by the hair and pulled me up.

'You fucking stinking Paki, we don't want you here.' Then he pushed me roughly against the glass bus shelter. 'I'll shove your head right through it if you ever get in my way again.'

I'd only been at Holly Field for a day, and already someone was trying to break a bus shelter with my face.

As Webster and his gang walked off up the lane, I heard him say something and then everybody laughed. My heart sank when I saw him come running back towards me.

He stood inches away, cleared his throat and spat in my face.

'That's for hitting me with the tray.'

Chapter 13

When my R.E. teacher, Mrs Boothroyd, gave me a Bible, I knew my mother would be angry. I'd lost count of the number of times she'd told me, 'You're not a Christian like Estie. If they ever say prayers at school, just move your lips and pretend.'

When I got in from school with my Bible, I went straight to the toilet; it was the safest place to read it without getting caught. I sat on the floor and flicked through the pages. It had never dawned on me that it was full of stories. I suddenly realized how limited my education had been, but I knew I had to brush up on Christianity in order to get through the lessons; I didn't want to be the only person in the class without a voice.

Some of the stories were fascinating – the passage about an eye for an eye struck a particular chord with me and I learned a fun new word: 'fornication'.

When I showed Egg the Bible, she shrank away from me, almost as though I was a leper, and warned me to be careful not to let Mammy see it.

The next day, I forgot to take it to school with me, and when I got home my mother and Climax were waiting for me: I'd hidden the Bible under the mattress, but they'd still found it.

'Whose is this?' Mammy asked, her face flushed with righteous indignation.

'Mine,' I replied, and tried to grab it from her.

'You unholy little brat. This has no place in a Muslim home. I'm so ashamed of you.'

She tossed it into the bin.

As I went to retrieve it, she said: 'Take it out and I'll break your hands.'

'See what I mean, Gongal?' Climax sniped maliciously. 'You've got no idea what goes on at that school. They're filling Dilly's head with all kinds of nonsense. Today it's the Bible, tomorrow who knows?'

'Mind your own business, you interfering old bat,' I snapped.

Climax's breasts made a sudden, heroic attempt to escape, but somehow they were held back by her equally heroic kameez. 'Old bat!' she barked, as she slapped my face angrily. 'Who the fuck do you think you're talking to?'

'That hurt!' I shouted.

Climax snorted aggressively. 'That was nothing, just wait till your father gets home. I'm going to tell him how rude you are, and then you're going to get what you deserve.'

It wasn't the threat of violence that made me uneasy – I was used to that – but the growing realization that I was living two lives, and was struggling to keep them separate. At school, I had to keep my teachers happy by conforming to the British way of life; then, when I came home in the evenings, I had to flick a switch in my mind and become an Asian to keep my family happy. It was getting harder and harder to keep the two worlds separate.

*　　*　　*

The moment my father stepped into the house, two furious women pounced: while Climax was blowing her top about my lack of manners, my mother was yelling that the West was corrupting the children's minds – and by the way did he know that Dilly was now a Christian, and she'd brought a Bible into the house, which thanks to her quick thinking was now in the bin.

'Daddy!' I shouted, 'It's not mine, it belongs to the school!'

'Shah, she called me an old bat!' Climax shrilled.

'Daddy, she hit me!'

'She bloody deserved it!' Climax yelled. 'Why the hell don't you control her?'

'What are you going to do about Dilly?' my mother demanded.

'For the love of God, will you all shut up!' my father bellowed. 'How am I supposed to think straight with you harridans yowling like bitches on heat?'

As we all fell silent, Daddy pushed his way through to the kitchen and fished the Bible out of the bin.

'My God, have you no shame?' he asked my mother. 'This is a holy book. How dare you treat it with such disrespect?'

Folding her arms, she said: 'I'm not having it in my house.'

'Why not? Monkey and Doc have both got one.'

'What?' Mammy screeched, and Climax shook her head in disbelief.

'Is it any wonder they hid them?' Daddy asked. 'Sometimes you two are so ignorant.'

While I was wondering how I was ever supposed to keep up with my parents, when they seemed to delight in baffling me with conflicting expectations, he suddenly announced: 'Come on, Dilly, I've had enough of this madhouse. Get your sisters – we're off to Toadie's.'

In a matter of moments, I'd gone from dread and confusion to joyful anticipation. Toadie's was the elixir for all pain.

The minute I walked through the door, I felt like Mr Benn as he stepped into a magical kingdom.

I stared greedily at all the sweets, unable to decide what I wanted. On the shelves there were scores of glass jars, lined up neatly; each one had a label, naming the contents and the price for a quarter. Should I ask Daddy to buy me some pear drops? But no, I wanted mint humbugs. Then I changed my mind when I saw the Yorkshire Mixture, and changed it again when I spied the bright-orange aniseed twists. Or maybe the sherbet pips . . . They were deliciously sour, and would stick to the paper bag. The only way to get them off was by chewing the paper as well, and then spitting it out later. But could I leave without getting some strawberry fizz bombs? They gave you a gobful of sweet spit that you could actually feel bubbling in your mouth. The candy letters were a firm favourite, always painful to eat because they were so hard. Egg and I would play word games with them. Whoever made the longest word got to eat it. Egg's longest word was 'little', spelt 'lickle', and mine was 'bastard'.

On the countertop was a large flat box full of liquorice sticks, which had heads of blue sprinkles. Next to them were the drumstick lollies, the bright-pink foam shrimps, and tins of Victory V lozenges – strong enough to burn the tongue.

And then there were the small pouches of Gold Rush gum and Anglo bubble gum and banana-split toffee, which was yellow on one side and a lemony brown on the other.

There were yards of strawberry laces and small packets of dipping sherbet. The Coca-Cola Spangles were flat and golden brown. They looked like Tunes, but tasted like sunshine and cola. If you sucked them long enough, they would split in two inside your mouth.

'What would you like?' Daddy asked, shaking me from my trance.

'I want rainbow drops,' Daisy said eagerly.

'Can I get a traffic-light lolly, please?' Poppy asked, as she held on to the counter and jumped up and down.

Egg asked for some sarsaparilla drops from a jar on the top shelf. Toadie glared at her over the top of his glasses. He was a hunchback who couldn't reach the higher shelves without a ladder. If my father hadn't been there, he would have sworn at Egg and refused to serve her; instead, he politely struggled his way up the rungs, while Egg and I helped ourselves to handfuls of Bazooka Joe gum.

Toadie puffed and panted his way down the ladder and weighed out Egg's sweets.

'What are you having, Dilly?' my father asked.

'Can I have one of everything off the top shelf, please?'

As Toadie looked at my father in despair, Daddy said, 'She'll have five white mice.'

'Thanks, Mr Shah. That daughter of yours is a bugger.'

Chapter 14

I was helping my father to dig the back garden, when the gate opened and a burka-clad woman came in. She scuttled past us without saying a word. Daddy hardly noticed her; it would take a lot to distract him from a steaming pile of manure, freshly bought from the farm. The anonymous woman was in the kitchen for a few minutes, and then slipped out just as silently as she'd arrived.

Mammy came out into the garden and said she needed a lift to Asif's house in Keighley, as his wife, Shamim, wasn't well. Asif and Shamim lived with Asif's widowed mother; both women were tall, with massive hooked noses. They were very sweet, and were always kind to Egg and me, but we still called them the Halloween Witches.

'Can I come too?' I asked hopefully. I loved going to Asif's house. Shamim was an even better cook than Climax, and her gulab jamuns were the best I'd ever eaten.

My stomach had just started a little dance at the prospect of warm rose-flavoured syrup leaving a sticky trail down my chin, when Mammy said: 'Not today, Dilly, you can stay here and sort dinner out.'

She urged my father to abandon his manure. 'Can you hurry up? We've got to go. She's really sick.'

I wondered what was wrong this time. I expected Shamim had a cold, and my mother was exaggerating

as usual. It was always the same with Mammy and her
friends. They seemed to derive some sort of perverse
pleasure from their bizarre medical conditions. Sipping
tea in someone's kitchen, or hanging around in the back
alley while their kids played, they'd exchange horror
stories of botched operations and difficult pregnancies.
They belonged to the Sick Wives' Club. You didn't have
to be ill to get in; being a convincing hypochondriac was
enough.

The club members were constantly trying to outdo
each other: if one had a headache, another had a migraine,
then they'd both be trumped by someone with a brain
tumour. If one had toothache, another had an abscess.
Anyone with backache had a friend with a spinal injury.

And when they got sick of talking about themselves,
they'd gossip about so and so from six doors down, whose
son had twisted his bollocks climbing a wall. Or how her
at Number 4 was pissed off because her husband had a
cotton bud lodged in his ear, and was slowly going deaf
while he was waiting for an operation. I learned some
amazing medical facts by eavesdropping on my mother
and her friends: one quack in black taught me that you
can miscarry by drinking too much water, but moving
heavy furniture when eight months pregnant is fine.
Another said if you drink milk every day, you might not
lose your milk teeth until you're thirty-two. A third case
study proved that the remedy for a vomiting child is to
tie his hands behind his back (poor Doc had been treated
that way after he'd eaten some unripe pears, and spent all
night writhing in agony, unable to retch properly because
he could hardly move). And any pregnant woman in the
street who was past her due date was urged to drink a

cup of cooking oil so the baby would slip out 'like a turd after a red-hot curry'.

I'd never heard my mother tell her friends that she was actually feeling fine. When asked: 'So how are you, Gongal?' in time-honoured tradition, she would reply, 'I've not been well.'

And now she was off to Shamim's, so the two of them could sit together over a slap-up meal, and compare notes on who was going to die first.

In fact, Shamim had more than a cold. She'd suffered a stroke, and the left side of her body was paralysed. When Mammy returned with the news, she spent the next hour in the back alley, updating her friends. I was racked with guilt for even thinking that Shamim had been faking it, whereas my mother wore a smug expression as she announced to all and sundry that she'd warned Shamim often enough that lily-of-the-valley bubble baths would be the death of her, so she really had no one but herself to blame.

Chapter 15

My heart sank as my mother handed me the shawl. 'Here you are, Dilly' she said, smiling. 'I'd like you to wear this.'

The smile on my own face froze as soon as I realized what was going on. The shawl was huge – about six feet long and three feet wide – a deep-purple nylon with a flowery pattern running through it. The material felt cold and watery in my hands, and the smell of mothballs made my stomach queasy, and reminded me of old people and piss.

'What's this for, Mammy?' I asked, even though I already knew the answer. The shawl was worse than the Ban; it was the end of an era. I was only ten years old, but by giving it to me she was telling me I was already a woman.

'Don't you think it's pretty?' she asked cheerily.

I wanted to tell her exactly what I thought, and where she could stick her stupid shawl. I wasn't ready to grow up; there were still so many things I needed to do, and I couldn't do them if I was an adult. For me, wearing a shawl and observing purdah meant being stifled. There'd be no more running or climbing over walls. No more cycling or skateboarding in the alley. No more cricket or football. And I knew it wouldn't be long before she made me give up my dolls. How would Hamble cope without me? I'd have to be demure, coy, discreet and well-behaved. I didn't have any of these characteristics, and I didn't want them.

'Is Egg gonna get one?' I asked hopefully.

'No, not yet.'

'Why not? She's a girl; you should treat us the same. It's not fair. I'm being victimized.'

'She's still little. You're too old to be running all over the place without covering up. Every other Pakistani girl your age can wear one, so why shouldn't you?'

'But I'm not Pakistani, I'm British.'

'Hah! If that's what you think, go outside and ask a white person what you are.'

'This is so unjust,' I thought to myself. 'Surely there's some law against making me wear a shawl?' First, there was the salvaar kameez. Then the Ban. And now the shawl. My parents were squeezing the sunshine out of my life, drop by drop.

The heaviness of the shawl in my hands was much more than the weight of the material: it was the dead weight of conformity, loss of liberty, and, most terrifying of all, the crushing realization that, little by little, my mother was turning me into a younger version of herself.

Over the next few weeks, Hamble wore the shawl more often than I did. When I could persuade her to part with it, the shawl became quite versatile. Not only was it the perfect miniskirt, ball-gown and wedding veil, but whenever a doll was injured, she'd be carried to hospital on a deep-purple stretcher. Midnight picnics in the bedroom became much more colourful events now we had a new tablecloth. The shiny nylon material made a great sledge for Egg to sit in, while I pulled her over the tiled passage floor. And whenever Egg and I were lost at sea, we'd wrap the shawl around the clothes-line stick, and wave it to attract the attention of passing ships. If Egg was ever unfortunate enough to die in the deep snow on a mountain top, the shawl made a perfect shroud.

And, joy of joys, I found a way of getting revenge on my mother. Whenever she asked me to go into the back garden to fetch garlic or some other vegetable, I'd tell her I couldn't possibly go out without my shawl, which was 'somewhere upstairs', and then I'd take ages searching for it, even though I knew exactly where it was. Three minutes of not-really-looking was always enough time for my mother to lose patience and go and fetch the garlic herself.

Chapter 16

Zarqa Patel lived at 44 Gomshall Road. She and my mother were best friends. Like my mother, Zarqa could leave by the front door only when she was with her husband, and even then she had to be covered head-to-toe in a black burka.

Her gardens were arranged Pakistani-style: vegetable plot at the front, concrete yard at the back. The front garden, with its beautiful rows of perfectly planted vegetables, was her pride and joy – even though she hadn't sown a single seed. She could often be seen sitting in her front window, admiring her husband's hard work, and cooing with pleasure at the vivid and colourful contents of this magical wonderland.

Zarqa had made it quite clear that she didn't like me, because she saw me as a bad influence on her daughter, Sara. I hated the blue-eyed old witch, and would flick two fingers at her on my way home from school.

In June 1977, Zarqa was told by her husband that his brother and sister-in-law would be moving in with them. She was absolutely furious, and came over to our house so she could bitch with my mother about hated relatives.

While they were trying to outdo each other in the garden, I decided to entertain Sara in our kitchen.

First, I sang her a school-yard rhyme:

> Milk, milk, lemonade,
> Round the corner chocolate's made

While I was singing, I did the actions – pointing to my chest, pubes and backside. There was a stunned silence, then Sara burst into embarrassed laughter, and said, 'Oh my God, do it again, Dilly.' So I did, to more laughter and acclaim.

'I know another one as well,' I bragged, as I jumped around the kitchen with excitement.

'Yeah, what?' Sara asked.

'Promise you won't tell anyone,' I said.

'Why?'

''Cos it's mucky.'

'Come on, Dilly, tell me,' she laughed.

'Okay,' I said, then I sang:

> Ee ba gum,
> Can yer belly touch yer bum?
> Do yer tits hang low?
> Can ya tie 'em in a bow?
> Is yer cock made of brass?
> Can ya shove it in a lass?

'Teach me the words, Dilly,' Sara pleaded, tugging my arm enthusiastically.

So I did, and she went home as happy as Zarqa was miserable.

Later that evening, I was in the kitchen, modelling my new swimming costume for Egg, when Zarqa, face like thunder, exploded through the back door. She stopped in her tracks as she saw me prancing about in my swimming costume and flower-topped cap. She made a half-hearted attempt to cover her face so she wouldn't have to look at me.

'Auntie Zarqa,' I said. 'Do you like my costume?'

'You're too big to behave like that,' she yelled. 'What the hell are you doing? Your bum's hanging out.'

I did a pirouette for her.

'Where's your mother?'

'She's upstairs spying on the neighbours. Shall I get her for you?'

'No! You cover yourself up now! My God, girls these days have no modesty. You should be ashamed of yourself, running about the house dressed like that.'

I stuck my tongue out at her back as she went in search of my mother, then hurriedly slipped out of my costume and got dressed.

There were raised voices coming from upstairs, and the unmistakable sound of two angry women coming to get me.

'Dilly,' my mother said, 'what did you teach Sara?'

'Nothing.'

'You're a liar,' Zarqa hissed. 'You've been singing dirty songs. Anyway, what's this "Milk, milk" rubbish, and "Ee ba ba"?'

Egg spluttered.

'Gongal, your daughter's Satan,' Zarqa said, smouldering with rage. 'She forced Sara to learn those bad words.'

'I never did,' I responded. 'She begged me to teach her.' Once I'd said it, I knew I'd fallen straight into her trap.

'Hah, so you did do it,' Zarqa said. 'Gongal, this cartoon of yours is going to give you nothing but a bad name if you don't control her. Keep her out of my way; the next time she misbehaves, I'm going to beat her.'

She reminded me of the wicked witch from *The Wizard of Oz*. As my mother followed her to the gate, I resisted the urge to call after them, 'Fly, my pretties!'

I told Egg that Sara's days were numbered.

But five minutes later, it was me who was sitting in the corner, nursing a slapped face and crying my eyes out.

The next day, it was my mother's face that was wet with tears. Out of the blue, a letter arrived from Chowki: her younger sister had died. She was devastated. When she said she was going to Pakistan to be with her family, Daddy told her he wouldn't let her go on her own, so she'd have to take Climax with her. I was suddenly filled with dread. Daddy was useless around the house – how would we cope? And what would happen if Mammy decided not to come back?

Over the next two weeks, I monitored progress with a rising sense of panic.

Flights arranged.

Tears shed.

Pounds converted to rupees.

More tears shed.

Long list of requests for Western goods received (via Asif, as he had a phone).

Presents duly bought for relatives.

More tears shed.

Favour asked of Zarqa to keep eye on children (especially Dilly).

Last-minute warnings not to leave house without stupid shawl.

Children kissed.

More tears shed.

And then they were gone.

Chapter 17

I'd endured almost a year of school life at Holly Field, and at the end of each day the same thought went through my mind: would Webster catch me and give me a good kicking, or would I manage to sneak home without him seeing me?

I'd often see him and his gang waiting for me at the school gates. It hadn't taken me long to discover all the sneaky routes out of school. It meant I was always late home, but nobody seemed to notice, and at least I didn't get the crap kicked out of me.

Webster reminded me of Bully Beef from *The Dandy*. He had violent acne, and wasn't really popular; he had his hangers-on, but most of the kids were scared of him and kept out of his way. He claimed to be 'Cock of the School' and no one had the nerve to argue.

He never tired of tipping the contents of my school bag over the wall. He would roar with laughter as the wind ran away with my school work. For Webster it was a game; for me it was public humiliation. Sometimes, he'd wait till I was within earshot, then he'd tell jokes to his friends, like:

'How many people would die if you dropped a bomb on Pakistan?

'Don't know,' someone would reply.

'None, 'cos they're all over here.'

Or:

'What's green and full of shit?

'Tell us, Webster.'

'A Paki in a parka.'

Or:

'What's transparent and lies in a gutter?

'Dunno.'

'A Paki that's had the shit kicked out of her.'

When he saw me queuing for the nit nurse, he slapped me on the back of the head, and said: 'If you've got any nits, Paki, they're dead now.'

My only consolation was in knowing that my first year was also his final one, and the last day of term would mean no more bullying. Fox Hill had been a haven, but Holly Field, thanks to Webster, was a nightmare.

A few days before the end of summer term, I was on the bus home when Webster got on, chased me up the stairs, and used my pigtail to drag me all around the top deck. When I finally managed to break free, I got off at the next stop, and walked the rest of the way home.

I was still feeling miserable when I got in. Monkey was in the kitchen, mopping the floor.

'Oi!' he said. 'Don't walk across it, I've just cleaned it.'

'Aw shurrup, you stool sample. I wanna get a drink.'

He came over and punched me in the stomach. 'Don't be fuckin' cheeky,' he said.

I sat on the front steps and mulled over what had happened that afternoon. Monkey hitting me wasn't a big deal as far as I was concerned; he was my brother. But Webster, he was an entirely different proposition. What gave him the right to single me out? Why did he think it was acceptable to hit me?

I wondered if my brother would be able to beat Webster in a fight. Monkey was sixteen years old, and well over six feet tall. He certainly knew how to handle himself, and spent a lot of time playing football and rugby. And he had a BB gun. On many occasions I'd toyed with the idea of borrowing his gun for a day, and putting a pellet in Webster's eye.

I wanted to ask Monkey if he'd sort Webster out for me. But why would one bully want to stop another? They'd most probably join forces and take turns to smack me around.

Leaving the front door on the latch, I headed cautiously into the street. It was a beautiful, sunny afternoon, but I was feeling too glum to enjoy it. Mary Mumbleweed was pegging out her pink bedsheets at Number 33, and Rita from Number 35 was taking Hepburn, her Fox Terrier, for a walk.

I ended up outside Zarqa's house. The net curtain twitched. A few seconds later, the front door flew open and Zarqa stood there. 'Dilly, what are you doing outside?' she demanded.

'I'm playing,' I said, as I leaned on the gate, swinging it back and forth.

'Hey, stop doing that. You'll break it,' she said. 'You go home now.'

'You're not my Mammy,' I said tartly. 'And I don't have to listen to you.'

'Yes, you do have to listen to me.'

This felt good. I knew I was winding the old witch up. I also knew that I was perfectly safe; she didn't have permission to come out of the front door without her husband. The silly bitch was housebound without her owner, and he was still at work.

I sat down on the little black picket fence.

'Dilly, you get off there now. Look at the size of you. You're going to break it.'

'Up yours,' I said, flicking her a V sign. I jumped onto the fence. It wobbled precariously, and I lost my balance and landed inside the garden.

'Get out of there!' she shouted, waving a fist at me.

'Make me,' I said.

For the next minute, there was a stand-off between us. She was in the doorway, red-faced and fuming, and I was sitting by the immaculate vegetable patch, wondering how to make her face even redder. A turnip caught my eye. I reached over and plucked it out of the ground. It was small, round and white, soft brown soil still clinging to the roots.

'Look what I found,' I said, holding it up for Zarqa to see.

'You never found that!' she shouted. 'You better get out of there. I mean it, Dilly – otherwise I'm going to have to come outside.'

'Yeah, right,' I said, as I hurled the turnip on to the path. It landed with a crack, and the soil shuddered as it slipped off the roots and rolled along the flagstones.

'Hey, you've got lots of stuff in here,' I called, pulling up another turnip and giving it the same treatment as the first.

Spitting with fury, she made it look like she was going to step out of the house, but I knew she was just bluffing.

There was a thick clump of garlic, swaying gently in the breeze. I uprooted it and threw it in the air; the pungent smell clung to my fingers, and made my nose burn. 'Your garlic smells great – much better than ours,' I said as I sniffed my hands.

'Your mother's going to hear about this.'

'Good,' I replied, goading her even more. I pulled up onions, coriander and spinach, and tossed them all over the fence and on to the pavement.

'Stop it, for God's sake, stop it,' Zarqa whimpered. As she gripped the door, grinding her teeth and shaking her head in defeat, Zarqa looked like the life force was draining from her. Only a heart of stone could have felt no pity.

'You can make a nice salad with all this stuff,' I said, playing football with the turnips and potatoes that littered the path. Then I ran around, kicking the remaining vegetables the way a small child kicks a pile of leaves in autumn; everything that had once been green and lush was now flattened to a pulp.

'Dilly, I'm telling your father what you've done.'

'He's not home,' I said smugly.

'Oh yes he is – I just saw his car.'

I raced through the front gardens of Numbers 42 and 40. Heart pounding, I let myself into the house and dashed into the kitchen to wash the incriminating evidence off my hands.

Moments later, my father strolled into the house carrying a box of groceries. 'Hi, Daddy,' I said. 'Do you wanna cup of tea?'

'Yes, in a minute,' he replied, then hurried upstairs. I heard the farts coming from the toilet. There were hundreds; he must have been holding them in all day, and now they were going off like fireworks.

I heaved a sigh of relief – he obviously hadn't seen me outside. I filled a pan with water and put it on the hob. The next few minutes would be critical. Would Zarqa stay away, or would there be a knock at the back door?

As it turned out, I was lucky this time. The knock never came.

Chapter 18

The last day of term arrived, and with it came the wonderful knowledge that I'd never have to see Webster's face again. I hoped that, wherever he was going, there'd be a bigger bully than him, someone who'd make his life as miserable as he'd made mine.

Angie told me she wouldn't be back in September. Her father had taken a job in London, and the family would be relocating during the summer holidays. I didn't even know where London was – for me it might as well have been on the moon.

As we emptied our lockers at the end of the day, I told her how much I was going to miss her.

'I'm going to miss you too, Dilly, but we can keep in touch. Why don't you come and visit? It'll be great.'

'I won't be allowed to,' I responded flatly.

She handed me a pair of Scholl slippers as a parting gift. My stomach suddenly felt tense with embarrassment, as I didn't have anything for her; I wasn't accustomed to receiving presents from friends, and was caught off guard. But if she was disappointed, she was too gracious to let it show.

We left the school grounds, and I knew I wouldn't see her again. She hugged me warmly and got into her dad's car. As they drove away, I waved and envied.

Fed up of waiting for a bus, I decided to walk home. I'd been warned hundreds of times by my parents never to go anywhere on my own while the Yorkshire Ripper was still on the loose, but they weren't around to stop me.

I'd just reached the end of Holly Field Road when I heard footsteps approaching from behind. I spun round to see not the Ripper, but Webster. I clutched my bag to my hip and ran, with my tormentor in pursuit.

'Wait a minute,' he called after me. 'I wanna say sorry.'

I had no intention of stopping, even though I was beginning to get a stitch in my side.

'I'm leaving, and I wanna say sorry.'

Webster hadn't said sorry all year, and now he'd said it twice in one minute. I came to a standstill and waited for him to catch up. His face was red, and his spots seemed to stand out even more than usual.

'I didn't want to leave without apologizing for the way I treated you.'

'Well, you've said it now. I've got to get home.'

He laughed. 'Why? You're not scared of me, are you?' When I didn't reply, he said, 'I know I did some real shitty stuff to you and I'm sorry. Can we shake hands?'

I placed my hand in his, and as soon as I felt his grip tighten, I realized what an idiot I'd been. He squeezed harder and harder – it felt like he was trying to break my hand.

'You're hurting me!' I cried.

'Guess what? I never meant any of that stuff, you silly bitch.'

'Let go!' I shouted pathetically, trying to push him away. But he just kept jerking me back and forth, refusing to let go.

'So then, Paki, how do you feel now you know I'm leaving?'

He finally let go of my hand, only to give me a sharp push that sent me sprawling to my knees. My bag fell on the ground and he kicked it across the pavement.

'You bastard. You're a fucking bastard,' I cried.

'Yeah, and you're a chocolate,' he said scornfully. As he waited for me to get to my feet, he sang his favourite song, "Cadbury's take Pakis and they cover them in chocolate . . ." I'm gonna miss you Paki, 'cos it's been great fun beating you up. I've got a present for you, I've been saving it all year.' He pushed his face up close to mine and spat a huge mouthful of snot all over me. I closed my eyes as I felt it rolling down my face.

'See you around,' he laughed, then turned and strolled cockily away.

Humiliation and self-loathing swept over me. I was a fool and I wanted to kick myself. As I walked home, I imagined Webster would grow up to be just like my father – the kind of man who beats his wife for fun.

When I got home, the house was empty, so I went up to the room Monkey and Doc shared; it smelt of damp trainers and sweaty socks. Egg and I had hidden in the wardrobe one day, to see where Monkey kept his sweets, and we'd been surprised by his cunning. His secret stash, that we'd never been able to find, despite searching his room from top to bottom, was concealed inside the huge transistor radio he'd found in a skip. This was the radio that was so old, we swore we could hear German soldiers talking in their trenches. You could listen to five different languages while tuned into Radio Luxembourg.

I prised the back off the radio, took out a jar of peanut butter, and scooped a fingerful into my mouth.

The whole house was filthy. Ever since my mother had gone to Pakistan, the work had piled up and there were always hundreds of jobs demanding attention. But it wasn't a case of everyone being given a job and then getting on with it. Fairness was an alien concept in Sharnia, where the girls were given the work, the boys went out to play, and my father spent most of his spare time playing cricket, or pottering about among his plants.

Ignoring the mountain of housework, I decided to go and irritate Zarqa. At first, I'd been really surprised that she hadn't complained to my father about her garden. This was totally out of character for a woman who raged like fire, spitting and crackling with bitterness and anger. Eventually, I'd realized what she was doing: biding her time until my mother returned. She knew she'd never get anywhere with my father – he probably wouldn't even speak to her – so she was saving everything up until my mother got back.

Assuming I was untouchable for the next few weeks, I took a Stanley knife from my father's toolbox and hurried down the alley to the back gate of Number 44.

I pulled myself up on to the wall. Zarqa was nowhere in sight, but her washing line was within reach. The clothes on the line were almost dry and ready for the ironing pile. There were small puddles of water up and down the path, and a lovely smell of soap powder in the air.

Grabbing the line, I sliced through it; it snapped with a twang, and everything parachuted to the ground.

It looked like Zarqa, whose husband had never bought her a washing machine, would have another load on her hands.

As a final gesture, I carved 'I woz ere' into the gate, and then ran back home.

I was safely back in my own garden when I saw Zarqa's dupatta-covered head go bobbing down the path as she ran towards the laundry. She struggled with the line, but it was too heavy. After a while, she gave up and leaned against the wall, saw me watching, and put two and two together.

'This was you, wasn't it, you little bugger?' she shouted.

'It's not my fault your washing line's crap,' I said.

'Crap! I'll show you crap when I beat it out of you.'

We were separated by only two gardens; all she had to do was climb over the walls, and I'd be for it. But she just stood there and glared at me.

'Your eyes are really ugly, Auntie Zarqa,' I goaded.

'What did you say?' she squawked.

'Your eyes remind me of currants. They're so small and ugly, you look like the gingerbread man. Only trouble is, you're too white. You need to go back in the oven a bit longer.'

Spluttering with rage, Zarqa rocketed straight towards me. The back of Gomshall Road became *Planet of the Apes*, and one of the ferocious gorillas was scrambling over the garden walls to get me. I ran into the house and managed to slam the door and lock it, just as she came pounding on it with her fists. 'Open up!' she yelled. 'I'm going to kill you.'

I went upstairs and opened the toilet window. She looked up from the path below. 'Get down here!' she shouted.

I filled my mouth with spit, paused for a second to summon the strength into my cheeks and then launched a perfect air-to-ground mucous missile. If gobbing on enraged pink-faced witches was an Olympic sport, this would have won me gold. In slow motion, the globule floated serenely downwards, trailing a wonderful glow of inevitability in its wake. There was a loud semi-liquid splat, followed by a moment's silence. I felt as though I'd purged the humiliation that had been bottled up inside me since Webster had done the same thing to me. By spitting on Zarqa, I'd forced her to join the Bullies' Victims Club that had previously had only one member. It felt so good to share.

Poor Zarqa. If she'd been allowed out into the front garden by her husband, there was no doubt she'd have made mincemeat out of me when I destroyed her vegetable patch. But I knew her weaknesses and I preyed on them. She was like a shadow, and because she wore the veil she was faceless, shapeless and sexless. She was a zero, a blob of nothing dressed in black, the property of a man who chose how she lived, where she could go, what she could do.

I felt sorry for her in a way – she was a slave to both her husband and her culture. She'd wait patiently all day for her man to come home and take her for a walk, like a dog. But unlike a dog that runs ahead and sniffs the air with excitement, Zarqa would have to walk a respectful ten paces behind, her veiled face always angled downwards.

The whites would tease her with cruel and ignorant mockery; in 1970s Bradford, anything that looked exotic was fair game for the small-minded bigots who lived on every street. But a contest between faceless black-clad nonentities imprisoned by their own husbands, and Westerners with the freedom to taunt them, was no contest at all. Even at the age of ten, I knew which side of the fence I was on.

Chapter 19

'Who's missing?' Egg asked, having counted the dolls we'd lined up against the wall. 'There are only six children at school today.'

'Hamble's not coming in,' I said.

'Why not? She's already missed a day,' Egg said as she wrote Hamble's name on a piece of paper, and then put a cross next to it.

'Well, she's not feeling too clever. I tried to get her an appointment with the doctor, but he was fully booked,' I said.

'I don't care,' Egg sniffed. 'You tell her from me that she's in detention when she gets back to school.'

'What for? She's ill – how can you give her a detention for that?'

'I have to be strict. So many children don't come to school, and they miss a lot of work. I bet Hamble's not even sick.'

Daisy came and sat down by the dolls.

'Miss Egg, can I play with you?'

'I wanna play too,' Poppy said, then picked her little button nose and wiped her finger on Daisy's back.

Egg thought about it for a moment, and then said, 'Yes, of course you can. As we're already one child short, you can make up the numbers. I need parents to help today.'

'Why, what are you gonna do?' Daisy asked, as she sat her one-legged teddy bear down next to Poppy's doll, Ragapoo-poo.

Ragapoo-poo was one of my creations; I'd stitched her from an old pillowcase my mother had thrown out. She was plug-ugly, had a really lumpy face and two purple sequins for eyes. One of her legs was longer than the other and her hair was made from thin brown wool. Poppy didn't have a rag doll, so I'd semi-loaned her Ragapoo-poo with the threat that if she ever annoyed me, the doll would lose its head.

'Well, today we're going on a trip to the seaside,' Egg said enthusiastically as she put her sheet of paper away and crossed her legs.

'What?' I squawked. 'You never said anything about a trip.'

'A letter went home.'

'When? I never got a letter.'

'I'm sorry, Mrs Shah, but if your child doesn't take letters home, it's got nothing to do with me,' Egg said seriously. She handed out chunks of yellow chalk that she'd taken from her real school.

'I don't believe you; this isn't fair,' I snapped, beginning to lose my temper. 'Hamble would have come if she wasn't sick.'

'What's wrong with her, anyway?' Egg asked, getting up to rearrange the toys.

I gestured to Daisy and Poppy.

'I can't tell you in front of these people.'

'Why, we're not gonna say anything,' Daisy said as her teddy went flying into the air and landed on top of Ragapoo-poo.

'I don't know what to do with Hamble at the moment,' I said, glaring at Daisy. 'You see, she's the way she is because of your bear.'

'How come?' she asked.

'You know she was going out with that moron. Well, she's pregnant.'

'Oh my God,' Egg squeaked, and burst into fits of laughter. 'What a tart.'

'Hey, you're not allowed to say stuff like that about your pupils. It's not her fault; Daisy's bear is always jumping on the girls. Poppy, you better watch Ragapoo-poo, she might end up pregnant an' all.'

'What's pregnant?' Poppy asked as she grabbed her doll.

'Having a baby,' Egg replied. She took her sheet of paper out again and wrote on it.

'What ya doing?' I asked.

'Writing down why your disgusting daughter's absent,' Egg said scornfully.

'You can't do that. Stuff like that's private, and anyway you've spelt it wrong. Pregnant doesn't have an "i" in it.'

'Are you sure it was Ted what did it?' Daisy asked. She picked up the culprit, tied his bonnet into place under his chin, and hopped up and down the path with him.

'Of course it was him. You know what, Daisy? You're gonna have to give him to me now, 'cos he has to marry Hamble.'

'No way. It's not his fault; it might be someone else's baby,' defended Daisy.

'So how pregnant is she?' Egg asked.

'Dunno, but I can't show my face for the shame. I'm not ready to be a grandmother, and that bloody doll wants to breastfeed.'

A roar of laughter went up.

'It's not funny,' I said, as I went inside to fetch Hamble. I'd stuffed a sock up her dress and secured it with a ribbon, and rubbed some of my mother's red Max Factor lipstick on her face to make her look sick.

Egg howled with laughter as she took Hamble and sat her down. 'Oh my God, she looks bad. When's it due?'

'Soon, I think,' I said. I took a piece of chalk and drew a huge butterfly on the path. When I'd finished, Poppy got to her feet and jumped over it, while singing:

> B. A. Y.
> B. A. Y.
> B. A. Y.
> C. I. T. Y.
> With an R. O. double L. E. R. S.
> Bay City Rollers are the best.

I laughed. 'Where did you hear that?' I asked her.

'It's a skipping song,' she said. 'We play it in real school.' She picked Hamble up and squeezed her. 'Dilly, where's the baby gonna come from?'

'From her bellybutton,' I said, suddenly feeling quite knowledgeable and grown-up.

'No way.' Egg laughed. 'I thought it came out of the bum.'

'It's a baby, not a turd,' I said.

'You lot know nothing,' Daisy said. 'Babies come out of fannies. Granny told me.'

'You're not in Jallu now, you savage,' I snapped. 'Now come on, let's go to the seaside.'

*   *   *

Daisy used a trowel to dig a hole in the vegetable patch, which Poppy filled with water from a bucket. The dolls took it in turn to swim. Everybody was enjoying themselves, but I noticed how scruffy Daisy and Poppy were. Their clothes were covered in dirt, and both of them needed haircuts. Daisy's fingernails were black, and the soles of Poppy's feet were grimy.

Egg said she was hungry, so I went to get some food. I was in the kitchen emptying the biscuit tin onto a plate, when I heard a scream and lots of shouting. I couldn't believe my eyes: Zarqa was climbing over the garden wall . . . again!

'Run! Run! Get inside, quick!' I shouted as I shot outside, just as Zarqa dropped from the wall into the garden, like a huge spider.

'Now you're for it, and this time there's no escape, Dilly,' she said, as she came towards me.

I realized that, while Zarqa was bearing down on me, my three dear little playmates had taken my advice and scurried into the house. I heard the kitchen door being locked; they'd left me to my fate at the hands of the pink-faced banshee.

Making a mental note to kick the crap out of them later, I sprinted across the garden and clambered up on to the brick outhouse roof, dodging Zarqa's clawing fingers by inches.

I knew I was safe there. I doubted if Zarqa would try to climb up, but, even if she did, every back garden in the street had one, and if I'd wanted to I could easily have made my getaway by jumping from one outhouse to the next.

So I stayed where I was and sang:

I'm the king of the castle
And you're the dirty rascal.

Zarqa folded her arms and waited. I decided to entertain her some more:

There was a fat donkey called Zarqa,
Whose husband ran off to Denmarka,
When she phoned and asked why,
He replied with a sigh,
"Cos your arse is as big as a sharka.'

There were some loose bits of stone on the outhouse roof. I picked one up and threw it at her; it hit her on the arm.

'Who the hell do you think you are?' Zarqa yelled.

'I'm Princess Dilly, and my mother said she's not bringing anything back from Pakistan for you, and she doesn't even want to be your friend any more, 'cos she's made new ones. She told my dad she hates you 'cos you stink.'

The kitchen door opened, and my father stepped into the garden like a daddy duck; Egg, Daisy and Poppy were the nervous ducklings following behind.

'What's going on?' Daddy demanded as he surveyed the scene.

'She was rude to me,' Zarqa said, covering her face with her dupatta so my father couldn't see it.

'What ya doing that for?' I asked, feeling a lot more in control now the cavalry had arrived. 'We already know you're an ugly cow.'

'I want you to sort Dilly out,' Zarqa said. She was talking to my father, but looking at the ground. 'She's bad-mannered and foul-mouthed, and she's got no respect for her elders.'

'How dare you come into my garden and tell me what to do?' my father bristled. 'Go home, you foolish woman. And if you ever try anything like this again, I'll have words with your husband.'

Humiliated and defeated, Zarqa walked down the path towards the gate. Once again, the beautiful Princess Dilly had banished the evil witch Zarqa from the Kingdom of Sharnia. As she passed beneath me, I whispered, loud enough for her ears only, 'Shame.'

She shot me a look of pure hatred. 'I'll get you, Dilly,' she promised. Then she stepped into the alley and slammed the gate behind her.

Later that afternoon, our grumbling stomachs led us into the kitchen, where we found my father making stew. 'Did you do something to upset that blasted woman?' he asked me.

'No, Daddy, ask this lot. We were playing.'

'I can't understand why she thought she could just come into the garden and try to hit my kids,' he said. 'From now on, I want you to keep out of her way. If she's outside, you come straight back into the house. I don't want to catch any of you talking to her. We all have to live on the same street, and I don't want any trouble. Is that understood?'

'Yes, Daddy,' we all chorused in unison.

After dinner, Egg and I went into the garden to clean up the mess from the trip to the seaside. We found poor Hamble, still floating in the muddy sea. She was in shock, so we rushed her to the hospital in my shawl. But it was too late; she'd already lost her sock-baby. Ted wanted to visit her in her ward under the dining table, but Hamble refused to see him.

I wanted to torment Zarqa some more, but my father had made it quite clear he didn't want to see us anywhere near her. Of course, he hadn't said how long the curfew would be in force. As far as I was concerned, that kind of ban expired at midnight. Tomorrow, I'd be free to think up new and inventive ways to torture the wicked witch, knowing that she couldn't rely on my father to defend her.

Chapter 20

It was strange that an educated man like my father couldn't seem to work out how to use a washing machine. He took every opportunity to tell my mother how stupid and useless she was, how she wasn't right for him because she didn't have a college education, and how she was fit for nothing but cleaning and raising children. But, while she was in Pakistan, my father's own domestic shortcomings were plain to see. The front garden was immaculate. It looked as though the rows of fruit and vegetables had been set out with geometric precision; the tomato vines and runner beans stood tall in perfect formation, like Russian soldiers marching across Red Square. People would come down our street just to coo with admiration at the display.

Their reaction would have been a bit different if they could have seen inside the house. Piles of dirty washing overflowed from the laundry basket. The drainer was stacked high with dirty dishes, while under the sink, there were milk bottles so old that their contents had turned green and furry. No one thought to open any windows, so the whole house stank of sweaty children and curry.

Once we'd run out of clean crockery, instead of washing up, Daddy bought paper plates from Bargain Stretcher. Bins of rubbish cluttered every room, the carpets were sticky with mud and food and the tide mark around the bath got darker every Sunday evening. The bedding hadn't been changed since my mother left. The new stray cat that we'd brought into the house had given birth under my father's bed, and nobody knew until we found the kittens while playing hide and seek.

All it needed was for my father to take charge and sort things out, but he wasn't the person to do it. The garden was the mistress who'd seduced him away with promises of earthy pleasure. He lavished his time and energy on her, and neglected his dull boring wife, the house. The more she nagged, the less he listened.

So, unbelievably, I was really pleased to see my mother when she came back, a week before the end of the holidays. And I was ecstatic when I realized that Climax wasn't with her.

From the moment Mammy got back, I noticed something different about her: she was happy! It seemed that the time she'd spent away from her husband and kids had done her the power of good.

As she stepped through the back door, even the sight and smell of weeks of domestic neglect didn't wipe the smile from her face. She'd been in the house less than a minute, and hadn't even had a chance to take off her new brown burka, when the back gate flew open and a seething Zarqa bustled into the garden.

'Shit,' I thought. 'Now I'm gonna get it.'

But my mother didn't even let Zarqa through the door; she just told her she was tired and to come back another time. Zarqa was outraged. She tried to reel off all the things I'd done to upset her, but Mammy just yawned, said, 'I'm exhausted, I'm off to bed,' and sent her on her way.

Once again, the evil witch Zarqa had been banished from my kingdom. I knew my luck couldn't last forever, but, for now, I was happy to gloat at her misfortune.

The next day, our house was filled with expectancy. Mammy had brought bags of gifts from Pakistan, and we all gathered round her in the back room.

Doc had been looking down in the mouth ever since he'd been told that his mother wouldn't be back until October, because she 'had some family business to attend to', but his spirits soon lifted when Mammy handed him and Monkey two new cricket bats and a shiny red ball.

As the bags were emptied, the room became a blaze of bright colours: bangles, scarves, salvaar kameez suits, dried fruits, biscuits baked by Rasheeda, embroidery threads, Urdu books, halwa, henna, sweets and a thousand other trinkets and gewgaws were handed out.

Mammy gave gifts to all the children, but I was overjoyed to look around the room and see that my pile of presents was by far the biggest. The best gift she gave me that day, though, was the promise of spending time with me; she said she'd show me how to stitch, using the lengths of pure white Egyptian cotton and beautiful silk threads she'd bought. My new improved mother continued to score full marks.

After all the presents had been handed out, the other children went off to play, leaving Mammy and me alone. She pulled a suitcase out from under my father's bed, and told me to lock the door because she wanted to show me something. I was so excited I bounced across the room. She only ever locked the door if there was something she wanted to hide, like sweets or cakes.

She opened the case.

'Oh gosh, they're beautiful,' I said, as I gawped at the exquisite clothes inside.

She took out a pink salvaar kameez and handed it to me. It was covered in filigree silver embroidery and felt as soft as tissue paper in my hands. There was also a green suit, with long trousers that flared at the bottom, and it came with a matching chiffon dupatta.

Also in the suitcase were sandals, long silk ribbons, Tibet Snow skin-lightening cream, talcum powder and green glass bangles. Mammy opened a small red box and took out two rings, one gold and one silver.

'Wow, who's all this stuff for?' I asked, secretly hoping it was for me.

'It's for you from someone in Pakistan.'

'But Mammy, who's it from? And why?'

'Eat the mangoes, Dilly, don't count the trees,' she replied.

'When can I wear the rings?' I asked.

'Patience, Dilly, there's something I need to discuss with your father first. Now please don't mention this suitcase to your sisters; you'll make them jealous.'

'Okay, Mammy, but why is it such a big deal? I thought we weren't supposed to have secrets.'

'Dilly, there are lots of secrets in our family,' she said.

Despite my pestering, she wouldn't say anything more about the gifts – but she did tell me some family news from Pakistan: my mother's uncle's son, who was nice but poor, had married my mother's auntie's daughter, who was a fat lazy pig.

My head was spinning as I tried to work out who was who. 'Is this stuff allowed, Mammy?'

'Of course it's allowed. They're cousins. Dilly, you're such a fool sometimes. Now go and put your presents away, and when you've done that, come and help me with the cleaning, this house looks like a tip.'

My father kept well out of the way as we set to work. Every time Mammy uncovered more piles of filth, she would waddle to the front door and shout, 'You useless tramp, I'll break your bloody kneecaps!' at the sheepish gardener. She filled a bin bag with the cheesy milk bottles and hurled it down the front steps. Dirty paper plates became Frisbees and were sent flying at Daddy's head.

While my hands were busy with the housework, my mind was occupied with thoughts of my inbred relatives. The family tree was in danger of becoming a tangle of poison ivy wrapped around a choking trunk, but it was impossible to know which branch was the host and which was the parasite; if I wasn't careful, when I grew up I might find myself marrying a crazy cousin and having to call my mother 'Auntie'.

When I wasn't thinking about my relatives, my thoughts turned to the mystery suitcase under the bed. My curiosity was pricked: who was this person in Pakistan who'd sent me such beautiful gifts, even though they'd never met me? Since when was I so important that someone had gone out of their way to send presents to the ugliest member of the Shah household?

Chapter 21

'There's no need for you to take that tone, young lady. It's school policy.'

'Sir, nobody told me anything about this. I have to bring a packed lunch – my dad can't afford to pay for meals any more.'

'I'm sorry, Dilly, but if you want to eat that, you'll have to leave the school premises.'

'But it's cold outside, Sir.'

'I don't make the rules,' Mr Brown said. 'Now get out.'

I grabbed my lunchbox and went into the playground. Egg was standing there, looking bemused.

'Don't tell me, you're not allowed to eat your packed lunch in school,' I snapped, taking hold of her arm and guiding her to the gate.

I'd been looking forward to the new school year (especially as Egg had just started at Holly Field, in the year below me) but this was halfway through the first day back after the holidays, and already things were going wrong. While Egg had been going to Fox Hill, I'd been allowed to have a school dinner because she and the twins went home at lunchtime but, thanks to a telegram Climax had recently sent, Daddy was now diverting funds to another cause – buying farmland in Jallu that had just come up for sale – so there wasn't enough money to go round.

Egg and I sat in the bus shelter with our cold meal of congealed omelettes and parathas, most of which ended up in the bin. She looked unusually smart in her new green school uniform, but it was obvious to anyone who saw her that she was in the first year: her tie was around her neck, rather than sticking out of her pocket, and her white socks were pulled up to the knees. Every item of clothing was too big. She'd complained, of course, but Mammy had just said, 'Stop whining, you'll grow into them.'

'Look, Egg, don't say anything to Mammy and Daddy about what happened,' I said.

'Why not?'

''Cos it'll only worry them.'

That was a lie. The real reason I wanted to keep it a secret was that, whenever anything went wrong, whenever my parents needed someone to blame, they didn't hold a trial and call witnesses, they just assumed that somehow I must be responsible. The less they knew the better.

'But I don't wanna do this all the time,' Egg said. 'Can't we hide in the cloakroom instead?'

The next day, we tried Egg's idea. Mr Brown told us to get out, and I told him to sod off.

I spent half an hour outside the headmaster's office, waiting to be summoned. This was a part of the school I'd never seen before. It looked as though the head considered himself too important to mingle with his subjects, and had created his own palace on the outskirts of reality. I had plenty of time to watch the secretary coming and going. She was a sickly white colour, with alarming blue-rinsed hair, and wore clumpy shoes with chunky heels. She was all disapproving looks and frumpy clothes.

Eventually the summons came, and in I went. Mr Barratt was sitting behind a huge desk. There were lot of trophies in a cabinet behind him, and I wondered if he'd won them all for being a champion smartarse.

'Sit down,' he said, as he peered at me over his spectacles. I stared at the bald patch in the centre of his head, and tried not to laugh as I took a seat on a squeaky leather chair.

'What's your name?'

'Dilly Shah.'

'I'm sure you know why you're here, so why don't you explain to me why it is that I have to speak to you,' he said sternly.

'Don't you know why?' I asked bluntly.

'I beg your pardon?' he said, clearly taken aback.

'Sorry, Sir, what I mean is, didn't . . .'

'Quiet! How dare you talk to me like that?' he roared. '*I* know why you're here, but I want to know why *you* think you're here.'

I didn't know what to say without making everything worse, so I stayed silent.

He picked up his pen and scribbled something on the notepad. He looked like a doctor, and I wondered if he was writing me a prescription for some 'good behaviour' pills.

'Well? I'm waiting.'

'I was rude to Mr Brown,' I said, as I clenched my teeth and waited for him to hit me. When the slap didn't come, I let out a deep breath.

'That sort of behaviour is unacceptable. I want to see your parents.'

'Sir, I'm sorry, it won't happen again.'

'I know it won't! I'm not prepared to have you at my school if you go around hurling abuse at my teachers.'

'Sir, please, I didn't mean it, it just kinda slipped out and it was too late, 'cos the damage was done.'

Mr Barratt raised his eyebrows and looked at me as though I was an alien life form. 'So what do you intend to do to rectify this matter?' he asked.

I had no idea what 'rectify' meant, but it sounded bad. 'Absolutely nothing at all, Sir.'

'Are you sure about that, Dilly?'

'Yes, Sir, I'm sure.'

'Fine, then I have no choice but to call your parents in. A letter will go home tonight, and I want a response back in the morning. Do you understand?'

'Yes, Sir.'

'You'll be on yard duty for a week. I want the yard spotless; if you see a scrap of litter, you pick it up. Is that clear?'

'Yes, Sir.'

'Oh, and another thing: why are you having a packed lunch? The school operates a policy which clearly states that no pupil may consume anything other than that which is provided on the premises.'

I wished he'd talk plain English so I could understand what he was going on about, but then he was the head, and he was a dick.

'I've got too many brothers and sisters, Sir. My dad can't afford for all of us to have school dinners, but we can't get free meals 'cos he works.'

'What does he do?'

'He's a librarian, Sir.'

'Is he now? Well that's a surprise.' Mr Barratt smiled at me as though he'd just found life on Mars. I guess it had never occurred to him that a Paki could have a proper job.

'Where does he work?'

'The Central Library,' I said. My bottom was sticking to the chair, but I was worried about moving in case it made a farting sound.

'I see, very well. It's highly improbable that he'll be able to attend a daytime meeting, so I'll dictate a letter to him. Now get out, I don't want to see you in here unless it's for something positive. And if you're ever rude to a member of my staff again, you're out for good.'

It was with relief that I escaped from the leather chair and went back to class. By now, news of my disobedience had spread, and the kids in my class were all smiling at me with admiration. I'd done something that none of them would ever have dreamt of doing – I'd been lippy to a teacher.

After lessons, the secretary handed me an official-looking envelope and told me to give it to my parents. When I got home, I went up to the toilet and opened the letter.

Dear Mr and Mrs Shah,

I regret to inform you that your child Dilly was involved in an incident today which requires your attention. I would very much like to discuss this matter with you at your earliest convenience.

Would you please contact the school office to arrange an appointment to see me.

Please sign and return the attached slip as confirmation of receipt of this letter.

Yours faithfully,

D. H. Barratt

Head Teacher

I forged my father's signature and returned the slip to the school office the next morning. I knew there was no way they could check up on me; we didn't have a phone, and my mother couldn't read or write English, so any letters addressed to my parents would be easy to intercept and destroy before my father got home from work.

That lunchtime, Egg and I tried loitering in the playground, but a supervisor saw us and shooed us out. So we went exploring down a side road, and ended up walking past a row of beautiful detached houses with perfectly tended lawns. One of the front gardens had a big hedge of plum trees, laden with fruit. We shook the trees, feasted on plums with our parathas, and went back to school with our lunchboxes full of the plums we couldn't eat.

Over the next few weeks, we discovered many new and interesting places to eat lunch. The area around the school was full of fields; the further up the hill you went, the more rural the landscape became. But, as the weather got colder, Egg's complaints grew louder. It was proving harder and harder to persuade her not to tell my parents what was going on. I was desperate to keep her quiet, as I was sure I'd get the blame. Sometimes she was so unhappy she'd refuse to eat at all, and a sheep would get to try my mother's cooking.

*　　*　　*

It was a grim October day, with the smell of frost in the air, when Egg and I found ourselves exploring a new field in search of shelter from the biting wind. We climbed a wooden gate, set our coats down on the damp grass and tried to smile as we chewed our way through our miserable picnic. Every lunch was the same: cold omelettes and parathas, with a tin of fruit, and a pink plastic Thermos flask of lukewarm milk, tea or water. I longed for a scoop of mashed potato.

I'd just started to open the tin of pears, when I heard a dubba-da-thubba-da noise.

'What the . . . ?' I looked up, to see Egg sprinting for the gate. As the sound got louder, I saw what she was running from: a massive black bull was thundering towards me. This was a real matador's bull, with ivory-coloured horns and a brass ring through his nose; he was huge, grunting, frothing, and clearly outraged that we'd trespassed on his land.

The pears would have to wait. I ran for my life, and made it over the gate moments before the bull arrived. Egg and I backed away as he thumped his head against the fence, which shook and looked as though it could give way at any moment. Anyone with any sense would have just kept running, but I was hypnotized by the long gluey ribbons of snot streaming from the flaring nostrils.

Egg yelled: 'Come on, Dilly, let's go!'

'We can't, Egg, we've left our coats in the field,' I replied, but she was already disappearing rapidly from view down the lane.

The bull seemed to lose interest, and turned away from the gate. I watched his tail swinging across his big black backside, but only for a few seconds. All he was doing was giving himself some space for a run-up. He turned back towards me, and charged the gate. Just before what seemed like a certain impact, he dug his hooves into the ground and stopped. Then he did all the things an angry bull is supposed to do – pawing the ground, snorting, bobbing his head.

This was the moment when a tiny sign on the gate caught my eye: 'Beware of the bull'. I'd seen bigger warnings on aspirin bottles.

Then I heard shouts from across the field. A man in the distance – I guess he was the farmer – was waving a stick and calling the bull by name. I couldn't believe it: this mobile meat mountain that should have been called Hercules or Satan was actually called Albert. As he trotted off towards his owner, I took my chance and grabbed my things.

Egg was unusually quiet on the way home from school that afternoon. I could tell there was something on her mind, and I didn't have to wait long to find out what it was. As we all sat down to eat that evening, she said in a loud voice, 'We got chased by a bull today.'

Several mouths fell open. My mother, who'd been gobbling her food like a hungry farm animal, froze in surprise, and a silence descended.

'I said, we got chased by a bull today.'

This time there was a noise – the sound of my father choking on his food.

'What do you mean, you got chased by a bull?' he asked between splutters. 'What the hell was a bull doing in the school?'

'No, Daddy, you don't understand.'

I kicked her under the table, but the little snitch wouldn't keep quiet.

'The bull was in a field.'

'Oh, did you go on a trip?' Climax asked, looking a healthy brown from her months under the Pakistani sun.

'No, you silly woman,' I wanted to say. 'We were in a shitty field, eating crappy cold eggs, and we got chased by an enormous fucking bull.'

'No, Auntie, you don't understand,' Egg said. 'We weren't at school.'

'Well, where the hell were you?' Mammy shouted angrily. 'I bet this is all Dilly's fault.'

'It was her idea to go in the field,' Egg said. 'We go exploring every lunchtime, 'cos we're not allowed a packed lunch in school.'

'What?' my father asked, finally finding his voice. His timing was terrible; he tried to speak just as he was taking a gulp of water from his glass, and began to choke again.

My multi-tasking mother started to thump his back, point a finger of blame at me, and still managed to act the drama queen.

'Dilly, Dilly, Dilly. Whenever there's something dodgy going on, it's always that girl at the bottom of it. She'll be the death of us all.'

'Will you stop hitting me, woman!' my father shouted as he pushed her hand away. 'How long has this been going on?'

'Since September,' I said, as quietly as I could.

My mother shook her head, rigid with disapproval. Climax tutted.

'I don't believe this!' my father wheezed. He smashed his fist down so hard on the table that the crockery jumped in the air. 'You mean to tell me the two of you have been leaving school every day to eat your lunch, and you never thought to say anything?'

'I was scared, Daddy' I said, as I burst into tears. 'I thought we'd get into trouble.'

'The girl's mad,' my mother hissed.

'I can't believe those bastards have been sending my children out of school,' my father raged. 'I'm going up there tomorrow, and that headmaster is going to regret the day he was born.'

Relief washed over me. For weeks, we'd been braving the elements just to comply with a stupid school policy. And now my father the hero was going to take that policy and shove it up Mr Barratt's arse.

Chapter 22

Mr Barratt was lucky to escape with his life, and Egg and I were overjoyed to leave Holly Field behind and embark on a new phase of life at Titus Middle School.

It felt wonderful going to a place where half the kids were Asian; I already knew lots of my classmates from mosque. Mr Sandy, the headmaster, made us feel very welcome, all the teachers were nice, and the lessons were fun. Best of all, it was close enough to Gomshall Road that we could go home for lunch.

But I suppose it was too much to ask for everything to work out perfectly. Just when I found true happiness at school, the crap really hit the fan at home.

Mammy had been in good spirits ever since she got back from Pakistan. Her attitude towards me had changed dramatically; she had become more tolerant and understanding, and was taking more of an interest in what I wanted to do. Even though I still couldn't persuade her to take me shopping, at least we seemed able to exist in the same place without being at each other's throats all the time.

She'd been spending a lot of time with me, teaching me how to embroider with the silk threads she'd brought back from Pakistan. My willingness to learn seemed to please her. What a transformation. I found myself starting to love her; she was my Mammy, and she was great. We put the cookery books she'd brought back from Pakistan to good use. Neither of us was very good at cooking, but we were spending time experimenting with all the recipes, and it seemed to bring us closer.

Together we learned how to make chutney with fresh coriander and mint from the garden. She showed me how to pound up the leaves with the pestle and mortar, how much salt to add, when to put the green chillies in and how much yogurt to pour in to make a smooth, creamy paste. We learned how to use chilli powder, lemon juice and salt to turn homemade chips into a gastronomic delight; how to marinade chicken in ginger and garlic paste; and how to make the crispy layered parathas that the family loved. And we baked date pies, with thick sweet crusts and creamy custard.

Every now and again, Climax would stroll into the kitchen and examine the contents of whatever bowls or pans we were working with, chuckle condescendingly, shake her head, and stroll out again. But, apart from these interruptions, the kitchen was warm and alive with happy sounds. My old mother, the one who hated me, had vanished.

The more time I spent with Mammy, the more grown-up I felt, and the more time Egg spent with the twins. I noticed the close bond the three of them were developing. On one occasion I told Egg off for playing outside, and she accused me of sounding just like my mother. It was then that I started to wonder: was Mammy deliberately distracting me with interesting things to do indoors to keep my mind off the idea of going out to play like a normal child? Or was there some other reason why she was so keen for me to learn new skills?

Those questions were answered a few days later. I was in the kitchen when I heard my father's voice booming from the back room.

'What? Both of them? How could you do it without asking me? I'm their father.'

I was surprised when I heard Monkey's voice, deep and angry. 'You've got to be fucking kidding me! There's no way my mother is gonna choose who I marry!' He ran out of the house, slamming the front door behind him.

'She'll show you,' continued my father from the back room. 'Just you wait and see – I know what she's like. This is going to end in tears.'

'*She*'? Surely he meant '*he*'? I thought to myself.

'Why are you so angry?' came my mother's voice. 'Thank God I even managed to find someone for her.'

By now, I'd worked out that 'her' could only be Egg, Daisy, Poppy or me. I found myself hoping it was one of my sisters, but deep down I had a horrible feeling it wasn't any of them. My heart was hammering, my hands were icy and I could taste salt in my mouth. I felt like I was going to be sick, but my legs were shaking so much I couldn't stand up to go to the toilet.

'In case you've forgotten,' my mother shouted, 'Rasheeda was all ready to marry her off to one of your useless nephews, and you wrote to her and said don't bother, she's too ugly.'

As soon as I heard the word 'ugly', I went into a panic. I retched violently, but nothing came up. I couldn't breathe; the pain around my heart was suffocating me. There was only one ugly person in the world. They were talking about me! None of this would be happening if only I was beautiful. Why couldn't I look like Doris

Day? My mother loved her, she always said she was gorgeous.

My father called, 'Dilly! Come here!'

I inched inside the room, while my heart continued its drum solo.

'Your mother has something to tell you,' he said.

'Leave it,' she snapped. 'It's nothing to do with her.'

'If you won't tell her, I will,' he said. 'Dilly, you're engaged to your cousin Adam, and Monkey's engaged to your cousin Afeeka. They're your Auntie Nonna's kids. Their father, Samir, is your mother's brother and they're all low-life bastards.'

'I'm not getting married, Mammy. Your nephew can go to hell.'

'I made a promise to my brother,' my mother said. 'And we've exchanged gifts. I've got the rings and clothes from Nonna.'

'You didn't exchange gifts,' Daddy thundered. 'You exchanged daughters. You got theirs and you gave them ours.'

'You swapped me!' I cried hysterically. 'How could you?'

'I'm your mother, and I know what's best for you,' she said. 'In a way I did swap you, but it's a good swap.'

Shaking my head, I said, 'I'll never do it.'

She turned to my father for support, but he was smiling smugly. 'What are you looking at me for?' he asked. 'I'm not going to force her into it.'

It looked as though this was one battle I wouldn't have to fight on my own.

That night, when we switched the light off, unhappy thoughts assaulted me. Like soft brown moths with dusty wings, they fluttered around inside my mind. The biggest thought-moth said: 'Your mother's a bitch.'

Another one fluttered into view, saying: 'Your mother, originally a vicious hag, transformed herself into a nice, warm woman. Are you so stupid you didn't realize it was all just an act?'

As the moths fanned their wings inside my mind, I felt the tears slipping down my cheeks. I thought about my father and what he'd done. Was he as bad as my mother? Or worse? How could he write to Rasheeda and tell her I was ugly? That really hurt, but now he was a surprising ally, a vital part of an uneasy coalition. He was the loud, blustering buffalo that I'd have to rely on to protect me from my two-faced hyena of a mother.

Tossing and turning, I listened to the steady breathing of my sisters, tucked up and sleeping peacefully. It was okay for Egg and Poppy – they were slim and attractive. They wouldn't have to work as hard as me, because their looks would help them along. And Daisy didn't have to worry; no man in his right mind would be interested in an otherwise pretty girl with a severe skin disease.

I thought about the close relationship that had developed between Egg and the twins while I was busy trying to please Mammy. Desperate to win one friend, I'd lost another.

The last thought-moth that fluttered through my mind that night, before I finally surrendered to sleep, warned me that I was in danger of becoming a younger version of my mother. I'd always had a vague idea that when I grew up I'd escape my parents and live my own life. Surely, once I was an adult, I'd be free to do as I pleased. But if my mother got her way, I'd soon be married to her nephew, and then I'd never be rid of her. It was bad enough having her as my mother, but now she wanted to be my auntie as well.

Even worse, if my husband moved into my parents' home, I'd be stuck forever with no way out. For the first time in my life, I knew the true meaning of despair. Unlike Doris fucking Day.

Chapter 23

A cagey and enigmatic woman called Mrs Baba lived at Number 30. Sometimes, when we were playing in the back alley, she'd peer out to see what all the commotion was about, and speak in a mysterious low voice that was little more than a whisper. She reminded me of a tightly bound mummy, or one of the unconvincing monsters from *Scooby-Doo*, dressed from head to foot in dark swathes of cloth, with her head wrapped in hessian-like material.

From my vantage point on top of the garden wall, I'd sometimes see her as she hung out the washing, and I'd wonder what went on in that house. What strange creatures resided there? Despite the dangers, Princess Dilly of Sharnia longed to explore the dark and secretive Kingdom of Baba Land – but not on her own, obviously.

In 1978, on the first anniversary of my auntie's death, Mammy held a remembrance service at our house. She invited a few of her closest friends to join her and share the food she'd persuaded Climax to cook for the occasion. After the guests had gone, there was some food left over, and she asked me to take a bowl of semolina round to Mrs Baba's. Yes! My heart leapt with joy at the prospect of venturing into the unknown. Maybe I would meet unicorns and armour-clad knights on white steeds, for these things must surely exist in Baba Land. However, I had no intention of exploring this shadowy realm on my own; I'd need the services of my dim but faithful handmaiden. I called Egg, who was only too happy to tag along.

We headed up the alley. On the way, I prodded the pudding to see how firm it was. It was set all right, my thumb print just stayed there. I nibbled on some of the almond flakes, grated pistachio and threads of saffron that were scattered on the top.

When we got to the back of Mrs Baba's house, I was disappointed to find that the gate was bolted. My quest to uncover the closely guarded secrets of Baba Land had come to a sudden and premature halt.

There was only one thing left to do, and that was to go round to the front. I knew I'd be in trouble with my fire-breathing-dragon father if I was seen, but I decided it was worth the risk.

I rang the bell. Nothing happened, so I rang it again, and then peered through the letterbox. I'd expected to see an empty passageway, but no – Mrs Baba was making her way towards the door. But she wasn't walking like a normal human being; she was down on the ground in a squat position, moving like a huge cockroach. My mouth fell open; this was really weird. But it was also great – I'd already discovered my first strange creature in Baba Land, and I wasn't even through the front door yet. I let the letterbox snap shut.

Very slowly, the door opened and a low voice whispered, 'Come inside, quickly.' A flicker of excitement ignited deep within me. This adventure was turning out to be more gripping than I'd hoped.

Bravely, I pushed Egg in first. She could act as a decoy,

just in case there was an ogre hiding in the passageway, waiting to pounce.

'Go through to the back,' whispered Mrs Baba.

Egg and I made our way to the kitchen, with Mrs Baba half-shuffling, half-crawling behind us. This was the first time I'd seen her up close, and I was mesmerized. She had the hairiest top lip I'd ever seen on a woman.

As Egg stood with her mouth hanging open in aston-ishment, I couldn't resist trying to make her laugh, by catching her eye and then slowly stroking my upper lip.

'Sit down,' whispered Mrs Baba, signalling to us.

'What?' I asked distractedly. I'd become fascinated by the kitchen windows. I couldn't see out; they were painted white. This was seriously weird stuff. I'd always assumed the Shahs were the most screwed-up family on the street, but there was no way we could compete with this.

We squatted on the floor, and I knew it would be impos-sible to stay in that position for long without farting. I shot a glance at Egg, and could see from the look on her face that the same thought was going through her mind. As the first little bubble of gas squeezed its silent way out, I hoped all its friends would be equally innocuous. Egg was teetering on the brink of uncontrollable giggles. One loud parp would be enough to push her over the edge, and she'd take me with her.

'My mother sent this for you,' I said, handing Mrs Baba the semolina. As she took it from me, I saw close-up just how startlingly white her hands were. They were riddled with spidery blue veins.

Instead of standing, she shuffled across the floor and reached up to the sink; she moved her fingers about among the pile of crockery on the draining board, clasped a bowl, took it down and poured the semolina into it, using her finger to scrape the remains out.

I was unable to hold my tongue any longer. 'Auntie, why can't you get up and do that properly? Who painted the windows? Why are we sitting on the floor?'

'Quiet, girl. Don't raise your voice, it's not good.'

I wanted to run outside and tell everybody what was happening in this house. It was brilliant, but nobody was ever going to believe me. I'd stepped through the wardrobe, and ended up in a Narnia for weirdos.

'Auntie, who painted the windows?' I asked again, as Mrs Baba rocked back and forth on her heels.

'Mr Baba painted them so nobody can see into the house. He likes his privacy.'

'But you can't see out.'

'I don't need to.'

While I was mulling over her words, the phone rang; it made me jump.

'Aren't you going to answer it?' I asked.

'Mr Baba doesn't let me use the phone.'

Now I knew for sure that nobody was going to believe me. They'd all say I'd made the whole thing up. What sort of fiend would do this to his own wife?

As Mrs Baba moved to get comfortable, her shawl fell away from her face, revealing a chin covered in hair. I suppressed the surge of laughter that rose inside me, and wondered if I had the nerve to call her 'uncle'.

My feet had started to get pins and needles, and the need to fart was overwhelming. I stood up quickly, and said, 'We have to go.'

'Thank your mother, and tell her to come and visit. I haven't seen her for a long time.'

Egg got to her feet and made for the passage, but Mrs Baba stopped her. 'Go from the back of the house – you're too big to be coming and going from the front.'

Back in the safety of the alley, I let out a huge breath. 'Oh my God, that was great!'

'The woman was giving me the creeps,' Egg shuddered. 'I can't believe she's got a beard.'

We burst into the house, to find my mother waiting for us. 'Where have you two been?' she asked impatiently.

'Sorry, Mammy, Mrs Baba took a long time to come to the door.'

Egg and I excitedly told Mammy about everything that had happened. She didn't believe a word of it.

As I lay in bed that night, I kept going over the afternoon's events. I couldn't understand what drove a man to be so cruel to his wife. I'd never liked Mr Baba, with his ridiculously long, pubic beard and huge pot belly. He was always telling Monkey off for not going to mosque, or for playing his music too loud. He was uncouth, uneducated and couldn't speak English properly, but he still strutted about the street as though he owned it.

And why did Mrs Baba allow him to treat her like an animal? Were there other women living like her, or was she the only Crawlosaurus in captivity?

I knew she had grown-up children, but I hadn't seen them for a while, and I wondered if Mr Baba had done something terrible to them. Maybe he'd imprisoned them in the cellar, like my mother used to do to me.

As I fell asleep, I made a mental note to myself: first thing in the morning, I had to check in the mirror for any sign of hair. I was ugly enough already; the last thing I needed was a moustache.

Chapter 24

As far as the Shah kids were concerned, Doc was more a
brother than a cousin. He was sensitive, studious when
he wanted to be, always helpful around the house, and,
when backed into a corner, the most aggressive of all of us.
He had the same pale complexion as his mother, but was
considerably better-looking. He'd broken his leg playing
rugby when he was thirteen, and had walked with a limp
ever since. It was the one thing he hated about himself,
because it excluded him from a lot of sports, and made it
even harder for him to emulate Monkey.

I felt sorry for him because my father was always picking on him, punching him, and telling him he was good
for nothing. Daddy liked to beat him, and Climax liked
to stand by and watch. In many ways, Doc and I were
alike. After me, he was the blackest sheep of the family;
we shared a bond because we both knew what it felt like
to be unwelcome in your own home.

With Monkey and me engaged, it wasn't hard to work
out who was next. It was Doc's turn to start twitching
nervously. He was fifteen – the ideal age to get engaged,
according to his mother. Doc's idea of a perfect girl was an
English-speaking blonde; he always said that when he grew
up he wanted to marry a Farrah Fawcett-Majors lookalike
– and there weren't many of those among my cousins.

It wasn't long before Climax let slip that she had been trying to arrange a match for Doc with one of her nieces (whom Mammy called 'Rhino Arse', for obvious reasons). But my father said that Rhino Arse was an ugly excuse for a woman and when her mother had washed her hair with DDT to kill the nits, it had damaged her brain instead; and there was no way he wanted that cerebrally challenged tart in his house. Climax said she hadn't got a clue what he meant, and she wished he'd stop talking like a college professor, because he was just a book-stamper taking orders from a white woman.

As soon as Doc found out what was going on, he threatened to run away, saying he knew his mother was a bitch, but he couldn't believe she could sink so low as to want him to marry the family troll.

Any doubts he might have had about wanting to leave home were erased after he went swimming without permission. When he came home, Daddy smacked him in the face and dragged him around the back garden; then, soon afterwards, he was accused of stealing cigarettes from Toadie's. Doc denied it, but Climax punished him anyway, and gave him a whipping with a leather belt. Doc said it wasn't fair: how could his own mother believe a shopkeeper over him?

So when Doc first saw the Army recruitment office in Bradford city centre, it must have seemed like an escape route from everything he'd grown to hate. It may as well have had an 'Emergency Exit' sign above it, with a little matchstick man showing him the way to freedom.

Doc signed up – not to join the professionals, but to leave the psychopaths. Here was his opportunity to hold on to his sanity and start a new life; he grabbed the chance with both hands, and held on tight.

He signed up in the summer of 1978, when he was still only fifteen, but the Army said he couldn't start his training until he was sixteen. From the moment his mother found out, until the day he could pack his bags and go, Doc knew he'd be in for a rough ride.

Climax tried to talk him out of it, but that didn't work. So she pleaded, and that didn't work either. In desperation, she took to her bed and made out that the stress was killing her, but Doc wasn't fooled. She told him he shouldn't be fighting for the Queen, because good Muslim boys didn't go on Crusades. She even said if he was normal he'd want to be a doctor or a pharmacist, or at the very least, a dentist. She said she'd undoubtedly have a heart attack if he left home. She made many threats, and he ignored them all.

I couldn't understand why she was so desperate to keep him at home anyway. It was my father's abuse that was driving Doc away; perhaps if she'd been as persistent in defending her son, he might have stayed.

While Climax was having her pretend fainting fits like the heroine of a Victorian melodrama, my father was openly delighted by Doc's news, and spent his days bouncing happily around the house like a superball. He, at least, didn't hide his true feelings. Doc's limp wouldn't go unnoticed, and Daddy was convinced he'd fail the medical. This would be a wonderful opportunity for my father to crush Doc's spirit once and for all, to tell his hated nephew that he was so useless that even the brainless white uniformed morons didn't want him, and that he wasn't even good enough to march to his death.

But Doc proved him wrong, and passed the medical. He got a letter of acceptance, inviting him to join the Army the following March. The moment he read that letter, all his worries seemed to vanish, and his thoughts turned to the new life he'd soon be starting. His body was still at home, but his mind had already packed its kitbag and cleared off. I was pleased for him; now at least he would be free from Sharnia.

It was a hot summer morning, and Daddy and Climax were still arguing about the effects of DDT on the human brain, when a letter arrived in the post from Pakistan.

We all crowded round to have a look. Daddy opened the envelope, saw what was in it, and disdainfully tossed the contents on to the table. 'Help yourself,' he said to my mother, as he grabbed his cricket bat and headed for the door.

Mammy took out two big glossy photos that had obviously been taken in a professional studio. The first picture was of Monkey's fiancée, Afeeka, who looked like a Zeenat Aman wannabe. She was standing straight, arms by her sides, a coy smile on her face. She was slim and pretty, with huge breasts trying to escape from her skin-tight pink kameez. The boys both looked on approvingly.

'Mmm, nice jugs,' Monkey murmured.

'Blimey,' Doc said. 'She'd be dangerous with those on a cold night. She could poke your eyes out.' He turned to Monkey. 'Don't worry, mate,' he said. 'At least you'll have somewhere to hang your hat.' He laughed, then added, 'Or somewhere to shove your helmet.'

The second picture was of Adam. I felt myself cringing with embarrassment. Monkey was engaged to a nymphet with huge melons, and my fiancé looked like a low-life Mexican bandit from a Clint Eastwood film.

There's no justice in the world, I thought, as I threw the picture on the table and stormed out, with the sound of laughter ringing in my ears.

A few days later, a letter arrived from my father's younger brother, Ilyas. There were no photos, but plenty of opinions, and – in case we didn't already know – he felt duty-bound to inform us that Adam was a college drop-out, a jobless sponger, and an idiot.

That letter was the ringing bell at the start of another round of the long-running Big Daddy vs Ranting Mammy bout. I bet the neighbours were fed up with the arguments, the yelling and the slamming doors. Every once in a while, tempers would cool, and things would calm down a little. All it needed from me was, 'Mammy, I'm not marrying that bastard,' then I'd go off and play with Hamble, while my reignited parents brawled all over again.

But we'd received photos, so my mother said it was only right that we return the favour. Somehow, she persuaded my father to take Monkey and me to the photographer's studio. Monkey looked quite smart in his new suit. I, on the other hand, felt quite ridiculous in the baggy purple salvaar kameez I was forced into. Mammy smoothed down my hair with so much Brylcreem that it ran down my neck like an oily river.

As we got ready to leave the house, she said, 'Whatever you do, Dilly, keep your mouth shut. I don't want your buck teeth ruining the photos.'

However, when the pictures arrived in the post, it wasn't my teeth that my mother was looking at; it was the hole in my shoe where the upper had come away from the sole. It showed up beautifully in the snaps, even though I'd done my best to hide it by colouring the toe of my sock with a black crayon.

'Oh my God! I don't believe it!' she fumed as she shook the photograph about wildly.

'What's wrong with you?' Daddy asked, sipping his tea.

'She's got a bloody hole in her shoe.'

Daddy took the picture. 'Oh, just get a marker and colour it in – no one will even notice.'

I felt like I'd won a battle without even trying; it hadn't occurred to me that the hole in my shoe could do so much damage. I'd managed to get one over on my mother and I was feeling victorious, when Monkey brought me crashing back down to earth.

'You're such a silly cow, Dilly,' he said. 'Look at this picture; you've ruined it.' He sounded genuinely irritated.

'No I haven't – and anyway, why should you care? Don't tell me you actually want to get married?'

'Shut your mouth, you stupid black bitch.'

I was surprised by his reaction. We were supposed to be on the same side, but now it looked like he was changing his mind. Maybe it was out of a sense of loyalty to my mother, or maybe it was the size of Afeeka's jugs, and the promise of nights spent resting his head between those soft welcoming pillows. Whatever the reason, I hated him for it.

Afeeka's photo was given pride of place on top of the TV. Whenever I walked past, I'd give it a flick with my finger and send it tumbling to the floor. My mother never missed a chance to tell her friends how fortunate she was to be getting such a beautiful daughter-in-law. She was the first Asian woman on the street to have secured a partner for her son, and there was no way the neighbours were going to avoid her victory cries. She'd lie in wait in the back alley like a sniper, and pounce on unsuspecting passers-by. And then she'd thrust the photo of Afeeka into their hands, and crow gleefully.

It wasn't long before all the women on the street were doing their best to arrange cousin-cousin marriages in their attempts to keep up with the Shahs. Even Zarqa, who'd been keeping a low profile, was caught up in the wave of enthusiasm, and came over one day to find out how Mammy had done it.

'Oh, it was so easy for me to find partners for Monkey and Dilly,' my mother bragged. 'I went to Pakistan and my family were begging me for their hands in marriage.'

I'd heard this speech a thousand times.

'I feel sorry for Dilly's poor fiancé. She'll ruin his life,' replied Zarqa.

I'd heard enough. 'You stupid fat cow, don't feel sorry for him. Feel sorry for me – she wants me to marry a loser. And Zarqa, what are you doing here? My dad told you to get out once; if you had any brains you'd have got the message the first time. I guess that makes you an idiot, you bastard.'

The world held its breath. There was silence as my mother and Zarqa looked at each other, and then at me. Then my mother charged at me like an angry heifer, and sent me to the ground with a single slap to the face. 'I swear to God I'm going to kill you.'

From my horizontal position I could make out a look of satisfaction on Zarqa's face. She'd waited a year for this, and now her patience was finally being rewarded. I took off my shoes and threw them at her.

She shouted, 'See what I mean, Gongal? I don't think your family's ready for Dilly, God help them.'

'She's a pain in the arse, and I'm going to show her who's boss,' Mammy hissed. 'Get up now. I'm sick of you.'

She dragged me to my feet by my hair and shook me.

'She's going to ruin that poor boy. He won't know if he's coming or going,' Zarqa added. 'Why don't you warn him?'

'Why don't you piss off?' I shouted.

My mother sent me sprawling across the floor, just as Daddy walked in. Zarqa took one look at him and scarpered.

'What the hell's going on?' he asked.

'It's your bloody daughter,' my mother seethed. 'She's gone mad, and you won't control her, you don't do anything.'

'I'll never marry him!' I shouted. 'I'll never marry your idiot nephew. Only total wasters marry their cousins. It should be illegal.'

'I married my cousin,' my mother spat angrily.

'My point exactly,' I spat back.

'That's it, I'm going to kill you!' And she came after me with murder in her eyes.

My father the hero stepped in her way and caught hold of her. 'Leave it, Gongal.'

'She needs to be taught a lesson,' she shouted.

'I hope Adam dies!' I yelled. 'I hope Afeeka dies. I hope you die!'

Daddy had two jobs to do now. As head of the house, he knew he had to take charge of the situation. But at the same time, he had to fight back the laughter that was threatening to overwhelm him. 'Dilly, get upstairs now.'

'Tell her, Daddy, tell her she can't do this to me. I'm never marrying that shitbag.'

He tried as hard as he could to keep a straight face, but failed and found himself almost convulsed with laughter, while trying to hold on to my mother so she couldn't get to me.

'You're loving this, aren't you?' she shouted, fists flailing, but heavily restrained by a manly hand holding her by her pigtail.

'Oh, give it a rest, woman, you've got nobody to blame but yourself. I told you, you're on your own. Dilly, upstairs.'

I ran up to my room. Egg looked up from her Plasticine models. 'What happened to you?'

'Shut up! Don't talk to me!' I screamed, as I kicked the wall and cried. 'I hate her! I hate her! I'm never going to marry that loser, never!'

'Did you see Zarqa downstairs?' Egg asked calmly.

'I threw my shoes at her,' I spat.

Egg burst out laughing.

'And I'm going to go and get them back.'

My parents were sitting in the kitchen, acting out a scene from a bad amateur dramatics production. My mother was pretending to faint, and my father was pretending to care.

'I'm dead, I'm dead,' she lamented randomly. 'My family's ruined, my feet are like ice, and my blood pressure's up – look at my ears.' She was so high-pitched, she sounded like an ice cream van.

'Gongal, calm down,' my father soothed, as he rubbed her arm. 'Your ears look fine to me.'

When she saw me, my mother stopped her acting for a second, gave me a look of pure venom, and then continued with her drama. I was angry with my father for comforting her. It wasn't fair. It was time to stir things up again.

'I'm never gonna do it, Mammy. You can't make me.'

Considering she was dying of a thousand different ailments, she shot out of her chair remarkably swiftly. But my father grabbed her and held her back. As I went upstairs to play with Egg, I could hear her cursing her bad luck for having me as her daughter.

Chapter 25

When I was eleven, a letter arrived from Pakistan. It was just a single page, handwritten in Urdu: Rasheeda, my mother's nemesis, was sick, and wanted to come to England for urgent treatment. Because she was too ill to travel alone, she wanted to bring her son Ilyas with her.

Mammy was ecstatic about Rasheeda's illness, but filled with horror at the prospect of having the mother-in-law from hell land on her doorstep.

'God's punished her. She treated me like shit when I was living in Jallu.'

'Is she going to be okay?' I asked.

'Who gives a flying fuck?' my mother tittered. 'You can't believe a word those savages say, it's all lies. She's not as sick as she's making out. She's been trying to get to Bradford for years, and your father's such a simpleton he believes whatever those donkey-herders tell him.'

'Can I have the letter, Mammy? I wanna show it to Egg.'

'No, you bloody well can't. Anyone would think Egg was the Prime Minister – what do you want her to do, stamp the lying cow's visa, so she can come and live here and make my life hell? Go on, get lost.'

When Climax found out her mother was sick, she just shrugged her shoulders and said, 'If that hag comes here, I'm leaving.'

But when my father read the letter, he looked as though he was about to cry. He told Mammy he was going to Pakistan as soon as he could buy a ticket, but she wasn't having any of it. She tried to convince him that Rasheeda was as strong as an ox, and would live forever. After all, how many times had he received news that someone or other was sick? If he flew back home every time someone sneezed, he'd be bankrupt.

Over the next few weeks, there was a lot of arguing as Daddy sent money and presents to Pakistan; whatever he sent was never enough, according to Rasheeda, and way too much, according to my mother.

My poor father was caught between two conflicting loyalties, and he couldn't win. Mammy wore him down so much that Rasheeda never received the invitation she'd asked for, and my father never made the journey to Pakistan to see his sick mother.

They said the First World War would all be over by Christmas. The Shah 'should I stay or should I go?' battle would have raged for years, but Rasheeda's death brought it to an unexpected end on New Year's Day.

Chapter 26

It was no surprise that Daddy was crushed by the news of his mother's death. I'd never seen him so subdued; he spent most of his time in a daze.

What was more surprising was my mother's reaction. In fact, she had two, depending on who came to the house. Rasheeda's death was either a sad loss to humanity, or not before time.

Whenever my father or Climax was around, she was red-eyed and tearful, every bit the grieving daughter-in-law. And when they were out, her smug look would reappear, and she'd bitch non-stop about Rasheeda and the rest of the family in Jallu.

My mother took duplicity to new heights, and it was embarrassing to witness the hypocrite in action. As my father's friends started to arrive at the house to offer their condolences, my mother shed the required number of tears in front of the wives, told everyone how heartbroken she was, and how she couldn't believe that such a good and noble woman was dead. I heard the same old speech from Mammy time and again, as she performed her new production, *The Grieving Daughter-in-Law*. On Pennine Radio, Elkie Brookes was preaching 'Don't Cry Out Loud' but she was wasting her breath as far as Mammy was concerned.

It was a different story when my mother's friends called round. The gloves would come off, and she'd tell them exactly what she thought of Rasheeda. When Zarqa came over to pay her respects, Mammy told her not to bother with the tears, and asked her if she'd like a Garibaldi with her cuppa.

'I'm so glad that evil bitch is dead, she's nothing but hell's tinder now,' Mammy said as she poured the tea. 'She made my life a misery.'

'Well, she can't make anyone miserable now,' said Zarqa, with paper-thin sympathy. 'You're lucky that she's kicked the bucket.'

My mother chuckled. 'And not before time. I thought she'd live to be a hundred – the women on that side of the family don't want to die. And while they're alive they try to squeeze the life out of everybody else. I hope she's dancing with the Devil.'

'Are you going to the funeral?' Zarqa chirped.

Mammy tossed back her head and laughed. 'Are you kidding me? Why the hell would I waste my time? They can pour yogurt on her and throw her in the street for the dogs, for all I care. Go to her funeral, my arse! She was a cunt! She treated me like a slave, and then she had the bloody nerve to ask if she could come and stay with us.'

Not to be outdone, Zarqa said, 'She's done you a favour by dropping down dead. Thank God she never made it to Bradford, or you'd be suffering the way I am.' She went on to whinge about how she was stuck with a lazy, good-for-nothing sister-in-law, who spent all her time playing with the hot water, and flushing the toilet, because she'd never seen a tap or a cistern until she came to England.

And so it went on for hours. Just as Zarqa finally got up to leave, the doorbell rang, and in came Estie to pay her respects. My eyes lit up at the sight of the home-baked Jamaican ginger cake she'd brought with her.

'I'm so sorry to hear the news, Gongal,' she said. 'How's Shah taking it?'

'Who gives a shit?' Mammy said, as she poured the tea. 'I'm so glad that evil witch is dead. She's nothing but hell's tinder now. Come on, let's have some of that cake, and see if *Rainbow*'s started yet.'

It was weeks before things returned to normal. We were in the back room when Monkey told Daddy he wanted to train to be an accountant when he left school, and Daddy smiled and nodded approvingly. So I thought it was only right that I share my ambitions with him too, saying, 'I want to be a newsreader, like Angela Rippon.'

His reaction was a bit unexpected. As I lay in a heap on the floor, with pain throbbing in the side of my face where his fist had been just seconds earlier, he told me he'd break my legs if I tried to go out to work before I was married, and that my only job was to help my mother around the house. Just to make sure I'd got the message, he said he'd kill me if I dared to defy him.

As I got to my feet, I hoped the next fatality in his family would be soon. With any luck, it'd be his father, and then he'd be in a sombre mood for months.

As soon as I got the chance, I looked up 'defy' in the dictionary. It wasn't worth dying of ignorance.

Defy   To resist openly or boldly; to challenge, baffle, obstruct; to resist successfully.

I could see this was going to be difficult; I'd spent all my life defying someone, and I had no intention of stopping now.

Chapter 27

I loved school, and was really upset the day my teacher sent me home with suspected chicken pox. The next morning, I was a mass of red spots, and spent the day feeling sorry for myself.

In the afternoon the electricity man came to read the meter, but my mother didn't let him in because my father didn't like strange men in the house when he was out. An official-looking orange card was pushed through the letterbox; it was a request to call and arrange a convenient time to have the meter read. I hid it under the TV where Mammy wouldn't find it.

Dr Johnson also came to visit that afternoon; he wasn't a stranger, so he was allowed in. He wrote out a prescription for some ointment. When he'd gone, I produced the orange electricity card and said, 'Look, Mammy, this is a note from the doctor. He said I have to rest. I'm not allowed to do any housework till I'm better.'

'Okay,' Mammy said. She had to take my word for it; she'd been stuck in Early Reader books for years, and the only English she could read was 'My name is Brenda. I am a doll' and 'Topsy and Tim go on holiday'. If Climax had been at home, I wouldn't have been able to get away with it, but she had gone to visit her friend Amina in Dewsbury.

My chicken pox was really bad. The fact that I had eczema as well meant the scabs took ages to heal, and I was off school for nearly three weeks. I was still at home feeling sorry for myself when the truant officer, who was a regular visitor to Sharnia, hammered on the door. My mother talked to him through the letterbox.

'What do you want this time? Have any of my bastards been skiving again?'

'Hi, Mrs Shah. I need to know why Dilly isn't in school.'

She opened the door, told him to wait in the passage, and came running into the back room. She rummaged around in the drawers, and then said, 'Dilly, where's that sick note the doctor gave you?'

I told her it was under the TV. She lifted up the set and grabbed the orange card, then she hurried back to the truant officer, clearly pleased that for once there was a genuine, fully documented reason for my absence. I poked my head round the door and saw the look on his face as my mother puffed up her chest and triumphantly presented the paperwork.

'Mrs Shah,' he asked, 'are you joking?'

'Look, look, look! Read it!' She prodded it with her finger. 'It's from the doctor.'

He put on a supremely condescending voice. 'No, it isn't.'

I saw the back of my mother going from proud cockerel to punctured balloon in a matter of seconds. 'What the hell are you talking about? Are you calling me a liar? Are you saying this isn't a sick note?'

'It's from the Electricity Board, wanting to know when the meter man can come round, Mrs Shah.'

I dived into the bed and pretended to be asleep; seconds later, the door flew open, and a red-faced mother came marching in. The duvet was pulled off me.

'There!' she said, pointing at me, as though it wasn't obvious where I was. 'See, she's sick. Dilly, get up and show this man your spots.'

'There's no need, I can see she's not well, Mrs Shah.' He handed her back the card. 'I suggest you keep this.'

She snatched it from his hand, saw him out of the front door, and came racing into the back room.

'You little bitch. If you weren't so sick, I'd kill you. I'll be the laughing stock of the Education Department. Did you hear that sarcastic bastard? He talked to me like I was a village idiot. It's all your fault. I'm so embarrassed; wait till your father gets home tonight. Keep out of my way today, or I swear I'll kill you, pox or no pox.'

That evening, Daddy was subjected to a barrage of incessant nagging: she felt worthless; she'd been mocked; what were things coming to, when her daughter could make her look like such a fool?

Two weeks later, Miss Goode, the English tutor, turned up. She visited for two hours at a time, three evenings a week, and there was homework as well. It wasn't long before Daddy was moaning that his mealtimes were being ruined because his wife was spending too much time improving herself and not enough time looking after him.

So, after a few weeks, things returned to normal. Miss Goode was sent packing, my father got the meals he wanted, and my mother went back to being a semi-literate village girl with no ambitions and no future.

Chapter 28

Every afternoon when we got in from school was the same for me: try to figure out what sort of mood my mother was in, help her with the housework even though she'd been at home all day, then get ready to go to the mosque in Oakwood Road with the other kids from our neighbourhood. For the half hour before religious instruction started, it seemed like every child in Bradford was on their way to mosque. The streets were a sea of colour and calm acquiescence; the atmosphere was more like a carnival than a journey to school, with everyone chatting and playing games along the way.

Once inside, the sexes were segregated: boys in one room, girls in another. Altogether, there must have been more than a hundred children. We were supposed to spend the time praying and learning about our religion, but somehow we always managed to find the time to natter about *Starsky and Hutch*, Kevin Keegan's hair, and all the other things that were important to us. We weren't allowed to mix with the boys, so we just talked about them instead.

There were eight teachers in all, and they could all be seen outside the mosque before the start of lessons, selecting the thinnest branches from the trees in the courtyard to use as canes. My teacher's name was Mr Ibrahim, but we all called him Molvi Sahib. He reminded me of a billy goat, but he was relatively nice most of the time, and everyone preferred him to the other teachers – especially Molvi Aap, who taught the boys; he was fat and scary, and used to spread himself out like a beached whale. All the boys had bad stories about him and how creepy he was.

My school teachers were allowed to cane naughty pupils, but the mosque teachers took punishment to another level: as well as the canings, there were plenty of slaps, punches and kicks, even for the teenage boys who were bigger than the molvis. All the parents approved of this physical abuse; they said discipline was good for us.

Molvi Sahib liked to pick on me because I was left-handed. He'd tell me I was Satan's spawn, and took special care to make sure I only used my right hand when I was in mosque.

Egg and I were on our way to mosque one afternoon, being swept along on the tide. As usual, there were hordes of kids heading in the same direction, then we bumped into Nelly and her mother. Nelly was one of the girls in my class at Titus Middle; she was a snob who lived in a big house, and I hated her for having all the luxuries that I didn't. All the girls called her Nelly to her face, and Bitch-Face behind her back.

As I fell into step with Nelly, her mother took one look at me, shuddered and tutted. Then she sniffed the air theatrically, and said to Nelly, 'Why are you walking with that girl? She's smelly and dirty. I don't want you to hang around with children like that. Come on, darling, hurry up.' They quickened their pace to get ahead of me.

I felt humiliated. Egg and I stopped walking and stared at each other in bewilderment. I looked around for something to throw at Nelly's mother, but couldn't find anything hard enough. They continued on their way, and didn't even appear to notice that we were no longer tagging along behind them.

When we got to the mosque, Egg and I sat next to a girl called Sofia, who lived at 54 Gomshall Road. She was born and raised in Bradford, and spoke perfect English, but, for some reason I never understood, she insisted on speaking with a Pakistani accent.

As I opened my prayer book, she turned to me and said, 'Last night my dad threw the murderers down the stairs.'

I stopped reading and looked at her in surprise. 'How did the murderers get into your house?'

'Through the door, of course,' she said scornfully.

I was trying to figure out if I'd missed something, and then I saw Egg's shoulders going up and down in silent laughter.

Sofia continued. 'My mum told my dad, "Get the murderers out," so he did.'

'Why didn't he call the cops?' I asked.

Sofia eyed me cautiously, as though she was trying to work out if I was taking the piss. Then she said: 'He's a big man; he didn't need the police.'

By this time Egg was on the floor, laughing hysterically. I told her to shut up because Molvi Sahib would hear us, but she ignored me.

Sofia shook her head in disgust and said, 'You two are so thick. What's so funny about that? Are you trying to tell me you don't sleep on your murderers, Dilly?'

'Why the fuck would I sleep on a murderer?'

Egg shouted out loud: 'Dilly, you idiot, she means *mattress*.'

I kicked Egg to shut her up, and that's when Molvi Sahib saw me. We were supposed to be studying verses from the Koran in preparation for the annual mosques competition. As I looked up, I saw Molvi Sahib hurdling the patlers*, and racing across the room towards me.

There was nowhere to run, so I sat and waited for the punishment. It wasn't the first time that week I'd been beaten in mosque; it was becoming so routine I'd grown to expect it. Most of the other kids got beaten as well – for me, the difference was that the beatings made me feel right at home.

Molvi Sahib picked up my Hafti and brought it crashing down on my head. Then he did it again, and again. By the third time, I was seeing stars and had a howling headache. As I cowered lower and lower, holding my hands over my head, he whacked me on the neck and back instead.

'You should be studying. We have a competition next week and we have to win. Come with me.' He grabbed my arm and dragged me to the front of the room, then picked up his cane from the desk and struck me across the palms.

'Why were you talking?' he demanded.

My head was killing me, but I had to think fast or I knew I was in for more of the same, or worse.

'I was telling Sofia about my mum,' I said.

---

* A long low wooden table used in a mosque for children to sit at, while keeping them separate – a bit like a cross between a pew and a row of desks, but all the children sit on the floor.

'What were you telling her that's so important it can't wait till you've left? This is God's house – show some respect.'

'I was only telling her that my mum died. And it's you who doesn't have respect – you're not supposed to hit me with my Hafti.'

He looked shocked. 'When did she die?'

'Last week' I said.

'How did it happen?'

'She had a headache, and then her head burst. The doctor said her brain was bleeding.'

He looked at me, then at the book he'd just hit me on the head with, and asked, rather sheepishly, 'So why are you here?'

'Me and my sister came to pray for her soul,' I said. The deeper I got into these lies, the harder I was finding it to keep a straight face.

Molvi Sahib looked at me sympathetically. All thoughts of beating me had obviously fled from his mind, as he took a fifty-pence piece out of his pocket and put it in my hand.

'You don't have to come tomorrow,' he said generously. 'Go and sit down.'

Fifty pence was more than adequate compensation for the headache; it bought a lot of sweets for Egg and me that evening, and went some way towards soothing the ego that Nelly's mother had demolished.

Chapter 29

I saw Nelly at school the next morning, but by then my hot fire of vengeance had burnt itself out, and had been replaced by icy hatred. That hatred increased when I heard her telling other girls that she couldn't play with me because I was a tramp.

When I told my mother, all she said was, 'Well, you don't have to hang around with her, do you? If she doesn't want to talk to you, then don't talk to her either. I don't see what the problem is.'

Unlike Mammy, I could see the problem quite clearly. The other girls in my class were getting guidance from their mothers on how to take care of themselves: how to dress, how to look after their bodies, and how to maintain personal hygiene. I, on the other hand, had a mother who didn't seem to care how I looked or smelt, as long as I dressed like a frump and took a bath once a week.

Two days later, a few of the girls I hung out with decided to sneak out of school at lunchtime to find some older boys to chat up. I was invited along, but said I'd better not go because I already had a fiancé.

Eyebrows were raised in surprise, and then everyone fell about laughing. Nelly said, 'Yeah right. Pull the other one, Dilly. Who in their right mind would wanna go out with you?'

'It's true. I'm engaged to my cousin Adam,' I said.

Leela, who was my closest friend at school, said, 'Show us the ring, Dilly,' and I could tell that even she didn't believe me.

'I can't. My mam won't give it to me yet; it's too big.'

Nelly laughed. 'You're a liar.'

She sneered at me and snooted away in a huff, with the other girls following in her wake. They all went off in a sniggering huddle, and I was left in the playground on my own, wishing that I'd never mentioned Adam, and wondering what warped sense of loyalty to my mother had persuaded me to behave as though I was already the property of a man I'd never met.

But I was eager to prove to Nelly and Leela that I'd been telling the truth, so that evening I asked my mother if it would be okay to take one of the rings to school. She handed me the silver ring, and warned me not to lose it.

The next day, we were sitting at the back of the class in the science room when I took the ring out and passed it to Leela.

'It's really pretty,' she said, slipping it onto her finger.

'Let me see it,' Nelly demanded, her fat dimpled face screwed up with jealousy.

Leela handed it to her. 'This isn't an engagement ring,' she scoffed. 'I've got loads like this from Pakistan. It's really cheap. You can get them in the markets for a few rupees.'

'Just give it back,' I said, resisting the urge to slap her.

She rolled it across the table towards me. I pushed back my chair and tried to grab it, but it fell onto the floor and through a gap in the floorboards. There was a mad scramble to try and fish it out, but we couldn't reach it. Even the science teacher tried to hook it out with a piece of wire, but eventually gave up.

'You stupid cow, Nelly, look what you've done.'

'Oh shut up, Dilly, just go and get another one from the bubble gum machine. Here's ten pence.'

When my mother found out I'd lost the ring, she was furious. She slapped me, then appealed to my father to dish out a more serious punishment, but he just laughed and said, 'The marriage is obviously jinxed.'

The next day, when Leela and I were sitting on a step in the playground at lunchtime, she asked me if I'd been telling the truth about my engagement. I told her all about Adam and Afeeka and how life at home was unbearable because of all the fighting over my mother's plans.

She looked at me with her heavily made-up eyes. I really envied her, the way she always strutted around in flouncy skirts and heels. Even if I'd managed to lay my hands on any clothes like that, I wouldn't have made it as far as the front door before one parent or the other had thrashed me and sent me back to my room to get changed.

'Your parents are mad,' she said. 'I thought only people in Pakistan did stuff like that. If I were you, I'd tell them to get lost. Your mum and dad are living in the Stone Age.'

'Leela, what's it like having a white mam and a Pakistani dad? Does he push her around?' I asked, trying to imagine what it would be like to have a white mother.

'God, no, it's the other way round. My dad's lovely, but he's a real wimp. If he tries anything, my mam just tells him to bugger off. She's the boss in our house. She drinks beer and eats pork as well, and that really winds him up. But he won't kiss her till she's brushed her teeth. I eat bacon sarnies an' all.'

I was stunned. How could people live such different lives? My father was still killing animals in the back garden so we could eat halal meat, and every Sunday afternoon in my house was spent baking our own bread and cakes, because the ones from the shops contained non-halal animal fat. If my mother had dared to drink beer and eat pork, there would have been murder in Sharnia.

I opened my lunchbox and took out a soggy paratha. Leela took out a bundle of cheese sandwiches wrapped in clingfilm.

'Wanna do swapsies?' she asked. 'I can't remember the last time I had a paratha.'

One bite of the sandwich, and my tastebuds were singing. The bread was soft and the cheese filling was buttery, sweet and smooth; I'd never experienced anything like this before. It was a far cry from the hard homemade bread I was accustomed to, and the dry crumbly salty cheese my father made once a month.

'Oh my God, Leela, where did you get this cheese?' I exclaimed. 'It's delicious.'

She looked at me as though I was mad. 'Morrisons. Why, where do you get yours? It's only Dairylea.'

Having gobbled the paratha down in a matter of seconds, she took a lip-gloss from her bag and applied a generous slick of pink shimmer to her lips.

'Sure you've got enough on?' I asked, looking at the glass bottle with the roller ball in the top, and longing for one of my own.

'This cost thirty pence,' she said, handing it to me. 'Go on, have it – I've got another one.'

'Really?'

'Yeah. If you want, I can get you one from the chemist on Oak Lane. They only have cherry flavour, though.'

'Do you want money for it?' I asked, hoping she'd say no. I didn't have thirty pence.

'Nah, it's okay, my mam got me it.'

'Wow, does your mam let you wear make-up?'

'Yeah, she doesn't mind.'

This was another surprise. I'd always assumed Leela applied her make-up on the way to school, and took it off again on the way home. Lots of girls in my year did that.

'Hey, Dilly, what's going on between you and Bitch-Face?'

I told her about Nelly's mother, and how much she'd upset me.

'Don't worry about her. She's just a stupid Paki,' she said. We both laughed, then Leela said, 'Er, don't take this the wrong way, Dilly – I'm telling you this 'cos you're a mate. Bitch-Face's mum's right: you do smell. You need to wash more often.'

'What?' I shrieked.

'Sorry, Dilly, but it's true. You stink of sweat. You've got B.O.'

'What's that mean, "bloody 'orrible"?' I was so embarrassed by my ignorance, I tried to turn it into a joke, but it wasn't funny.

'Body odour,' she said, totally oblivious to my discomfort. 'It's no big deal. Just get some deodorant.'

'Oh, and I suppose you can get that from the chemist on Oak Lane as well?' I asked angrily.

'Yeah, you can. Want me to get you some?'

'No thanks. My mam can get it for me,' I said, knowing there was no chance of her buying me anything like that. 'How come you know all these things and I don't?' I asked enviously.

'My mam tells me; she talks to me about stuff like that. We go shopping on Saturdays and we always have a really good time. We go to the market, and we have lunch and she lets me buy whatever I want.'

I felt as though I'd been squashed into the ground with a sledgehammer. This was so unfair; Leela had the mother I'd always wanted. Ever since I could remember, I'd longed to go shopping with my mother, and it had never happened. I wasn't allowed to go shopping at all, unless my father took me, and then I'd have to carry all the bags and walk ten yards behind him. Sometimes he'd walk so fast I'd lose him completely, and I'd frantically try to find him again before that scary madwoman Old Anna spotted me on my own, and came at me with her big stick.

And Leela went shopping with her mum every weekend, and just took it for granted.

'Dilly, have you started your periods yet?' she asked as we walked across the playground, dodging small groups of boys playing football.

'Yes,' I replied glumly.

'What do you use?'

'Cloth,' I said, feeling even more depressed. No doubt Leela was about to tell me she used something else, and it was available in cherry flavour from the chemist on Oak Lane.

She stared at me in surprise. 'What? Cloth? Are you serious?'

'Yes, I'm serious. Cloth, Leela – cut-up pieces of old bedsheets,' I said, feeling totally deflated. 'Why, what do you use?'

'Sanitary towels, you fool. Why do you use bits of sheets?'

''Cos that's what my mam gives me.'

'Your mam's a savage. What's her problem, man?'

'Yeah, well, we can't all have perfect mams.'

'Shall I get you some towels?' she asked kindly.

'No,' I replied, trying to fight away tears of embarrassment.

'They're called sanitary towels. Tell your mam to get you some. Look, I've got to go, I've got an appointment at the dentist's. Are you gonna bring a paratha tomorrow?'

'Yeah, if you bring Dairylea.'

As I watched her walking over to the gate in her new black suede boots and short skirt, I realized I envied everything about Leela. In the space of a few minutes, she'd told me more about B.O. and sanitary towels than I'd ever learned at home. She knew all this stuff because her mother had taken the time to educate her. What made the situation more upsetting for me was the fact that there were two women at home, and neither of them could be bothered to talk to me about simple things like feminine hygiene. It wasn't fair. I made a mental note to beg Leela's mother to adopt me the very next time I saw her.

My heart felt heavy as I put the gloss in my bag. I knew I'd never be allowed to use it, but I thought I'd keep it anyway. Then, making sure no one was looking, I raised my arm and sneakily sniffed my armpit. Leela was right, I did smell. It was a horrible acrid stench, and I hadn't even realised until someone else had been brave enough to tell me about it.

That afternoon during cookery, I was suddenly struck by the realization that the boiled mincemeat smell I'd been noticing on and off for months was actually my own B.O. Nelly's mother was a stuck-up old cow, but she'd been telling the truth after all. I spent the rest of the day squirming.

Chapter 30

When I got home that afternoon, I was greeted by the smell of daal and garlic. Mammy and Climax were both upstairs in the boys' bedroom, spying on the neighbours. While I did my chores, I kept thinking about my chat with Leela. She'd been surprisingly upfront, and in a begrudging sort of way I admired her for her honesty. As outspoken as I was, I don't think I'd have been brave enough to tell even a best friend they smelt. I didn't bear Leela any malice. I reserved that for my mother, and I decided it was high time to do a bit of snooping, to see exactly what it was she'd hidden away in that chest of drawers in the back room – the one no one was allowed to look in. I knew she kept her make-up in there – maybe there was also some deodorant I could borrow.

The coast was clear. I sneaked into the back room, pulled open the top drawer, and had a good root around.

Contents: a golden powder compact with a black rose-bud on the lid, from her dead sister in Chowki; a pot of Atrixo hand cream; red Max Factor lipstick; a bottle of Soir de Paris perfume; a pot of Astral hand cream; a squeezy plastic bottle of Oil of Ulay that Monkey had given her for Mother's Day; a Boots N°7 lipstick; some black hair pins; an open pot of Germolene with years of accumulated hair and fluff where the lid should have been; a packet of blood pressure tablets; and three bottles of something called MUM. I didn't know what it was until I read the label. Roll-on deodorant! I couldn't understand why Mammy needed three bottles, when I didn't have any. I helped myself to one, and moved on to the next drawer. It was a real disappointment; all it contained was my father's undergarments. Nothing very interesting and definitely nothing worth taking.

But when I opened the third drawer, I was shocked to find a white plastic carrier bag full of packets of sanitary towels. I felt defeated. I'd been forced to use folded squares of cloth, cut up from old cotton bedsheets, and I'd been suffering from sore, chafed thighs every month. I'd been humiliated in class because the material wasn't absorbent enough to last the day, and sometimes blood would leak through my clothes and onto the chair. I'd borne the pain of rough green paper towels that I'd had to stuff down my knickers to get through the day. I'd been having to wash the blood off the squares by hand, so I could have clean ones ready for the next month. It was unbelievable that while I'd been rubbing clots the colour of chopped liver out of my blood-stained, homemade sanitary towels, my mother had been using Dr White's, and bleeding in comfort.

I took two packets, hid them in my wardrobe, and went to ask my mother for money.

Doc was sitting on his bed, reading *The Gods Themselves*, and Mammy and Climax were both perched on the same chair by the window, monitoring the progress of the building works at Number 49, which – to my father's joy – was being converted into a mosque.

As Mammy turned to look at me, I noticed her eyes were red; it looked like she'd been crying again. I casually wondered what the problem was this time. Then I noticed some packed bags on the floor.

'What's going on?' I asked.

'My son's leaving me in the morning,' Climax sobbed dramatically.

Doc threw down his book in disgust, and stormed out of the room. Mammy called after him, 'I can't believe he wants to leave.'

'I can,' I said coldly. 'And I wish I could go with him.'

'Why are you standing there, like the Angel of Death? Go away and let us cry in peace,' Climax lamented.

Ignoring her, I said, 'Look, Mammy, I need some money.'

'Oh my God! The world's been plunged into darkness. We're drowning in despair, and all this selfish brat can think about is money. Get lost.' She turned back to the window, and started to sob.

After dinner, I was doing the dishes when Doc came into the kitchen. He was looking smart in his grey sweatshirt, drainpipe denims and new Army haircut. He handed me an orange Morphy Richards hairdryer.

'Oh wow, thanks,' I gushed, and wondered if Leela had anything as flashy as a hairdryer. Doc was a lot taller than me, so I had to stand on tiptoe to hug him.

'I've got some money, but I'll give it to you when Mammy's not around,' he whispered. 'I cashed my giro.'

As soon as Doc left the kitchen, my mother grabbed the hairdryer off me. She put it in the cupboard in the back room, told me it was going to be part of my dowry, and said if I touched it again before I was married, she'd smash it.

Doc waited until Mammy went to take a bath before he gave me five pounds. I knew exactly what I was going to do with it: the very next chance I got, I was going to sneak out of school and treat myself at the chemist's on Oak Lane; I was going to buy everything in cherry flavour that I could lay my hands on.

Before leaving for school the next morning, Egg and I said our farewells to Doc and wished him all the best.

When we came home that afternoon, none of the housework had been done. Doc had gone but, unfortunately, he'd left Climax and Mammy behind. Both of them were lying in, of all places, his bed, feeling sorry for themselves as they tried to compete for who was going to be affected the most by Doc's departure. Climax was moaning that the bed was still warm from when Doc had slept in it. When I said that the bed was warm because their fat arses had been lying in it all day, Climax reached for her sandal and threw it at me.

That evening, Climax demanded centre stage as she forced out as many crocodile tears as she could muster, and asked a barrage of questions that nobody could be bothered to answer:

'What has the world come to when children have no respect for their parents?'

'Why am I so plagued with bad luck that my only son has run off and left me here to rot?'

'Isn't it Judgement Day when your children deliberately disobey you?'

'Why did I waste my time carrying him in my womb for nine months?'

'Isn't anyone bothered how painful my stretchmarks still are?'

'Who's going to look after me when I'm old and sick?'

'Will I still be alive tomorrow?'

'If I drop down dead, will anyone care?'

'Will that good-for-nothing son of mine even bother to put flowers on my cold, lonely grave?'

It was going to be a very long night.

Chapter 31

For the Titus Middle School spring show, Mrs Horton announced our class would all dress up as flowers, and dance around on the stage for the entertainment of our families. I instantly knew I wanted to be a sunflower, so, while Nelly, Leela and the rest of the girlie girls debated whether they should be daffodils, tulips, roses or pansies, I raced ahead and looted the stock room.

First, I cut a thick strip of cardboard to fit around my face, then I stapled my hair band inside it to make a more solid base. After that, I set to work, making petals from the vibrant yellow, orange and red tissue paper that I refused to share with anyone else. Once I'd glued all the petals to the card, I placed my sunflower over my head, and used some ribbon to tie it securely under my chin.

A quick check in the mirror confirmed that my creation was every bit as beautiful as I'd hoped.

I lifted the flower off my head, and took it over to the drying racks. It was quite heavy and I could feel the glue where it had soaked through the tissue paper. My fingers felt stiff from all the PVA I'd deliberately rubbed on them. Everyone else was still busy snipping and sticking, so I amused myself by peeling bits of dried glue off my hands, rolling them up until they were black, then shouting, 'Bogey attack!' and flicking them at Nelly the daffodil.

At the end of the lesson, Mrs Horton told us all to leave our flowers in the classroom so they could dry overnight, ready for the show the next day.

I knew very well that my parents wouldn't be coming – Daddy would be at work, and Mammy would find any excuse not to bother. Even if I arranged for her to be carried there on a throne like the Queen of Sheba, she'd still prefer to sit in front of the TV. So I appealed to Mrs Horton to let me take my sunflower home, as I was desperate to impress my family with my creativity, and then, hopefully, lap up their praise. She refused at first, but my persistence soon wore her down and she relented.

When I walked into the kitchen, my mother took one look at my headdress and said, 'Is that what they teach you at school these days? Anyone would think you were on *Take Hart*.'

'Don't you like it?' I asked in surprise. 'I might actually send it in to the Gallery once the show's over.'

Climax laughed and said, 'What is it anyway?'

'It's a sunflower,' I snapped, holding it closer to her face. 'Surely you can see that?'

She made a humphing sound in her throat and said, 'It doesn't look like any sunflower I've ever seen. What a pile of crap – is that the best you could do?'

I scowled. 'Is that what the midwife asked you when Doc was born?'

As Climax reached for an apple from the fruit bowl, I legged it out of the kitchen. Behind me, I heard the apple thud against the wall.

Determined to get some praise from anyone in the family, I poked my head back round the door.

'Where's Daddy?' I asked.

'Who knows, who cares?' my mother responded casually.

I found him in the front garden, chatting over the fence with Estie and Nathaniel.

'Look what I made,' I interrupted.

Estie and her husband both clapped their hands warmly. My father said, 'Where's your common sense, Dilly? The proportions are all wrong.'

After lunch the next day, the air was filled with the excited buzz of children waiting to impress their parents. I knew I would just have to leech off someone else's joy. I watched in silence as Leela's mum and dad walked into the playground, holding hands, followed by other parents who'd actually made the effort to be there for their children.

Nelly's mother looked me up and down, then made a huge show of cuddling her daughter. Nelly threw me a smug look. I could feel my blood boiling, and the urge to smack her face made my fingers twitch automatically.

As the children were ushered into the classroom, everybody rushed to get ready at once. 'Keep the noise down,' Mrs Horton said calmly. 'There's no need to raise the roof with all that racket. If you want to colour your faces, there are some paints on my desk.'

I hurried over and grabbed a black tablet of paint. It was thick and creamy, and smelt like the matt emulsion my mother had often used to paint the kitchen walls. The mirror over the sink was being monopolized by a noisy bunch of poppies, so Leela kindly offered to hold her compact mirror up for me while I blackened my face.

To save time getting ready, I was already wearing my green leotard; I'd put it on under my clothes before leaving for school that morning. I undressed, wrapped my arms in green crêpe paper, and put my headdress on.

Mrs Horton said, 'Come on, everyone, time to go.'

I could feel my leotard sticking into my butt crack, and I tried to pull it out, but was swept up on to the stage with the rest of the class.

Mrs Horton said a few words to the audience about how happy she was to see that so many parents had turned up. There was some clapping, and then Mrs Bond, the overenthusiastic music teacher, started thumping out 'Greensleeves' on the piano. I was scouring the crowd in vain for any sign of a family member, as the children began to skip clockwise around the stage. Distracted, and half-blinded by the drooping petals on my headdress, I turned anticlockwise, and danced straight into Nelly, who pulled an angry face, stamped on my foot and then smirked in the direction of her mother.

I shoved Nelly roughly; she stumbled backwards into Lisa (or Herculisa, as we called her), who happened to be the biggest, butchest girl in the class. Lisa shoved Nelly straight back at me. Desperate to avoid the collision, I stepped to one side and fell off the stage.

I landed with a thud, the music stopped, and there was a gasp from the audience. Someone tittered. I heard footsteps, then Mrs Horton helped me up.

'It's broken,' I cried. 'Nelly broke my bloody flower. She's nothing but hell's tinder now. She's a cunt.'

'Dilly!' Mrs Horton squawked as the audience erupted into embarrassed laughter.

I clambered back up on to the stage, where Nelly was waiting for me, fists clenched, petals bobbing up and down angrily.

'You bitch,' I spat. 'You did that on purpose.' I slapped her face as hard as I could, she slapped me back, then we were rolling on the stage, pulling each other's hair and swearing.

'All right, break it up!' boomed Mr Sandy. I looked up to see the headmaster, red-faced and glaring, towering over us. Behind him stood Mrs Horton, visibly shaken.

'She started it!' I shouted as I got to my feet.

'No I didn't, she did!' Nelly shouted back.

As I was being frogmarched to the head's office, I shouted over my shoulder: 'You and me, Bitch-Face. After school.'

'I'll be there, you smelly fucker,' Nelly fired back. 'You're gonna regret this.'

It wasn't long before we both regretted it. I had a lonely ten minutes, sitting on a chair outside Mr Sandy's office, listening to the muffled sound of 'Greensleeves'. Then the music stopped, and soon afterwards Mr Sandy was marching down the corridor towards me, dragging Nelly behind him like a rag doll.

As he shoved us into his office, I noticed he had black streaks of paint on his light-brown jacket.

He had three canes on his desk, and he reached for the thickest.

'Dilly Shah, you are a disgrace,' he barked. 'Hold out your hand. Now!'

I did as I was told. The cane made a hissing sound as he brought it down swiftly onto my palm. I flinched and tried not to make a sound. The back of my neck prickled with pain and the hair on my arms stood on end as the sting from the cane ran through my body. My hand felt like it had its own heartbeat; I could feel it thumping angrily. I wanted to cry, but would wait until I was alone before I surrendered to the tears. Crying now would mean that Nelly had won.

He hit me three times, then Mr Sandy turned his attention to Nelly.

Through my own pain, I watched with perverse delight as she leapt out of her skin with each lash of the cane. She had no problem with the tears. I'd won!

It wasn't often that my father came to school; when he did that afternoon, he didn't look at all happy. Still in my green leotard, I was marched across the playground and thrown into the car. He drove through the streets like a psycho, the muscle in his jaw twitching angrily. Not once did he attempt to speak to me.

When we got home, he dragged me through the house and into the back garden. Then he picked me up and dropped me feet-first into the water butt, which was nearly full of ice-cold rainwater, and had a film of dead insects floating on the surface. As I came up for air, gasping with shock, he said, 'If I ever have to come to your school again, I'll break your legs.'

Chapter 32

In May 1979, the new mosque at Number 49 opened. It didn't make a lot of difference to me, as it didn't have a children's centre, but it was an entirely different proposition for the men in Gomshall Road – now, no one had an excuse to pray at home. And so, every evening, half an hour before prayer-time, the job-dodgers would come hunting the mosque-dodgers. A gang of Pakistani men, all of them unemployed, would strut down the street, hammering on doors, ringing bells, demanding to know if there were any men inside, and, if so, why they weren't at the mosque.

At the head of this gang, like some modern-day straggly bearded Witchfinder General, was none other than the ghee-bellied Mr Baba, dispensing opinions and threats of hell for the damned. Uneducated, stupid, moronic – the thesaurus just didn't have enough adjectives to do him justice. And yet, by surrounding himself with people who were even more ignorant than he was, he'd somehow managed to assume the role of a sage, the Oracle of Gomshall Road. The man was living proof that 'in the land of the blind, the one-eyed man is king'. Why on earth anyone would take the advice of someone who wore black socks with sandals was beyond me, but Mr Baba wielded real power; when he and a dozen of his friends came knocking on a door, it was a brave man indeed who had the balls to tell them to get lost. In fact, there was only one man in the whole street who ever stood up to the mosque posse – and that was Monkey.

But Mr Baba was a persistent man, and wouldn't take no for an answer. One evening, things finally came to a head, when Mr Baba and his merry men rang the bell as usual. Egg and I peeked through the front window, saw who it was, and ignored them. The ringing went on and on, and eventually Monkey came downstairs, flung the door open, and said, 'You again? What do you want this time? I've already told you a thousand times, I'm not interested.'

To which, Mr Baba replied, in time-honoured tradition: 'Why aren't you at mosque?'

Back came Monkey's usual reply: 'It's got nothing to do with you. I'll go when I want, not when you tell me to.'

'You should be ashamed, talking like that,' Mr Baba snapped. 'Everyone else goes to mosque.'

'Oh yeah? Funny how you never bother the whites, isn't it? Go and ring their bells.'

'You shouldn't be telling me what to do, boy,' Mr Baba said. 'Learn some manners.'

'Fuck your manners. Get yourself a good dentist – you're gonna need one if you ring that bell again. Got it, shithead?'

With that, Monkey slammed the door in Mr Baba's face, muttered 'twat' under his breath, and disappeared upstairs. As the sound of Fleetwood Mac boomed from his room, the doorbell started to ring again. I took a look out of the window, and felt my jaw drop. There was Mr Baba on the front step – thumb on the bell, with his beard trapped in the door. A few of his gang had grown bored and wandered off, but a hard core were standing around him, pointing, cracking jokes and sniggering. Mr Baba was tugging desperately on his beard, but couldn't free it.

Above the cacophony, I heard footsteps thundering down the stairs.

'Right, that bastard's dead this time,' Monkey said. As he opened the door, the suddenly released Mr Baba stumbled backwards down the steps and into the crowd of onlookers; without a word, he turned and walked hurriedly back down the path.

Shortly after, my father came home. He was furious, and said Monkey would have to go and apologize to Mr Baba. When Monkey refused, Mr Baba called a crisis meeting at the mosque, and it was agreed that the Shahs were to be banned. Not only that, but Daddy was to be kicked out of the cricket team. As Mr Baba put it, 'if a man can't even control his own children, he can't possibly have what it takes to play for the York Shah Terriers.'

Daddy wasn't so bothered about having to drive to the mosque in Oakwood Road; after all, he'd done it for years before the new mosque opened. What really annoyed him was having to watch Mr Baba and his team on their way to play cricket in the park.

One Sunday evening, the cricketers were returning home while I was helping Daddy to creosote the fence in the front garden. As Mr Baba strolled by, in his white jumper and trousers, bat tucked under his arm, Daddy flicked the brush, and creosote splattered on to Mr Baba's clothes.

'I bet you lost again, didn't you?' my father asked scathingly.

'At least I'm playing, Shah,' huffed Mr Baba. 'Not only am I the opening batsman, but I've been voted the new captain. And as we don't have any Shahs in the team, we've got a new name as well.'

'What's that, then?' asked my father. 'Back-Stabbing Bastards XI?'

'No,' preened Mr Baba. 'We're called the York Baba Terriers.' He waved his cap at Daddy. 'Here, look.'

I had a special interest in this – I'd spent hours embroidering 'York Shah Terriers' on to all the caps for the team. The gold 'Shah' had been crossed through with what looked like black marker pen, and above it, in childish scrawl, was the word 'Baba'.

Daddy roared with laughter. 'Baba, you're a buffoon. When you have your next English class, ask your teacher what a pun is.'

'Yes, I will, Shah. And when you have your next cricket lesson, be sure to ask them what a captain is.' With that, Mr Baba strutted off home.

The next evening, a sheepish Mr Baba appeared at our front door on his own. He said he wanted bygones to be bygones; my father was a great man indeed, and he hoped they could be friends again. After all, it would be madness if they let such a strong friendship be ruined by a petty squabble. Oh, and by the way, could my father possibly help him fill in a form he'd got from the dole office?

Chapter 33

Monkey came into the kitchen with a big grin on his face. 'Are you guys ready? It's "Hop Home, Mister" time. And the going is good to firm.'

We all made our way out into the back alley. It was no longer raining, but there were deliciously huge puddles everywhere. There was already a gaggle of kids waiting for us. I did a quick headcount – fourteen – and nodded in Monkey's direction. 'We're ready. And this time, we're gonna win.'

'Dream on, lass,' Monkey said as he pulled a little blue notebook out of his parka pocket. He systematically worked his way through the crowd, collecting twenty pence from each child in turn, dropping the money into a freezer bag and adding their names to his list.

Scully appeared and said, 'Okay, kids, prayers have started. Let's go.'

We all hurried through the house; I was last one out, and made sure the front door was on the latch. We hid behind the fence in the front garden; from there it was easy to see the mosque across the road at Number 49.

'Daisy, you first,' Monkey said, shoving her into the street. 'And make sure you don't get caught.'

Everyone watched Daisy as she headed for the mosque. She disappeared inside, and seconds later emerged with a shoe in her hand. As she made her way back to Sharnia, Poppy set off. When their paths crossed, they both giggled excitedly. Soon, Poppy was heading back, and Sofia set off, and so it continued until every child except me had a left shoe in their possession.

Scully nudged me and said, 'Hurry up, Dilly, get a move on.' Pulling the purple shawl from my head so it wouldn't slow me down, I clutched it in my hand and ran across to the mosque. Tiptoeing up to the doorway, I could feel my heart pounding with anticipation as I heard the gentle murmur of men at prayer coming from inside. Just by the door, there was a large pile of shoes; there was everything from flashy Nike trainers to tatty plastic flip-flops.

I rummaged through the pile and grabbed an open-toed leather sandal. It looked just like the sort that Mr Baba had been wearing earlier that day. I was so excited at the prospect of what was about to happen next that I had to crush the urge to laugh out loud. I couldn't wait to see all the stolen shoes flying through the air onto the railway embankment, or to watch the furious men hopping home. Maybe this time we'd hit the jackpot – if any of the kids had managed to get Mr Baba's shoe, we'd collect our winnings of forty pence from Monkey, but the real reward would be hiding behind a hedge, watching Mr Baba hopping, wobbling, panting and desperately struggling to stay upright as he tried to avoid the puddles on his way home.

Emerging from the doorway, I saw the others urging me to hurry. I was halfway across the road when there was a blood-curdling bellow behind me. I turned to see Mr Baba and my father charging out of the mosque,

followed closely by a horde of barefooted men, all shouting and shrieking with fury. Throwing down my shawl,
I ran for my life. As I sprinted into the front garden, the
other kids scattered in all directions, like a herd of gazelle
with a lion in their midst, peeling off into the safety of
any garden with a hedge big enough to hide in.

I flew up the steps. The front door opened and, to my
horror, Mammy and Climax were barring the way.

'Move!' I cried. 'Daddy's coming.'

'No shit,' Climax said. 'And about bloody time.' She
slammed the door in my face and I heard the latch click.

'Oh crap, I thought. 'Now what?'

I didn't have to wait long to find out. Egg and the twins
were kicked into the garden by my father, while up and
down the street I could hear the same sounds – angry
men shouting, and children yelping. One by one, the shoe-
stealers were dragged unceremoniously into the front
garden of Sharnia, or deposited on the pavement outside.

An awkward silence descended. Children fidgeted
uncomfortably, Climax and Mammy watched intently
from the window, and men stared at my father, waiting
for him to take control of the situation. Standing there
with my hair a tangled mess, I sneaked a quick look at
him; he was holding my dripping-wet shawl in one hand,
and a black Reebok trainer in the other.

When he eventually broke the silence, his voice was
a low rumble. 'Monkey, you bastard. Have you got no
shame, running a book like a professional gambler?' He
threw the Reebok at Monkey's head. It landed with a
thwack and bounced off into the bushes. 'I want to see
that book of yours later. But first, I have to deal with this
bitch.'

Taking a deep breath, I tried to swallow myself up into my clothes. I felt strangely naked without the purple material. As he came for me, green eyes flashing fire, I realized that, for the first time in my life, I was outside the house wishing I was on the other side of the door.

Chapter 34

I was in the front room reading the *Oxford English Dictionary* when there was a loud banging on the front door. I looked out of the window to see a mountain of a man, dressed in a black pinstripe suit and sunglasses. He was about to thump on the door again when my father opened it, and asked him what he wanted.

'I'm here to see Mr Monkey Shah. Is he home?'

'Why? Who are you?'

'Let's just say he and I have some unfinished business to attend to,' said Mr Pinstripe.

'Business?' my father asked. 'What sort of business?'

'Is he in or not?' the man demanded impatiently.

My father bristled. 'Now just a minute. Who the hell do you think you are, turning up on my doorstep and throwing your weight around?'

'My beef isn't with you, it's with Monkey. My boss, Mr Cherry, has sent me round because Monkey's missed a payment on the money he owes.'

My father looked flabbergasted. 'How much money are you talking about?'

'Enough to make Mr Cherry very unhappy. So I'm sure you'll agree it's in all our interests to make sure Monkey coughs up pronto.'

'Stop talking in riddles. How much does Monkey owe?'

The man took a pen and paper from his pocket, scribbled something, and handed it to my father, who said very calmly: 'I'll need a few hours, can you come back this evening?'

'I'll be here at seven o'clock.'

As the man turned on his heel, my father closed the front door.

'Has he gone yet?' Monkey called from the top of the stairs.

There was an almighty roar: 'You son of a bitch, what the hell have you been up to?'

As Daddy went racing upstairs, Monkey turned tail and fled into his bedroom, locking the door behind him.

For the next few minutes, there was a stand-off, as my father banged on the door with huge whumps, Monkey refused to come out, Mammy and Climax hovered uselessly nearby and all the children looked on.

Just when it seemed as though my father was going to knock the door off its hinges, Monkey relented and let him in. Daddy went charging into the room, with all of us piling in behind him. He caught hold of Monkey and started to slap him around the head.

'Get the fuck off me,' Monkey yelped, as he tried his best to ward off the blows.

He pushed Daddy away, and ran downstairs, everyone close behind, with my mother shouting, 'Keep the noise down – the neighbours will hear,' and my father shouting back, 'All of your bastard children are nothing but trouble. Have you any idea what he's done?'

The fight continued in the back room.

'You lay another finger on me and I'm going to the cops,' Monkey shrieked.

A knuckle-filled fist smashed against his face and silenced him.

'Who the fuck do you think you are, messing with that gangster Cherry?' my father yelled. 'Pack your things and get out of here!'

Having ordered Monkey out, he then prevented him from leaving, as he continued to rain blows down on him.

'Mammy, stop them!' I shouted.

'What can I do?' she said. 'What if one of them hits me?'

Kicking and squirming, Monkey managed to wriggle free, and sprinted for his life. From the relative safety of the street, he shouted, 'You're gonna get it this time. I'm calling the cops.'

'Fuck you, you stupid bastard,' Daddy shouted back. 'Put one foot inside my house and I'll kill you. If Cherry doesn't get you first.'

My father was in a foul mood for the rest of the day. He divided his time between verbal outbursts, simmering silence and random bad-tempered threats aimed at anyone who strayed too close. My mother was on top form with her acting; she was far too distressed to cook or eat, so she just stayed in bed and tried to die.

When Mr Pinstripe returned that evening, it wasn't cash that Daddy paid him off with; it was the gold bangles he'd given Mammy as an anniversary gift.

Funnily enough, my father (who'd been driven to the edge of insanity by his useless children) and my mother (who was just one heart attack away from a life-support machine) still managed to heartily scoff down the dinner that Climax made, then they settled themselves down in front of the TV and watched the whole of *The Good, the Bad and the Ugly* without having to make a single 999 call.

Chapter 35

The next day, I was sitting in the upstairs window, spying on the street below for any sign of Monkey, when another familiar figure appeared and came strolling serenely up the garden path.

'Shit,' I thought, hoping my eyes had deceived me. But no, it really was Molvi Sahib down there. Mammy, who was supposed to be dead, was in the back garden weeding. The bell rang several times. Daddy called from the front: 'Dilly, make a cup of tea – the molvi's here.'

He spent half an hour in the front room with his guest, then, once the molvi had gone, Daddy came into the kitchen and asked Mammy how she was feeling.

'What?' she asked scathingly. 'You've got a nerve. You've thrown my son out and you're asking me how I feel? How the hell do you expect me to feel?' She wiped her nose with the corner of her apron, and glared angrily at my father.

'Give it a rest, woman. At least you're alive.'

'What?'

'Well, Molvi Sahib came to pay his respects; he was under the impression you were dead.' He chuckled. 'Anything you'd like to say, Dilly?'

Realizing there was no way I could dig myself out of trouble, I decided to tell the truth. 'Well, I couldn't help it – he was hitting me really hard,' I said. 'I had to think of something to make him stop, and that was the first thing that came into my head. I'm sorry, Mammy, I didn't mean to say you were dead.'

'What else can I expect from you?' my mother sighed balefully. 'You're just waiting for me to drop dead. And the way things are going around here, you won't have to wait much longer; you'll get your wish soon enough.'

I was baffled at how I'd managed to escape a beating from my parents for telling lies in mosque. But there was still the prospect of having to face Molvi Sahib that evening, and I knew he wouldn't be as forgiving. But I needn't have worried, because Mammy announced that, as I was now having periods, I was too old to go to mosque any more.

I was bitterly disappointed. Since the Ban, the mosque was the only place outside of school where I got to hang out with my friends; it was like a youth club, with added R.E. Mosque was a temporary escape from Sharnia, one of the few things in life I looked forward to with great excitement. It was a chance to belong to a big happy community, to receive the sort of attention and encouragement that was so lacking at home, and to share the food that other children's mothers would prepare for our regular Friday feasts.

I pleaded with my mother to change her mind, but she refused. After I pointed out that the molvis wouldn't object to me going, as long as I took a week off every month like the other girls who'd started their periods, she let slip the real reason for keeping me at home: it had nothing to do with piety; it was just that she needed more help with the housework, because she was busy planning a wedding and trying to think of ways to lure her son back home.

But, as the days passed, it looked more and more like Monkey wasn't coming back. The rumour on the street was that he'd gone to work for Mr Cherry and his mob in Lumb Lane. It was hard to get much information about what was going on, because no one had the nerve to go and hammer on a gangster's front door. When Mammy suggested that Daddy should go, as it was all his fault, he told her that Monkey wasn't welcome under his roof any more, and he'd be happy if he never saw him again.

When Mammy asked Climax to go round, she just laughed and said, 'What planet are you living on, Gongal? Have you seen Cherry's Dobermanns? The sodding things have got balls the size of Creme Eggs.'

All the neighbours were talking about Monkey, and my mother was sick of her friends popping round to get the latest news. She said they were making toast while her house burnt, and were laughing behind her back. It was ironic, really, considering how much time she'd spent bragging about what an expert she was at running her son's life.

With all the gossip flying around, Mammy was worried that her brother Samir would get wind of what was going on and call off the wedding. So she sat down and wrote a letter to Samir's wife, Nonna, explaining that Monkey had got into trouble with his father and had left home after an argument, but everything was under control. My mother's writing wasn't very good, but her persistence was world-class. It took her hours, but finally she was satisfied with her efforts.

I kept my fingers crossed that Nonna would realize what a bunch of losers the Shahs were, and bring both engagements to an end.

Two weeks later – disaster. A reply arrived from Nonna, saying boys will be boys. I guess she was as desperate to marry her kids off as Mammy was. Nonna said she was far too busy on the farm to spend hours writing letters, and wasn't it time we got a phone? She expressed surprise that we didn't have one already, because every cat and dog in Pakistan had one.

Nonna said she'd accepted Monkey as her son-in-law, and that no matter what happened her daughter would be travelling to England as soon as she got her visa. Afeeka had been promised an English husband, and Nonna sincerely hoped that Mammy wasn't about to go back on her word.

It was beginning to look as though the most important thing that Monkey possessed wasn't his good looks or his fine physique, but his ability to make his fiancée a British national.

Chapter 36

By the end of the summer holidays in 1979, the plans for Monkey's wedding were devouring all our lives. My mother was like a runaway train; we'd been forced aboard, and there'd be no stopping her until the wedding had taken place. She certainly wasn't going to let Monkey's absence derail her plans; she just carried on making arrangements without him.

There were plenty of people telling her to be patient. If she prayed to God, they said, her son would return home. The new owner of Number 44, a nice middle-aged woman called Naveeda, gave my mother some advice: 'Write his name on pieces of paper and hang them on your pear tree. When the wind blows the paper away, it will bring Monkey home. But don't tell anyone what you're doing, or it won't work.'

Soon afterwards, the tree in the back garden wore little decorations: Monkey's name, written in Urdu on tiny pieces of white paper, rolled up and tied with black string. And before the wind got a chance to blow them off, I sneaked out, took them down and gave them to Poppy, telling her they were fairy food. This went on for a few days, until Poppy showed my mother what she'd been feeding the fairies with; I was called a 'black witch' and there were no more notes after that.

Meanwhile, Daddy finally gave in to my mother's persistent demands, and had a phone installed. In theory, this meant Mammy could now call Nonna whenever she wanted; in practice, using carrier pigeons would have been easier. Virtually every call to Pakistan was answered by a very polite operator saying, 'Sorree, all the lines are bizzee right now; please try lay turrr.' Whenever there was no one else around, Egg and I would call Nonna's number so we could have a laugh at the operator's accent.

What I found difficult to understand was how accepting of the wedding Daddy had become. I watched him with bemusement and scorn as he showed just how spineless he was. For a man who'd made such a song and dance about how unacceptable the situation was, and how he'd never allow his son to marry Afeeka, he'd caved in remarkably easily, and started to go along with his wife's demands.

I resented Daddy for being such a coward, and grew increasingly concerned that, once Monkey had been led to the altar, my turn would be next, and my father would stand by and watch me suffer the same fate. But my mother still had moments of doubt; if she hadn't heard from Pakistan for a few days, she'd start worrying about Afeeka's parents changing their minds, and then she'd pester them for reassurances until they put her mind at rest. The more my mother and Nonna talked about Monkey and Afeeka, the more they sounded like two farmers discussing their livestock.

The biggest fly in the ointment was Monkey himself, who was happily oblivious to the stress his absence was causing at home; he hadn't even come back for his things, even though he was living only a couple of miles away.

*   *   *

Once the new school term started, my mother was on her own during the day; she had no one to share her thoughts with. While my father was at work, Climax would take herself off to Dewsbury to be with her friend Amina, so, as soon as Egg and I came in from school, we'd be subjected to a day's worth of pent-up anxieties, all at once, with no escape.

One afternoon, I hadn't even got through the back door when she started to rant at me.

'I wish that bastard brother of yours would swallow his pride and come home. He's got no idea what I'm going through; my God, your father's family are going to have a field day if this goes wrong. I can't bear it. All the stress is going to put me in an early grave.'

'Why do you care so much about what other people think, Mammy?' I asked, as I sat down to eat Weetabix and jam. 'You should be worrying about what happens if Afeeka turns up and she's got no one to marry.'

'Monkey has no choice,' she spat angrily. 'And neither do you.'

Chapter 37

One cold autumn afternoon, Egg and I got in from school to find my mother in very high spirits – no illnesses, no tears, and no loud sighing. For once, she wasn't sitting in front of the TV waiting for *Playschool*; she was actually humming a tune to herself as she prepared the evening meal. The kitchen was lovely and warm and the smell of onions frying in a pan filled the air. Whenever Mammy was in a good mood, I felt suspicious: what had happened to put a smile on her face? She was even wearing make-up. There was a hint of lipstick on her mouth, she had kajal in her eyes, and her shiny brown hair was combed and tied in a lumpy plait that hung down her back like a dead mouse.

She smiled at us and asked us how our day had been. I hid my surprise and tried to figure out what on earth she was up to.

We were soon to find out. As we sat down to eat dinner that evening, she told my father that Monkey was coming home. I was horrified. How had she managed to talk him into it? And if Monkey was so easy to manipulate, then what chance did I have?

'My son's coming back, my son's coming back,' she crowed.

'I heard what you said, dammit,' my father snapped. 'How do you know?'

'He came to see me,' she said as she scooped some daal in her mouth, and chewed noisily. 'He dropped in this morning,' she added between gobbling snorts.

'I thought I told you I don't want that bastard to darken my doorstep again.'

'Well, that's just stupid. Here, have some salad,' she said.

'Why don't you shove the salad?'

She ignored him, and carried on eating. She'd managed to spoil his meal, but appeared to be enjoying her own.

'You know what your problem is?' my father asked. 'You don't see the bigger picture. He's a loser. If he can't get a decent job, how's he supposed to support a wife? I'm not going to give him any money.'

'Oh be quiet. You should be rejoicing that your only son's coming home.'

'Just make sure you keep him out of my way, or I'll belt both of you.'

'Daddy?' Poppy interrupted, looking quite angelic in her blue polyester dress.

'What is it?' he asked grumpily.

'Are you the Ripper?'

'What the hell makes you think that?' he spluttered.

Poppy shrugged her shoulders: 'Someone on *Look North* said the Ripper's a madman and he hurts people. So I thought it might be you.'

'Gongal,' my father spat, 'keep this little bugger away from the television.'

The next evening, Monkey came home with his tail between his legs. He looked embarrassed and uncomfortable as he slinked sheepishly in through the front door.

I thought he should have come through the back door, because he was such a woman.

Daddy took one look at him, ground his teeth, flared his nostrils, and stormed out of the house without a word.

I was livid with Monkey for being so pathetic. I didn't care if he got married or not, but by coming home he'd given the kiss of life to my engagement as well as his own.

Over the next few months, Daddy took every opportunity to ignore Monkey. Mammy, on the other hand, treated her son like royalty. She would follow him from room to room, fawning creepily.

'How many sugars do you want in your coffee?'

'When should the girls make your dinner?'

'How much curry powder would you like in your baked beans?'

'Can I give you some money for your bus fare into town?'

'Did the girls clean your room well enough?'

'Shall I get you anything from the Littlewoods catalogue?'

When Monkey was around, he was Mammy's golden boy. She'd sing his praises ('You're such a good son'; 'I'm so proud of you'; 'You've proved to your father that you're a man by standing up to him') or tell him what was waiting for him ('I'm going to give you a wedding that people will talk about for years'; 'Afeeka will make you the happiest man in Bradford').

But when he was out at the Job Centre, it was a different story ('Typical man – he's useless without his mother to look after him'; 'Couldn't hack it in the real world'; 'The bastard had better get a job soon').

I hated my mother for her hypocrisy; I hated my father for giving in and letting Monkey come home; and now I hated Monkey for being such a pushover. He'd sold his soul to the Devil for a quiet life. He'd learned to swim with the tide, and I'm sure he was looking forward to having a lot of fun doing the breaststroke with Afeeka.

Chapter 38

On Friday, 21 March 1980, I celebrated my thirteenth birthday. I got two presents: a pair of green slippers from my mother, and a five-pound note through the post from Doc. Egg gave me a card that read: 'Happy Birthday Granddad'; she'd crossed out 'Granddad' and written 'Dilly'.

Estie came over with a huge homemade chocolate sponge cake, which was haemorrhaging strawberry jam and thick whipped cream. She gave me a warm bear hug, plastered my cheeks with sloppy wet kisses, and called me her little devil. Then she polished off a bottle of Lucozade and three parathas, struggled to her feet, and said it was time for her to go home.

After she'd gone, Egg asked me if she could have Hamble, because I was a teenager now, and teenagers shouldn't play with dolls. I told her to get stuffed.

As I went upstairs, it dawned on me that Egg had a point. Mammy had forced me to give all my other dolls to my sisters, but somehow Hamble had always managed to slip through the net. I knew our luck would run out soon.

But I was damned if I was going to give her to Egg; I couldn't bear the thought of anyone else enjoying her. Sitting on my bed, I cradled Hamble, and thought about all the years she'd been in my life. She was old and tatty;

one of her eyes had stopped opening, she had a bald patch where her hair had been combed away, and she'd lost one of the fingers off her left hand. But she was still the best doll ever. We'd shared so many good times together.

The following Monday, I made a big fuss about taking the bins out for my mother. I got Hamble out from under the mattress where she'd been hiding, put her in a carrier bag, took her down to the bottom of the garden, and tossed her into the bin. As the bag landed on top of the pile of rubbish, I could see Hamble's little black foot sticking out, just as it had all those years ago at the jumble sale. My heart sank. I picked her up and kissed her forehead. It was hard to say goodbye, but I knew I'd rather destroy her than let Egg have her. I placed her gently back on her deathbed, and waited.

As I heard the sound of the lorry in the back alley growing louder, the lump in my throat got bigger.

The back gate flew open, and one of the bin men came in.

'Hello, love, you waiting for me?' he asked cheerily as he lifted the bin high onto his shoulder.

'Yeah, my mam wants me to make sure all the rubbish goes,' I said.

I followed him into the alley, and watched as he emptied the bin into the back of the lorry. I knew I'd made a mistake – I wanted Hamble back – but it was too late. She was gone with the press of a button and the whirring of some strange machinery.

'There you go, love, it's done,' said the executioner. He put the bin down by the gate and went to get next door's rubbish.

He was right: it was done. I hadn't wanted to grow up, but it had happened anyway. For me to make the transition from child to teenager, it was poor Hamble who'd been made to pay the ultimate price. I'd never play with her again, but at least I'd made sure nobody else would either.

After school, I asked my father if it would be okay for me to visit Estie. I was still feeling depressed about Hamble's death, and needed a cuddle. He chaperoned me across the road, said, 'When you're done, give me a call and I'll come and get you.' With that, he headed back to Sharnia, leaving me to wonder what exactly he thought I might get up to if I was allowed to walk the fifty yards on my own.

Nathaniel opened the front door, said Estie wasn't feeling well and told me not to give her any Lucozade. He ushered me through to the back room, and then left.

As usual, the house was immaculate and smelt of vanilla and cinnamon but, rather than bustling around as expected, Estie was slumped in her rocking chair, grey and drained. Her eyes were puffed up and she was shivering. She didn't look up as I went in.

'Estie, it's me, Dilly,' I whispered.

'Ah, you little devil, stand where I can see you,' she said.

'What's wrong with you?' I asked. I didn't tell her I was standing in front of her.

'I don't know,' she sighed.

We chatted for a while, but it was painful for me. I wasn't expecting to see Estie like this. Days earlier, she'd been in Sharnia, singing 'Happy Birthday' in a booming voice. But now she didn't even have the energy to sit up. It wasn't fair; I'd only gone there seeking comfort for my own woes, but Estie was too ill to pay me any attention.

Two days later, Mammy and I went over to Estie's house to see if she was feeling any better. She was lying in bed. I climbed up beside her and gave her a cuddle. She offered me some Melba toast; normally, I would have scoffed the whole packet, but I was too upset to eat.

Mammy told Estie the wedding plans were going well, and Estie said she really wanted to meet Afeeka.

'Hurry up and get better, then. And when she comes, we'll celebrate.'

Estie shook her head slowly and said, 'I'm not going to get better, Gongal. I see angels waiting for me.'

My heart felt like it had been snapped in two like a pencil. Taking my hand, Estie said, 'You, my little devil, you were my favourite. Always my favourite.'

When we went home, Daddy asked how things were. Mammy said she had smelled death. I wanted to punch her.

The next evening, the phone rang. Daddy answered, and then ran out of the house without speaking. He didn't even bother to put the phone back in its cradle. I stared wide-eyed at my mother; she stumbled to a chair and sat down.

Daisy came running into the house. 'Mammy, there's a crowd outside Number forty-three.'

Mammy put her hands over her face and started crying.

My heart seemed to somersault as I headed for the door. Sure enough, the street was full of people. I ran, not caring about the consequences of defying the Ban. When I got to Number 43, the front door was open. Someone was crying. I rang the bell. Nathaniel came out, mopping his eyes with a handkerchief.

'Come in,' he said. 'Estie's dead.'

He stepped to one side as I ran upstairs. Daddy stood at the top, blocking the way.

'Look, love, you might not want to go inside.'

'Please, Daddy, let me.'

Estie lay in the bed, eyes closed. She looked like she was sleeping. I touched her face; it felt warm.

'You're all wrong,' I said happily. 'She's warm – she's not dead.'

I got onto the bed, put my arms around Estie and nuzzled her neck.

'She's dead,' Daddy said firmly. 'Come on, Dilly, time to go.'

Chapter 39

As it was my final year at Titus Middle, it was time to choose an upper school for the following September. All my friends at Titus wanted to go to Oxley High, because it was the only all-girl school in the area that would take Muslims. So naturally I hoped to go there too, and told my father I wanted it to be my first choice. He said it was my only choice: going to a mixed school wasn't an option, so if I didn't get in to Oxley High I'd be off to school in Jallu come September.

In April 1980, the news I'd been praying for finally came: I'd been offered a place at Oxley High, so I wouldn't have to worry about going to Jallu. The same day, we got a call from Nonna. Afeeka had been granted a visa. She would be coming to England as soon as everything was arranged.

My good news barely caused a ripple, but Nonna's news changed the mood in the house dramatically. Mammy became unbearably excited, like a child on the eve of Eid; she went round kissing and hugging everyone, and the more she rejoiced, the more discomfort she created. Daddy, Climax, Monkey and I all had different reasons for dreading Afeeka's arrival, but I realized we'd all been pretending that it would never happen. The granting of the visa shattered the illusion, and forced us all to accept that Mammy had won the battle.

For Daddy, it meant his only son would soon be marrying a pauper from the wrong side of the family; having made that mistake himself, he didn't want his son to suffer the same fate, but it was too late to do anything about it.

Climax was even more put out than Daddy – she was livid at the prospect of her territory being invaded by a younger, more attractive, competitor.

But, whereas the adults were aggressive with their feelings, Monkey and I knew that expressing our concerns would be a waste of time. There was no one within the four walls of Sharnia we could talk to without being ridiculed, so we both let our personal miseries consume us quietly; unable to express our fear of the future, we became sullen and withdrawn.

Mammy decided it was time to give the house a makeover. The solid oak furniture Daddy had lovingly collected over the years – armchairs, bookcases, a writing bureau, coffee tables, beds and coat stands – it all had to go. When my father refused to get rid of it, my mother waited until he was out of the house and then got Egg, me and the twins to drag it into the back garden, where she smashed it up with the sledgehammer, and set fire to it. Climax wrapped twenty potatoes in foil and roasted them in the bonfire. When the wood had turned to ash, we feasted on hot potatoes with melted butter and ground black pepper.

New furniture was purchased to replace the old. It was expensive in price but cheap and nasty to look at; the sofabeds for the front room were so flimsy that we were told not to open them in case they broke. The back of the new pine bookshelf came unglued the minute I stacked it with books. And the mirror on my mother's new dressing table fell on Egg's head.

Next, all the carpets were ripped up; the ones my mother liked were washed and hung on the wall to dry; the twins dumped the others on the railway embankment.

While my mother was preparing for Afeeka's arrival, Nonna was preparing for her departure. She organized a big party and invited all my father's relatives from Jallu, so she could remind them that it was her daughter who would soon be off to England.

When my father's family realized how easy it was for someone to get a visa if they were engaged to a Brit, letters started to arrive from uncles, aunts, cousins, even relatives we'd never heard of. They all wanted the same thing – to marry their son or daughter to any of the Shahs who might still be single. My father's cousin Yaga wanted me to marry her son, who was called Conk on account of his enormous nose (he'd had it rearranged by the irate brother of a village girl he'd been stalking). Yaga accepted that he wasn't the best-looking bloke in Jallu but she insisted he'd still be a better match than that useless Adam.

Many polite enquiries were made about Egg and Poppy. Even diseased Daisy had admirers. But, if none of my sisters were available, maybe we knew some other nice British girl who might be interested in a wonderful Pakistani man?

My mother was in such a good mood that, when my school had a jumble sale, she allowed me to go. Daddy brought the car round to the back of the house, and Egg, Daisy, Poppy and I all happily piled in.

When we got there, Daddy gave us some money and sent us off to have fun. We didn't see him again for hours; perhaps he'd gone off to have some fun of his own.

To say thank you for allowing me out of the house, I bought my mother two presents: a bracelet, and a silver ring set with a huge sparkly stone. I also bought myself a set of twelve little coloured bottles of perfume that were lying in a leather box on a bed of straw. Each bottle had a minaret-shaped top, which, when unscrewed, released a mystical Arabian aroma, that hung in the air like a million stars in a velvet-blue sky. I convinced myself that the previous owner must have been a fairy-tale princess.

When we got home that evening, my joy turned to bitterness when Mammy took the perfumes off me, and put them alongside the hairdryer in my dowry cupboard.

Chapter 40

22 October 1980 was Loss of Independence Day. Daddy and a very pale and quiet Monkey had gone the night before to collect Afeeka from Heathrow. I saw the torment on my brother's face, and thought, Serves you right, loser.

It was the half-term break and the house was already clean and tidy, but my mother still insisted on getting Egg and me out of bed early, so we could help her wipe up any lingering particles of dust.

For once, Mammy made an effort to look present-able; her house coat and bed slippers were replaced by a dazzling new blue salvaar kameez and toe-post sandals. On went the red Max Factor lipstick, black kajal and a generous squirt of Soir de Paris eau de toilette. Not to be outdone, Climax poured herself into the tightest dress I'd ever seen, a golden brushed-nylon number with a plung-ing neckline and big bell sleeves. It accentuated her back breasts as much as her front breasts, and made her stom-ach jut out like a six-month pregnancy.

While Climax and Mammy were in the kitchen, prepar-ing a banquet and singing along with the radio, Egg and Poppy were sitting in front of the mirror, slapping on make-up in an effort to outdo each other.

For a twelve-year-old, Egg was quite adept with a blusher brush, but ten-year-old Poppy still had a lot to learn. She rubbed large circles of blusher on to her cheeks; every so often she would pause, smile at herself and then carry on with the rouging process. When she was happy with the results, she moved on to the blue eyeshadow, which she slapped on enthusiastically.

When Daisy came in, she took one look and said, 'Hello, Coco the Clown, what the fuck have you done to your face? You look like a whore.'

Poppy burst into tears. The more she cried, the more her make-up smudged, and the more Daisy howled with laughter. Poppy ran into the bathroom, slammed the door and had a major tantrum, stamping her feet as hard as she could.

Mammy, who was in the kitchen directly beneath, shouted up the stairs, 'What the hell's going on up there? I don't need this today; for one day, please just give me some peace and quiet.'

I was sent to peg out the washing. There was a howling gale, and leaves were flying into the garden that my mother had obsessively swept the day before. Bent against the wind, I was fighting to get the washing on the line when I heard a car coming down the alley.

A slender hand pushed open the gate, and there stood Afeeka. My mouth fell open in shock – she was tiny! Mammy had described Afeeka to all of us in great detail, but somehow she'd forgotten to mention that Monkey's fiancée wouldn't have looked out of place somewhere on the Yellow Brick Road. My six-foot-three brother was about to marry a Munchkin!

My mind was racing. On automatic pilot, I went to greet her. She was dressed in a thin pink cotton salvaar kameez and flimsy strappy sandals; very fetching, but totally inappropriate for Bradford in October.

As she stepped into the garden, she stumbled. I grabbed hold of her arm to steady her. 'Oops!' she said, and giggled childishly.

Mammy bounded into the garden like an excited puppy, flung her arms around Afeeka in a wild embrace and plastered her cheeks with zealous kisses. Arm in arm, they disappeared into the house, while Daddy called me into the alley to help carry the suitcases.

When I went into the kitchen, I could hear laughter and excited conversation coming from the back room. It looked as though everyone was in there, chatting and having fun. I felt too awkward and embarrassed to just open the door and walk in; even though the room was full of my closest relatives, at that moment they may as well have been strangers. So I stayed where I was, wondering what to do with myself. After a few minutes, Mammy came to find me, asked me what the hell I thought I was playing at, and ordered me into the back room.

Afeeka was sitting in my father's bed, with his duvet wrapped around her. I tried not to let my surprise show; his bed was out of bounds to everyone except him, and now there was this newcomer sitting in it, looking quite at home.

The room fell silent.

'This is Dilly,' my mother said, as she pushed me forward.

Afeeka shot me a dazzlingly white smile – it was huge, she had so many teeth. Then she looked me up and down and said: 'Your clothes are really old-fashioned, Dilly. You're too young to carry off such a flappy salvaar. Giving you a makeover is going to be a real challenge.'

I felt myself wilting under her scrutinizing gaze.

Pleasantries over, my mother ordered me back into the kitchen to make chapatis. I was relieved to escape.

Everyone else stuffed their faces in the back room, while I ate a lonely meal in the kitchen. I comforted myself with the thought that at least I didn't have to endure my mother's slurps and snorts. While I cleared the dirty dishes from the room, Afeeka opened her suitcases and impressed the family with the cheap gifts she'd brought from her local Rupee-Stretcher.

I was washing up when Monkey sneaked into the kitchen. He'd been ordered upstairs, because he wasn't allowed to communicate with Afeeka until they were married. He wasn't even permitted to see her face, but that didn't stop him from hounding me for information about the future love of his life. Was she as pretty as her photo? Could she speak English? Was she nice? How big were her jugs? Were they like hard like melons, or squeezable like grapefruit?

The questions were endless.

'Look, Monkey,' I said. 'Are you trying to tell me you've travelled all the way from London with this woman, and you don't know the first thing about her?'

'I know she's got a really annoying laugh, but Daddy wouldn't even let me look at her. I had to sit in the front, and she hid under a blanket on the back seat. I don't even know what colour her eyes are.'

'Trust me on this, Monkey. It's not her eyes you wanna worry about. Have you seen her standing up yet?'

He looked startled. 'I went for a leak at the airport. When I got back to the car, she was already in it.'

'Oh, I see.' I nodded. 'Now if you'll excuse me, Gulliver, I've got loads to do.'

As I turned back to the washing-up, I whistled, 'Hi ho, hi ho, it's off to work we go . . .'

Chapter 41

Afeeka spent more time in bed than John Lennon. Until the wedding, she and Monkey wouldn't be allowed to share a room, so she got Daddy's bed in the back room, and Daddy had to sleep on one of the new, already broken sofabeds in the front room.

From the day Afeeka arrived, she was determined not to leave the bed any more than she had to. She saw herself as our guest, so it was up to us to look after her. There was no sign of all the things she was supposed to be able to do: she didn't cook, she didn't clean, she didn't sew. Her only contribution to the household chores was to lift her feet so I could vacuum around her.

She was quick to express her horror when she realized we didn't have any servants; she'd obviously been led to believe that we were a wealthy family with no shortage of maids. I wondered who could possibly have put that idea into her head.

Someone had told Afeeka that life in Bradford would be one big party. So she was shocked when my father told her she was confined to the house until the wedding; she'd be allowed out only on special occasions, and only then if she wore a veil and was chaperoned.

She'd been promised visits to the grandest hotels that

England had to offer, but all she got was prison food at HMP Sharnia.

She spent the first few days in floods of tears.

Before long, Afeeka decided she'd had enough, and told my mother she wanted to go back to Pakistan. I could tell from the look on Mammy's face that she could see the wedding plans slipping away, and she was damned if her dream was going to be ruined by something as trivial as the bride's feelings. She told Afeeka to grow up and stop acting like a spoilt brat.

Afeeka was probably expecting more sympathy from her own mother but, when she called her, Nonna told her the same thing. It turned out that Afeeka's family had already mortgaged their farm to pay for a mock wedding in Pakistan, so they could see her dressed up as a bride, and there was no way she could go back and humiliate them now.

Afeeka was trapped, and decided that, if her life was going to be miserable, she might as well make everyone else suffer too – by whinging like crazy. She complained about: the cold weather ('It's playing havoc with my skin'); being cooped up all day ('My legs are stiff from sitting around with nothing to do'); Climax making fun of her height ('It's not my fault I'm small; at least I look like a woman'); Mammy's cooking ('I'm getting spots from all the oil she uses'); Daddy's bad temper ('No one can relax when that bully's around'); having to climb up the stairs to go to the toilet ('All the houses in Chowki are on one level'); the broken bathroom window ('It's like trying to wash at the North Pole'); all the spiders in the house ('I *hate* spiders'); and the grim terraced houses ('In Pakistan, I was surrounded by countryside').

And so it went on.

She'd been in Bradford a little over two weeks when she suddenly exclaimed: 'I'm sick of looking at those plastic roses on the mantelpiece. I haven't seen a real flower since I left Pakistan.'

That evening, there was an extra item on the shopping list – a bunch of flowers. My father came back from the supermarket with the most pathetic, droopy carnations I'd ever seen. The petals were soggy, and the leaves were already going brown.

'Here you go, Gongal,' he said with a chuckle as he handed Mammy the bunch. 'That's the best I could find.'

My mother put them in a vase and carried them into the back room. 'Here are some real flowers for you, darling,' she gushed enthusiastically. 'Your uncle bought them specially.'

'He shouldn't have bothered,' Afeeka said, bursting into tears. 'They're hideous. All they'll do is make me homesick for Pakistan, where the flowers are so much prettier.'

One evening, when Afeeka went to the toilet, she caught a glimpse of Monkey. She came running downstairs, shrieking, 'Are you kidding me? Look at the size of him! He didn't look that big in his picture. He's taller than a bloody ladder!' She started to cry hysterically.

'At least you know what he looks like,' I chuckled. 'He still thinks you're normal.'

'What do you mean?' she wailed. 'There's nothing wrong with me. Good things come in small packages.'

'That'll be Monkey on his wedding night,' I replied, as Egg and I fell about laughing.

'Auntie!' Afeeka called out. 'Dilly's making fun of me.'

When Mammy appeared, before Afeeka had a chance to tell her what had happened, I said, 'Oh look, here comes Snow White to see what's wrong with Dopey.'

My mother was hopping mad.

'So which one am I engaged to, Mammy? Sleepy? Sneezy?' I asked. I was trying to think of the other names, when my mother slapped the laughter from my face with the clothes brush.

I ran up to my room and locked the door, thinking that would be the end of it.

But Mammy was still angry, and Afeeka was still crying, when Daddy came in. So he was sent upstairs to sort me out.

There was a violent banging on the door. 'Open up if you know what's good for you. I'm not going to tell you again,' my father threatened.

I knew what was good for me, and that's why I didn't want to let him in. The door was the only thing standing between me and a beating. His fist hammered on one of the wooden panels, and I heard a splintering noise. Reluctantly, I got up and unlocked the door.

He was fuming as he came into the room; his teeth were clenched and I saw the little muscle begin to twitch in the side of his face. Behind him, my mother was ranting. My father stood facing me, and I felt my legs tremble. He slapped me across the face. It was a hard smack that stunned me and blurred my vision.

'Why can't you behave?' he bellowed. 'Why must you be so rude? I shouldn't have to do this. You know that Afeeka's not as intelligent as you; there's no need to pick on her for something she can't help.' He raised his hand

and hit me again. This time I went sprawling onto the bed. He pulled me up by my arm, and hit me again. I thought I'd pass out: his fists were as hard as flint. I could still hear my mother's incessant ranting, but it sounded distant, like next door's TV.

'She needs pulling into line . . . She thinks she's better than everyone else . . . She's going to give me a heart attack . . .' Blah blah blah blah blah . . .

'You put a foot wrong and I'll slaughter you,' my father hissed.

He turned and went downstairs. Through my tears I could see a look of sadistic pleasure on my mother's face. Her eyes were lit up with the thrill of the violence she'd just witnessed, and she was purring like a cat.

'It serves you right. Maybe now you'll show Afeeka some respect.'

Chapter 42

'Egg's so sweet. She's the perfect sister-in-law,' Afeeka announced, and that teaspoon of praise was enough for Egg to decide she preferred Afeeka to me.

The two of them started to spend all their spare time together, lounging about and chatting happily.

When Egg told me that she wanted to learn how to dance like the Indian actresses in the movies, and that Afeeka had promised to teach her, I was at a loss for words. I'd known Egg all my life, and if anybody had asked me about her likes and dislikes I wouldn't have been able to tell them. I had no idea she liked dancing – when had that happened?

I found it hard to accept that Egg was growing up. She'd spent twelve years in my shadow and now she was making her own choices, and I didn't like it.

Once Afeeka realized she had a friend, the whining stopped and we started to see a different side to her. She was nice to everyone, and lavished attention on the twins in a way Mammy never had. She played dolls with Poppy, and even helped Daisy with her ointments.

With growing alarm, I realized that all three of my sisters now preferred a newcomer to me.

Afeeka was into hair and beauty in a big way, and would often comment that our long pigtails were old-fashioned.

Although Daddy had a shaved head, he'd made it quite clear that none of the girls were ever to cut their hair.

One Saturday, while my parents and Climax were buying wedding clothes in Bombay Stores, Afeeka decided to ignore Daddy's rule and give us all haircuts. Egg went first. Afeeka had a very sharp pair of hairdressing scissors, and in three quick snips Egg's tail of hair was lying on the carpet, with the red ribbon still tied at the bottom.

'Are you sure about this, Afeeka?' Egg said. 'Daddy's gonna be angry. I've never had my hair this short before.'

'Don't worry. He's a man – he probably won't even notice,' Afeeka tittered girlishly. 'Besides, I know what I'm doing, I've got plenty of experience. I used to practise on our donkey back home.' She ran her fingers through Egg's hair, and continued to snip and trim with gusto.

Within a few minutes, Egg's waist-length hair had been reduced to a very mannish bob, with a severe fringe that made her look like Batool's Mongol granddaughter.

'Oh my God, it really suits you!' Afeeka cooed. 'I never realized how green your eyes are; this cut really brings out the colour.'

As Egg admired herself in the mirror, Afeeka said, 'Okay, Poppy, you next,' and the whole process was repeated.

After Poppy, it was Daisy's turn to be ushered into the chair for her transformation from village girl to Ringo Starr. When she'd finished with Daisy, Afeeka said, 'Come on, Dilly, time for you to enter the eighties.'

'Don't you think three Friar Tucks are enough for one family?' I chuckled.

'You're so silly,' she replied. 'This is how all the trendies in Islamabad look.'

She soon gave up trying to coax me, and turned her attention back to Poppy. Out came the tweezers and, in less than half an hour, ten-year-old Poppy had the eyebrows of an eighteen-year-old catwalk model. They were plucked to perfection; gone were the shaggy caterpillars, and in their place were two thin arches of black hair.

When the shoppers returned, Daddy went crazy. What surprised me was that his fury wasn't directed at his short-haired daughters, but at Afeeka. She, who claimed never to have been hit by her own father, was given a sound thrashing by mine.

That evening, while Daddy was calming down in the mosque, Afeeka said she'd had enough of our madhouse, and was going to pack her bags and leave. Mammy tried to reason with her, but she was inconsolable.

'The man's an animal,' Afeeka wailed. 'He had no right to hit me.'

'You got what you deserved,' Climax said. 'You had no right to cut the girls' hair.'

'But he hit me.'

'Oh, shut your face,' Climax snapped scornfully. 'He hits everybody. The sooner you get used to it, the better.'

Chapter 43

It was late November 1980 when the registry wedding took place. I wasn't allowed to go because Mammy overheard me telling Egg that if the registrar asked if anyone knew of a reason why the couple shouldn't wed, I was going to shout, 'Yes! She's too stupid to marry my brother!'

Afeeka took her time getting ready. She applied several coats of mascara to her lashes, and batted them at her reflection in the mirror. She swanned about in her shimmering white salvaar kameez, looking like a Christmas tree, with all the sparkly bits of glitter catching the light. Her arms were heavy with thick gold bangles that Daddy had bought, her fingers were stuffed tight with garish rings, and she wore chunky gold earrings that hung like chandeliers. Under all the razzle-dazzle, she looked stunning.

When Egg came downstairs in her best pink salvaar kameez, she batted her eyelashes in exactly the same way Afeeka had done.

'How do I look?' she asked.

'Lovely,' I said truthfully.

Pity I couldn't say the same about Climax, who was wearing a black sequinned sari and a long blonde wig. She looked breathtakingly hideous. When Mammy saw her, she had to do a double take.

'What the Dickens . . . ?'

'Oh, shut your face, Gongal,' came the reply. 'Every wedding has some rare beauty who upstages the bride. And I guess that'll be me.'

She scrutinized my mother – who was busy tucking her baggy salvaar into red wellington boots – and said: 'I didn't know it was fancy dress. Are you going as Paddington Bear?'

Chatting and joking, everyone set off for the register office, leaving me feeling angry and excluded. I spent the time sitting in the kitchen eating green chilli pickle from a catering jar. My ears felt like they were going to explode from the heat of the pickle, but I carried on until I was almost squint with pain. When I'd eaten as much as I could stomach, I went up to the front bedroom, and sat waiting by the window.

Eventually, the car pulled up outside; Daddy emerged and strode through the snow, fists clenched. The women came through the back door, just as my father came hurtling into the house like a freak gust of wind.

'How dare she show me up in front of all those people?' he bellowed at my mother. 'She's lucky I didn't knock her teeth out.'

'Calm down, it's all sorted out now,' Mammy shrugged, as a very red-faced and sheepish bride slunk into the back room.

'That girl's a disgrace,' my father continued. 'It's up to you to control the women in this house – and if you can't, I will. Your daughter-in-law has made us look like asses. You wanted her here, so now teach her how to behave. I'm warning you, if any of the women in this house do anything to show me up again, it's your throat I'm going to slit.'

Once Daddy had stormed off to the mosque, Egg explained what had happened. Afeeka had refused to marry Monkey, saying she didn't feel she was ready to settle down and have children – and didn't anyone care that her father-in-law-to-be had beaten her up for being fashionable? When Mammy had said, 'Don't you think it's a bit late in the day to be having cold feet?' Afeeka had replied: 'That's easy for you to say: you're wearing wellies.'

Daddy had asked the registrar if it was okay for him to have five minutes alone with Afeeka outside. When they came back in, she said, 'I do' without a moment's hesitation.

When Monkey came home, he looked stunned. Not only was he mortified by the realization that everyone had concealed the eighteen-inch height difference until he'd got to the registry, but he'd also had to listen to his mate Scully ribbing him all the way home.

'Oh Jesus,' Monkey said, as he slumped into a chair with his head in his hands. 'Four feet nine and thick as shit. What the hell have I just done?'

Chapter 44

On 26 December 1980, it was time for Monkey and Afeeka to get married again. In the eyes of the law they'd been Mr and Mrs Shah for more than a month, but nothing else had changed. Before Monkey could get his hands on his wife, he'd have to go through a religious wedding.

It was snowing outside, and with front and back doors wide open to let the guests in there was a howling gale whipping through the passage.

Daisy and Poppy had been set to work to clear a path for all the women who'd be coming to the house via the back alley. They chatted happily as they took turns to shovel the snow; unlike the rest of the family, they actually appeared to be enjoying themselves.

Afeeka wore a sparkly red sari and a big smile. Monkey wore a grey suit and a grimace.

The ceremony took place in two rooms of our house: the men were in the front, and the women were in the back. Molvi Sahib commuted between the two, read some verses from the Koran, received various promises, and the whole thing was over in a few minutes.

Sadly, that was just the start of what would be three days of miserable 'celebrations', during which hordes of neighbours and people I'd never seen before took it upon themselves to traipse through the house in search of food and entertainment. The kitchen windows steamed up with all the cooking that was going on. Climax, who'd been promised caterers for the event by Daddy, struggled to keep up with the demand for more chapatis every few minutes, while Egg and I ran back and forth, with trays of steaming food, and drinks.

On the first day the bride and groom spent hours receiving guests, and presents which mainly consisted of hastily rolled-up five-pound notes. By nine p.m., all the visitors had disappeared for the day and my father took himself off to the mosque. Monkey bounded upstairs with a big eager smile, and shortly afterwards my mother and Climax escorted Afeeka up to the marital room.

An hour later, Monkey came down, looking flustered and angry. My mother and I were in the back room, tidying up, when he came in and said, 'Mammy, we need to talk.'

My mother told me to get lost. Normally, I would have eavesdropped, but there was too much housework to do. Not that it really mattered, because Monkey naively assumed that confidential chats with my mother would be just that: confidential. The reality was rather different. My mother's definition of keeping a secret was to tell one person at a time, and ask them not to tell anyone else. Or to tell a group of people, and swear them to secrecy. Or, sometimes, to tell the whole back alley, but in a hushed voice.

So it wasn't long before she was entertaining Egg and me with the particulars of Monkey's plight. The details were as follows: Afeeka wouldn't let him near her; she said he'd have to sleep on the floor; if this went on much longer, he'd need a wheelbarrow for his testicles; he wanted to leave home.

The details of my mother's advice to Monkey were as follows: be patient; if necessary, tie a knot in your sac; for God's sake, don't mess this marriage up; feel for your father – the bank account's empty, we haven't got two pennies to rub together, and we've got another two hundred people coming tomorrow; show some concern for your mother – my blood pressure's up and I don't think I'm going to make it through the night.

Next morning, Monkey was on the warpath. 'Why did you do it? Why did you make me marry that empty-headed midget? I spent the whole night trying to get my hands on her, and she spent the whole night running away. It was like a *Benny Hill* sketch.'

'That's nothing,' Mammy replied. 'I spent all last night looking for my blood pressure tablets.'

As Monkey stormed out of the kitchen, Afeeka flounced in. My mother took one look, put her head in her hands, and gave out a low moan, while Egg and I hummed the *Benny Hill* theme tune.

'Auntie, I need to talk to you right now,' Afeeka said. She was trembling with rage.

'Just a moment, Afeeka,' my mother sighed. 'Dilly, Egg, get out of here now, and no buts, I'm not in the mood for your crap.'

Without a word, Egg and I walked into the back room, and pressed our ears up against the serving hatch.

Mammy: 'Make this quick, Afeeka, the visitors are going to be here soon; you need to get dressed and I've got food to prepare.'

Afeeka: 'Auntie, this won't take long. I just want to let you know what an animal your son is. He tried to force himself on me.'

Mammy: 'What happened?'

Afeeka: 'He lay on his back on the bed, and told me to lick him down there.'

There was a long silence.

Afeeka: 'I haven't lost anything to that sweaty savage.'

Mammy: 'Why are you telling me? This is between you and him.'

Afeeka: 'If you'd taught him anything, he'd know how to behave.'

Mammy: 'Oh my God. I was working all day yesterday, I was up all night with my blood pressure, and now you're trying to humiliate me.'

Afeeka: 'There's no way he's ever going to lay a finger on me. How dare he tell me to lick him? What am I? A dog?'

Mammy: 'You sort it out – I'm busy.'

For the next few days, Monkey and Afeeka avoided each other as much as possible, and my mother avoided both of them. My father looked edgy, and my mother looked exhausted.

Chapter 45

The snow on New Year's Eve was beautiful, but the view from the kitchen window was spoilt by a mountain of black bin bags awaiting collection.

Egg and I were in the kitchen eating our lunch, when Daisy drifted in and started to let rip with violent farts. Despite our protests, she refused to go to the toilet. She'd been in England for five years, but was still so scared of sitting on the toilet seat that she'd developed numerous bowel problems. Her phobia had been nurtured by Egg and me, who'd encouraged her to believe that a toilet wolf lived in the sewer, and was waiting for her to go for a dump so it could swim up through the S-bend and bite her on the bum.

There was a wet parping sound, and we watched in horror as Daisy thrust her hips forward, and a little brown marble rolled out from the bottom of her trousers onto the kitchen floor.

'Oh, you disgusting little cow!' Egg shouted. 'If you're not in the bog in ten seconds, I'm gonna make you eat that.'

'But the toilet wolf . . .' she started.

'Right, that's it, I've had enough,' I said, and jumped out of my seat, threw her into the passage, and slammed the door shut behind her.

As I sat down, my father came in, looked around, sniffed, grimaced, and went out without saying a word. A minute later, my mother came in and walked across to the sink. On the way, she trod in Daisy's freshly laid egg.

'What the . . . ?'

'It's okay, Mammy,' Egg said. 'It's just one of Daisy's.'

The back door opened, and in came Naveeda.

'Hi, Naveeda,' my mother said. 'Give me a minute while I get this shit off my slipper.'

She disappeared outside for a moment, then came back in, washed her hands and cleared a place at the table.

'Sit down, Naveeda. Would you like some tea?'

'No thanks, Gongal. I've just popped in to see your daughter-in-law.'

'So why didn't you come to the wedding? You were invited.'

'I'm sorry, I was ill – it was another migraine.'

'Oh, I know. Migraine, yes,' agreed my mother. 'There's a lot of it going around. The one I had last night was so bad, I thought I was going blind. Climax is in bed with one now. Dilly, go and tell Afeeka to come down.'

When I went to fetch Afeeka, it was a depressed-looking Monkey who came to the door. 'Yeah, what do you want?'

'Tell Afeeka to get downstairs. Mammy wants her.'

As I headed downstairs, I heard Daisy straining in the toilet.

'Nnnnnnn, nnnnnnn, nnnnnnn.'

'Oh my God, the toilet wolf's coming!' I shouted, and then slid down the banister as the yelping began.

Half an hour later, there was still no sign of Afeeka, and Naveeda's patience had run out.

'Why don't we go up and say hello?' she said, getting to her feet and making her way to the passage.

A few minutes later, they were back. Naveeda was livid because Afeeka had told her to go away, saying that a lady's boudoir was no place for socializing with the neighbours. My mother, flushed with embarrassment, tried to make excuses, but Naveeda was having none of it.

'If she was my daughter-in-law, I'd make sure my son gave her a damn good beating. If you let her get away with that sort of behaviour, you'll regret it later.' With that, Naveeda trudged her way home through the snow.

My mother, Egg and I trooped into the back room. Poppy was on the floor, playing with her Lego, and my father was sitting on his bed.

'Has she gone?' he asked.

'Yes,' my mother said. 'I'm really embarrassed. I took Naveeda up to see Afeeka, and she didn't even let us through the door.'

'You did what?' he thundered. But before she could reply, my father jumped off the bed and smashed his clenched fist into my mother's face. There were two thuds, first the sound of his knuckles on her jaw; then, as she fell backwards onto the floor, a hollow thumping as the back of her head struck the wall.

'You bitch!' he shouted, his face crimson with rage, as he stood over her. 'How dare you? It's private.'

I couldn't understand why he'd hit her, or what he meant by 'private'. It made no sense to me.

My mother groaned and opened her eyes. There was blood seeping from a deep cut in her lip, and the skin around her nose had already puffed up. As Egg and I helped her to her feet, my father yelled, 'I'm sick to death of the lot of you. I've had enough. I can't take any more.'

He turned to the wardrobe, flung open the doors, and pulled his clothes out, tossing them onto his bed. He grabbed his overcoat and threw it on top of the pile of clothes. Then he pulled the sheet off the bed and tried to make a big bundle, with all the clothes inside.

'You can't go,' my mother gasped.

He shot her a withering look, then gathered up the bundle in his arms. As he walked into the passage, the bundle fell apart, and most of the clothes tumbled to the floor. He grabbed as many clothes as he could carry, and roared, 'Open the Goddamn door for me!'

I ran past him and opened the front door. An icy-cold wind tore through the passage. My father paused on the top step, turned to me and said, 'I'll be back for my pans later.'

Egg, the twins and I crowded by the front door. Daddy took one step outside and skidded on the ice. As he put his hand out to grab the railing, his clothes dropped to the ground.

'Get some ruddy salt!' he boomed as the neighbours' nets started to twitch.

Poppy raced inside. My father was still gathering up his belongings when she reappeared, holding a plastic Saxa container, and started throwing salt on top of his clothes.

'Get that stuff out of my face!' he thundered.

Rita's irate voice came from across the road: 'Keep the bloody noise down – our Seamus is trying to sleep.'

'Fuck Seamus,' my father shouted back. 'Get a life. It's New Year's Eve, you dumb arse.'

'Shah, is that you? You should know better than to use language like that, you being a librarian an' all.'

'Get back in your house, you rancid old hag.'

'You cheeky pillock, I'll set Hepburn on you.'

'Drop dead, bitch.'

My father slithered down the path and out into the street, dropping clothes as he went. My mother's plaintive voice came from the back room, 'Dilly, don't let him leave – people will talk.'

I slammed the front door, bolted it, and put the latch down so Daddy wouldn't be able to use his key if he changed his mind. We all piled into the back room.

'He's gone,' I smiled to my mother.

'You don't care, do you?' she sobbed.

'No, Mammy, I don't. Come on, you lot, let's see what's on telly.'

I sat down in my father's favourite armchair, and prayed silently that he'd never come back.

Chapter 46

'Peace at last,' I said smugly, as I stretched out my legs and toasted my feet in front of the fire.

'You should've stopped him,' my mother whined pathetically.

I shrugged my shoulders. 'Why would I want to do that? We're better off without him.' I found it hard to believe she was still taking his side after what had just happened. 'Mammy, what are you gonna do?' I asked.

If only my mother had paused for a moment, considered the situation, then said, 'I've decided I'm getting a divorce. There's no way that creep's going to lay a finger on me or my children ever again. I'm going to get myself a good lawyer, then I'm taking him to the cleaners. I want the house, the car, the savings, the land in Jallu, everything.'

It was difficult to imagine what it would be like never to be hit by my father again, and never to hear him bellowing with fury. I'd spent all my life being afraid of him. Just the sound of his voice, or the look in his eye before he exploded, was enough to make my insides turn to water. All Mammy had to do was say he couldn't come back, and I'd have walked through fire for her.

But, being a fool, she had the wrong answer on the tip of her tongue.

'I'm going to wait until he's had some time to cool down,' she replied quietly, as she gingerly dabbed her cheek with a damp flannel. 'And then I'm going to ask him to come home. All he did was lose his temper. You know he's been under a lot of stress because of the wedding. He's the head of the house, and if he doesn't come back soon people are going to start gossiping.'

'But Mammy, we all hate him. Call the police and have him arrested. You don't have to worry about being alone – I'll look after you. Just stop making excuses for him.'

But I couldn't get through to her. She tried to fob me off with a pack of lame excuses about not being white, about knowing how to behave because she was Pakistani, about being prepared to compromise. I realized I was using logic to battle against something far more persuasive: her culture, her tradition, her religion. I was trying to fight everything she'd been brought up to believe in. I didn't stand a chance.

'So you're going to let him get away with it again?' I asked.

She stared at me balefully, as though she couldn't understand why my thoughts were so different from her own.

'If I ever need advice on my marriage, you'll be the last person I come to. Why don't you go away – your face is making my eyes hurt.'

Everything about the situation was unfair. I didn't want to live my life in fear. I wanted to be like Leela and Nelly. They didn't have to worry about being beaten up by their parents. My only hope now was that my father would get to enjoy his bachelor life, and decide never to come back.

Lying in bed that night, mulling over the events of the last few hours, I found myself warming to Afeeka. She was a stupid, irritating pain in the backside. But I had to admit that in a few months she'd achieved the one thing none of us had been able to do in years – she'd got rid of my father.

The next few days were agony and ecstasy.

Word soon got round that Daddy was staying in a room at the back of the mosque – it was the talk of Gomshall Road.

It felt wonderful not having him around. We slept late, ate late, and watched whatever we wanted on TV. No longer could my mother use the 'wait till your father gets home' threat to keep us in line. Climax went one stage further: without her brother to watch over her, she didn't even bother to come home at night, and we began to wonder if we would ever see her again. She would just phone in the evening to find out if Daddy was back yet and, when we said no, she stayed another night with Amina in Dewsbury.

But every time I tried to relax and enjoy myself, Mammy would be there to spoil things. She took every opportunity to accuse me of being selfish, and told me time and again how much I'd disappointed her. Her incessant nagging was like new shoe leather rubbing against a burst blister. No matter how hard I tried to ignore her, she was always there.

On 4 January 1981 the Ripper was in custody, but my father was still at large. It was the last day of the Christmas holidays, and Egg and I were taking turns to do our gymnastics routine in the kitchen, when Mammy walked in. The bruise on the side of her face had blossomed into a kaleidoscope of colour, and I stared at it enviously and wished I had one like it.

She sighed, and did her best to spread an air of misery around the room, but I wasn't fooled – I'd seen her like that often enough to know it was all an act. As soon as she saw the smile on my face, she muttered to herself: 'What's there to be happy about?'

Egg raised her arms high and balanced on one foot.

'Four point five,' I said.

'You bastard, that was worth at least nine. Come on, Dilly, you're not being fair. I gave you nine point seven, and I'm Olga Korbut,' Egg whinged.

'Olga Korbut, my arse, that was more like Ronnie Corbett. It was four point five – do it again if you want a better score.'

Egg lost her balance, stumbled and fell backwards, shunting my mother into the sink.

'Are you blind?' Mammy spat as she reached out and slapped Egg across the back of her head. 'You slut, stop dancing around my kitchen.'

'I'm sorry, I fell off the beam.'

What we had in the kitchen that evening was two girls who wanted to rejoice in their new-found freedom, and one bitter woman who wanted to make them feel guilty for being happy. Even after my father had left, my mother still tried her hardest to ruin my holidays. Yet again, I couldn't wait for them to end, so I could get back to Oxley High. I must have been the only teenager in Bradford who actually wanted to be at school.

The new term arrived, and that's when I fell in love for the first time, though the object of my affection was hardly aware of my existence.

Steve, as far as I was concerned, was the hottest thing on two legs. He was tall and handsome, with a dazzling smile and big blue eyes. The minute I saw him, I lost all sense of perspective. The only problem with falling for Steve was all the girls in my year wanted him to notice them as well. Behind his back, we called him 'Steve'. To his face, we had to call him 'Mr Maxwell' or 'Sir'. It was amazing how a new teacher could inspire so many girls to study Applied Science.

'I think he's sexy' Tanya said, as we sat in the cloak-room eating crisps.

'Oh God, every time I see him my stomach jumps up and down,' I said happily.

'He's so hot. I can't even speak sense when I'm around him,' Tanya added.

'Do you think he's got a girlfriend?' I asked, suddenly aware that Mr Maxwell might already be taken.

'I hope not,' said Leela, joining in the conversation. 'And even if he has, it's not as if she's here.'

'I hope he stays forever,' Tanya said.

'Mmmm,' we all sighed dreamily as the bell went to signal the end of lunch.

That afternoon when I left school I was feeling very happy, but the minute I stepped in to Sharnia, it was back to the same old routine.

Chapter 47

My mother was desperate for my father to come back. If she'd just put on her burka and gone across the road to the mosque, she could have spoken to him. But her pride wouldn't let her, so she channelled all her energy into trying to persuade me to do her dirty work for her.

She bombarded me relentlessly. I felt like I was trapped inside a Space Invaders game; no matter how much I tried to dodge her, she was always there, blasting away. But the harder she tried, the more I dug my heels in. Any reasonable woman would have accepted defeat, but my mother, with her dogged determination, refused to let go.

Oddly enough, I was the only one she asked. Afeeka wanted to go – she was straining at the leash to race across the road and steal the credit for bringing my father home, but Mammy wouldn't let her. And, as far as I knew, she never asked Monkey, Egg or the twins. I'm sure they'd have done what she wanted; they were all much keener to please her than I was. But they never offered to go and get Daddy, and she never asked them to. Maybe she didn't want to subject any of the others to my father's rage, but she obviously didn't have a problem sending me out of the trench and across no man's land.

As the days passed, and there was still no sign of my father, it slowly dawned on me that I had a brilliant opportunity to use this situation to my advantage. I knew it was only a matter of time before his rage subsided and he realised he needed my mother to look after him, and then he'd be back. I also knew that when he turned up at the door my mother would welcome him in.

So I found myself thinking that maybe it wouldn't be such a bad thing if I did what my mother was pestering me to do. If I talked him into coming home, it would give me the chance to bask in the glory of my mother's praise for once. I wanted to be the hero, to hear her telling the others that I was great and they were useless.

If I was going to do it, I knew I would have to act fast. If Afeeka beat me to it, she'd get all the credit, and I'd be forever treated with contempt. My reluctance to help my mother in her time of need would be dredged up and force-fed to me at every mealtime for months.

My mind was made up one afternoon, when I was in the kitchen painting my nails black. My mother was painstakingly making parathas the way Climax had taught her; they were huge and flaky, and you could peel off each layer without disturbing the layers underneath.

As she rolled out another ball of dough and spread a generous amount of ghee on it, she said, 'Dilly, if you go and get him, I promise you that I'll get Climax to make a wonderful meal to celebrate his return, and everybody will know it's because of you.'

Up until then, I'd been dithering, but she'd managed to push the right buttons, and my conceit took over. However, I didn't want Mammy to know what I'd decided yet; I wanted her to beg some more.

'Can you put butter in mine instead of ghee, and make it nice and crispy, please?' I asked greedily.

'Wouldn't it be lovely if your father was here to share these?' she said, pointing to the stack of freshly cooked parathas. 'You know how much he likes them with a nice cup of tea. Look, Dilly, will you do me a favour? Can you go and tell him I'm making his favourites, and he's welcome to join us?'

I watched the ghee sizzling on the tawa; a swirl of smoke from the hot fat rose in a plume over her head. 'I might,' I said. 'But I'm hungry, can't I eat first?'

'Why do you want to rush yours? Go and talk to your father, and when you get back I'll make you the best you've ever had – nice and hot.'

I wanted to see how far I could push my luck, so I asked her if she'd buy me a pair of the red wedge sandals I'd seen Naveeda wearing; Naveeda had bought them for six pounds from Begum, the woman from Bangladesh who made her living by selling cheap tat to all the ladies in Bradford who weren't allowed to go shopping for themselves. My arithmetic was hopeless, but I knew that six pounds divided by twenty pence a week pocket money was too many weeks. By the time I'd saved up for those sandals, they'd be out of fashion.

At any other time, my mother would have refused – she wasn't keen on me strutting around like a peacock, full of my own self-importance – but on this occasion the stakes were high.

'Look,' she said, through gritted teeth, 'I'll get you the sandals. Now go, before I change my mind.'

Victory was mine. The evil and corrupt Queen of Sharnia had admitted defeat; she'd even resorted to bribery to get what she wanted.

But it was dark outside, and I was scared of going on my

own – I needed the services of my faithful handmaiden. I found her in the back room sitting on the floor, watching *Blue Peter* with Daisy and Poppy; they should all have been in mosque, but standards had slipped recently.

Mammy hovered in the passage as we put on our coats. We were just about to leave when Afeeka came flouncing down the stairs. Her breasts jiggled up and down inside her pink and brown kameez, and I wondered if Monkey had milked the silly cow's udders yet.

'Dilly, why are you going out?' she asked.

'I want to spend some quality time with Daddy,' I said. 'My social worker recommended it.'

When Afeeka found out what I was really doing, she insisted on gatecrashing my party. I could see the opportunity to get the sandals slipping away.

We crunched our way through old snow that no longer felt like polystyrene underfoot; it had hardened into slippery little islands of ice. Egg and I linked arms and Afeeka tried to keep up, in her tarty fuck-me shoes.

When we got to the mosque, we hammered on the side door with our fists. A few seconds later, it was flung open, and there stood my father, looking fierce and angry.

'What the hell do you want?' he barked.

'Uncle,' chimed Afeeka, 'I've come to take you home.'

'Oh for God's sake, don't you realize? I left you bastards for a bit of peace and quiet. Damn you all to hell.'

'We can't go home without you, Daddy – Mammy'll kill us,' I said.

My father growled angrily. 'Tell her I want a divorce.'

Here was an interesting and very unexpected development. At last I'd be able to say I came from a broken home.

There was a scramble as we hurried back to give Mammy the news.

'Well?' she demanded eagerly, as I pushed past her into the passage.

'He says he wants a divorce,' I said. 'Does that mean I won't get my sandals?'

'What?' she spluttered. 'Go back and try harder.'

Egg had turned her attention to a bowl of mushroom soup, so it was just Afeeka who went with me this time.

As he opened the door, Daddy wore a self-satisfied, triumphant look on his face. It was almost as though he'd been expecting us.

'Well? What's the message?' he asked, arms folded victoriously.

I said, 'Mammy says she's sorry about everything, and she's really missing you. She wants you to come home now. She'd have come herself, but her blood pressure's up.'

'Hah, I knew she couldn't live without me. Less than two weeks, and she's shitting in her salvaar.'

'So what shall I tell her?'

'Tell her I'll be home later.'

'At last,' I thought smugly. 'New sandals and prestige – what more could a girl want?'

As we walked home, Afeeka told me how homesick she was feeling, how much she hated Bradford, and how she didn't think she'd ever be able to forgive her parents. Even though I found her annoying, I couldn't help feeling sorry for her. It must have been such a shock to travel all the way to Bradford, just to end up with the Shahs. I tried to imagine how she must have felt when she realized her parents had tricked her into agreeing to marry Monkey.

She'd sacrificed her happiness for her family's sake. And I'd just done something similar – I'd persuaded my father to come home just to please my mother.

An hour later, the bell rang. My mother rushed to open the front door, and in strolled my father. There were no kisses or cuddles on the doorstep, no 'darling, I missed you'.

'Make me a cup of tea, you fat cow,' he said.

'You owe me, big time,' she replied. 'Thank your lucky stars I didn't call the police.'

'You, call the police?' he laughed. 'You're so thick you'd get all the nines mixed up. You should put some make-up on that bruise.'

He walked past me into the back room, just as three disappointed-looking children came scurrying out. It looked like our days of watching unrestricted TV were over.

As my mother went into the kitchen to make tea, I asked her if she was happy now.

'Not yet – he still hasn't apologized. But the night is young, and one way or another, he will say sorry.'

'And what about me, Mammy?' I asked, conscious of the fact that she still hadn't thanked me for the part I'd played.

'What about you?'

'Well, I brought him back for you.'

'What do you want, a medal? You should have gone to get him when I first asked you. A dutiful daughter wouldn't have made her mother grovel, but you've got no shame.'

'But, Mammy, you promised we'd all sit round the table for tea and you'd tell everyone what a good daughter I've been.'

She scowled at me. 'Well, I've changed my mind. Good daughter? Hah! A good daughter wouldn't try to profit from her mother's pain. It's the end of the world when Satan whispers in your children's ears.'

'But, Mammy . . .'

'Not another word! Now leave me alone. I want some time with your father. Your paratha's there if you want it.'

For the next couple of weeks, Daddy was on his best behaviour; Mammy strutted and crowed as though she'd won a famous victory, and I was ashamed of myself for being so easily manipulated. But then it served me right: it was my own selfish pride that had tripped me up.

The promised meal never happened, and I wasn't elevated to the glory I'd so desperately sought. But she did buy me the sandals, and I was so furious with her that as soon as she gave them to me I sliced off the heels with my father's saw.

Chapter 48

Afeeka was standing by the stove, peering lustfully into the cooking pot.

'Dilly, come and look at this,' she said.

Climax had cooked aloo ghosht. Beneath a garnish of finely chopped fresh coriander leaves, I could see chunks of lamb, thick wedges of potato and long slivers of green chillies, all bobbing up and down in a rich sauce that was simmering away gently, and filling the kitchen with a mouthwatering aroma.

Climax appeared from the garden. 'Afeeka, put the lid back on that pot right now, and come away from the stove. Don't even think about helping yourself. And Dilly, did you get the Avon book for me?'

'You'll need more than Avon to sort out that face,' Afeeka tittered. 'If you're trying to compete with me, you'll have to eat less and exercise more.'

'Compete with you?' Climax spat back. 'You're an idiot, your brother's an idiot, your parents are losers. What the hell have you got to be so proud of? And the first time you squeeze out a baby, that figure of yours will be history.'

'It doesn't matter how many babies I have – thank God I'll never look like you,' Afeeka replied. 'Admit it, Climax, you're just jealous because I'm a size-eight teenager and you're a fat old bag.'

With that, Afeeka skipped out of the kitchen like a little girl.

There was a loud hammering on the back gate.

'Sounds like someone wants to come in. Are you going to see who it is?' I asked Climax.

'Of course not; that's your job,' she replied angrily, clearly smarting from Afeeka's remarks.

'Whatever,' I said, and went outside. There was more knocking on the gate. 'All right, hang on a second, will you?' I shouted as I strolled down the path.

It was Naveeda's daughter, Billi, wanting to know if Poppy fancied a go on the yellow space hopper her dad had just bought her from a car boot sale.

'Sod Poppy – I want a go,' I said, and bounced around the alley for a while, until I suddenly remembered I was supposed to be making chapatis.

The kitchen was deserted as I set to work. I was still busy half an hour later, when Mammy came in and told me to fry up a stack of poppadoms as well.

As everyone sat down to eat, Climax lifted the lid from the cooking pot. She was visibly taken aback. As she ladled some of the aloo ghosht into a huge bowl and handed it to my father, her expression changed from surprise to annoyance.

'I can't figure this out – where have all the potatoes gone?' she said, looking from one face to the next. 'All right, which one of you bastards took them?'

It was as though someone had squeezed out a silent fart. Everyone put on an offended 'well, it wasn't me' look, at the same time scrutinizing everyone else's face to catch a sign of guilt.

When no one owned up, Climax jumped to the

conclusion that it must have been Afeeka, because she'd seen her peering into the pot.

Afeeka laughed uncomfortably, but was silenced by a slap from my father. He jumped to his feet.

'Did you do it?' he roared as he towered over her.

She shrank into her chair. 'No,' she wailed thinly.

'Liar,' he said, then picked up his bowl, and tipped his dinner over Afeeka's head.

'If your Auntie says you did it, then you did!'

Afeeka sat rigid, too stunned to move, as sauce ran down her face.

Then Daddy lifted the cooking pot and poured the entire contents into Afeeka's lap. Fortunately for her, the stove had been off for a while.

'Steal from us again, and I'll break your hands.'

Later on that evening, Egg and I were playing hide-and-seek. I'd just managed to crawl under my father's bed, when I heard Mammy and Climax coming into the back room. I lay as still as I could, and listened.

'She said I was ugly, Gongal, so I decided to teach her a lesson.'

'I can't believe you'd do something like that, just to get your own back. If she finds out you hid the potatoes, there's going to be hell to pay.'

'I don't give a shit.'

'I'm warning you, Climax. If you can't get on with her, just leave her alone. And as for you, Dilly, I know you're under there. You breathe one word of this to anyone, and I'll cut your tongue out.'

Chapter 49

A few days later, Mammy was trying to teach Egg to knit, but things weren't going well. The teacher was losing her patience, and the pupil had lost interest a long time ago. I was quietly doing my homework when in flounced Afeeka, wearing a skin-tight green salvaar kameez with a matching dupatta draped fashionably over her shoulders, her hair pinned back with a silk clip.

'That's it, Auntie, I've had enough,' she said dramatically, but Mammy didn't even look up.

'Me an' all,' Egg said, as she tossed her knitting to one side. 'I can't be bothered with this crap – can't we just buy a jumper from C&A?'

Afeeka huffed. 'I've had enough,' she repeated.

'You've had enough?' Egg asked. 'You wanna try spending hours doing this knit-purl bollocks. I've gone squint from all this yarn to the back and yarn to the front. Whoever invented knitting should be shot. Can I go now, Mammy?'

'Auntie!' shouted Afeeka, stamping her foot childishly. 'I – have – had – enough!'

Egg held up her knitting. It was full of holes. 'You've gotta be joking if you think I'm wearing this. I'll look like a total prat.'

'Actually it's not for you; it's for your father,' my mother said.

'Oh, that's all right then. It's finished.' She gave up all pretence of knitting, and started to play catch with the ball of wool.

'Auntie! I want a divorce!' Afeeka announced wildly, hoping everyone would stop what they were doing and listen to her.

'You'd better ask your husband, then,' came the curt response.

I glanced up to see a look of disbelief on Afeeka's face.

'I'm bored,' she whined. 'There's nothing to do here.'

'You'll soon get used to it,' my mother said nonchalantly. 'Just give it time.'

'Time!' Afeeka squawked. 'My God, I don't have time. My youth and beauty are fading in this prison.'

'You need to make more of an effort. Your husband's out all day looking for a job, and what are you doing for him?'

'Why should I do anything? I'm not his servant.'

'You can't clap with one hand,' my mother said coldly. She was about to say more, but Afeeka had already gone.

Later that evening, Egg and I were busy tidying up the kitchen when Monkey came in, clearly in a bad mood. 'Oi, Dilly, where's the old lady?'

'In the back room. Why?'

'Mind your own fucking business.'

He disappeared into the back room, and closed the door behind him.

Without a word, Egg and I walked over to the adjoining wall and pressed our ears against the serving hatch.

Mammy: 'Ah love, I need to talk to you about Afeeka.'

Monkey: 'Snap. I wanna talk about that fraud as well.'

Mammy: 'What do you mean, fraud? That's not a very nice thing to say about your wife.'

Monkey: 'Well, that's what she is. I've had to look at those massive gazungas for two months, and she wouldn't even let me touch them. And now I know why. I finally managed to get her bra off, and her tits fell on the carpet. She's as flat as a pancake.'

Mammy: 'Keep your voice down. Have you got no shame?'

Monkey: 'Why should I have any shame? Did you have any, when you conned me into marrying her? I blame you for this mess, Mammy. You spent years telling everyone what a catch she was. Well, you could've fooled me. Fuck it, you *did* fool me. She told me that if I try to bounce her, she's gonna go back to Pakistan. Unbe-fucking-lievable. I've got a wife I'm not even allowed to shag. So what exactly is she here for, Mammy? 'Cos she's certainly not doing what she's supposed to be doing.'

Mammy: 'Wait till you get to know each other a bit better. It's not that bad.'

Monkey: 'Not that bad? My bannocks won't fit in my Y-fronts any more. She doesn't even get undressed in front of me. Every night it's the same: she hides under the duvet until the light's off.'

Mammy: 'Keep your voice down. If your father hears you, I'm in deep shit.'

Monkey: 'Like I give a fuck. I haven't even given her a pearl necklace yet. I should be getting my nuts up to her guts by now.'

Mammy: 'Monkey! No shame!'

Monkey: 'I don't fucking care! She can fuck me or she can fuck off! Tell her that!'

Mammy: 'I'll tell her no such thing.'

Monkey: 'You know what, Mammy? I never knew what real happiness was till I got married. And now it's too late!'

Mammy: 'Leave it with me, I'll see what I can do.'

The front door slammed.

My mother came in, muttering, 'Pearl necklace, it's not as if she hasn't got enough jewellery.'

She wandered over to the sink, and we watched in silence as she made some tea and piled a plate high with gingernuts and Jammie Dodgers.

'So many problems,' she grumbled to herself. 'It's just as well they've got me to sort things out for them. I think I've managed to get through to Monkey; all I've got to do now is talk some sense into Afeeka.'

Chapter 50

Afeeka and Egg became best friends. While I did the housework, they sat around, drinking coffee and chatting. Or they went out shopping together, claiming that each was the other's chaperone. Their selfishness was infuriating. Every time I asked Egg to help out, she'd tell me she was too busy – although she always seemed to be able to find time if Afeeka needed something.

My mother would grumble about having two lazy cows in the house, but rarely did anything about it.

It was difficult to believe that Afeeka was a married woman; she was more like a child than the twins. She loved nothing more than to lie on her bed, with Egg beside her, popping gum, flicking through fashion magazines, and telling jokes about Climax.

I'd managed to tolerate sharing the same living space as Afeeka, until the day I caught her cutting up my black kameez with Mammy's dressmaking scissors.

I was horrified. 'What are you doing, you silly tart?' I asked as I snatched the kameez from her hands.

'Making some ribbons for the girls from this old rag I found in your wardrobe.'

'You've gotta be kidding me,' I said indignantly. 'You had no right to go in there – how would you like it if I cut up your clothes?' And then, before I could stop myself, I gave her a rough shove, and she fell on the floor.

Moments later, she was downstairs, wailing: 'Uncle, Dilly hit me.'

I was summoned into the front room. As soon as I saw the look on my father's face, I lost my nerve, and headed for the safety of the stairs, but he was right behind me, and as I reached the first step I felt a punch in between my shoulder blades. It was so hard it winded me, and I lost my balance and found myself falling awkwardly. I instinctively put my hands out to cushion my fall, and instantly regretted it, as my fingernails took the full force of my weight, and I felt them snapping and ripping away from the skin underneath. Excruciating pain shot through my body; I got to my feet and ran upstairs in silent agony. My heart was thumping and I could feel the goosebumps rising on my neck. As I reached the top of the stairs, I turned to see Afeeka standing at the bottom, looking anxious.

I went into my room, sat down on my bed and whimpered.

'Are you okay?' Egg whispered.

'What do you think? I got punished 'cos Afeeka ruined my kameez.'

'No, you got punished 'cos you hit someone older than you.'

A sheepish-looking Afeeka came into the room. 'I feel awful. I didn't think he'd hit you. Can I have a look at your hands?'

When I showed her, she said: 'I'm really sorry, Dilly, what a nightmare. I know how long it takes to grow your nails.'

*　　*　　*

That night, the pain was so bad I couldn't sleep. As I lay in bed, I thought about how crap my life had become. Without realizing, I'd turned from a couldn't-care-less child into a miserable, bad-mouthed, angry, spotty, wiry-haired loser of a teenager.

I counted the pleasures in my life.

1) Going to school.
2) Climax's cooking, especially when she did roast chicken with all the trimmings, followed by thick-crusted apple pie and custard.
3) Sitting in the back garden in summer, sunning myself through my salvaar kameez.
4) Reading at night, tucked up in bed, lost in a private world.
5) Knitting.

I couldn't think of any other good things.

So that was it – I was fourteen years old, and I had exactly five good things to live for. I began to feel really depressed.

Then I started to count the bad things in my life, but that served only to depress me further. And my heart sank even deeper, when it dawned on me that I had something in common with Climax, after all – there was no one in the house I liked any more.

The next day in my art lesson, everyone wanted to know why I had so many plasters wrapped round my fingers. I said my eczema was playing up.

As I sat at my desk, paintbrush held gingerly, eyes closed, head down, I struggled to stay awake long enough to create a masterpiece for Mrs Turner, my art teacher. Apart from Mr Maxwell, she was my favourite teacher, and I always looked forward to her lessons. She had long blonde hair worn in a ponytail, piercing blue eyes, and a lovely slender figure. She was always elegantly dressed, and wore sexy high-heels. All in all, she was a class apart from the assortment of frumps who inhabited the Oxley High staff room.

For instance, there was Mrs Murray, who taught accounts and typing. She was a short, vicious bulldog of a woman, who seemed to dislike me from the moment she first set eyes on me, and took every opportunity to put me in detention.

And then there was Mrs Earl, an obese sari-wearing hippo with a massive arse permanently swathed in yards of brightly coloured material. She'd waddle about, making me feel queasy at the sight of her loose spongy stomach flab. She had so many rolls, she could have opened a baker's shop. Somewhere under all that blubber there must have been a midriff once, but her narrow waist and broad mind had changed places long ago. Mrs Earl was sour and vindictive, with a mean streak as wide as her knickers. She loved to hide in shadowy corners, eavesdropping on conversations that were none of her business, and interrupting to give people the benefit of her twisted and racist opinions (in a nutshell: brown = good, white = bad). She'd gatecrash Mrs Dobbs' needlework lessons and demand that she be measured for a new sari blouse, as her weight had 'fluctuated' (i.e. gone up dramatically) again. But there were never any volunteers willing to wrap a tape measure around that marshmallow monster.

Mrs Gilmore was my English Literature teacher. There must have been times when the poor woman felt like I was stalking her; I'd track her down during afternoon breaks, even banging on the staff-room door, to insist she read my latest short story, which I'd hastily scribbled at lunchtime. It was her own fault; her passion was infectious, and it rubbed off on me.

I loved my P.E. teachers: Miss Fryer, with her contagious laugh, and Miss Dexter, who couldn't seem to make her mind up – when I was up a rope, she'd be telling me to come down; when I was down, she'd be telling me to climb up. She must have thought I was the Grand Old Duke of York.

To be fair, with the exception of Mrs Murray and Mrs Earl, all the teachers at Oxley High were nice, and I loved them.

The end-of-lesson beeps jerked me awake. Slightly dazed, I watched the other girls as they scraped back their chairs, placed their artwork in the drying racks, and left for lunch. I wondered whether I could be bothered to open my packed lunch; it was yet another Mammy's Special: rigor mortis paratha and cold congealed omelette. I'd have loved to have had the salmon fishcakes and chips from the canteen, but I was skint as usual.

Mrs Turner waited until the class was empty, then she slapped my homework book down on the desk in front of me.

'Well, madam, what exactly is this?' Her expression was bemused rather than stern.

'It's good, isn't it, Miss?'

'Oh yes, Dilly, it's very good. But when I asked you to draw something from your kitchen, I expected a free-hand sketch.'

'And?'

'Are you trying to tell me you drew this knife freehand?'

'Yes, Miss. I held it on the paper with one hand, and drew round it with my free hand.'

Mrs Turner shook her head in exasperation. 'I'm never going to make an artist out of you, am I? What were you thinking? You must have spent all of two minutes drawing this. Why is your homework always so rushed?'

I could have told her it was because in Sharnia the housework came first, and some nights I'd still be up at 3 a.m. trying to do my homework because I'd spent all evening helping my mother. So even if I managed to finish my homework, it was never very good because I was too tired to concentrate. But I didn't want Mrs Turner to know about my private life, so I just said: 'I had to be quick – my mam wanted the knife back to chop the onions with.'

'Next time I set you homework, I'm going to make sure it's something you can't trace around. Like a tree.'

I noticed she was staring at my fingers. 'Is there anything you want to tell me, Dilly?'

'Nothing, Miss.' There was no way I was going to run the risk of word getting back to my parents that I'd been talking about them behind their backs.

Chapter 51

In June 1981, Afeeka visited Bradford Royal Infirmary maternity unit. When she came home, she was carrying a little plastic wallet containing four ultrasound pictures. She was in shock – not only was she pregnant, but she was expecting twins.

The empty-bannocked Monkey took to swaggering around the house, with a permanent self-satisfied smirk on his face. He had a job working in a bakery, a wife, and now two little chimps were on the way. It was the happiest he'd been for years. Afeeka, on the other hand, looked miserable. The thought of having stretchmarks like Climax's filled her with horror. Her only consolation was that, surely, at least one of the babies would be a boy, and then she wouldn't have to go through the stress of childbirth again. She'd begged the midwife to tell her the sex of the foetuses, but the midwife just said, 'You've got to be joking; I know what you lot are like.'

When Mammy found out she was going to be a grandmother for the first time, she took gloating to new heights. For her, two good things had come out of the pregnancy. One, it was time to heave a sigh of relief and put away her blood pressure tablets; she knew there was no way Afeeka was going anywhere now she was up the duff. Two, she could hold her head up high in front of her friends again: her daughter-in-law had done her duty, and it was time to crow at all the women on our street who were unfortunate enough to have unmarried sons. Out came the knitting needles, and there were half-knitted cardigans and booties left conspicuously all around our kitchen whenever my mother's friends came calling. Even Naveeda, who still hadn't forgiven Afeeka for her rudeness, had been taken down a peg or two; both her sons were still single, and she was green with envy at being left at the starting post, while my mother took gold at the run-your-son's-life Olympics.

Chapter 52

The more time I spent with my friends at school the more I realized that my world was completely different from theirs. They didn't have to watch the evening news; they got to see programmes like *Top of the Pops* and *Dallas*, and they had posters on their walls of their favourite pop stars. I had a poster of Shakin' Stevens, hidden away inside my science book. If I'd put it on the bedroom wall, my mother would have ripped it and me to shreds.

I would listen silently to my friends, as they made their plans for the weekend. There was always someone visiting someone else, and more often than not they would all meet up in the town centre and then go shopping. I longed to be able to go with them, but it was out of the question.

I invited Tanya over one Sunday, so we could natter about Steve, but it was a disaster – it felt like visiting time in a prison; we had to sit in the front room, and my mother sat with us the whole time.

Tanya was really upset. When I invited her again, she refused, saying: 'My mum won't let me until you've been to ours.'

'But I can't,' I replied. 'I'm not allowed.'

'It's up to you, Dilly. If you can't come out then don't expect other people to drop what they're doing just to visit you.'

That evening, I appealed to Climax. I thought if she offered to chaperone me to Tanya's, I might be allowed to go. But she just told me that if I wanted to hire her as an escort I'd have to pay the going rate.

The next day in class, I told Sameena how hard it was for me to see my friends out of school. Sameena was a rebel who seemed to hate her life as much as I hated mine. She had a reputation as a hard-case, and was always in trouble with the teachers, so the other girls kept away from her. Sameena said she'd be happy to come over for tea one evening. I didn't have the heart to tell her she wouldn't be welcome in Sharnia because she was too westernized.

So it came as a bit of a shock when Sameena burst into my bedroom that evening. Her breath reeked of alcohol, and she was dressed like a Bananarama wannabe – miniskirt, lace and ribbons everywhere, bright pink lipstick and blue eye-shadow. I did a double-take. 'What the fuck?' I hissed, as she flopped down on my bed. Egg looked up from her homework in disbelief.

'I hate him,' Sameena said drunkenly. 'I'm fed up of my dad hitting me all the time.' She rolled over, buried her face in my pillow, and sobbed angrily.

Egg whispered to me, 'Who let her in?'

I shrugged my shoulders. 'Sameena,' I said, 'you shouldn't be here. You're gonna get us all into trouble. Go home.'

She sat up and stared at me. Her eye make-up had smudged all over her face.

'What sort of friend are you?' she asked accusingly.

'I could ask you the same thing, you silly tart,' I spat.

'Have you any idea how much shit we're in? Egg, go downstairs and humour Mammy. She's gonna kill us.'

Egg shot out of the room, squawking, 'Get rid of her, Dilly,' as she went.

'Your mum doesn't like me,' Sameena giggled. 'She tried to stop me coming up; she called me a bitch.'

'Hey, don't take it personally; I'm her daughter, and she calls me that all the time.'

'I need some money, Dilly,' she sobbed. 'Get your dad to lend me some – I'm gonna run away.'

My mother came stomping into the room. 'What's going on in here?' she demanded, shooting Sameena the dirtiest scowl she could muster.

'I came to see Dilly,' Sameena said. She looked my mother up and down. 'Have you got a problem with that?'

'Get out of my house,' my mother said instinctively, then frowned and asked: 'Who the hell are you, anyway?'

'I go to school with your daughter. I'm in her class.' Sameena pointed at me, then lay back on the bed and closed her eyes. 'I wish this sodding room would stop spinning.'

'Why are you dressed like a white woman?' Mammy asked. 'This is a respectable house; you're not welcome here. My God, if my husband sees you dressed like that, he'll have a fit.'

'I can wear what I want,' Sameena replied. 'It's a free country.'

'Don't you have anyone to control you?' my mother asked, glaring at her in disgust.

Sameena sat up slowly, gripping the side of the bed to steady herself. 'Mrs Shah, I have to tell you,' she said, as though she was a doctor, about to diagnose a mystery illness, 'you're too strict.'

My mother's mouth opened, but nothing came out.

'You're way too strict,' Sameena confirmed. 'Dilly told me.'

'Sameena, shut your face,' I said. 'Mammy, take no notice of her. She's lying.'

'Mrs S, calm down,' Sameena giggled.

'Leave right now!' my mother shouted. 'Get out of here!'

Sameena got to her feet, flung her arms round my mother's neck, and slurred, 'Lend us some money, Fatty – I'm gonna run away from home.'

'I'll do no such thing,' my mother hissed as she disentangled herself. 'You're a disgrace.'

Sameena shrugged. 'Ditto. I tell you what, Dilly, you were right: she's a cow.'

I'd heard enough. Grabbing Sameena by the arm, I led her out of the room.

'You've got no idea what you've just done,' I said, as she let me guide her downstairs. As I dragged her through the kitchen we ran into Climax, who was just coming in wearing her brown fake-fur coat.

Sameena shrieked. 'Dilly! Have you got a gun? There's a fucking grizzly coming for us!'

I didn't know whether to laugh or cry. Sameena clasped my wrist, and whispered, 'Sssh! I don't think it's seen us. Tiptoe as quietly as you can.'

I shoved her out through the garden and into the alley. 'You've gotta go, Sameena. I mean it. Fuck off. Go home,' I said. I slammed the gate, and bolted it.

Back in the kitchen, Mammy and Climax were waiting for me. It suddenly dawned on me that I'd abandoned

Sameena in the alley, at no point pausing to think about how she was going to get home. Oh well, that was her problem. What worried me was how I was going to get through the next few hours.

Chapter 53

'Can I keep her, Mammy?' I asked hopefully as I came waltzing through the gate into the back garden. I had my school bag in one hand, and my new little friend in the other. The scrawny-looking pigeon tried her best to escape, but I held on tight, and I could feel her heart thudding with fright.

My mother, who'd been busy pulling up coriander from the herb patch in the garden, stopped what she was doing and looked up.

'Where did you find that thing? And what's wrong with it?'

'She was in the alley,' I replied. 'She can't fly properly, and there's something wrong with her foot.'

'Don't you think it would be better to put it out of its misery?' Mammy asked. 'It looks like it's about to die anyway.'

'I wonder if Dr Johnson ever thinks that about you.'

'Don't be cheeky. If you want to keep it, it can stay in the shed.'

'Can't I keep her in my bedroom?' I pleaded.

'No bloody way! Shed or dead, your choice.'

I found an old budgie cage in the garden shed, and locked my new pet in it. She started to panic, flapping wildly and bashing herself against the bars.

'It's all right, Catch. Don't worry, everything's fine,' I cooed. 'Mummy's here; I'll look after you.'

I left her in the shed, and went upstairs to get changed out of my school uniform. I felt a bubble of excitement in my stomach – I had a pet! At last I had something to love. I hadn't felt this happy since my father had run away from home. I rummaged around the bedroom looking for some paper, and came across a back issue of *Philip in the Nude*, the newspaper that Egg and I had made, consisting mainly of drawings of Prince Philip with nothing on. I shoved it under my arm and headed downstairs.

I grabbed some stale paratha and ran down to the shed. I was glad to see that Catch had calmed down – she'd stopped flapping, and was hobbling slowly around her cage on her one-and-a-half legs.

I tore up the paper and scattered it on the bottom of the cage. Placing the paratha on top of the paper, I whispered, 'I'll be back later to bring you into the house, but you'll have to wait till Mammy's gone to bed.'

When Mammy asked me to get some meat from the freezer in the cellar, I refused. I hadn't been locked in there since the Great Escape, but I was still afraid of it.

'Ask Egg, she's not scared.'

'Egg? The invisible girl? I don't know what's got into her – she never has any time for me.'

'You know very well what's got into her, Mammy. She's a lazy cow and you always let her get away with it. I bet she's up there with Afeeka, talking bollocks as usual.'

My mother sent Poppy upstairs to fetch Egg. She was back within a minute.

'Egg says she's busy, and you're to tell Dilly to do whatever needs doing.'

'Well, this is going to be a brilliant dinner tonight, with no meat. One daughter's scared of the cellar, one's too lazy to come downstairs, and the other two are so small if they climbed into the freezer they'd never get out again.'

Poppy was sent for a second time. Moments later, she was back.

'Egg says she's still busy, and you're to get Dilly to do it.'

She was sent a third time. While Poppy was delivering the latest message, I asked my mother why she didn't just go and get Egg herself.

'Why should I?' she replied. 'I'm not here to run around after you lot. I've already got two holes in my arse from all the work I have to do. Now, if your father would get a stairlift installed, I'd be whizzing up and down all day.'

'If that had been me who was upstairs, you'd have come up and kicked the crap out of me by now.'

My mother was about to explain why she had different courses for different horses, when Poppy reappeared.

'Egg's in the toilet. I told her through the door that it's her last chance, and she said, "Whatever."'

My mother's face reddened. 'Get back up there and tell her she's to come down right now.'

'What, again?' moaned Poppy. 'Do I have to? I'm getting dizzy from all this upping and downing.'

She was sent for a fourth time. I couldn't work out what was going on in my mother's head. Why was she prepared to give Egg so many chances?

Poppy reappeared. 'Guess what?' she smiled. 'Egg's doing Afeeka's nails. She says she might be down in an hour or two, if she can be bothered, and you're not to cook anything special for her, 'cos she's not hungry.'

Poppy was sent a fifth time. I couldn't wait to see what the next excuse would be. It was amazing how long Egg's luck had held out.

Poppy returned. 'Egg said, "Piss off."'

I studied my mother's face; her cheeks had turned crimson, and her lips were pursed into a thin line. She angrily shouted upstairs, 'Egg, get down here! Now!'

'About time,' I thought. 'You should have done that ages ago.'

With no sign of life upstairs, she shouted again.

Climax came in from the back garden, carrying a bag of sweets. 'Hi, Gongal,' she said. 'Here, I got you a Flake. Don't bother cooking for me. I'm eating at Amina's tonight.'

'Why are you giving her chocolate?' I asked. 'She's already too fat to get up the stairs.'

'Will you shut up, Dilly,' my mother snapped. 'Climax, love, do me a favour. I'm sick to death of Egg. I must have called her a hundred times. Give her a slap, then send her down to me.'

'No problems, Gongal – I'm on to it.'

Climax strode manfully upstairs, with me hot on her heels. If there was any slapping going on, I wanted to watch. As we reached the landing, I heard raucous laughter coming from Monkey's room. As soon as Climax opened the door, the merriment ceased.

Climax was across the room in two strides. She seized Egg by the arm, hauled her up off the chair and slapped her face.

'Your Mammy wants you, so move.'

Egg stood her ground. 'You bastard!' she shouted.

Climax smiled as she slapped her across the face again. She was so much bigger and stronger than Egg that she might as well have been King Kong picking a fight with a twig. She frogmarched Egg across the room, and out onto the landing.

By the time I got downstairs, Egg was already in the kitchen screaming at my mother.

'It's no more than you deserve,' Mammy snarled. 'How many times have I called you down?'

'You never called me!' Egg shrieked.

'Five times! I sent your little sister up to get you five times!'

But when Poppy was interrogated, she just shrugged her shoulders and said she'd forgotten five times, because she'd been busy doing something else – and besides, she had a lot on her mind. She wasn't even punished.

This was adding insult to injury for Egg, who was already fuming from the slaps that Climax had given her.

She shouted, 'I'm sick to death of you, you're a crap mother.'

The next slap she got that afternoon was from Mammy. As Egg turned and ran from the kitchen, I had to admire the way she'd managed to get out of doing any house-work again. The meat was still in the freezer, and Egg was back upstairs.

My mother was shaking with fury. 'I'm going to make damn sure her father sorts her out. She can't talk to me like that.'

Half an hour later, Mammy got her chance. As soon as my father strolled nonchalantly into the house, asking,

'What's for dinner, Gongal?' my mother replied: 'Your dinner's in the freezer. Or you can eat that flea-ridden pigeon that Dilly locked in the shed.'

'Pigeon?' he enquired.

'Never mind that. I need to talk to you about Egg. She's out of control.'

But Daddy wasn't listening; he was only interested in seeing Catch. As he walked into the back garden, my mother spluttered indignantly behind him: 'Go on, then, don't answer me – I'm not worth it. All I'm here for is to put food on the table.'

'Better get started, then,' he replied. 'I'm starving.'

He spent the next ten minutes tending to Catch's foot. It didn't make sense to me – how could a man who was so violent towards his wife and children be so gentle and compassionate with this bird? As I watched him applying Elastoplast with love and care, I found myself wishing I was a pigeon so he'd be kind to me.

Meanwhile, my mother was scrambling eggs as psychopathically as she could. She looked as though she was trying to make a hole in the bowl with the fork.

'Don't bother with my tea just yet,' he told her. 'I'm popping out to Wickes to get some straw.'

'Why don't you take the damn thing to the BRI and see if you can get it a private ward? That bird's been in the shed five minutes, and it's getting more attention than I've ever had. I could drop dead right now, and you wouldn't give a shit.'

'How do you know – you've never done it,' he scoffed.

'What am I supposed to do with this food? It's almost ready.'

'Feed the kids. I'll be back later.'

My mother's shoulders sagged. She flopped down at the dining table, put her head in her hands, and sobbed. I fleetingly thought about giving her a cuddle, but I knew she'd push me away. Besides, I wasn't very good at all that touchy-feely crap, so I just left her to it.

Chapter 54

Somehow, I managed to make it to the end of the summer term without being expelled from Oxley High, even though I'd set fire to my ex-friend Rupi's eyebrows with a Bunsen burner. I got thumped by my chemistry teacher, Mr Bentley, for showing a total disregard for health and safety, but it didn't go any further.

For the first time in years, and despite the prospect of six weeks under house arrest, I was actually looking forward to the holidays. It was 1981, the year of the Royal Wedding, and I couldn't wait for 29 July, when Charles and Diana were going to get married in St Paul's Cathedral. Di-mania had taken the entire country by storm; I thought she was beautiful, so for months I'd collected every photograph of her that I could lay my hands on, and stuck them into a scrapbook I'd made at school.

Afeeka spent a lot of time in front of the TV, eating gherkins with salad cream, and watching every news item about the Royal couple with relish. One evening, she misunderstood a report on *Look North*, and thought the government had passed a law saying that all babies born that year had to be called Charles or Diana.

She was beside herself, and ran around the house, saying, 'Charles Shah? Diana Shah? I was thinking more along the lines of Amitabh or Rekha.'

I told her not to be so stupid, but she wouldn't listen.

We had a huge argument, which ended with her bursting into tears, and my mother so angry that she grabbed a kitchen knife, pushed me to the floor, sat on top of me, and shouted, 'Say sorry now, or I'll cut your tongue out!'

She was waving the knife around, and kept trying to grab my tongue.

It wasn't the first time my mother had threatened me with a knife, but it was the first time she'd done it to defend Afeeka. I wasn't only embarrassed; I was also deeply concerned about how much further my mother would be prepared to go just to keep Afeeka sweet.

Not long after the knife attack, my mother dragged my father down to Oak Lane to buy some white cotton fabric, which she said I was to make into a prayer shawl for her. She handed me a thick reel of gold Lurex thread, traced flowers on to the material, and then told me to keep my big trap shut and get on with the stitching. I loved embroidering that shawl; it was the most beautiful thing I'd ever made, and I beamed with pride when I presented it to my mother.

Two days later, Naveeda came round for a natter. Since Zarqa had moved to a bigger house on the other side of Bradford, Naveeda had become my mother's new best friend, and she often dropped in for a chat. On this occasion, she was wearing the shawl I'd made; she said my mother had given it to her as a present. I was so angry I cried, but when I confronted Mammy, she said she couldn't see what the problem was – it had been her shawl, so she could do what she wanted with it.

*   *   *

The impending Royal Wedding had created renewed demand for our *Philip in the Nude* newspaper, and we had our hands full churning out daily issues and charging five pence a copy. We spent most of the profits on orange Juicy Lucy ice lollies, and Egg started saving up to buy clothes for Afeeka's babies.

Fired up with inspiration at the success of *Philip in the Nude*, Egg decided she was going to carve out a career for herself as a romance novelist. She gave me her first manuscript to read, and I was seriously impressed – if a little baffled by a recurring feeling of déjà vu. It was only after I'd finished reading all one hundred pages that she told me she'd written it entirely by copying chunks from various Mills and Boon books that I'd given her. She was all ready to send her manuscript off to a publishing company in London, until I told her they'd put her in prison for theft. She threw her work in the bin, saying, 'What's the point if I can't copy it from someone else? What am I supposed to do? Make it up myself?' After that, she didn't write again, she just spent the summer hanging out with Afeeka, or playing in the garden with the twins.

Egg's writing career might have come to a premature end, but her creativity in dreaming up new ways of avoiding housework was flourishing, and the work rota became nothing more than a timetable to show when her next excuse was due.

Egg was a freeloader, but at least she wasn't a professional sick-note like Daisy.

I'd have loved to have been as sick as she was; the little diva even had her oranges warmed for her, because Mammy claimed that a cold orange might give her a chill. She was the only child in the family allowed to have peaches. The first time I saw a peach was when she was holding one. Daisy, being a spoilt brat, sat and ate half of it in front of me, then threw the other half in the bin.

No matter what Daisy said or did, she was never smacked. Mammy claimed it was because she was 'frail and of a delicate disposition' but I think it was because her skin was so sore that there was nowhere for anyone to hit her without leaving evidence.

Her true colours came to light one afternoon, when Toadie hammered on the front door: he'd caught Daisy helping herself to money from his cash register. When he threatened to press charges, Daddy just laughed and said, 'Toadie, don't be daft, can't you see the child's sick? I'll make sure it doesn't happen again. Help yourself to anything you want from the front garden.' Daisy got away with it, without so much as a slap or a telling off.

During the summer, Daddy became the Bird Man of Bradford. It all began innocently enough with Catch, and then Climax brought home a cockatiel one day, saying, 'It's name's BJ. Don't even ask where it came from.'

Daddy took an instant shine to BJ, whose cage got pride of place in the front room.

Not long afterwards, my father persuaded some of the men from the mosque to cancel a cock fight they'd been planning – he told them they had no right to force animals to fight each other for their entertainment, and he'd be happy to buy the birds off them. I don't know if it was the moral or the financial argument that convinced them, but either way we ended up with two cockerels in the garden shed, making unbearable noise from dawn till dusk. When my mother complained, my father told her to shut up, and she said he'd made it quite clear to her where she came in the pecking order. But when he said he was going to get some hens as well, she made such a fuss that he decided not to push his luck for the time being.

Then Tommy from Number 31 sold Daddy a cage full of innocent-looking finches. The cage went on the passage floor, where my mother would trip over it on a daily basis, while trying to vacuum up all the spilt Trill. The finches were incredibly noisy little things, chattering away non-stop until the cover went over the cage at night. Daddy was always the first person up in the mornings and he'd make a point of removing the finches' cover, to make sure they woke everyone else up with their incessant twittering. It got to the stage where I couldn't take it any more, so I left the cage door open one night, hoping they'd escape. The end result was even better than I could have imagined: a rat from the cellar got into the cage, and killed them all. When my parents saw the carnage the next morning, my father blew his top, while my mother did a happy little jig, and offered a reward of five pounds to whoever had left the cage open. For once, I kept my big mouth shut.

Daddy's favourite birds may have been slaughtered indiscriminately, but mine was positively thriving. My father had clipped Catch's wings so she couldn't fly very far, but he needn't have bothered, because she never showed the slightest interest in going anywhere. She'd set up her home in Sharnia, and seemed more than happy pottering about in the shed, or sunning herself in the garden. She was so tame she'd sit on my shoulder when she felt like it, and if she wanted to come into the house, she'd tap on the kitchen window with her beak until someone opened the door and let her in.

As the holidays wore on, Afeeka became more and more difficult to be around. She spent most of her time with her head in the toilet, probably wondering who Armitage Shanks was. I tried to cheer her up by persuading Egg to hide a toy tarantula under Afeeka's pillow, but judging from the screams that came from Monkey's room, I don't think it helped much.

Apart from the Royal Wedding and playing with Catch, the summer holidays were shit, and I was glad to get back to school in September. On the first day of term, Catch watched me set off in the morning, and when I got back home in the afternoon she was sitting on the windowsill outside my bedroom. As soon as she saw me, she flew down, landed on my shoulder, and cooed a pigeon 'hello'; after that, she did the same thing every school day.

By now, Afeeka was heavily pregnant, and everyone, except my father and Climax, was very excited about the birth.

When Monkey brought home a double buggy from Mothercare, Mammy, who'd only ever carried her babies on her hip, almost fainted at the price, saying she couldn't believe something like that could cost more than a hundred pounds. Afeeka, who'd never seen a pram before in her life, suddenly became Lady of the Manor and, from then on, everything had to come from Mothercare.

Throughout her pregnancy, Afeeka received letters from Nonna, all carrying the same message: she didn't see why she should miss out on the birth, and she wanted her daughter back to have her babies in Pakistan. Every letter caused a row between Afeeka and my mother. Afeeka would say, 'I'm going home,' and my mother would say, 'Oh no, you're not.'

But when Afeeka was eight months pregnant, she finally made up her mind: she was going back to Pakistan to have the babies, and absolutely nothing would persuade her otherwise. We were in the kitchen when she broke the news to my mother, who just said: 'How are you going to get there, you idiot? They won't let you on a plane in your condition.'

This had obviously never occurred to Afeeka, who looked stunned.

'Why not?' she asked. 'Do the babies need travel documents? I've got photos of them from the hospital. Will they make me buy three tickets?'

My mother put her head in her hands, and mumbled, 'Let's hope the babies take after their father.'

'I need my mummy to hold my hand,' Afeeka said. 'I can't do this without her.'

'Why are you making such a fuss?' I asked. 'All you're gonna do is open your legs. It'll be like doing a big crap. Can I watch when you give birth?'

'Urgh, you're sick,' Afeeka replied. 'Do you think I'm going to do it in front of an audience?'

'Why not? I've seen it all before.'

'When?' Afeeka enquired in surprise.

'They showed us a video in Biology. This woman had a baby. It was gross – I nearly threw up.'

'What? You saw it in school?' she asked in amazement. 'That's disgusting.'

'You're telling me,' I said. 'There was loads of water, then the woman started screeching and swearing, and then you could see the top of the baby's head in the woman's fanny, which is when the bleeding started. Then the baby came out, and it was purple and all scrunched-up.'

Afeeka sat in silence, eyes wide open, as I continued: 'And then the best bit was when they cut the cord with a pair of scissors.'

'Now I know you're lying,' Afeeka said. 'That's not what happens; whoever heard of anything so stupid?'

Chapter 55

It was a bitterly cold November evening when Egg and I got home from Oxley High to find my mother in a state of panic.

'Afeeka's not well,' she sobbed.

'What's up with her?' I asked, not sure I wanted to hear the answer. 'Has the doctor been? Have you called an ambulance?'

'I was waiting for you to come home,' she said pathetically.

I dashed upstairs to Monkey's room. My mother waddled behind me, wailing, 'Oh my God.'

Afeeka was writhing on the bed, crying in agony. She was dripping with sweat.

'Dilly, I think I'm dying,' she wept.

'I'm gonna get you an ambulance,' I said, trying to disguise the fear that was gripping me.

I raced back downstairs and phoned Dr Johnson, who said he'd send an ambulance straight away; Afeeka was to be kept as calm as possible, and not given anything to eat or drink.

Back upstairs, I found Mammy busily forcing Afeeka to swallow Disprins dissolved in water; I snatched the beaker out of her hand and tossed it across the room.

*   *   *

Half an hour later, Afeeka was still screaming with the pain and Mammy was wailing, 'She's dying. God forgive her, she's with children' and there was still no sign of an ambulance.

When the doorbell finally rang, it was my father who strode in, with the midwife close behind.

The midwife said a curt 'Hello' and ushered Mammy and me downstairs while she examined Afeeka. A minute later, she came flying down, grabbed the phone and made a call.

'Where's the ambulance?' she asked in a calm but forceful voice. 'Get it here now.' She reeled off some blood pressure readings, and then said: 'Half an hour's no good. I need it here now.'

Then the bell rang again. This time it was the emergency doctor. He and the midwife hurried upstairs.

As my father and I retreated to the kitchen, he asked me in a quivering voice, 'What's wrong with her? And where the hell is Climax?'

'I don't know,' I said. I nodded in the direction of my mother, who was sitting at the table with her head in her hands. 'You'd better ask Mammy.'

But my mother was in no state to take part in an interrogation. She just muttered 'My God' to herself, over and over.

The midwife called from upstairs: 'Mr Shah, we can't wait for the ambulance. We're taking her to the hospital. Are you coming with us?'

He was about to reply when the doorbell rang again, and this time it was the ambulance crew. A few minutes later, Afeeka was strapped to a stretcher and on her way to hospital.

'Come on, Gongal, we've got to go,' my father urged. 'Be quick. I'll wait for you in the car.'

My mother put her hand to her breast. 'I don't think I can go – my legs feel wobbly.'

'Well, you'll just have to wobble to the car, then,' he snapped as he headed outside.

'Monkey's going to blame me for this, I know he is,' my mother lamented. 'He'll say I killed her. He's never going to forgive me.'

'I can't believe you didn't call for an ambulance,' I said.

My mother replied in a feeble half-whisper, 'I didn't know how to.'

'Mammy!' I exploded, thinking it was very bad taste to be joking at a time like this. 'Are you kidding me?'

'Since when have I known how to use the phone?' she sobbed.

'All you have to do is dial nine three times!' I shouted. 'It's not exactly rocket science, even for you.'

She scowled but said nothing. I desperately wanted to argue with her about the benefits of an education, but I could hear the car horn blasting from the street, and I knew I'd have to wait until the next time she told me that going to school was a waste of time.

'Look,' I said, 'just go.' I grabbed her coat and veil, shoved them in her hand, and pushed her to the door as fast as I could.

The car horn was now blaring constantly. As I looked out, I was momentarily taken aback: it looked as though the whole of Bradford had turned up to see what was going on, and there were hordes of people milling about on the pavement, or watching from windows. The Shahs couldn't even do childbirth quietly.

Chapter 56

The next day, my mother had some urgent business to attend to. Her agenda was as follows:

1) Check what had happened to the bedding that had been soaked when Afeeka's waters broke.

I told her it was all still on the bed, and she told me I was a lazy cow.

2) Attract the attention of neighbours.

She wrapped up warm, and strutted up and down the garden path, making as much noise as possible; this involved slamming the shed door and the back gate, and lifting the bin lid and dropping it back with a clatter, all the while singing loudly to herself.

3) Prepare for visitors.

She ordered Egg and me to tidy the place up. Then she sat herself down in the kitchen and waited.

4) Hold court.

Ten minutes later, the back gate opened, and in came Naveeda (wearing the shawl I'd made for my mother), her daughter Billi, and the elusive Mrs Baba, who'd been given a day pass by her husband. They were invited in, given tea and biscuits, and fed stories of how my mother had bravely and single-handedly saved two babies' lives after one of them had decided to come into the world feet first. I'd been commanded to keep my big mouth shut, on pain of death; so I brought Poppy's old Fisher-Price telephone downstairs, put it on the dining table, and pretended to make phone calls. Mammy told her friends to ignore me, because I was clearly mental.

Wave upon wave of visitors called, all wanting to know about the babies, and tutting with disappointment when they found out that both of them were girls. The kitchen was filled with throngs of women, all saying 'never mind', 'she can try again in a few months' and 'girls this time, boys next time'. In between shooting me 'wait till these people have gone – that phone's going up your arse' looks, my mother took great pains to tell everyone that she was thrilled to have two granddaughters. Even girls were a gift from God, she reminded them; and further-more, didn't they know the Shahs were trailblazers? Apparently, although I hadn't realized it until that day, we were a new breed of Asian, who loved boys and girls equally. After all, hadn't my mother herself been blessed with four wonderful daughters? None of the visitors had the balls to say, 'No, Gongal, you've got three wonderful daughters and Dilly,' but I'm pretty sure that's what they were all thinking.

Once all the well-wishers had gone, Daddy said, 'Come on, we're off to the hospital.' We piled into the car as only an Asian family can, two in the front and a scrum in the back, with everyone trying to get a window seat. My mother told us to stop fussing, and didn't we know that they can get six people on a motorbike in Pakistan.

As soon as I set eyes on my new baby nieces, I was smitten – Gadafi and Zia were absolutely gorgeous. I wanted to pick them up and cuddle them, but they were in the special care unit, and the nurse wouldn't let us touch them.

Everyone in the family cooed adoringly at the new twins, and I could already tell that here were two little girls who were going to be spoilt rotten as soon as they got home to Sharnia.

Afeeka was distraught. She kept saying, 'All that pain for nothing. Two babies and not one dick between them.'

Climax voiced what I'm sure my parents were thinking: 'How the mighty have fallen. It looks like you'll just have to go through it all again and again, until you get it right.'

Chapter 57

I always thought that Monkey would end up a psycho like my father, but he proved me wrong by becoming the soppiest, most attentive dad on our street. His daughters were now the centre of his universe in a way that Afeeka never was, and never would be.

Unfortunately for Afeeka, Gadafi and Zia didn't seem to need much sleep, and the endless broken nights soon began to take their toll. Egg and I became unpaid live-in nannies and nappy-changers, while Afeeka caught up on her sleep, or lay in bed, crying dramatically and being oh-so depressed about her stretchmarks, her Caesarean scar and the shadows that had stolen across her face from lack of sleep.

It didn't take Daddy long to work out that he was now single-handedly supporting eight losers and two babies, without so much as a penny's contribution from anyone. He demanded to know where Monkey's salary was going, and it turned out Afeeka was sending most of it to Nonna – which was very nice of her, but it didn't seem to go down too well with my father. So, after a few heated arguments over housekeeping, Monkey agreed to start paying a third of each gas bill. This was a small victory for my father, but a huge disaster for everyone else, because Afeeka got into the habit of sneakily turning the boiler temperature right down, and bath time became a race to get clean before the hot water ran out.

When Gadafi and Zia were a few weeks old, Afeeka began to make noises about taking them to Pakistan for a holiday. Mammy had convinced herself that, once the babies were born, Afeeka's yearnings for home would be a thing of the past, and she would, at last, settle down to a life in England. How wrong she was: the twins' arrival just added fuel to the flames of Afeeka's homesickness. She spent a lot of time writing to Nonna, and each letter that arrived from Pakistan begging Afeeka to return home would cause another argument to erupt between her and my mother.

Eventually, Afeeka announced her mind was made up: she was going. Once word got around, the shopping lists began to arrive from Pakistan, and she was off to town to spend money like it was going out of fashion. Monkey's pay was squandered on anything with a flashy label that might impress the folks back home: clothes from Marks & Spencer, gold from Ratner's, French perfume from a market stall in John Street, packets of Yeoman mashed potato powder, imitation silver necklaces (five for a pound), plastic flip-flops, even batwing sweaters from Begum, the street's supplier of all things crap.

The more Afeeka planned her holiday, the more irate Mammy became. Not only was Afeeka refusing to be controlled, but all my mother's friends were sniggering. Suddenly, every woman on our street knew how to control a wayward daughter-in-law, and they all wanted to pass their extensive knowledge on to my mother. Naveeda said that 'a daughter-in-law shouldn't be allowed to go back to Pakistan until she's had at least six kids', whereas

Batool, the old crone next door, advised my mother to take a harder line: 'The only way to keep a daughter-in-law in her place is to slap her around until she obeys.' I don't think my mother ever tried slapping Afeeka around, though I'm sure the thought must have entered her head – it certainly entered mine often enough. The combined efforts of Naveeda, Batool and all the other tea-sipping visitors certainly increased the tension in the house, but they didn't actually change anything – Afeeka was going, end of story.

Afeeka always maintained that she was going to Pakistan for only a month, but she was secretly planning an altogether longer vacation. I think her real objective was to take Gadafi and Zia back home and live there permanently, while Monkey stayed in Bradford and sent her money. But she hadn't counted on the shambolic state of British bureaucracy in 1982; she was told that, because she didn't have a British passport, she could only be out of the country for a maximum of three months. If she stayed in Pakistan any longer than that, she might not be allowed back into Britain without having to go through masses of paperwork, which could take years. So Afeeka decided to keep things simple by applying for a British passport. When she was told it would be ten years before she got one, she ran about the house, shrieking, 'Ten years! Ten bloody years! I can't stay in this shit hole for ten more years!'

My mother's sniggering knew no bounds. Every now and then, she'd wind Afeeka up by making comments like, 'They don't give out passports like sweets, you know'; and 'Everyone's in such a rush these days; whatever happened to patience?'

But Afeeka decided that three months in Pakistan was better than nothing, and off she went, dragging a reluctant Monkey behind her.

Four weeks later, they were back. Monkey was full of stories about his holiday:

1) Afeeka's mother, Nonna, was the sweetest person he'd ever met; he said it wasn't fair that someone as kind and caring as her should have such a hard life.
2) Afeeka had only made things worse – she just dumped the twins on Nonna, and went off shopping with her friends for hours on end.
3) Monkey had loved every minute of his stay in Chowki. He hadn't wanted to come back.
4) Afeeka had tried to persuade Monkey to let her stay on without him for a few more weeks, but he didn't trust her to come back at all – and besides, it wasn't fair on Nonna.
5) He was planning on doing regular overtime so he could send more money to Nonna, because if anyone needed it she did.

Whereas stories one to five were happily shared with the whole family in the back room, Monkey reserved the final stories until he could get me on my own.

6) Afeeka's father, Samir, was suffering from senile dementia. There were times when he couldn't remember who he was, and he had trouble recognizing his own wife and children. Nonna even had to brush his teeth for him. Every morning, he'd shuffle

to the bus stop, but by the time the bus came he'd forgotten why he was there. The doctor had said that there was no chance of him recovering; it was downhill all the way.

7) My fiancé, Adam, was the village idiot. He made Afeeka look like Brain of Britain. He spent most of the day sitting in a field, watching the corn dancing in the breeze.

'Don't mention a word of this to anyone, Dilly,' Monkey said. 'Mammy and Afeeka made me promise not to tell you, but it's only fair you know what they're getting you into.'

From the kitchen window, I could see my mother pegging out the washing in the sunshine. Catch was sitting on the wall, Poppy was cycling up and down the path, Egg was digging up some weeds, and Daisy was dangling her teddy bear from the washing line. It was a picture of domestic bliss; and while they were all happily going about their business, I could feel myself slowly wilting with defeat.

Chapter 58

Egg and I came home from school one afternoon to find my mother holding a bundle of Adam Ant posters in her hand.

'Hey, those are mine,' Egg squeaked as she tried to grab the posters.

'It's good of you to admit it,' my mother hissed, pushing Egg away. 'You've saved me the trouble of finding out who they belong to.'

She tore the posters up. 'I won't have this garbage in my house. I don't send you to school so you can drool over men, you whore.'

'Come on, Mammy, it's not such a big deal,' I said.

'Shut your mouth, Dilly.' She shot me an accusing look. 'Have you got any?'

'No, I haven't,' I sniffed, offended. How dare she suggest I had a crush on a loser like Adam Ant?

My mother turned her attention back to Egg. 'How many more have you got?' she asked.

'None,' came the reply.

She slapped Egg's face. 'How many?'

'None.'

'I'm going to tell your father.'

'Why?'

'He needs to know what you get up to when you're meant to be at school.'

'Mammy, please don't tell him,' Egg begged. 'He doesn't need to know.'

'What's the problem, Mammy?' I asked. 'It's only Adam Ant. Anyway, all the girls at school have got posters.'

My mother kept her attention firmly on Egg. 'If you didn't know it was wrong, why did you hide them?' she demanded, apparently unashamed that she'd just confessed to snooping around our room while we were at school. It was odd how my mother rarely had time to do the housework, but had plenty of time to spend on her hobbies, like snooping and being annoyed.

When Egg didn't answer, my mother pushed her out of the way and struggled up the stairs. We followed her into our room, where she proceeded to tip the contents of all the drawers onto the floor. When she couldn't find anything incriminating, she lifted up the mattresses and looked underneath them.

'I know you've got some more hidden somewhere,' she said as she put her hands on her hips and surveyed the room for likely hiding places. 'So where are they?'

'I told you, I haven't got any,' Egg said. 'The only ones I had were the ones you just tore up.'

'I know you're lying. If you ever bring pictures of a man into my house again, I'm going to kill you,' she said. 'I mean it. I'm not having it, do you hear me?' She slapped Egg across the face again, shot me a vicious look, said, 'Clean up this mess,' and stomped out of the room.

'Where are they?' Egg whispered conspiratorially.

'On top of Monkey's wardrobe,' I whispered back.

When my father came home, my mother wasted no time in telling him what had happened, and he wasted no time in deciding that Egg and I were no longer to be trusted. So, from now on, our bags were to be searched before and after school. I wondered if Sharnia could get any more like a prison. What would be next? Pyjamas with arrows on them? Bars on the windows? Guard dogs?

That night, as I lay in bed, I felt quite depressed with the state of my life. In fifteen years, I'd never been on holiday; I'd never been on a plane or a train; I'd never seen a pantomime or been to the theatre or the cinema; I'd never been ice-skating or ten-pin bowling. I'd been to the seaside only once, and that was on a school trip. I'd never even been to a café, never mind a restaurant.

For most of my childhood, my father had promised to take me to the zoo, and every weekend for years I'd skipped around the back garden singing, 'Daddy's taking me to the zoo tomorrow . . .' But the only wild animals I'd ever seen were the ones I was living with, and what I should have been singing was, 'Daddy's telling me more lies tomorrow . . .'

Chapter 59

'I came top in English,' I said to the back of my father's head. He gave no indication he'd heard me above the sound of the February rain splattering against the windscreen, and the depressing whine of the wipers as they rattled up and down. He took a sharp corner on two wheels, and Egg and I involuntarily slid sideways along the back seat. Like the *Millennium Falcon*, our orange Datsun Sunny didn't look like much, but she sure had it where it counted.

'Mrs Gilmore says I'm doing really well,' I called out to Shah Solo in the front seat.

'You're not going.'

'But, Daddy . . .'

'It's inappropriate for a girl of your age.'

'Everyone else is going.'

'Everyone else can go to hell.'

'Mrs Gilmore says I have to see it, or I'll fail the exam.'

'That woman should be ashamed of herself. No daughter of mine is going to see *Romeo and Juliet*.'

The journey home from the after-school cookery club was strained, and I was glad when Daddy brought the car to an unruly halt at the top of the back alley. He revved the engine impatiently as he waited for us to get out. I watched the car as it disappeared around the corner, and felt like screaming with anger and frustration. The way my father was going on about it, anyone would have thought that Shakespeare was X-rated. I desperately wanted to do well at school, especially in English; but how could I, when I was always being held back by my bloody-minded parents? It wasn't fair. All I wanted to do was watch a play, but no matter how much I scratched my head, I couldn't think of a way to change his mind.

'I hate that man; he's so stubborn,' I said to Egg as we walked down the alley.

'You might as well accept it, Dilly, you're never gonna see it,' she replied. 'He's made his mind up, and I bet you any money he won't back down.'

I let her go in front of me and she karate-kicked the gate open. She stopped in her tracks just inside the garden, and I heard her gasp.

'Move your butt,' I said, keen to get a word in with my mother about the play.

Reluctantly, she stepped to one side.

Catch was lying motionless in the middle of the path. I ran over and knelt down beside her. As I scooped her up in my hands, her head lolled to one side, and I could see a blood-stained hole in her neck. Blood was gently oozing from the wound, matting her feathers. She was still warm, but I knew she was dead. It felt as though an icy hand was clutching my heart, as I knelt there on the path, holding Catch's pathetic lifeless form, bawling my eyes out.

Egg crouched down beside me, looking sad and bewildered.

'She's been shot,' I said between violent sobs. 'Someone shot my baby.'

I looked down at the path where Catch had lain. There was a little red puddle, where her blood had mixed with the rain.

Climax came out into the garden. 'I see you've found it, then,' she said. 'Mark shot it.'

'And you didn't do anything?' I shouted. 'You just stood and watched?'

'What sort of fool do you think I am? He had a gun, for God's sake. What if he'd shot me? The bird just got unlucky. When fortune turns against you, even jelly breaks your teeth. It's only a bloody pigeon; leave it in the garden – let one of the cats have it.'

'You've got no compassion,' I cried.

'Bloody hypocrite. I don't remember you offering me any comfort when Doc left me. But now your vermin's dead, you expect me to act like it's the end of the world?'

I was so angry, I couldn't control myself. 'Doc left you because he hates you, you fat old man!'

My fury rapidly turned to panic as Climax came thundering towards me, fists clenched. I was expecting her to hit me, but instead she grabbed Catch out of my hands and slapped me across the face with the dead bird. Blood splattered everywhere.

'Cheeky little bastard,' she growled.

She was about to slap me again when Daddy ran into the garden and started to give her a lecture about treating animals with dignity and respect.

'Shah, for God's sake, stop your preaching,' she interrupted. 'It's a fucking pigeon. Get over it.'

Chapter 60

In June 1983, my parents told me they were planning a trip to Mecca for the Hajj, and they wanted me to go with them. I was delighted – at the age of sixteen, I'd still never been abroad. For the first time in my life, I was able to tell my classmates that I was going away for the summer.

My mother bought yards of white cotton from Attique Cloth House in Oak Lane and spent hours cutting out burkas and salvaar kameez suits for the two of us. As I was now adept with the sewing machine, thanks to Mrs Dobbs' needlework lessons, my mother asked me to stitch up all the clothes that we needed for the trip. Although it was a lot of hard work, and took many hours, the eager anticipation made it enjoyable.

When all the clothes were washed and dried, Mammy told me to iron them and give them to Egg, as my parents had decided to take her instead.

I was too upset to speak. Holding back tears, I headed off into the back garden. It was a lovely afternoon, and Sultan, Batool's cat, was sunning himself on the wall. I kissed him on the head, but he was too busy doing nothing even to acknowledge my existence.

I felt a pang of envy as I heard the chatter of children playing in the alley. Those children didn't understand what it was like to be a prisoner like me, but the little girls would be finding out for themselves, soon enough. I wondered if, when I had daughters of my own, I'd lock them in the house, the same as my mother had done to me. It seemed to me that my only hope would be to find a husband who wasn't too strict, one who wanted his children to be free. In other words, nothing like my own father.

I heard a noise from the house, and turned to see my mother tapping on the window and motioning me to go back in. I knew the look on her face well enough, just as I knew that within the next few seconds she'd be saying to me, 'What the hell were you doing out there? There's work to be done in here; get on with it.'

I left the cat to its easy slumber, and traipsed sullenly back into the house for yet another fun-filled afternoon in HMP Sharnia.

The summer holidays that year were crap. Most of the time, it felt as though I was just muddling through, waiting for the pilgrims to return. Climax spent all her time in Dewsbury, and, as expected, all the housework became my responsibility. Afeeka seemed quite content to let me get on with it, while she stayed in her room, watching Indian videos and giving makeovers to her infant daughters.

Whenever I had time, I'd amuse myself by sitting in the window, watching the street below. More often than not, the local eccentric, Frontcrawl-Man, would be walking up and down, pretending he was swimming, pursued by a posse of laughing kids. Or Rita would be leaning over her gate chatting amiably with Mary Mumbleweed, while Hepburn limped around the garden, yapping in vain for attention.

And there'd be Daisy and Poppy. If they weren't indoors watching TV, they'd be playing with Doc's old skateboard, or hopscotching on the pavement, while Billi zoomed in between the parked cars on her little red scooter.

Sometimes Scully's mum, Lana, the most glamorous woman on the street, would be hanging out her washing, dressed in tight-fitting clothes that left little to the imagination. In warm weather, her blouse would always be knotted at the front to show off her toned midriff. When Lana was reaching up to peg and bending down to grab, the street's normal activities ground to a sudden halt, and didn't resume until she'd gone back indoors.

Then there'd be fat Mr Baba and skinny Mr Ali, the Two Ronnies of Gomshall Road, standing by the lamp-post outside the mosque, deep in conversation. And Lulli, in clown-sized shoes, who'd be running frantically back and forth across the road, delivering milk in the middle of the afternoon, always in his curry-coloured duffle coat, no matter what the weather.

Occasionally, the Playspace camper van would turn up, and a horde of eager children would gather to cheer wildly, while half a dozen long-haired hippies performed street theatre to the sound of 'Echoes'.

In the late afternoon, Gabby and her high-heeled prostitute friends could be seen teetering off to their hunting grounds in Lumb Lane, wearing fluorescent boob tubes and impossibly short skirts. As soon as they emerged from their bedsits, all conversations would stop, and many heads would be shaken in disapproval, but their wiggling arses would be studied intently all the way up the street.

Towards the end of August, Monkey chaperoned me to school to get my exam results. I was the proud owner of one O Level (English Language) and six CSEs (Applied Science, Arithmetic, Dress & Needlecraft, English Literature, Home Management and Humanities). Not brilliant, but good enough to enrol for the Sixth Form. I knew Mammy would be furious when she got back from Mecca – she'd made it quite clear that the Fifth Form was as far as my education would go – but I went ahead and did it anyway.

When I got home, Afeeka was sitting in the back garden, sobbing quietly into a handkerchief while both pairs of twins played in the playpen that Monkey had made. She said she'd just got off the phone to Adam. Apparently, he was desperate to get married, and now that I was sixteen and finished with school, could we please set a date?

Afeeka asked me what message she should pass on to Adam.

I told her to tell him to go and fuck himself.

Chapter 61

At last, Egg was back! While my parents set about unpacking, I took her to one side and handed her a quarter of pear drops. I told her how much I'd missed her, and asked her if she felt any different now she'd completed the Hajj. She said she hadn't enjoyed the experience; she didn't feel any different mentally; she was fed up of camel meat and cheese, and my mother had run her ragged with constant demands to fetch and carry for her. She said she was glad to be home.

All summer, I'd been harbouring a faint hope that the trip to Mecca would change my mother for the better – some hope. Within minutes of arriving, she was rubbing her finger along the work surfaces, and tutting. Her first words to me were: 'This house is filthy. What the hell did you do all summer? I bet you didn't clean it once while I was away, you lazy cow.'

I wanted to tell her she should be pointing the finger of blame at Climax and Afeeka, who hadn't done a thing to help me, but I didn't get a chance; Daisy gleefully told Mammy that Poppy had been having nightmares because I'd let them watch the *Thriller* video. My mother accused me of being negligent as well as useless. Then Batool and Naveeda arrived to offer my mother congratulations on performing the Hajj, and wanted to know if she'd brought them any gifts.

When they finally left – clutching bottles of holy water, packets of dates and cartons of henna powder – my mother spent hours deep in conversation with Afeeka. Eventually, I managed to get her on her own. She was in the kitchen, stuffing huge chewy Saudi dates into her mouth. When it suited her, her blood pressure ruled all our lives; at other times, she didn't give a damn. She'd been ordered to limit her calorie intake, but I knew it was a waste of time saying anything.

As she devoured yet another date, I told her about the conversation I'd had with Afeeka, and that there was no way I was marrying Adam.

'Your marriage isn't negotiable,' she replied. 'Now stop giving me earache, and help me weigh out these dates.'

We filled paper packets for distribution to the neighbours, and I asked her what she and Afeeka had been talking about.

In a hushed voice, she told me I was to leave Afeeka alone, because she was going through a very difficult time. Her father wasn't well, and her mother was struggling to look after him on her own, because Adam was always busy on the farm. Mammy announced that she'd decided it would be best for everyone if the wedding was brought forward, so I could go to Pakistan and help Nonna. She promised me this arrangement was temporary, and that as soon as Samir was up and about, I could come back to Bradford while Adam waited for his visa.

I was grateful to Monkey. If it hadn't been for him, I would have swallowed this story without question; my mother was such a convincing liar. I wondered what had persuaded him to tell me the truth about Samir and Adam, even though he must have known it would eventually get him into trouble with his wife. A long time ago, I'd lumped him into the 'bully' category along with Webster. What had mellowed him so much? Was it because he had children of his own that he'd started to consider other people's feelings?

Mammy continued: 'Wait until you see Nonna's farm in Chowki, Dilly – it's absolutely beautiful. You'll love Pakistan . . .'

I'd heard enough.

'Please, stop talking crap. Adam's an idiot. Samir's senile. And you're a liar.'

There was a gasp behind me; I hadn't heard Afeeka come in.

'My father? Senile? What are you talking about?' she squeaked.

'Monkey told me everything,' I replied. 'I know your dad's demented.'

Both women looked at me in surprise, then looked at each other.

Afeeka burst into tears. 'Auntie!' she sobbed. 'She'll never go now.'

'Damn right!' I shouted. 'Find yourself another mug.'

'You can't do this to me, Dilly. We had an agreement. I'm here, so now you have to go to Pakistan.'

'Mammy made the agreement. If she's so keen to help Nonna out, she's welcome to do it herself. After all, Samir's her brother – I don't even know the bloke.'

My mother flew at me; her fist struck me on the jaw. Before I could do anything to defend myself, she was all over me. I tried to push her away, but she was too heavy. She just kept hitting me wherever she could land a blow.

I started crying, not because of the pain – I was used to that – but because of the injustice.

'You're nothing but trouble,' she panted as she stepped back, satisfied that she was victorious: she'd made me cry. 'You ask for it, Dilly – you don't know when to stop.'

Chapter 62

In September 1983, Daddy faced a dilemma, and it was all because of Egg. She was about to start in the Fifth Form at Oxley High, and couldn't legally be removed for another year. My father didn't trust her to behave, so he needed someone to keep an eye on her while she was out of the house.

He asked Climax if she would be willing to escort Egg to and from school, but she just told him to get lost.

So, as it turned out, there was only one person who could do the job. After much pacing of the floor, Daddy announced he'd had a marvellous idea, and said I could go back to school, provided I made sure that Egg behaved herself. If I could guarantee that Egg would keep her scarf on her head, stay on the school premises all day, stay away from boys and study hard, he would guarantee that I could do my A Levels. But if I let him down, it would be me, not Egg, who would be paying the price.

When he told my mother of his decision, there was uproar.

'It's time to keep our side of the bargain,' she shrieked. 'Nonna's waited long enough. What the hell am I supposed to tell her?'

'Tell her I make the decisions around here,' he replied quietly, and strolled out of the kitchen.

Without him to shout at, my mother rounded on me.

'I've been waiting forever for you to finish at that blasted school. We need to make plans for your future.'

'This is a plan for my future!' I replied.

I knew that my only realistic prospect of ever escaping from my parents was by getting enough qualifications so that I could become financially independent. Of course, I couldn't tell her that, so – frustratingly – I had to lie, by pretending that my interest in education was purely so that I could be a better person. She accused me of arrogance and laziness; in her eyes, I was deliberately avoiding my responsibilities at her expense, or, as she put it, 'riding on her back to glory'.

When Afeeka heard the news, she burst into tears; whatever plans she'd made for my future were slipping like sand through her fingers.

'Auntie, you can't go back on your word,' she sobbed.

'What can I do, Afeeka? It's only for another year.'

'But she's got to go now. Mummy needs her, she can't cope with Daddy on her own.'

'Your mummy can go to hell,' I shouted.

'You're going to be the death of me,' my mother said, and she grabbed hold of a steel ladle and brought it crashing down on my head.

Pain hissed through me. Here we go again, I thought to myself as I sat in silent defiance and let her hit me for a second time. It made her even madder.

'Look at her, Afeeka. She's so stubborn, she just sits there and takes it.'

Afeeka smirked as my mother raised the ladle again, but before she could bring it down on my head for a third time I reached out and wrenched it from her hand.

Turning to Afeeka, I said, 'How would you feel if one of your daughters was being treated the way I'm being treated? Look at your girls, and then imagine them in my place.'

Afeeka started to say something, had second thoughts, then fell quiet.

Chapter 63

It was spring 1984 when Daddy came waltzing into the back garden, carrying the latest addition to the Shah family: a brown and white baby goat. He said I could keep it as a pet.

Mammy wasn't happy. 'Next it'll be a bloody camel. This isn't Pakistan – people are going to complain.'

'Let the girl raise it,' Daddy said. 'It's nice to have some reminders of home.'

Egg cooed. 'Aw, it's so cute.'

'He's mine,' I said quickly, just to make sure she knew the score. 'But you can help me look after him.'

Daisy wanted to know what the goat was for. 'Are we going to eat it?'

'No, you barbarian. It's a pet,' Egg answered scornfully.

'Big deal,' Poppy said. 'We've eaten pets before.'

'Well, you can't eat this one,' I announced. 'He's mine, and we can all take it in turns to play with him. I'm going to call him Duffle.'

Egg filled a baby bottle with milk. 'Look what I've got,' she shouted to Duffle, as she waved it in the air. Duffle let out a 'maah' and trotted over to Egg. He wrapped his mouth round the bottle, guzzled loudly, and within a matter of seconds the milk was gone.

'He must be missing his mother,' Poppy said as she stroked Duffle's nose.

'He can have mine,' I replied.

Over the next few weeks, Duffle proved to be more demanding than I'd expected. He was a constant source of hard work, always wanting to be fed or groomed, and bleating for attention whenever he was left on his own. But he was ever so sweet, and it wasn't long before he'd taken Catch's place in my affections.

He and I would sit in the garden for hours, with him leaning heavily on me, nuzzling his face into my arm, while I brushed his fur, and fed him chocolate from my mother's secret stash. It didn't take Duffle long to transform our once orderly back garden into a total mess. Vegetables and herbs were nibbled down to the ground. There was a huge pile of grass by the shed, which my father topped up every evening by raiding the railway embankment. And, of course, there were droppings and yellow puddles of wee everywhere.

Daddy seized every opportunity to take Duffle out for a walk, parading him up and down the street for all to see. Every time the two of them went for a stroll, my mother would cringe with embarrassment, saying she couldn't show her face any more because all her friends were laughing at her.

Duffle grew at an alarming rate. Within a matter of weeks, he turned from a cute little scrap into a greedy bearded monster, with sharp horns that he wasn't afraid to use. When he playfully head-butted my mother one afternoon, she made the mistake of slapping him, and he showed her who was boss of the garden by chasing her into the house.

One Saturday afternoon, when Duffle was four months old, Daddy strolled into the kitchen and asked, 'Dilly, where's the big knife?'

'It's in the cupboard,' I said. 'What do you want it for?'

'Well, love, there's a new molvi at the mosque, so everyone's going to cook something to celebrate.'

'And what are you cooking?' I asked dumbly.

'Duffle, of course.'

'What?'

'I'm going to roast Duffle,' he said, as he rummaged through the contents of the cupboard.

Shaking my head, I said, 'Daddy, you can't.'

'Don't be like that, Dilly. He's had a good life. But first of all, I've got to find the blasted thing to kill him with. Aha, here it is.' He held up the knife for me to see. It was a solid steel weapon, more like a machete than a knife, about fifteen inches long and three inches deep, tapering to a murderously sharp point. 'Come on, Dilly,' he said cheerily. 'You can help me.'

'No! Daddy, please, you can't do this.'

'Don't be silly, we can't keep him forever.'

'Mammy, please stop him,' I wept. 'Don't let him do it.'

My mother looked up from her stitching. 'Why, what's he doing?'

'He's gonna kill Duffle.'

'Oh good! About bloody time. Kids!' she shouted. 'Show time!'

Everyone came scurrying downstairs to witness the public execution. They all piled into the garden, and started to talk excitedly.

I was crying as I watched my father leading Duffle out of the shed. Poor thing, he must have sensed something was wrong; he nuzzled Daddy's leg affectionately, but he was shaking wildly, and looked bewildered.

'Dilly! Come here and help,' my father demanded angrily. His good mood had been swept away by my stubborn refusal to take part in the butchery.

'No, I can't,' I sobbed.

'Get back in the house then, you selfish bugger,' he shouted, struggling to control Duffle. Daisy skipped over to help him, and together they pinned Duffle to the ground with their knees. His terrified bleating was too much for me to bear; I ran back into the house and closed the door.

There was a moment's silence, and then the sound of laughter and cheering coming from outside.

I tried to look at the situation from my father's point of view. To me, Duffle was a pet, but to Daddy, he was a farm animal. I knew that, unless we were all going to become vegetarians, animals would have to die in order for us to eat. But I'd seen the affection my father had for Duffle, so I couldn't understand how he was able to switch his feelings off when the need arose. Was it because he'd grown up on a farm, where animal slaughter was an everyday occurrence? Or did he feel the same remorse that I felt, but had concealed it so he didn't lose face in front of his family?

Whatever Daddy's feelings were for Duffle, it was quite obvious he didn't care about how I felt. What sort of father would ask his own daughter to take part in her pet's killing?

That evening, the new molvi came to dinner. Only a few hours earlier, my pet had been innocently munching grass and filling the garden with his bleats; now it was the smell of his cooking flesh that filled the house. When I went down to the kitchen, Mammy was sitting at the table on her own, gnawing on what looked like Duffle's shin bone.

'Do you want anything to eat?' she asked.

'No,' I replied glumly.

'Well, I never knew goat could taste so good,' she said, smacking her lips together. 'You can say what you like about Climax, that hench beast certainly knows how to cook. Are you sure you don't want some?'

'What sort of cruel barbarian are you?' I shouted.

'Keep your voice down. The molvi's in the front room with your father.'

'I don't give a shit. You're eating my goat.'

'Oh, don't be daft, Dilly. You eat meat all the time.'

Daisy came into the kitchen, and said, 'Mammy, I want some more.'

My mother made a big show of carving the meat.

Daisy grabbed the plate greedily, gave me a sadistic grin, and went back to watch TV.

'You're all savages,' I said to my mother. 'You know how much I loved him.'

'Well, let that be a lesson to you,' she replied. 'In the end, everything dies. And that includes love.'

Chapter 64

In the summer of 1984, we got a phone call from Cyprus; it was Doc, saying he was coming home for a visit. Climax and Mammy were excited at the news; my father was indifferent. When the twenty-one year old turned up, he looked the picture of health. Being away from Sharnia clearly suited him. He was full of stories of how good life was in the Mediterranean sunshine: the women were beautiful, the alcohol was cheap, and he loved it.

As soon as he saw how mundane Monkey's life had become, Doc tried to inject some fun into it, and persuaded him to go out clubbing – something totally unheard of in our house. Climax, Afeeka and my parents were horrified; pubs, discos and nightclubs were all supposed to be out of bounds. Afeeka said she couldn't understand why Monkey wanted to watch white women dancing around in tarty clothes, when he had such a stunning wife at home. She even offered to put on a miniskirt and dance Bollywood-style for him. But it was to no avail; the boys went anyway.

When they came back in the early hours of the morning, Monkey got grief from his wife and both his parents, and decided it wasn't worth the aggravation. He settled straight back into his family-man routine, and Doc was back at square one.

The next evening, Monkey and Doc rented *The Empire Strikes Back*, and said we could all watch it together. The twins went mad with excitement; it wasn't often they got to watch films.

There was eager anticipation in Monkey's room as he fiddled with his second-hand video recorder, and tried to get it to work. Egg, Daisy, Poppy and I all sat on the floor, while Climax and Doc perched on the edge of the bed, sipping tea.

Afeeka sat at the dressing table, painting her nails, while Gadafi and Zia slept peacefully beside her in their cot.

As I waited for the film to start, I looked at the walls, and chuckled to myself. Peter Lorimer and Billy Bremner were still there, but only their football boots were visible; everything else had been concealed beneath glossy posters of Rekha swaying suggestively in the Alps, and Reena Roy frolicking in a fountain.

As soon as the movie started, Doc asked Afeeka to switch off the light, but she refused, so he got up and did it himself. No sooner had he taken his seat again, than Afeeka reached over and turned it back on. Doc scowled, and turned it off again.

Afeeka said, 'I need it on, otherwise I can't see what I'm doing.'

She switched it back on.

'Can't you go in the girls' room?' Doc asked, and took a sip of tea.

'Why should I? This is my room, and I want it on.'

Doc growled, got up, and switched the light off. Afeeka waited till he sat down, then she turned it on again.

If Afeeka had done her homework on the family she'd married into, she'd have known that the Shah men were renowned in the neighbourhood for their aggression; nobody messed with them for long. She'd also have learned two things about Doc in particular: first, that he never walked away from a fight; and second, that he didn't have a problem hitting girls – as I knew only too well, because he'd kicked the crap out of me often enough.

But Afeeka wasn't to know any of this. So she probably thought that if she kept switching the light on, eventually Doc would give in. I wasn't so sure, so I sat back and watched – it was a lot more interesting than the video, in which everyone else seemed engrossed.

The game of on-and-off continued a few more times, until Doc roared in despair, 'For God's sake, leave the fucker off!'

'Such vulgarity,' Afeeka snapped, eyes flashing angrily, as she reached over to switch the light on again.

'I'm telling you, leave it off, you thick bitch!' Doc shouted.

'Shut up, you fishmonger's bastard!' Afeeka shouted back.

Climax sat bolt upright, and glared angrily at Afeeka.

Doc looked puzzled. 'Fishmonger? What sort of insult is that?'

'If you were listening properly instead of jumping up and down all the time,' Afeeka spat, 'you would have heard me say "fishmonger's bastard".'

Climax growled menacingly, but Afeeka just screwed the top back on her nail varnish, and said, 'Doc, the man you call "Dad" isn't your dad at all. Everyone in Jallu knows your real father is Kashif the fishmonger. He's an ugly little runt, but your mother still screwed him.' She tittered gleefully.

Doc's mouth opened, but nothing came out. He turned to look at his mother, who was clenching her fists, as though she was about to swing a punch at Afeeka.

Doc put a hand on Climax's shoulder. 'Is she telling the truth, Mum?'

'Who the fuck do you think you are, interrogating me? I'm your mother; have some respect. You should be grateful I didn't get rid of you – that's what Kashif wanted.'

Without too much thought, Doc casually tossed the contents of his mug into Climax's face. Climax yowled like a scalded cat and jumped to her feet, with tea dripping from her hair. 'You bastard!' she screamed as she lunged at Doc. Fingers outstretched, she tried to scratch his face, but he was much too fast for her.

He caught her by the wrist, hissing, 'Don't even think about it, bitch.'

'You two, keep the noise down,' Monkey said, but he was too absorbed in Princess Leia to pay much attention to what was going on behind him. He turned the volume up really loud, unaware that he was the only one who was still watching the film.

As Doc held on to one of his mother's wrists, she used her free hand to grab his ear, which she pulled viciously. Doc caught hold of her and threw her on to the bed, shouting, 'Keep away from me! You're no mother of mine – I hate you!'

With a shriek, Climax jumped up and scraped her fingernails down Doc's arm. She probably thought he'd surrender – how wrong she was. He opened up his right hand, and brought the palm crashing against her cheek.

It made the most beautiful cracking sound, and the force of the impact made Climax's head fly back, drops of tea spraying in all directions.

But she bounced back, trying with all her strength to push Doc away. And he, with all his armed forces muscles, picked her up and threw her back on the bed again.

She took off her slipper and charged at Doc, her belly wobbling from side to side like a massive jelly. She backed him into a corner and slapped him repeatedly around the head, all the while shouting, 'You little bastard! After everything I've done for you!'

Doc cowered, his arms in front of his face, and eventually shouted, 'Monkey, give me a hand!'

Monkey finally realized what was going on, and went over to help. He'd just managed to grab Climax around the waist when the door opened and my father walked in. His mouth fell open.

'What the hell?' he barked.

Monkey dragged Climax across the room, while Doc fell away, panting heavily.

'I'm going to kill him,' Climax screamed, as she pushed Monkey away and ran at Doc again.

'Stop it!' yelled Monkey, as he caught hold of the back of Climax's kameez, and held on tight.

My mother appeared in the doorway, hands over mouth, eyes popping.

'What's going on in here?' my father bellowed. 'And turn that bloody telly down!'

As I switched the video off, Afeeka gave a little giggle. 'Uncle, I really don't know what their problem is. All I did was tell Doc about his real dad.'

'Right, you kids, get out,' my father said grimly.

Everyone was quiet as we made our way downstairs. We went into the front room to try to hear what was being said in the bedroom directly above us, but the voices were too low.

'Doc,' I said, losing interest in trying to eavesdrop, 'that was amazing. You're a hero.'

But Doc was sitting hunched over, chewing a finger-nail and looking worried.

'I'm in a lot of shit now,' he said glumly.

My mother came downstairs, poked her head round the door, said, 'You bastards,' then went back upstairs again.

My father came in and grabbed Doc roughly by the arm. 'I want you out of my house. And don't ever come back. You're no longer welcome here.'

I fought off the urge to shout, 'Hypocrite!' Whenever Daddy and I argued, and he couldn't win with words, he always resorted to violence. I'd witnessed that behaviour all my life – it was a family tradition, part of the fabric of our universe. My father had shown me that violence was a good way to silence your opponent; and since Afeeka had arrived, he'd even taken to hitting me on her behalf, just to keep my mother happy. So why did he have a problem now, just because it was his sister on the receiving end?

I stole a quick glance at his face, and was momentarily taken aback. There was anger there, of course – I was expecting that. But, for the first time in my life, I saw a glimmer of anxiety, maybe even fear, in his green eyes. I instinctively knew what his problem was. He was a control freak who couldn't cope with having his power challenged by a strong independent outsider, which is what Doc had become. Everyone else in Sharnia was still within my father's sphere of command, and feared him. But Doc was a loose cannon, who was no longer prepared to be dominated. His very presence threatened to destabilize the family dynamics that my father had painstakingly built up over the years.

Compromise and forgiveness were not words I ever associated with my father, and I knew there was only one course of action left open to him: he had to get rid of Doc, so he could regain control of his domain.

Chapter 65

Later that summer I passed three more O Levels: Drama, English Literature and Religious Studies. I may as well have passed wind, for all the congratulations I got.

I wanted to stay at school for another year to complete my A Levels, but I didn't think my parents were going to let me, bearing in mind all the arguments I'd had the year before. My only hope was for Egg to continue for another year, so I set about persuading her to sign up for the Lower Sixth. She wasn't really bothered either way, so it was easy to talk her into it by telling her that being a Sixth Former was really good fun, and that there were loads of boys she could hang around with during breaks – unlike the younger girls, the Sixth Form girls were allowed into the boys' school next door.

When Egg told my parents she wanted to go back to school in September, they offered little resistance; at sixteen she was still a baby in their eyes. Besides, she wasn't engaged yet, and there weren't any plans for her immediate future, so letting her go back wasn't a big deal.

My master plan proved to be amazingly successful: my father decreed that Egg could go back to school only if I was prepared to watch her. My mother and Afeeka were understandably put out, but my father had made it quite clear what was going to happen, and eventually they just resigned themselves to the fact that Nonna was going to have to wait a bit longer. My mother did her best to make me feel like nothing more than Egg's servant, but I didn't care; I'd got what I wanted.

As my father drove us to school on the first day of the autumn term, he made a point of reminding me that it was my responsibility to keep an eye on Egg. It was the same sermon he'd preached to me the year before: if Egg misbehaved, I would suffer the consequences.

As he drove away, Egg said, 'Thank God he's gone,' and whipped off her scarf. 'He's gotta be joking if he expects me to wear this damn thing all day.'

Over the next few weeks, my younger sister became the loudest, most annoying, attention-grabbing, boy-crazy floozy in school. If Egg had gone on *Mastermind*, her specialist subject would have been Boyfriend Theft. All boys interested her, but it was other people's boyfriends who were the most interesting, at least for a while, until she got bored, and moved on to the next conquest.

She was on a mission to have as much fun as possible, and the last thing on her mind was education, so keeping her in check was like trying to stop a tank with a spud gun. She started hanging around with a group of girls and boys who all seemed to think that having a good time was the only reason they went to school.

Every time I asked her to be discreet, Egg told me not to be so anal. But I knew things were getting out of hand when I caught her in the boys' common room, sitting in the lap of a boy called Kasim, squeezing his knee to see if he was ticklish.

That evening, we had a heated row. I told her to be careful; she told me to stop being so middle-aged and jealous, and to accept that she wasn't going to change her lifestyle to suit me. She went on to say that none of the boys in her gang fancied me, but that they wouldn't mind having me around, if only I'd learn to relax.

So I decided that, if I couldn't beat them, I might as well join them. Besides, I had a point to prove to Egg: she'd upset me by trying to make out I was unfanciable. I wanted to show her I could get myself a boy if I wanted to. From then on, I started hanging around the boys' common room – mainly to keep an eye on Egg, but also to check out the talent.

I soon set my sights on a boy called Amigo; he was tall, okay looking and quiet. However, two things went against him: (a) he had a Mexican bandit moustache, and (b) he always wore the same pair of trousers, which were two inches too short and flapped around his ankles. We had three dates in total, all of which involved a lunchtime walk to the High Street shops, and very little conversation (the longest sentence he managed was: 'Would you like a Rolo?'). He held my hand on the third date, which is when I decided to dump him. I didn't have the nerve to tell him to his face that I was chucking him because he was a dork, a loser, and embarrassing to be with; so I told Omar (one of his friends) that my father had seen Amigo and me together, and he'd said if he ever saw me talking to him again he'd run Amigo over with his car. I said I really liked Amigo, and it hurt like hell to have to end the relationship like this, but I was doing him a favour, because my father was a maniac.

Understandably, Amigo never spoke to me after that, and every time he saw me, he gave me the evils and crossed the road to avoid me.

As far as I was concerned, dumping Amigo was a liberating experience. All around me, girls were going out with boys; it was easy to get caught up in the moment, and do it just because everyone else was. But I'd tried it, and to be honest it was no big deal. What was a boy good for, anyway? Holding hands? I wasn't interested in all that soppy stuff. It was time to forget about relationships, and concentrate on my schoolwork.

But one thing had started to bother me greatly: if boys were so useless, why was I engaged to one? The crushing inevitability of my predicament dawned on me; if I didn't act fast, I'd be Adam's wife before long. And he wouldn't be as easy as Amigo to get rid of.

The stakes were raised just before the October half-term, when a letter arrived from Nonna. As soon as my father got in from work, he was confronted by my mother, waving the letter at him, and saying, 'Come into the kitchen, you need to read this.'

'Oh, for God's sake, now what? I've got some books to label,' he complained.

'Why didn't you do them at work? What do you do all day, anyway? Sit in the canteen and eat that shit you call cheese?'

'Just give me the letter, you silly cow.' He snatched it out of her hand, and sat at the dining table to read. But it was impossible; my mother, who'd already read it, insisted on interrupting him impatiently so she could tell him the nuggets of information he was trying desperately to read for himself.

There was one final interruption: 'Wait till you get to the next page; Nonna says if we don't send Dilly to Pakistan . . .'

Roaring with frustration, he reached over and punched her in the mouth, splitting her lip.

It was embarrassing for me to have to witness her humiliation at the hands of my father yet again. She knew how short his fuse was, but she never seemed to learn.

As he stormed out, she dabbed at the blood that was oozing from her mouth, and blamed me for everything.

'It's your fault he's like this. If you'd just agree to the wedding, I wouldn't have to put up with all this shit. All you have to do is go through with the religious ceremony over the phone like Nonna wants.'

'Get married over the phone? Are you mad?'

'What's the problem? Lots of people do it. Once you're married, your father'll calm down.'

I could hear her crying as I went upstairs. My father's sudden violence had made me realize that it wasn't fair to anyone for the current situation to continue. This engagement fiasco had been dragging on for years, and I'd had enough. It was time to do the right thing.

I took a sheet of paper from my notepad, picked up a pen and wrote:

Dear Auntie Nonna, I hope you are well . . .

Chapter 66

I was tidying the front room when I heard footsteps coming down the stairs, then Afeeka shouting for my mother.

I peered out; she was standing in the kitchen, still in her nightie, hair dishevelled, face void of make-up, lips trembling. For a woman who could spend hours in front of the mirror, it was a surprise to see her looking so unkempt; whatever she had to say to my mother was obviously urgent.

'What is it, Afeeka?' Mammy asked anxiously. 'You're scaring me.'

'I'm going to be ill,' Afeeka sobbed as she waved a sheet of blue paper in the air.

Suddenly, the penny dropped. At last, the reply to my letter had arrived. Whistling a merry tune to myself, I strolled casually into the kitchen. Afeeka glared at me with cold contempt.

'Auntie, you've got no idea what your daughter's done.'

'And she won't, until you tell her,' I giggled.

'How could you do this?' she quivered indignantly. 'You should be hanging your head in shame. Who the hell do you think you are?'

'Your future sister-in-law, twice over. Not.'

This was a deliciously sweet moment. I had Afeeka in a state of apoplexy, and my mother in a daze of idiotic confusion. If only I could have bottled the glee I felt. It must have been times like this that inspired the Germans to invent the word *Schadenfreude*.

Afeeka was so beside herself with fury, I thought she was going to hit me. I wished she had; it would have given me the perfect opportunity to slap her silly little face – something I'd been yearning to do since she caused the trouble that got Doc thrown out.

But, disappointingly, all she did was shriek, 'She broke it!'

My mother was still stuck in village idiot mode. 'Broke what?'

'The engagement. She called it off.'

Mammy turned a sickly pale; her legs wobbled, and she slumped into a chair.

'What?' she whispered. 'What are you saying?'

'That—' squawked Afeeka, pointing a finger in my general direction, 'wrote to Mummy, and said she isn't going to marry Adam.'

'Oh my God!'

'And what's worse is the stupid cow has written back to say that it's okay. She must be as mad as my father.'

'No, that can't be true,' my mother said. 'Nonna's just saying that so she doesn't lose face.' She snatched the letter from Afeeka, and read a few lines for herself. Then she started to hyperventilate.

I was so happy that Nonna had accepted my decision that I felt I needed to share my good news with Egg. As I went upstairs, singing, 'I'm in the mood for dancing . . .' to myself, I could hear Mammy sobbing hysterically. A normal daughter with a normal mother would have been moved, maybe even distressed, but I didn't care.

Egg was sitting on her bed, reading *2000 AD*. I tried to tell her what had happened, but she wasn't interested. She got up and rummaged around in the dressing-table drawer. 'I'm gonna enter this competition,' she said, as she turned to the readers' page in the comic, 'I could do with some extra cash.'

It was obvious she didn't want to talk, so I went back to cleaning the front room. I'd been in there for only a minute when my mother came in. Neither of us said a word. She sat down on the sofabed and watched me, and I could feel her eyes boring into me. I could smell her rage – the anger was wafting off her in waves – and I didn't need to look at her to know she was willing me to speak. When I refused to play her game, she said quietly, 'I hate you. I really do.'

Ignoring her, I took my father's books off the shelves, and put them in piles on the floor. I loved those books; there were hundreds of them – Dickens, Chaucer, Eliot, the Brontës, Shakespeare, Wordsworth, Thomas Hardy, D. H. Lawrence, C. S. Lewis, poetry compilations, Arabic books, atlases, encyclopedias, Wisdens, car manuals, and so on. But, out of all his books, my favourite was his massive cloth-bound *Oxford English Dictionary*. It was so old that it smelt musty, and all the pages were dog-eared and yellowing, and felt fragile to the touch. I'd spent many happy hours as a young child, thumbing through that dictionary in search of strange new words I could use to amuse Egg. 'Testicle' and 'flatulence' had impressed her greatly.

I picked up *Jane Eyre*, and wished I could dive into the pages. Jane Eyre had escaped her awful family; she'd found love and happiness. But that was just fiction – I couldn't see anything like that ever happening to me. I hugged the book close, feeling a sudden urge to dash out of the room, run upstairs and read it in bed – but there was a big problem of about fifteen stones that I had to deal with first. I turned to face her. She returned my stare. I was trying to decide which Womble she most resembled when she broke the silence.

'That's what's ruined you,' she said coldly. 'Those books, and your greed to know more than you need. You've always been greedy. And selfish.'

'What's wrong with knowledge? It's a good thing; don't make it sound dirty,' I replied, clutching *Jane Eyre* tighter, and longing to get upstairs so I could start reading.

'God only knows why your father lets you read those things,' she continued. 'I'd love to see you with your nose in a book when you've got a family to look after. Oh, silly me, I forgot – that's never going to happen, is it?'

She was stone-faced, and her eyes looked cold and flat. Why wouldn't she just leave me in peace? But she wasn't going anywhere, and as I dusted my father's books I had to suffer her indignation, while she shared her thoughts with me:

I'd ruined everything;

I was a bitter disappointment;

If I cared about anyone other than myself, I wouldn't have done such a terrible thing;

I was too arrogant at present to realize the damage I'd done, but one day I was going to look back on this moment and wish I'd listened to her;

I was in no position to choose what was best for me, because I was just a stupid teenager who knew nothing about boys;

Adam was the best man I could hope for;

I'd fall in love with Adam, if I only gave him a chance;

I'd let Egg and the twins down – what man in his right mind would want to marry one of them now?

People would say that Adam had dumped me;

Once my father's family found out what had happened, every single maggot in Jallu would be crawling out of the woodwork;

My mother was going to sit back and watch, while my father gave me to the worst of the bunch;

I was on my own;

It wasn't too late to change my mind.

The door opened, and Afeeka came in. I wondered how long she'd been standing in the passage.

'You threw your shame out with the bathwater,' she wailed at me.

'Oh God,' I thought. 'Here we go again.'

I'd been a fool to hope that this might all blow over in a day or two. The smile on my father's face lasted for weeks, but my mother and Afeeka were foaming at the mouth for months.

Chapter 67

My mother was right about the maggots! It didn't take long for word to get round that I was back on the market, and offers of marriage started to arrive from my father's relatives. Most of the letters were written by Uncle Ilyas, my father's younger brother, who'd become the mouth-piece of the family since Rasheeda's death.

Every time a letter from Ilyas arrived, my mother would hop around the house in a rage, saying it was all my fault. She said he was a sleeping dog that I'd poked with a big stick, and now he and his family were yowling at our front door.

I told her to ignore them, which is what I intended to do, but she had the bit between her teeth and life became one big argument. The nagging drove me mad; it was incessant. It got so bad, I couldn't think straight any more. I rejected all Ilyas's attempts at matchmaking without a moment's hesitation, and after a few weeks he must have realized I was more trouble than I was worth. But rather than give up altogether, he said I needed a cooling-off period, to get over the shock of being dumped by Adam. Then he moved on to the next Briti-Shah on his hit list, and, for the first time, the spotlight shifted away from me and beamed down on Egg.

The first indication of this welcome turn of events was in December 1984, when a letter arrived from Ilyas. As usual, Mammy put on her pink Marigolds before she picked it up, and said, 'That ugly motherfucker Ilyas's a dirt bag, and I don't want to catch his germs.'

The coast was clear (my father was out Christmas shopping with Egg and the twins), so Mammy did her usual 'petty villain from an episode of *Columbo*' routine: she held the letter over a steaming kettle, then carefully peeled open the envelope. I'd seen her do this a hundred times, and every time I couldn't help feeling sorry for my father – he had no idea what she was really like.

After she'd read the letter half a dozen times, scowling and cursing angrily all the while, she resealed it with a dab of Bostik, then ironed it flat. She asked me if I could tell it had been opened. As I examined her artwork, I marvelled at her ingenuity, and wondered how dangerous she would have been if she'd had a proper education, instead of just picking up the odd tip from daytime TV.

'I don't know why you do this, Mammy. It's so deceitful.'

'Oh shut up – since when were you my moral guardian?'

'I don't get it. You can't stand Daddy's family, so why are you always so desperate to find out all their gossip?'

'I didn't ask you to interview me,' she snapped. 'I asked you if the letter looks like it's been opened.'

'No, it doesn't,' I said.

'Good.'

When the shoppers returned, the kids disappeared upstairs to wrap their presents, and Mammy put the kettle on again. When Daddy came into the kitchen, she thrust the letter into his hand and he opened it without even looking at the envelope. She hovered over him as he read it. When he finished, he looked up and said, 'Ilyas wants Egg to marry Zulfi.'

Mammy put on her most shocked and aggrieved expression. 'You've got to be kidding me,' she said. 'He's way too old for her.'

'Well, I think it's a splendid idea,' he replied. 'I'm surprised I never thought of it myself. I'm going to write to Ilyas for more details.'

Over the next few weeks, there were raging arguments between my parents, as they debated whether or not Zulfi should become Egg's fiancé. Egg and I were perplexed; we'd never even heard of Zulfi before, and didn't know anything about him.

Ironically, while our parents were choosing a match for Egg, she'd already beaten them to it. She and Kasim were a serious item, and they were hoping to get married. So, despite more letters being exchanged between Ilyas and Daddy, Egg was living life to the max, skipping classes and hanging around Kirkgate Market with Kasim and his friends. They went out shopping, watched movies, went to the pub and ate pizza. Egg's school life had become one big party.

I must have been the most useless chaperone in history. I hadn't realized quite how bad things had got, until one day when Mr Dougal, Egg's geography teacher, told me she hadn't been to any of his lessons for a fortnight, and if she didn't show her face soon he was going to tell my father. When I confronted Egg, she went back to class for a few days, said she was bored, and started bunking off again.

As if her behaviour at school wasn't bad enough, she was also spending far too much time with Afeeka. They'd spend hours in Monkey's room, deep in conversation. I knew they were up to something, because every time I went in there, they'd stop talking and wait for me to leave.

February brought a new problem: our phone started behaving oddly. It would ring three times at exactly six-thirty every evening, and then stop. A moment later, Egg would go charging down the stairs, volunteering to take the washing off the line, or to put the rubbish in the bin. It was blindingly obvious to anyone with half a brain what was going on. It took my mother six weeks to comment on the curious phenomenon of the ringing phone; but when she mentioned it to Climax, she just said it was most probably a prank caller.

As the weeks went by, Egg continued to skate on thin ice, apparently unconcerned about the stress she was causing me. I faced a huge dilemma, and I couldn't see a way out. If I kept quiet, I was pretty sure that she'd be found out sooner or later, and then I'd be in big trouble.

But if I went to my father and told him what was going on, it wouldn't just be Egg who hated me – it would be half the boys in the common room. And, as she'd been messing about for so long, my father would be certain to punish me severely anyway.

It was a cold, wet, windy day in April when I found myself hanging around outside school at the end of lessons, wondering where the hell Egg was. I couldn't see her in the playground, so I headed back into the school, and wandered around the empty corridors looking for her. I finally gave up, and went into the office to ask Mrs Bates, the secretary, if I could call home. I told my mother that I had a revision period, and we'd be home as soon as it had finished.

As I stood in the playground in the pouring rain, with water soaking through the hole in my left shoe, I became so angry with Egg I decided enough was enough. She'd had plenty of warnings, and ignored them all. As soon as we got home, I was going to tell on her.

It was after five when she finally made it back to school. When she climbed out of Kasim's car, I told her that she'd blown it and I was going to tell my father everything. Instead of begging me to keep quiet, which is what I expected, she just shrugged her shoulders nonchalantly. But one of Kasim's friends, who knew my father really well, advised me to think again; he said if I grassed on Egg, he'd tell my father that it was me, not Egg, who had a boyfriend. Egg just smiled complacently.

As we walked home, she didn't speak to me, but every now and then she would give me a dirty look, and then sniff angrily like my mother. I was left wondering when she had become so selfish. Was this what she considered growing up?

For the first time ever, I was terrified of what Egg was capable of. I decided to keep my mouth shut.

Chapter 68

In Sharnia, Ramadan was always a month for quiet prayer and reflection. For me, it was much more than that. Going without food and water from dawn to dusk made me appreciate some things I seriously lacked: discipline, willpower and self-control. But the main reason I liked Ramadan was because my father became temporarily serene; it was very rare for him to lose his temper during Ramadan, and all bickering, backstabbing and idle gossip was put on hold until the day after Eid. My father was Mr Hyde for eleven months of the year, so it was relatively pleasant to have Dr Jekyll come and stay with us for a month.

At the end of Ramadan, we would celebrate Eid very quietly. My father and a reluctant Monkey would go over to the mosque for prayers. And we girls would help Climax with the cooking, and then get dressed in our new clothes. The second part of the day would consist of Daisy and Poppy going round to neighbours' houses with plates of food, while the rest of us tiptoed around Sharnia because my father was sleeping.

I usually found Eid quite depressing; it was never the huge explosion of bright colour that I expected. It was more like a damp squib, promising much but delivering little. It also marked the end of my father's good behaviour.

My mother always made a big fuss about Eid. She loved it so much that one year she even concealed news of the death of one of my father's cousins until after the celebrations, because she didn't want it to ruin her special day. All through Ramadan, she would savour the anticipation of getting everything ready, and then, when the big day arrived, out would come the gold jewellery and the make-up, and she'd spend hours getting ready in front of the mirror, even though she never went further than the back garden.

The first Saturday of Ramadan in 1985 was a quiet one. It was grey and miserable outside, and inside the mood was so gloomy that, even by midday, none of the children had bothered to get out of bed. Unable to sleep, I made my way downstairs to get my knitting, and walked straight into my mother.

She pushed me into the back room and closed the door behind her. Before I had a chance to speak, she slapped my face. 'Right, you little snake, start talking. Is Egg seeing a boy from school?'

I didn't know what to say, but from the way she was looking at me, I could tell she already knew something. My stomach growled uncomfortably as I sat down on my father's bed and wondered how I was going to get out of this mess.

'No,' I said sullenly. I knew that lying during Ramadan was a sin, but at that moment, all I could think about was self-preservation.

She slapped my face again. 'You pimp your sister out, and then you dare to lie about it? I know she's got a boyfriend.'

'If you know, then why are you asking me?'

She sat down next to me, caught me by my hair, and pulled me close. 'I promise I won't say anything to your father, if you just tell me what you know. All I'll do is have a quiet word with Egg, and after that, we can act like nothing's happened.'

Who was she trying to fool? Had I been a few years younger I might have fallen for that rubbish, but I was older and I knew that, to my mother, telling lies was as easy as slipping on ice. She had taught me loyalty, truth, honesty, fairness and respect, but only because she did the opposite of what a good person would do; by watching her do wrong, I had learned to do right – most of the time.

'Look, Dilly,' she said, in a low sinister voice. 'Egg's in the shit whatever happens. But you can save yourself a whole lot of trouble, if you tell me what you know.'

'I don't know anything,' I said.

'What's his name? When I find out who he is, I'm going to make sure the bastard never walks again.'

'How do you know he's not a cripple already? What are you gonna do if he is – take the wheels off his wheelchair?'

'Mock if you like. I know what's been going on; I've known for a while, actually, because Egg's been beating a drum all across Bradford. And she made a huge mistake – she confided in the wrong person.'

'Who?'

'Afeeka. Egg told her, and she told Climax, and Climax told me. So now I'm going to tell your father.'

I tried to conceal the dismay I felt, but I didn't do a very good job because my mother started laughing. 'You can go and warn the slut if you want, and tell her I know about Kasim.'

Upstairs in the bedroom, Egg was sound asleep. As I shook her awake, I was sweating with shock. At first, I'd thought my mother was trying to trick me, but she knew Kasim's name, and that meant it was time for some serious damage control. I was desperate to find out what Egg had already told Afeeka, so we could spin a web of deceit to hide the bits that my mother didn't yet know.

But then Egg told me she'd been confiding in Afeeka for months, and there was nothing Afeeka didn't know. I felt a wave of despondency wash over me. I couldn't see any way out of this mess.

We both sat on the bed and cried.

The door opened, and my mother walked in, looking smug. There hadn't been the usual sound of footsteps on the stairs, so I guessed she'd been standing just outside the door, listening in on the conversation.

'You dirty little bitch,' she said to Egg. 'You're a whore.'

Egg caught hold of my mother's arm, and begged: 'Mammy, please don't tell him. I'll do anything you want, but don't tell Daddy.'

'Have you slept with the boy?' Mammy asked. 'Are you still a virgin, or are you second-hand goods now?'

'No, I haven't, Mammy.'

My mother scowled, as though she didn't believe it.

'Mammy, I'm begging you. Don't tell Daddy,' Egg pleaded again.

I knew she was wasting her breath. My mother had been given the perfect opportunity for total control over two of her four daughters. Egg had handed it to her on a

plate: we would have been her willing slaves; she could
have made us do anything. From that moment onwards,
she wouldn't have needed to peel another onion or make
another bed or vacuum another carpet as long as she
lived. But she wasn't interested.

I took my mother's hand and stroked it.

'It was a mistake, Mammy, but you don't have to tell
him. We can sort this out ourselves; he doesn't need to
know. We'll do anything you want.'

She pulled free, as though she couldn't bear my touch.

'Get your filthy hands off me. You're no daughter of
mine.'

'Fine, if that's what you want, I won't be your daughter.' Turning to Egg, I said, 'Tell her it's over, and you
won't see Kasim again.'

'It's true,' Egg said. 'I swear I won't, just don't tell
Daddy. Once you tell him, you won't be able to stop him.
He'll kill me.'

'So what? You deserve to die. I hope he slaughters you
like an animal,' my mother said flatly. 'And it won't be
long now,' she added, as she glanced at her watch. 'He'll
be home soon, and then you'll get what's coming to you.'

Egg put her face in her hands, and started to rock back
and forth.

Chapter 69

The sound of the bell made me jump. As my mother got up to answer it, I dashed over to the bedroom door and barred her way.

'Move,' she said imperiously.

I wrapped my arms around her, in a hope that, even at this stage, I could soften her heart.

'Please, Mammy,' I sobbed, my throat thick with tears.

She pushed me aside, and said, 'I have to.'

'Why?' I cried, feeling hysteria rising.

'If I don't tell him, Climax will. It's better if it comes from me.'

She brushed past me, and walked down the stairs to let my father in. I wished that someone would be struck dead by a freak bolt of lightning – if not one of my parents, then I wouldn't mind it being me. Anything would be better than what I imagined was about to happen. When I went out on to the landing, I saw Afeeka peering out from behind her bedroom door.

'You fool,' I hissed. 'Why did you have to go and tell Climax?'

Without a word, she disappeared back inside her room. I turned to see Egg cowering behind me. For weeks, she'd been full of bravado; she didn't look so brave now. Leaning over the banister, I saw my mother slowly reach out to open the door. She knew I was watching; she was milking every second, relishing the way the tension was tearing my insides apart. I started to pray under my breath.

As my father stepped into the passage, he said, 'You took your time. What kept you?' He dumped two bags of shopping on the floor, and shrugged off his overcoat.

My mother replied, 'You had your blasted keys; why were you ringing the bell in the first place?'

'So I could see your lovely face,' he said sarcastically.

Then he went back outside to fetch more shopping from the car. As my mother grabbed the bags, she looked up at me, and I found myself not knowing whether to go down and help or just stay where I was. She didn't ask; I didn't offer. It took an eternity for all the shopping to be brought in; my father doing many trips to the car, and my mother huffing and puffing as she carried the bags into the kitchen.

'Gongal,' my father called. 'I'd better move the car – the kids are playing football in the road again.' He sounded like he was in a good mood – but for how much longer?

As he disappeared outside, I ran down the stairs to the kitchen. My mother turned on me instantly.

'Don't waste your breath.'

'Don't tell him. Why does he have to get involved?'

'Because he's your father, and he's got a right to know what you lot have been getting up to. It's about time he saw what you're really like.' She turned her back on me and started to put the shopping away.

When the doorbell rang again, I shot up the stairs to the landing. Egg was still there, shaking with fear. I heard my mother's slippers clicking on the tiles as she hurried through the passage to let my father in.

She muttered something, and he said, 'What's wrong, Gongal? Is the fasting getting to you?'

'No, it's not that,' she replied. 'I've got something to tell you.'

'What is it?' he asked.

'Congratulations, Shah. Let me give you the good news. Your daughter has a boyfriend.'

I felt my breath catch. I noticed how my mother had worded that sentence. *Your daughter has a boyfriend.* She'd probably been planning the exact words for hours, running different possibilities through her mind, until she found the one that promised maximum havoc, yet with minimum risk to herself. With just those five words, she'd distanced herself from any blame, and left him to guess which of the four daughters was the guilty one. Perhaps she hoped he'd leap to the wrong conclusion, and beat me senseless before she told him that, by the way, it was Egg, not Dilly, who deserved the punishment.

My father was too stunned to speak. He just stood there, clenching his jaw and grinding his teeth.

'Did you hear me?' my mother nagged, clearly disappointed that there hadn't yet been a major eruption.

'Yes, I heard you,' he replied twitchily, as if his blood was getting close to boiling point. It looked as though Dr Jekyll was about to leave early this year.

Whatever happened now, the cat was out of the bag, and no amount of pleading would be able to get it back in. There was nothing for Egg or me to do, except sit back and wait. There didn't seem any point in hiding in the shadows at the top of the stairs any more – we'd be able to hear my father well enough, no matter which part of the house we were in. I pushed Egg into our room, and closed the door. I thought about locking it, but decided against it; having to kick a door down to get to us would just make him even angrier.

My insides had turned to water, and my heart was so loud, it felt like the whole room was beating. I was afraid, but this wasn't like the fear I'd known when I was younger and had done something naughty, like hitting Daisy or swearing at Poppy. This was a different sort of fear; it even had its own flavour and, right then, as I sat awaiting my fate, I could taste it – it was salty and tart and was threatening to choke me.

Egg sat down on the bed quietly. She wasn't crying any more.

'He knows now,' she said calmly. 'I didn't think Afeeka would tell Climax. I thought they hated each other.'

My mother came into the room. She looked like a hungry Rottweiler that had just been let loose in a field full of baby rabbits, and told it could eat as many as it could catch.

'Move yourselves. He wants you both.'

When we got downstairs, my father was standing in the middle of the back room, rolling his prayer beads in his right hand. He glared at me; I stared at the floor. I was aware of him towering over me, willing me to look at him, to return his gaze – but I didn't dare. My mother pushed Egg into the room behind me.

In one stride, he was across the room. He reached out, seized Egg by the arm, and pulled her roughly towards him.

'Is it the boy I saw you with?' he demanded.

I felt my eyebrows rising with surprise. It looked as though something had already happened to arouse his suspicions, and I wasn't even aware of it.

'Yes, Daddy,' Egg said quietly.

He shoved her away in disgust, and said, 'You lied to me.' I wanted to ask them both what the hell was going on. When had he seen Egg with Kasim? How had she talked her way out of it? Why hadn't anybody mentioned it to me?

'My brain's not able to deal with this right now,' my father said. 'I can't think straight on an empty stomach.'

My mother folded her arms and glared at him. 'But that's just stupid,' she squawked. 'You mean you're going to let them get away with it, just because you're hungry?'

'No, I mean I refuse to deal with them while I'm fasting.'

'You're shameful,' she said. 'Using the fast as an excuse not to do anything.'

'You can nag all you want, but you're not going to ruin Ramadan for me,' he seethed.

Then he rounded on me. 'Dilly, you've let me down terribly. I trusted you, and you deceived me.'

I really didn't like the way this was going; things didn't look good at all. I could smell his anger, and my knees were knocking together with fear.

'Think yourself lucky you're in England. If this was Pakistan, I'd kill you.'

'Fine,' I thought. 'Just cut to the chase. I know how this works. Hit me, swear at me and then send me to my room. I can deal with it; you've been doing that all my life. These are the punishments that follow me around like my shadow. They belong to me; I own them. Do anything you want, but please don't stop me from going to school.'

I glanced at Egg; there was terror in her eyes. Finally, it had sunk into her thick skull – all those months I'd begged her to stop, and she'd laughed in my face.

'Come with me,' my father ordered. 'I'm going to teach you a lesson you won't forget.'

We followed him into the back garden, and watched as he went into the shed. When he emerged, he was carrying the length of electric cable that Egg and I often used as a skipping-rope. From the grim look on his face, I could tell he wasn't about to start skipping around the garden like a bald pansy. Egg let out a squeak. I felt sick.

He took Egg by the arm and stood her in the middle of the path. Without any expression, he whipped the back of her legs. The sound of the cable yowling through the air made the hair on my neck stand on end.

It was horrible, watching Egg getting whipped, seeing her distress as she ran around the garden, with my father in pursuit. I had to endure her screams, knowing that I would soon be getting the same punishment.

When my turn came, it was worse than any pain I'd felt before, like being pricked with a million hot needles. I stood as still as I could, the cable slapping down on the backs of my legs and bottom, time and again. I wanted it to be over quickly, but I didn't cry out, because I wasn't ready to give my father the satisfaction of knowing how much it hurt. My teeth ached from gritting them, and the palms of my hands bled where my fingernails had dug in.

When he'd finally finished, my father threw the cable on the ground and said, 'Get upstairs. I need to talk to your mother.' I didn't need telling twice. As I rushed past my mother, she flashed me a spiteful little smile.

'Dilly, what do you think they're planning?' Egg whimpered as she followed me into the bedroom. I was feeling sick with stress, and I contemplated just crawling into bed and pulling the duvet over my head.

'I don't know,' I replied weakly.

We didn't have to wait long to find out. Ten minutes later, my father came striding into the room like a medieval king, with my mother the court jester close on his heels.

'Shut the door,' he said to her.

He waited till she'd done as she was told, then he walked over to me, raised his fist high above me, and brought it down rapidly, landing an angry blow across my cheek. It was so hard, it felt like he'd broken my jaw. Everything inside my head rattled, and there was a whooshing in my ears. I thought I was going to pass out.

'The next time I tell you to do something, make damn sure you do it,' he barked.

My face was throbbing and I was too stunned to speak. I just slumped on to my bed and waited for the room to stop spinning. As my father turned, Egg stepped back to avoid his fists, but he wasn't interested in hitting her. Instead, he bent down and picked up my school bag.

'You won't be needing these any more,' he said as he tipped the contents out on to the floor. For good measure, he gave the books a sharp kick, scattering them across the room. 'You won't be leaving the house again until you're married.'

Turning to Egg, he said, 'And as for you, you slut. You're obviously desperate for a man, so I'm going to get you one as soon as I can.'

'What about that old-timer you found her?' my mother asked smugly.

'Zulfi's a good boy. Why should I ruin his life by shackling him to this whore? He deserves better.'

My mother looked like a cat with a canary in its mouth. As she followed my father out of the room, she looked over her shoulder and smiled. Her day was going remarkably well.

Chapter 70

On Monday morning, Daisy, the sister I'd hated for years, cuddled Egg, and asked her if she was okay. Then she hugged me, and said, 'Daddy's wrong, Dilly. He's blaming you for something he couldn't control himself. It's not your fault.'

I was struck by the thought that, had the tables been turned, I wouldn't have been trying to comfort Daisy – I'd have been laughing at her misery.

I felt ashamed.

Was this God's way of teaching me humility? It seemed that every bad thing I'd ever said or done to Daisy had come back to haunt me.

I watched as she and Poppy set off for school, and I was overwhelmed with sadness. It was a lovely sunny day, and I was stuck at home with Mammy and Climax, the two women I hated most in the world. I was supposed to be fasting, but the stress of the weekend had been too much for me, and I sneaked into the kitchen and ate two cold kebabs from the fridge. It was painful; my face hurt, my jaw felt tender, and every time I moved my head, I felt a sharp pain in my neck.

I went out into the garden, sat down on the wall, and spent half an hour of my pointless life wondering how I'd allowed myself to get into this mess.

My mother came outside to put some rubbish in the bin.

'What are you doing out here?' she asked accusingly.

I felt cold inside. How was it possible to detest someone so much? What had I done to her to make her so insensitive to my suffering? She hadn't been nice to me for years; I couldn't remember the last time she'd cuddled me or said a kind word to me. After all this time, I still hadn't worked out what made her tick.

Years ago, Mrs Gilmore had told me that I was an enigma, and she couldn't figure me out. I wonder what she would have said if she'd met my mother.

I wanted to hit Mammy so hard that I would knock the breath out of her; I wanted her to feel the pain that I was going through, to know the fear I'd known. But I suspected that once I started to hit her, I wouldn't be able to stop.

'Minding my own business,' I answered. 'And I suggest you do the same.'

'Don't be bloody cheeky. Get used to it, you're going to be at home for a long time, so there's no point moping around. Bear it: this is the life of a Pakistani woman.'

'I want to go back to school. I'm going to miss my exams.'

'I know,' she said, smiling at me. Her face was glowing. 'Why do you think I told your father when I did?'

'What are you talking about?'

'You humiliated me when you called off your engagement. Did you honestly think I was going to let you get away with it? Revenge is a dish best served cold, Dilly, and I'm loving every minute of this. It's one of the sweetest moments of my life.'

With a sudden jolt, I realized what it was like to be on the sharp end of someone else's *Schadenfreude*.

Gadafi came tripping out into the garden; she was wearing Egg's school shoes. Climax followed her, carrying a pile of washing, and started to peg it out on the line.

'No school today then, Dilly?' she asked.

'I didn't want to go anyway.'

My mother chuckled. 'We all know that's a big lie,' she said mockingly. 'You wanted to get your A Levels so you could go to university, didn't you, Dilly? You swan around, acting like you're better than everyone else. Well, guess what, Miss Clever Clogs? You and I have got a lot in common: we've both got no A Levels.'

Climax roared with laughter. 'Oh Gongal, you're so funny.'

'I can't wait to get out of this shit hole,' I said.

'And how are you going to do that?' my mother asked. 'You could've done, if you hadn't called off your engagement. But you thought you were so smart, and now you're stuck. You're just a slave now, and you don't need A Levels for that.'

Climax sniggered, and I knew I had to go inside to get away from the temptation to punch them both. I ran upstairs, and locked myself in the toilet.

Now I knew what it was like for Mrs Baba. I'd laughed at her, because she couldn't leave the house without her husband's permission, and I'd arrogantly sneered at her because she hadn't stood up for her rights. I'd often asked myself what sort of woman would be so weak that she'd allow a man to totally dominate her. Well, now I had the answer. For all my airs and graces, and my naïve belief that I was somehow different and better, I was under house arrest, just like Mrs Baba and all the other women in the street who were at the mercy of their menfolk.

Chapter 71

Afeeka told me she had a plan. But before she could carry it out, she had to wait until my parents and Climax were out of the house. She finally got her chance in late June, two days before the end of Ramadan. Daddy was at work, and the women had taken a taxi into town to do their last-minute Eid shopping.

Afeeka asked Egg and me if we were interested in getting our own back on Climax for the part she'd played in getting us banned from school. She was still smarting from Climax's betrayal, and felt stupid for having trusted her enough to confide in her about Egg and Kasim; if anyone had it coming, it was Climax, she said.

Egg and I refused, saying we were already in enough trouble with Daddy, without provoking him any more. Afeeka shrugged her shoulders and said provoking him was exactly what she had in mind; with any luck, she'd find some dirt on Climax that would make Daddy so mad he'd throw his sister out of the house and on to the street where she belonged.

She asked us to keep a lookout in case anyone came home unexpectedly, then headed up to Climax's room to do some snooping. It wasn't long before she reappeared, carrying a cardboard box with 'Dilly' written on it.

My hackles rose as I peered inside – there was the

hairdryer Doc had given me, and the bottles of perfume that Mammy had locked away in my dowry cupboard. It was enough to convince me that Afeeka might be on to something. She had a triumphant smile on her face as we headed up to the attic.

'Put things back exactly the way they were,' I said. 'If she finds out we've been up here, we'll be in big trouble.'

Afeeka raised the mattress, and said, 'Ooohh, what's this?' She held up an envelope; it was stuffed tight with twenty-pound notes.

'Where the hell did she get that from?' I asked.

'Who knows?' replied Afeeka. 'Let's ask her when Uncle comes home, shall we?'

I felt a ripple of excitement. Afeeka looked around the room. 'Dilly,' she said, 'if you wanted to hide something in here, where would you put it?'

'On top of the wardrobe,' I replied.

I was right. There was a battered old suitcase, which I pulled down and opened. Bingo! Inside it, were two packets of condoms, one of which was half-empty, a bundle of letters tied with a pink ribbon, a teddy bear wearing a T-shirt with the slogan 'Hard man inside', a paperback copy of the *Kama Sutra*, and some photos of Climax in a négligée with her arms around a man I didn't recognize. In one snap, he was squeezing Climax's breast.

'Come on,' I said, 'we've got enough here to have her kicked out ten times over. Daddy's gonna kill her for sure.'

'There's got to be more than this,' Afeeka suggested. She reached under the bed, and pulled out a little black carrier bag. Inside it, there was a video; on the cover was a picture of a blonde woman in a bikini stroking a horse. The title read: *Dobbie Does Dallas*.

Afeeka and I carried everything down to the front room, where we laid it all out on the table.

We didn't have to wait long for my mother and Climax to come home, weighed down with shopping bags.

As the women came through the door, Afeeka asked my mother to step into the front room, as she had something she wanted to show her.

My mother stopped short when she saw what was on the table.

'Where did all this come from?' she asked in surprise.

'Why don't you ask her?' Afeeka said, pointing to Climax. 'Your precious sister-in-law is a slag.'

Mammy picked up the envelope and exclaimed: 'Shah lent you a hundred pounds this morning for Eid shopping because you made out you were skint, and you had this all the time?'

I was disappointed by Climax's reaction. Instead of squirming with embarrassment, she rolled up her sleeves and went for Afeeka.

'You little runt – what gives you the right to go snooping through my things?'

She caught hold of Afeeka and was about to slap her, when Mammy pulled her away.

'Climax, it's over,' my mother said coldly. 'No whore is welcome in my house. Pack your bags. I want you out by the time Shah gets home.'

Climax gathered up her things from the table, said, 'Go to hell, the lot of you,' and stomped her way upstairs.

As soon as Daddy came in from work, Mammy told him everything that had happened. Without a word, he disappeared upstairs to the attic.

Hours later, the sun had set, and it was time to eat, but nobody had the balls to call him for dinner. We were halfway through a very sombre meal when he finally reappeared. With barely concealed fury, he took his place at the table.

'Uncle,' Afeeka asked nervously, 'when's she going?'

He glared at her, and said, 'She isn't. But you are.'

Two hours later, Monkey, Afeeka, Gadafi and Zia were gone. They didn't even say goodbye.

For the next few days, Sharnia was even more miserable than usual. The house was quiet, without Gadafi and Zia running around, and my sisters were all distraught without Afeeka to entertain them; Daisy, especially, took it hard, and spent most of her time sitting in Afeeka's wardrobe.

My parents argued incessantly. My mother kept saying she couldn't believe my father had kicked his only son out of the house, and how did he sleep at night not knowing where his grandchildren were. My father's reply was always the same: 'I'm sleeping very well, thank you. And as for Monkey, that loser will be back as soon as he's run out of money.'

Two weeks after the eviction, the phone rang. When I heard Monkey's voice, I hoped he was calling to say they were coming back.

'Hi, Dilly,' he said. 'We're at Manchester Airport. We're emigrating to Pakistan; we're off to live with Nonna.'

I was too shocked to speak.

I wished I hadn't taken the call – how was I going to break this news to my parents?

'I've gotta go,' Monkey said. 'Can you do me a favour? Tell Daddy, if he's ever in the neighbourhood, be sure to drop in. I'll make sure he gets a proper Shah welcome. See you around, lass.' The phone clicked, and the line went dead.

Chapter 72

Having too much time on my hands was a novelty that rapidly wore off. Every day was the same: when I wasn't doing housework, I had plenty of time to think about what a dull life I was leading. And the more I thought, the angrier I got with Egg. Not once did she try to make amends for the mess she'd created; no matter how much I asked her to speak to my father on my behalf, all she'd say was, 'Dilly, what's done is done,' as though that would somehow make everything all right.

The summer dragged by, and I reluctantly resigned myself to the fact that my father was never going to change his mind. Eventually, I gave up all hope of getting my A Levels and escaping from Sharnia.

On the last day of the summer holidays, my father casually announced: 'I've decided. Dilly can go back to school.'

Had I heard him correctly? The silence around the dinner table was deafening. As he reached over and picked up the water jug, he said to me, 'Why don't you give them a call in the morning and see if they'll take you back?'

'Are you sure, Daddy?' I asked, trying not to show my joy, in case disappointment followed.

'I wouldn't have said it otherwise,' he replied.

I glanced at my mother; she was chewing her food slowly and menacingly, but, surprisingly, she didn't say a word. When Daddy finished eating, he got to his feet and said, 'I'm going to watch *Antiques Roadshow*, so keep the noise down.'

Mammy waited for him to go, then turned and snapped at me: 'Don't even think about it. There's no way you're going back.'

'Oh really?' I chuckled, as I skipped around the table, clearing the dishes away. 'I think you'll find I am.'

I hurried upstairs to my room and pulled my school bag out from under the bed.

Half an hour later, I was called into the back room. My father was sitting on his bed, with lots of books and papers scattered around him, while my mother, ever the actress, was sitting in a chair, gently sniffing into her shawl.

'Dilly,' my father said quietly, 'I've changed my mind. You can't go back to school.'

My heart sank.

'But why?' I whispered.

'Your mother's been jumping around like a flea on a dog's back. She doesn't want you to go, so you can't go. Okay?'

'No, it's not okay,' I said angrily. 'What's it got to do with her? How come she's suddenly in charge? I thought you were the boss around here.'

My father fidgeted uncomfortably.

'You had your chance,' my mother said. 'It's my turn now. Naveeda and I are starting college next week, and you're staying here to do the housework.'

'That's all, Dilly,' my father said. 'You're dismissed. Go on upstairs.'

I was furious with him for going back on his word. What right did he have to treat me with such disrespect, as though I was just a possession? In his eyes, my feelings weren't important enough to be considered, even fleetingly.

I knew now that for as long as I lived in Sharnia, I could never be happy. For years, I'd thought of many ways to escape, but they'd all amounted to nothing. I knew what would happen if I ever ran away. I might be free, but at what cost? My selfish act would make the Shahs a laughing stock. A father who couldn't control his daughters would be ridiculed and ostracized. The stigma would be overwhelming. My sisters, even though they'd done nothing wrong, would be sent to Pakistan and kept under house arrest until they could be married off.

As far as my father was concerned, the threat of condemning all my sisters to a life of misery was a cruel but effective way of keeping me in line. What he didn't know was that I was too cowardly to run away; my sisters were a convenient excuse. I hated my parents for keeping me in the house, and I hated myself for being too pathetic to just pack my bags and leave under cover of darkness. I was the feeble prisoner of Sharnia who would fantasize about running away, but never do anything about it.

Anyway, where could someone like me go? I had no money, no qualifications, no job, no prospects and no balls! I was trapped, my parents had seen to that.

It was sad, really, when I thought about my life. I saw it in stages. When I closed my eyes I could see myself from the age of one right through to seventeen. At one time, all those Dillys had stood behind me and I, the eighteenth, was right up there at the front, peering back over my shoulder, watching each Dilly scaling the wall of injustice that my parents had built for me and then laughing at them because I'd managed to get away.

In the beginning, the wall had been smaller and easier to navigate, but, with each year that passed, the wall grew taller. I couldn't see over it now; there was no way of knowing what lay on the other side.

Seventeen Dillys had shinned over it and escaped forever, and now there was only me left. All I could do was look up and see that the wall was now too high for me to climb. I was trapped – stuck on the side where the evil King and Queen ruled, doomed to serve them until the day they saw fit to let me go.

Chapter 73

Over the next few months, Egg's state of mind became increasingly fragile. With every phone call and letter that was exchanged between Daddy and Ilyas, she became more and more anxious. And with good reason: not only was my father hell-bent on marrying her to a man she'd never met, but she also faced the possibility of having to relocate to Pakistan. My father wanted her future husband to come to England, but if the Home Office wouldn't allow it, Plan B was to pack Egg off to Jallu with very little chance of ever coming back again. This was no idle threat – we'd lost count of the number of girls on the street who'd been whisked off to Pakistan to marry a stranger. Some of them simply vanished without a trace on their sixteenth birthday; they just disappeared in the night, and, like Snowball in *Animal Farm*, they were seen no more.

By Christmas, Egg was still coping, but only because she was holding on to the dream that she and Kasim would one day be reunited. Then came the news that he had a new girlfriend, and had moved on with his life. Shortly afterwards, Egg told me she'd tried to kill herself by overdosing on Mammy's blood pressure tablets. She asked me not to say anything, but the days when I would cover for her were long gone.

I found my mother rifling through some papers she'd brought home from college.

'I'm worried about Egg,' I said.

'Don't you think you're locking the stable door?'

'Did you know she tried to kill herself? She took a load of pills.'

'Get lost, I'm trying to concentrate on my alphabet.'

'Look, Mammy, I'm telling you, Egg's not well. Which part of that don't you understand?'

'Oh, I understand all right,' she scoffed. 'I just don't give a shit. If she wants to take pills, that's fine with me, as long as she doesn't help herself to any of mine. Anyway, the dirty bitch is immune from all those aspirins you pumped into her when she was little.'

As soon as Daddy came through the front door, humming a little tune to himself, I pounced. I told him what Egg had been up to, and that, if the next suicide attempt was more successful, I'd tell the police that he knew what was going on and hadn't done anything about it.

'Leave it with me, Dilly. I'll sort things out.'

And he was as good as his word – things calmed right down after that. In fact, both my parents went out of their way to be nice to Egg. I was pleased to see that, for once, they'd listened to me.

Egg wasn't the only one going through emotional turmoil. Climax told Daddy she was feeling depressed, and needed some time away from Sharnia. I was really surprised. I'd never seen a softer side to her; I'd always considered her to be a hard-nosed battleaxe. I realized that, because she'd never discussed her feelings, I'd wrongly assumed she didn't have any.

She told my father that ever since the incident with Doc she'd been feeling miserable, and just needed to get away for a while. Daddy suggested that Climax should go and stay with her friend Amina in Dewsbury for a week. That soon put a smile on Climax's face, but then Daddy wiped it off again by saying it would be inappropriate for her to go without some sort of chaperone, and he suggested that I go with her.

While I was busily trying to decide whether I really wanted to spend a week with Grizzly Adams in Dewsbury, Climax glared at me, and said, 'Shah, if she shows me up, I swear I'll kick her arse.'

And so it was that I found myself wedged tight in the back of the car, with Climax on one side of me and my mother on the other. Normally, Mammy would have been sitting in the front with Daddy, but the passenger seat was piled high with Climax's luggage; she'd refused to put any of her bags in the boot, because it was filthy with bits of compost, wood chippings, oily tools, and the manure-crusted wellies that Mammy wouldn't allow in the house.

'Seriously, Daddy,' I gasped. 'Have we got time to clean the boot out? There isn't enough room in the back for me and these buffalos.'

Daddy choked on a cough, and pretended not to hear. Climax folded her arms, and sat back in her seat with her legs wide open.

'Do you have balls down there?' I asked.

My mother slapped me on the back of the head.

'Stop being so cheeky.'

'I'm not being cheeky. I mean, look at her – only blokes sit like that. And why the hell are you coming with us, anyway? You could have stayed at home.'

'Oh shut up with your whining,' Climax sniffed. 'I knew this was going to be a disaster. Why the hell did I agree to it?'

''Cos you're depressed, remember? And it's my job to cheer you up,' I said.

'God help us all,' replied Climax, and stared out of the window.

Daddy dumped me on the pavement outside Amina's back-to-back slum. He very carefully helped Climax into the house with her bags, gave her a cuddle, and said, 'See you next week, Sis.' All I got was a scowl and a 'Behave yourself, Dilly', then he was back in the car and speeding away.

Amina was a scrawny, sour-faced dog, with skin the colour of a charred onion bhaji. She looked surprised when she realized Climax had brought an unwanted house guest.

'It's okay, Mina – Dilly can do the housework,' Climax volunteered.

Amina shrugged her shoulders.

'She can stay, but don't expect me to run around after her.'

'I didn't want to come,' I snapped, determined not to feel guilty for being there. 'My dad made me; he obviously doesn't trust Climax.'

'Bollocks to him,' Amina snorted. Then she hugged Climax and said, 'Are you ready to paint the town tonight, girl?'

Climax nodded as she shrugged off her coat.

'Damn right, I've had a bellyful of Bradford. Are we going to see the lads tonight?'

The two of them giggled as they linked arms and headed for the kitchen. I tagged behind. This was the first time I'd seen Climax away from Sharnia; she seemed to be a completely different person – carefree and happy. I certainly couldn't see any sign of the alleged depression that was, after all, the only reason she'd been allowed to spend a week away from HMP Sharnia.

On that first night, Amina and Climax got ready in all their finery, and then drove off in Amina's car. I was woken at four a.m. by raucous laughter as they came tripping in through the door.

It was a similar story every night. By the end of the week, the only person suffering from depression in that house was me.

Unbelievably, I was actually happy to see Daddy's car pulling up outside. When I got home, I rushed upstairs to see Egg and tell her all my news. But she had some news of her own. She told me that the day I'd gone to Dewsbury, Daddy had given her an ultimatum: marry Zulfi, or he'd tie a rope round her neck and hang her from the rafters in the attic. She agreed to get married, after which Daddy casually mentioned that Zulfi didn't want to come to England, so Egg would be relocating to Pakistan to live with her new husband and stepchildren.

Apparently, my week with Climax had been a set-up; it was my father's idea all along. He needed to get me out of the way so he could bully Egg into submission, without me there to give her moral support.

Egg said that Mammy had taken great delight in explaining how Daddy had decided who Egg was going to marry. According to Mammy, there were originally five candidates from within the family, but, over the last few months, they'd been whittled down to just Zulfi.

Number One had looked promising, until he'd disgraced himself by falling out of a walnut tree, while spying on the village girls, and breaking both his legs. Daddy ruled him out, because he was a pervert who could only get around on a little wooden trolley.

Number Two was a cross-dresser who'd been caught wearing scarlet Swiss Miss lipstick, and his sister's bra and panties. Daddy hadn't ruled him out altogether, until he was told that the transvestite had been enlisted into the army by his father 'to make a man out of him'. Number Three had serious kidney problems, and was on the waiting list for a transplant. Daddy suspected that if Egg married him, she'd wake up on her honeymoon with one kidney and a scar. Number Four showed a lot of potential, but he ruled himself out by getting engaged to someone else and moving to Hong Kong.

Zulfi was candidate number Five. Daddy dithered over him for a while; he wasn't ideal because he was fifteen years older than Egg, with two children from a previous marriage. But, by a process of elimination, it became a one-horse race – Zulfi was to be the love of Egg's life, whether she liked it or not.

I was shocked. For the first time in my life, it dawned on me just how dangerous and manipulative my parents really were. Did they ever actually do anything just for the sake of it, or was there always some ulterior motive? How could I grow into a well-rounded adult when I was surrounded by such deceit? It seemed as though just as I was prepared to give them the benefit of the doubt, they would go and do something to destroy my faith in human nature again.

'Look at our lives, Dilly. What a pile of crap. And it's all my fault. I should have listened to you when you tried to warn me.'

'To be honest, Egg, I really don't give a shit any more. I wonder how long it'll be before I'm off to Dewsbury again.'

'What do you mean?' she asked. 'Did you have fun?'

'No, it was torture, but I'm sure they'll want me out of the way when it's time for one of the twins to have a chat with Daddy and his noose.'

Chapter 74

I ran across the landing, and slid down the banister; hearing the ratter-tatter of my mother's sewing machine coming from the back room, I peered round the door and saw her stitching masses of black fabric. In my innocence, I asked her what she was making.

'It's your burka for when you go to Pakistan.'

I had an instant flashback to the time when she forced the purple shawl on me. I shrank back as though she was pushing a naked flame in my face.

But that was nothing compared to Egg's reaction when she found out what was going on: the wedding date had been fixed, flights had been booked, and we would all soon be jetting off to Jallu. Panic and hysteria set in. She'd had weeks to prepare herself for this moment, but she was still shocked at the realization that there was to be no happy ending, no eleventh-hour reprieve. Kasim wasn't going to ride up on his horse and whisk her away. The man of her dreams was less than a mile away, but Egg was about to fly halfway round the world to marry a stranger.

And that wasn't all. When my mother told Egg that she'd decided not to bother going to her wedding, Egg just stared in disbelief.

I couldn't help but smile at the irony of the situation. I'd always wanted to go on a family holiday; it was something I'd hoped for ever since I could remember. And now, in the spring of 1986, it was about to become a reality – but what sort of family goes on holiday without their mother? I suppose it shouldn't have come as a surprise that we were leaving her behind; in the Kingdom of Sharnia, where bizarre was normal, something as mundane as a mother refusing to go to her own daughter's wedding was just business as usual.

And, as my mother wouldn't be going, she told me it would be my responsibility to arrange Egg's wedding. It was my turn to stare in disbelief.

It took Mammy a fortnight to make burkas for all the girls. Once they were stitched and ready, we were sent out into the garden to practise wearing them.

'This is crap,' I said. 'I can't see shit in this tent.'

'It's not that bad,' Egg replied. 'I think it's quite good fun.'

'How am I supposed to take you seriously, when you're standing there looking like Yoda? Where's your lightsabre?'

'No, we're more like *Dr Who* monsters,' Daisy said. 'I'm the evil Doctor Burka, from the planet Fat-Mammy.'

'You know what, Dilly?' Egg giggled. 'Think about it: we've got a big advantage with these on. No one knows who we are. It's like being invisible.'

'And? Your point is?'

'Well, we could go shoplifting.'

'Hey, yeah,' I said, suddenly seeing what Egg meant. 'Or maybe we could rob a bank? They wouldn't have a clue who'd done it.'

'Or we could kick the crap out of Mammy,' Egg laughed. 'And then say Mrs Baba did it.'

The black blob that had Poppy inside it suddenly tripped and fell; lying sprawled on the path, she looked just like a puddle of black rain.

'Bugger!' came a voice from behind the veil.

'Come on,' Egg said. 'Let's go out the back.'

We stumbled into the alley, where Egg tried to walk like a model, pretending she had three-inch heels on. She said, 'And Egg is wearing the very latest in black cotton from the Karachi Centre of Fashion and Design.'

Beads of sweat were building up on my forehead.

'It's hot in here,' I said. 'What's it gonna be like over there?'

'Hotter,' Egg called, as she did a pirouette.

'Seriously, though, I'm getting claustrophobic.'

'Me too,' said Poppy. She grabbed Daisy's hand and they started dancing. 'Have we gotta wear all our clothes underneath?'

'I don't see why,' I said. 'I mean, we could be butt-naked under here, and no one would know. I think I'll just wear one of Climax's big red thongs.'

The four of us made vomiting sounds at the thought of it, then my mother's head appeared round the gate. 'Are you going to be messing about out there all day? There's work waiting to be done in here.'

'We're busy,' I told her. 'We're preparing for our family holiday. You know the one, Mammy? The holiday that nearly all the family are going on.'

'Even under the burka you're a disgrace,' she snapped, and disappeared back into the garden.

Egg held her arms high and ran around in circles, making aeroplane noises. I couldn't help feeling uncomfortable about the way she'd been behaving recently; she was nearly eighteen, but had started to act more like a five year old, laughing one minute and sullen the next. It was obvious to me that the pressure was taking its toll.

A woman wearing a white burka came walking along the alley towards us. I instantly knew it was Mona, because she was the only Muslim woman on the street who wore Adidas trainers. Quietly confident I wouldn't be recognized under the veil, I started shoving Daisy around the alley.

'Hey,' the woman shouted, 'is that you, Dilly?'

'No, I'm Egg,' I lied.

'Dilly Shah, that burka's wasted on you,' she said scornfully.

We watched her as she trudged off up the alley.

'Any idea what colour knickers she's got on?' I whispered.

'Well,' Poppy scoffed, 'she's got her husband's trainers on, so maybe she's wearing his big baggy Y-fronts an' all.'

'Oi! Mona!' I shouted. 'Show us your Y-fronts!' But she didn't look back.

Chapter 75

The flight from Manchester to Karachi was booked for Saturday, 22 March 1986.

My mother and I argued for most of the day beforehand. Her indifference to Egg's wedding infuriated me, especially when she told me she'd never intended to go to Pakistan with us; if Egg wanted to get married to a man from my father's side of the family, then that was up to her – Mammy didn't see why she should be forced to travel all the way to Jallu just for the sake of showing her face. When I asked her why she was being so selfish, she shrugged her shoulders and told me to get used to it – in Pakistan, she said, I'd be overwhelmed by selfish relatives, all out for what they could get.

She told me she wanted me to have a miserable time at the hands of my father's relatives, as that would make me appreciate her more when I got back. Even now, when I was ready to make the scariest journey of my life, Mammy had nothing nice to say. No words of comfort to make me feel good.

I no longer regarded her as my mother; she was just a woman who was scared to lose control. As far as I was concerned, our relationship was over. Even if I spent the rest of my life under her roof, I knew I wouldn't forgive her for everything she'd done.

A few hours before our departure from Bradford, she cornered me in my bedroom.

'There's something I need you to do for me,' she said quietly. 'You have to promise you won't get married when you're out there.'

I'd spent all of my life listening to my mother telling me I would have to work hard to get a man, and now she was telling me not to get married if the opportunity arose. This made no sense to me. I shook my head in disbelief.

'Are you serious?'

'I mean it, Dilly. I don't know what your father's planning, but I know he's up to something. You're my black slave; you have to stay single for me. I don't want you working for anyone else.'

'That's bollocks,' I said. 'You couldn't wait to ship me off to Chowki to work for Nonna.'

'No, Dilly, you're the one talking bollocks. There was no way I was ever going to give you to her.'

'I don't get it,' I replied dumbly.

'How stupid are you?' she said sarcastically. 'Just because I made a deal with Nonna, it didn't mean I was actually going to go through with it. I got Afeeka over here, and that was the end of it. It just took me a while to figure out how I was going to get out of my side of the bargain without losing face.'

'But it doesn't add up,' I said. 'You went crazy when I called off the engagement.'

'It was all an act for Afeeka,' Mammy laughed. 'You belong to me, Dilly. So make sure you come back without a husband. Understand?'

I didn't make any promises. Not because I intended to get married, but because I was too dismayed to speak.

Up until then, marriage had never been a priority for me. I had other ideas for my future, and those involved somehow completing my education, starting a career and escaping from Sharnia. Finding myself a husband was at the bottom of my 'to do' list.

But later that night, as the coach cruised down the motorway towards Manchester, I stared dreamily out of the window and hid my smile behind my veil. I'd made up my mind: I was going to get married.

If I could somehow find a relative of my father's who was stupid enough to want to be my husband, there'd be nothing to stop me from getting married in Pakistan, returning to England and moving to a house as far away from Bradford as possible.

Any man who took me on would have to be independent enough to want to set up his own home; moving into my parents' house would be a disaster!

As soon as I'd escaped from Sharnia, I'd persuade my new husband to let me finish my education, and find myself a job. Then I'd dump him.

I didn't know if I could find anyone like that in Jallu, but I decided to give it my best shot. There was no other way. My evil father had already condemned Egg, my handmaiden, to a life of misery. I would do anything to avoid the same fate. Surely it was time for me to finally break free from the shackles of tradition? It was only right that Princess Dilly's story should have a happy ending.

But as I was busy hatching my plan, a man in Jallu was hatching a plan of his own. While I was preparing to divorce someone I hadn't even met yet, he was preparing to make sure we stayed married for the ten years it would take him to get his British passport.

But that, as they say, is another story.

Acknowledgements

I wish to thank: Darley Anderson and Zoe King for all their help in making a dream come true. Without you, this book would never have been.

Kerri Sharp, my editor, for her vision and strength, and for working relentlessly to pull everything together. I am eternally grateful to you.

Everybody at Simon & Schuster for their invaluable advice and support.

Janet Moffat, for her love and compassion.

Jenny Cox, for all the encouragement and kind words.

Mandie Frost, Sardah Boolaky, and Radek Dzik, for being my partners in crime.

And Janette Proctor, the bravest and most caring person I know. It is an honour to call you my best friend; you are like the stars in the sky – even when I cannot see you, I know exactly where you are.